C0054 23213

Widow's Welcome

D.K. FIELDS is the pseudonym for the writing
partnership of novelists David Towsey and
Katherine Stansfield. David's zombie-western
The Walkin' Trilogy is published by Quercus.
Katherine's historical crime fiction series, Cornish
Mysteries, is published by Allison & Busby.
The couple are originally from the south west
of England, and now live in Cardiff.

WIDOW'S WELCOME

Book One of the Tales of Fenest

D. K. FIELDS

HEAD
of
ZEUS

First published in the UK in 2019 by Head of Zeus Ltd

9 7 5 3 1 2 4 6 8

A catalogue record for this book is available from the British Library.

ISBN (HB): 9781789542486
ISBN (XTPB): 9781789542493
ISBN (E): 9781789542479

Printed and bound by CPI Group (UK) Ltd,
Croydon, CR0 4YY

Head of Zeus Ltd
First Floor East
5–8 Hardwick Street
London EC1R 4RG

WWW.HEADOFZEUS.COM

For Mike, for Vancouver

The Swaying Audience

Abject Reveller, god of: loneliness, old age, fish

Affable Old Hand, god of: order, nostalgia, punctuality

Beguiled Picknicker, god of: festivals, incense, insect bites

Blind Devotee, god of: mothers, love, the sun

Bloated Professional, god of: wealth, debt, shined shoes

Calm Luminary, god of: peace, light, the forest

Courageous Rogue, god of: hunting, charity, thin swords

Curious Stowaway, god of: rites of passage, secrets, summer and the longest day

Deaf Relative, god of: hospitality

Delicate Tout, god of: herbs, prudence, drought

Engaged Matron, god of: childbirth

Exiled Washerwoman, god of: sanitation, rivers, obstacles

Faithful Companion, god of: marriage, loyalty, dancing

Filthy Builder, god of: clay, walls, buckets

Frail Beholder, god of: beauty, spectacles, masks

Generous Neighbour, god of: harvest, fertility, the first day of the month

Gilded Keeper, god of: justice, fairness, cages

Grateful Latecomer, god of: good fortune, spontaneity, autumn

Heckling Drunkard, god of: jokes, drink, fools

Honoured Bailiff, god of: thieves, the dark, bruises

Insolent Bore, god of: wind, bindleleaf, borders

Inspired Whisperer, god of: truth, wisdom, silk

Jittery Wit, god of: madness, lamps, volcanoes

Keen Musician, god of: destiny, wine and oil

Lazy Painter, god of: rain, noon, hair

Missing Lover, god of: forbidden love, youth, thunder

Moral Student, god of: the horizon, knowledge, mountains

Needled Critic, god of: criticism, bad weather, insincerity

Nodding Child, god of: sleep and dreams, innocence

Overdressed Liar, god of: butlers, beards, mischief

Overlooked Amateur, god of: jilted lovers, the wronged, apprentices

Pale Widow, god of: death and renewal, winter, burrowing animals, the moon

Penniless Poet, god of: song, poetry, money by nefarious means

Prized Dandy, god of: clothes, virility, bouquets

Querulous Weaver, god of: revenge, plots, pipes

Reformed Trumpeter, god of: earthquakes, the spoken word

Restless Patron, god of: employment, contracts and bonds, spring

Scandalous Dissenter, god of: protest, petition, dangerous animals

Senseless Brawler, god of: war, chequers, fire

Stalled Commoner, god of: home and hearth, decisions, crowds

The Mute, god of: Silence

Travelling Partner, god of: journeys, danger and misfortune, knives

Ugly Messenger, god of: pennysheets, handicrafts, dogs

Valiant Glutton, god of: cooking, trade, cattle

Vicious Beginner, god of: milk and nursing, midnight, ignorance

Weary Governess, god of: schooling, cats

Wide-eyed Inker, god of: tattoos, colour, sunsets

Withering Fishwife, god of: dusk, chastity, flooding

Yawning Hawker, god of: dawn, comfort, grain

Zealous Stitcher, god of: healing and mending

Prologue

The night her sister left, Cora told her first story to the Stowaway. He was the member of the Audience for such tales: people coming and people going, growing up and leaving home. But not that other kind of leaving. The lasting kind. A story of that sort was better told to the Widow.

Cora's story for the Stowaway began with sudden waking.

It was the sound of breaking glass, somewhere downstairs, that pulled her from sleep. Then there was quiet, and that was worse than the shock of the noise. Her heart beat with a thump she could hear. The silence grew until the air of her bedroom felt sharp with it. Then there was a bump, a bang.

Footsteps below.

Her parents, returning from their engagement? They both liked a drink with company, and their meeting tonight was an important one. Her mother had talked about it all week. Perhaps her father had been clumsy with his nightcap. Perhaps that meant it hadn't gone well, whatever had been so important. Cora waited to catch his muffled apologies and her mother's scolding – safe, known noises – but neither came. It wasn't a night for such expected things; the night felt full of secrets and their dangers.

That was how the Stowaway liked it. Cora thought of the story she could tell, if she only knew a little more, and gently placed her feet on the floorboards. The wood was cold against her bare skin, but she couldn't find her slippers, and couldn't stop for them. She needed to get down there.

She snuck onto the landing, then to her parents' room, stepping as lightly as she could. Their door was open, their bed empty. She crept to her older sister's room. Ruth must have heard it by now. Ruth would go down with her.

'Ruth!' she whispered.

But Ruth wasn't there. Cora said her sister's name again, uselessly, as if Ruth might be hiding somewhere and this was her idea of a game, a joke, because Ruth did that sometimes, when their parents were out. She slipped behind doors, tucked her tall, thin frame into cupboards, where by rights a body shouldn't have been able to fit, then grabbed Cora as she passed, unsuspecting.

And now Ruth had left her in the house, alone, and people had come to rob them. Cora took an empty candlestick from Ruth's shelves, dislodging a pile of Seminary papers covered in her sister's neat writing, and held it up like a small but heavy club.

Cora wasn't entirely surprised by Ruth's absence. It had been the way of things recently. Her sister had kept late hours the last few weeks, not coming home when Seminary classes finished but disappearing into the darkness of the winter evenings, missing dinner. Their parents, usually so strict about their daughters sitting up to table with them, had seemed not to notice that their eldest child wasn't there. Nothing had been right for weeks. And now this.

At the top of the stairs, Cora paused. Below, in the hallway, light spilled from beneath the closed study door. Her parents' shared study: a room of locked drawers, glass-fronted cabinets, and animal heads mounted on the walls. The noises were coming from there. Perhaps her parents *had* come home after all, and there was business after the meeting that kept them from their bed. There had been worrying and fretting when they left the house earlier that evening. Cora knew better than to ask her parents about their work in the trading halls. They never welcomed such questions. That hadn't stopped Ruth asking them, again and again, in the last few weeks.

A shriek of metal sounded from the study. That couldn't be her parents, who never slammed a drawer, never even dropped a ledger.

Cora crept down the stairs, her grip on the candlestick weapon almost painful. A cold draught blew from under the study door and swirled around her. She took a deep breath, then kicked the door.

There was light, and... And she couldn't believe it: Ruth, a chisel in hand, looking as relieved to see Cora as Cora was to see her.

'Ruth! I thought you were a robber! What are you doing?'

'You should go back to bed.' Ruth bent over their father's desk and rammed the chisel into the top drawer's lock.

Cora moved towards her sister but as she did so she stepped on something sharp. At once there was pain, hot in her foot. Glass was scattered across the floor. The door of the cabinet beside Ruth was broken. The cabinet had been packed with wine-coloured ledgers, which were now spread across the floor, their cream innards spilling. And, beside them, small smears of blood. Cora's blood.

Ruth didn't look up from her frantic efforts. 'I didn't want you to... you should go back to bed.'

With some considerable effort, she wrenched open the drawer and grabbed a handful of papers from inside. She rifled through them then gave a cry – of joy or pain, Cora didn't know.

'You mustn't, Ruth! It's not allowed.'

Her sister appeared not to hear her, only glanced at the study window, which was wide open. Someone was out there, in the garden, a dark shape among the flowerbeds. Cora still held the candlestick and now she was ready to use it.

'Who's making you do this? I'll—'

Ruth's hand on her arm. Her thin face flushed.

'It's all here,' she said, and shook the papers, as if that should mean something. 'The whole place is rotten, right through the middle. You've been at the Seminary long enough; haven't you felt it?'

'I don't know what you're talking about.' Cora's foot throbbed.

'The Commission, Cora! Audience-sake, this whole city. It's built on lies. There's power in stories and a story of power.' She thrust the papers at Cora. 'This – this is the story of that power, and it consumes people.'

'Who? Who are you talking about, Ruth?'

But Ruth only shook her head. 'I didn't want to believe it of them, but I can't pretend anymore. I don't want any part of it and neither should you, Cora. Come with me.'

'Where are you going at this time of night?'

'Anywhere but here.'

And then Cora saw it: the bag by the window. She dropped the candlestick and it chipped the edge of a flagstone. Her mother would be livid.

'You're... You're running away?' she managed to stutter, though the question seemed ridiculous.

'I have to. Please – come with me.'

'But you've only got a year left at the Seminary,' Cora said. 'Don't you want to finish?'

'You're not listening! There isn't much time. They'll be back soon.' Ruth darted to the window, taking the papers with her.

'Wait – Ruth!'

Like a strange kind of echo, her sister's name was whispered urgently from the garden.

'Last chance, will you come with me?' Ruth said, sitting on the window ledge and lowering her feet over the other side.

But Cora was backing away. 'I can't.'

'Then you'll have to find your own way out.'

'Ruth—'

And then, if the Stowaway would believe it, her sister was gone.

As Cora sat on the bottom stair and tried to pull the glass from her foot, she began her story to the Stowaway. A story told through sobs – that didn't help the telling, but she hoped the Stowaway would understand.

It was only later, much later, that Cora realised the story would have been better told to the Widow after all: Ruth's leaving turned out to be a tale of death for everyone in Cora's house, one way or another.

One

The body was left there to be found. At least, that was how it looked.

Not dumped in the back doorway of the slop-shop, or the whorehouse, or the chequers' halls that ran the length of the alleyway. It hadn't been hidden behind the pile of rain-softened crates and their rotted food scraps that lent the early morning air a staleness it didn't deserve. The body was in the open, face-up.

A blue-clad figure stood watch beside it, glancing up and down the alley to the streets at either end, her hand gripping her baton.

'Expecting an ambush, Constable?' Cora called.

On seeing her, the young woman made an effort to compose herself.

Detective Cora Gorderheim, Bernswick Division, looked hard in her pockets for a few pennies. The gig driver, as grey and simple as his Clotham's uniform, showed no surprise when Cora paid the exact fare and no more. The gig lumbered off along Hatch Street, which was slow to rouse itself that morning, and Cora made her way down the alleyway to the constable.

'Jackson, isn't it?' Cora said, recognising the young woman from the station's briefing room. Recognising her buck teeth more, if she were honest.

'It's Jenkins, Detective Gorderheim.'

'Right then, Jenkins. Get yourself out on Hatch Street and wait for the stitcher – he's on his way.'

'Wait for him, Detective?'

'That's what I said.' Cora took her bindleleaf tin from the pocket of her old red coat and was annoyed to find she hadn't any rolled smokes among the loose leaves and papers. She snapped the tin shut. 'Get yourself out on the street. And once Pruett arrives, start knocking on doors to see what people saw or heard last night – that's if they'll admit to being anything but blind and deaf. I'll keep an eye on our friend here.'

Jenkins set off at a near trot towards the end of the alley.

'You're not going anywhere, are you?' Cora said to the body. She squatted beside him and felt the pull of the damage done to her foot all those years ago. The dull heat of the tendon, and of her anger too. She shook away the thought of Ruth, as she always did, and spoke to the dead man. 'I'd say you're not from around here.'

In fact, she'd bet her bindleleaf that the dead man was a Wayward. He was lying on one of their cloaks, the kind made of stiffened skin and lined with all manner of pockets. Lying on it, but not as if he'd fallen while wearing the thing. More like someone had spread it neatly beneath him. But that was where the niceties ended: this Wayward had joined the Audience after some violence.

His mouth had been sewn shut.

No wonder the constable had been nervous.

Daylight had just about regained its claim on the world and in its weak glow Cora took a better look at the man's face. Two lengths of string wound their way through his lips. No, something tougher than string. Cora touched one of the ends hanging from the Wayward's bottom lip. Feeling through the dried blood, she was sure the lengths were boot laces – the kind from sturdy work boots. One black, one white. Or, white originally. Now that lace was stained with blood. Blood that had also poured down the Wayward's chin and onto his smock. He was rusty with it.

She eased his chin up. Strangled was the story of the fat, purpled ring of skin around his neck. Pruett, the stitcher at Bernswick Station, would officially determine the cause of death, once he dragged himself from the depths of the cold room. Knife wounds and smashed skulls were Cora's bread and butter – she'd seen it all in this part of the city. Her part. But not this kind of mutilation. This was new.

She rolled a smoke and saw that the end of her coat had caught the murk that lay between the cobbles. A constant feature of the glorious city of Fenest, capital of the Union of Realms. Come rain, come sun, there was always something dark and dirty to be found in the gaps.

A single lamp still burned at the door nearest her. A lamp-man had found the body. He was in such a hurry to get to the station he'd abandoned his rounds and left one lamp unextinguished. Cora thanked him out loud, and used the lamp to light up, taking a deep drag.

Detective Sergeant Hearst, Cora's commanding officer, had also been in a hurry when he'd shaken Cora awake in a corner of the briefing room. He had a dead man and an address: the alley that connected Hatch Street and Green Row. The alley between the Swan's Teeth Inn and Mrs Hawksley's whorehouse was how Cora knew it.

'Everyone was in a hurry – except whoever did this to you, right, friend?' Cora said to the dead man.

Someone who had designs to sew a man's mouth shut wasn't about rushing things. That, and the cloak laid out all nice, made no sense for a back-alley mugging gone too far, or a fight over one of Hawksley's whores.

Maybe it was a Wayward thing? The Wayward people – and realms *were* people, not so much a place – spent their lives crossing the Northern Steppes and all the other lands of the Union, moving their herds and building other people's fences. That would wear away at you, make you capable of anything. It had certainly worn away at this man, Cora thought, looking down at him. He was about forty years of age, but it was hard to be sure. 'Weathered' would be a kind way of putting it.

Wherever you lived in the Union – Fenest, the Steppes, the Tear – life left its mark. Some said those realms that lived near the capital had it easier, that the Perlish and the Seeders were softer for that, and Cora could believe it. She'd heard stories about life down in the far south. How the Torn managed to not only live in the Tear but thrive there was no small wonder, and the Rustans likewise. For all their lofty peaks, the Rusting Mountains were still right in the middle of the Tear. And the Caskers on their boats weren't that far from it, either, when you stopped and stared at a map of the Union. This Wayward now at her feet looked rough as used nails. In her time in the police she'd seen plenty of Seeders looking no better. Perhaps nowhere in the Union offered a softer life. Certainly not Fenest at any rate.

Footsteps echoed at the end of the alley. Without looking up she said, 'This is a new one, Pruett.'

'Sorry to disappoint you, Gorderheim.'

Hurrying towards her was a stocky figure in a worn brown suit, a battered tub hat pulled low over his ears. Someone she hadn't expected, but knew all too well: Butterman, writer for *The Spoke*, Fenest's largest-selling pennysheet.

'Disappointed doesn't begin to describe my feelings on seeing you, Butterman,' she said. 'You're paying your sources well these days.'

'This one didn't cost us a penny,' Butterman said, his breathing laboured as he bent to look at the Wayward's face. 'They weren't wrong about the mouth. What will the Widow make of it, I wonder?'

'You knew about the mouth?' she said, unable to keep the surprise from her voice.

'The source was detailed. And insistent.'

'And here you are, before even the stitcher has seen the body.' She blew smoke into Butterman's face and was pleased when his coughing forced him to move away.

'How long until Pruett gets here?' he said.

Cora shrugged.

'Helpful as ever, Gorderheim. I've enough here to start the story, at least.'

'And in time for the afternoon edition,' Cora said. 'Why doesn't that feel like coincidence?'

'Hard getting space in any edition right now.'

'The election?'

Butterman grunted. 'For two months there's been nothing in this whole city *but* that. Trust me, I'd rather be covering fights over Mrs Hawksley's whores.'

'I thought you just made it all up anyway,' Cora said.

'Only when we can't be bothered to follow the tips,' he said, and grinned.

'So what made you get up early for this one?'

'Note said there was something special about it.' He nodded towards the sewn mouth. 'They weren't wrong.'

'Is the source one of your regulars?'

'Come now, Detective Gorderheim. You know I can't reveal that.'

'There's a difference between "can't" and "won't".'

Butterman ignored her and scribbled in his notebook.

She flicked away the stub of her smoke. 'At least tell me—'

'My job is to write the stories, Detective. Your job is to investigate them. I assume that's what you're doing when you visit the back room of the Dancing Oak? Or is that something more—'

'You know I can't reveal my sources, Butterman.'

'Then I s'pose we'll each keep our council, won't we? Now, any comment for the readers of *The Spoke* about another body found in the gutters of Fenest?'

Now it was Cora's turn to grunt.

'Thought not,' he said. Then something behind Cora caught Butterman's eye. 'But here's a man who might be less tight-lipped than you and the dead.'

Cora turned to see the stitcher, Pruett, making his way towards them from Hatch Street. Constable Jenkins had stayed with Pruett's assistant and the cart on the street.

'Morning, Pruett,' Butterman said cheerfully. 'Care to comment on—'

'The Audience won't want to hear your stories, Butterman, and neither do I.' Pruett opened his black stitcher's bag. Inside was a jumble of cloths and metal tools, none of which looked clean.

'Oh, I don't know about that,' Butterman said. 'My readers will be glad of a change from the election.'

Pruett reached into his bag and drew out a small saw, the teeth of which were flecked with white powder. Bone dust from the last person Pruett had opened. He pointed the saw at the pennysheet hack.

'The only stories I'm interested in hearing are those of the dead. So, unless you want to join them, I suggest you get back under the stone you've just crawled out from.'

Butterman backed away, palms raised. 'No need for that kind of ugliness, is there? I'll send a lad for the report.' And then to Cora: 'See you at the Oak, Detective.' He touched the rim of his battered tub hat and headed down the alleyway.

Pruett looked at the dead man for the first time. He didn't recoil on seeing the Wayward's sewn mouth, but a flicker of distaste passed across his face.

'No wonder the 'sheets are keen,' he said.

'Presses can't be stopped.'

'But do they have to see the bodies before I do? You let them get away with too much.'

'Butterman had a tip,' Cora said. 'He nearly beat *me* to it. Someone wanted this body found.'

'That so? Who is he, then?'

'Still unidentified. Discovered by the lamp-man just before dawn.'

Pruett began to rifle through his bag. He looked to have come straight from working in the cold room: the parts of his shirt visible beneath his tattered wool coat were flecked with blood and smears of something Cora didn't want to speculate on. At least he'd taken off his apron.

He knelt beside the dead Wayward. Cora knew better than to speak to him while he was assessing a body. She moved away to roll another smoke. More of the alley had revealed itself in the strengthening morning light. A rat scuffled in the crates of rotten vegetables. Two storeys up, a scrap of blue cloth was caught in the closed window of Mrs Hawksley's place. Cora briefly allowed herself to imagine the warm bed on the other side.

'Not dead more than a few hours,' Pruett said.

'And killed somewhere else.'

'I'd say so. No sign of a struggle hereabouts.'

'Risk of witnesses,' Cora said, 'that time of night. Mrs Hawksley's whores keep late company. Strangled?'

'Likely, but I'll know more when I've got him back to the cold room.' Pruett signalled to his assistant, Bowen, to get the stretcher from the back of the cart.

Cora stood back to let Pruett and the assistant move the body, and enjoyed the last of her smoke. Time to get back to the station and tell Sergeant Hearst what she'd found. Another body in the gutters of Fenest. Was that all it was? Just another victim of the city? Wayward weren't two-a-penny in Fenest, but they were just as likely to be killed over a drink, a bet, a woman as someone from another realm, and it was an election year, after all. That brought almost as many extra dead bodies as there were voters.

But the sewn mouth, and the tip to bring *The Spoke*?

Pruett and Bowen lifted the stretcher and Cora checked the cobbles beneath where the dead man had lain. Nothing out of the ordinary there. But as she stood, she saw something on the alley wall at eye level.

It was a smear of red-white dirt, directly above where the body had been. The mark was finger-length and crumbled at her touch. There were no other marks like it anywhere else that she could see.

Pruett had noticed her inspection and stopped.

'More of the city's filth?' the stitcher called back.

'Perhaps.'

Cora fished a grubby handkerchief from her coat and carefully collected some of the flaky dirt.

They went on their way again, the men bearing the Wayward, Cora just behind them. The unevenness of the cobbles meant the body teetered on the stretcher, jiggling the laces erupting from his mouth, as if the dead man were trying to tell his last tale.

Two

Back at the station, Cora and Pruett parted ways: the stitcher to the cold room beneath street level, where he would examine the Wayward's body, Cora to her cupboard-office opposite the briefing room.

She'd occupied the same spot since she'd made detective, more than ten years ago now, and had resisted all attempts to move her somewhere more in keeping with her rank – the kind of fancy rooms detectives had in other divisions. Part of the reason Cora had stayed in such a cramped office was the fact her parents would have been appalled by it.

A daughter in the police force was bad enough, after all that expensive Seminary schooling and a guaranteed job in the Commission's Wheelhouse. The Gorderheim name might not have had the power it once did, thanks to Ruth running off and the stories in the pennysheets, but her mother insisted it still counted for something. Cora was a chance to rebuild what was lost.

But a *police constable*, the lowest rung of one of the lowest professions in the city? That was hardly the kind of thing that would impress those who mattered in Fenest. Madeline Gorderheim had often been heard disparaging the police of Fenest at receptions and parties, even after her own daughter joined the force. And here Cora was now, all these years later, only a little further up the ranks and in a space no bigger than where the constables kept the coffee supplies. Not that Cora's parents would be coming to visit her office, of course, given that they'd both joined the Audience long since: her father in that terrible first week after Ruth had left, and her mother only five years later.

But just the thought of their disappointed faces was enough to lend her office-cupboard some charm. After all, windows were overrated, and if Cora had more space she'd only fill it with chequers' slips and the other detritus she seemed to collect. From her desk – an old card table – she could hear the constables in the briefing room that served as canteen, dormitory and the place where investigatory announcements were made. She could hear them even with both doors closed. That the constables often forgot that fact was no bad thing.

Sergeant Hearst forgot nothing. Cora had just inked her pen to start her report on the body in the alleyway when her commanding officer blocked the little light that found its way into her office.

'Well?' Hearst said, closing the door.

He was slight, a head shorter than Cora. There was a fine dusting of sandy-coloured crumbs on one of his elbows. He'd been feeding the pigeons on the station roof again.

'The lamp-man claims he found the body just before four this morning,' Cora said. 'That's his regular spring time for dousing in the alley. Does Hatch Street too.'

'And did our lamp-man see anyone else at the scene?'

'Only the rats,' Cora said.

'I've heard Mrs Hawksley's whores called many things, but that's a new one.'

'Same chance of catching something.' She put her pen back in the inkwell. 'But the girls and boys had finished for the night. No one about but our lamp-man.'

'Any reason to suspect he isn't telling us the truth?'

'None that I can find,' Cora said. 'I sent the new constable, the one with the teeth—'

'Jenkins,' Hearst said.

'I sent her door-knocking round that way. In the meantime.' Cora sifted through the papers on her desk until she found her notes. 'Apparently, the lamp-man has been dousing in the alley since he was old enough to lift the pole. He's a regular at the Seat of the Commoner and gives money to the Orphan Fund.'

'Sounds like one of our more commendable citizens. And Pruett's report?'

'I'm going down now,' she said. 'He should be ready to hear the Wayward's stories.'

'Wayward?' Hearst said, his voice losing its former lightness.

'That's right.'

Hearst noticed the crumbs of bird seed on his elbow and spent a moment picking them off. Cora waited.

'A Wayward in the alley behind Mrs Hawksley's,' Hearst said, checking his other arm for seed. 'No mystery as to what he was doing there, I suppose.'

'The whores don't usually sew their customers' mouths shut.'

His attention was on her again, his eyes wide. 'What?'

She told him about the laces through the Wayward's lips, and about Butterman getting to the scene almost as she did.

'Well, well,' Hearst said. 'Perhaps the afternoon pennysheets will tell us more. But in the meantime—'

'Pruett. I know. I'm going.' Cora stood with a practised care that didn't disturb the piles of paperwork.

Once they were out in the corridor, Hearst caught her arm.

'Sillian is to be kept informed about this one,' he said in a low voice.

'Sillian? Why?'

Hearst shrugged. 'As if she'd tell me. But I'm telling *you*: she wants to know.' He turned and went into the briefing room and Cora heard the constables scrambling to attention.

As she made her way down the steps that led to the cold room, Cora asked herself why Chief Inspector

Sillian, head of the Bernswick Division of the Fenestiran police force, was so interested in a dead Wayward behind a whorehouse. She hoped the stitcher had the answer.

Despite the bone chill that gave the cold room its name, Cora found Pruett in his usual state when examining: his old wool coat was hanging on the butcher's hook behind him – looking for all the world like a body waiting its turn on the table – and he'd rolled his shirt sleeves past his elbows. His grey apron was smeared, stained.

The Wayward was on the examining table. Pruett was behind his head, using pliers to grip one of the laces still threaded through the dead man's lips. The cold room was full of such tools and they winked in the light of the many lamps dotted about, giving a strange gleam to the dark purpose of the place.

'So, who is it that I've been getting to know?' Pruett said.

'Was hoping you'd tell me,' Cora said. 'Nothing to identify him in his clothes? No letters? Bills?'

'Bowen did the rifling.'

Pruett's assistant was mixing something foul-looking in a large mortar. He had to work it hard, which put a little colour in his cheeks, but his breath still misted in front of him.

'Not so much as a pennysheet,' Bowen said, wiping his forehead clear of cold sweat.

'Pity,' Cora said.

Pruett tugged at the lace. When it didn't give, he yanked it, and the lace came free of the small, ragged holes that lined the Wayward's top and bottom lips. A 'W', being un-inked.

'That's got you,' Pruett murmured. He dropped the lace into a small bowl and set about removing the one that remained.

Cora picked up the bowl and looked at the black lace. Other than being stiff with dried blood, it appeared ordinary enough. But it had been used to sew someone's mouth shut – that made it anything but ordinary.

She turned to look at the figure on the table. Now that he was stripped of his clothes, laid out on stone rather than his cloak, Cora asked herself if she'd still know he *was* Wayward. The contrast between his sun-stained face and arms and the chalky flesh of the rest of him was clear enough. But she'd seen as much on Casker dockers and Seeder farmhands. And the red glistening of his exposed guts would be as everyone else's. When Pruett got to someone with his saws and clamps, Bowen standing by with pails to catch the heart and lungs and all the rest, it didn't matter which realm they were.

Another yank and Pruett had the second lace moving. Like the black one, this slowly left the Wayward's flesh. As the lips parted at last, free of what had bound them, the dead man moaned.

Cora stumbled back from the table and knocked over a pile of tools, which made the floor's stone ring like the

Poet's bells. Pruett, unperturbed, widened the Wayward's mouth and peered inside.

'Nothing obvious here. Tongue looks healthy enough. Thought there might have been something stowed in the mouth to warrant the stitching.' He dropped the pliers into the bowl with the laces.

'And that... that noise?' Cora said.

'Air escaping. Happens more often than you'd think.'

'It sounded like he was speaking.'

Pruett gave a grim laugh. 'The dead *do* speak, Gorderheim, but not in any language you'd understand.'

'So what did this dead Wayward tell you?' she said.

'That he was in good health, up until he was killed.'

'And how *was* he killed?'

'Strangulation.' Pruett waved at the series of bruises that ringed the Wayward's neck. 'You saw the marks.'

'To crush someone's throat with your bare hands,' Cora said, 'you can't be rushing.'

'Which would tie in with you thinking the deed was done elsewhere and the body brought to the alley afterwards. But you're wrong about the bare hands.'

'What?'

'Those marks are too thin to be made by fingers.'

Cora bent closer to the Wayward, holding her breath against the cloying smell of blood that rose from the man's punctured lips. Bowen brought a lamp to aid her.

'A rope then?' she said. 'You think he was strung up?'

Pruett shook his head. 'Neck isn't damaged enough. Remember the boy found swinging from the North Gate last summer? The one who'd kept the women in the cellar?'

'The mob got to him,' Cora said.

'And his neck was broken from the body's weight.'

'You can't mistake a hanging,' Bowen called over, almost cheerfully.

'So what happened to our friend here?' Cora asked.

'Garrotted,' Pruett said. 'Sitting or standing.'

'And the weapon?'

'A thin length of cord, I'd say. Not too roughly made, given the lack of burn marks.'

'But thicker than these?' Cora picked up the bowl that held the laces. One black, one white.

'I'd put a mark on it, whatever the odds,' Pruett said, and looked at her slyly.

Cora shoved the bowl at him. 'What about the dirt I picked up?'

'Hm?'

'The mark on the wall, next to the body.'

Pruett waved in the direction of the shelves that lined the back of the cold room. 'Bowen put it in a jar, and if you're *really* lucky he might have added a label too.'

Cora saw the briefest curl of Bowen's lips before the assistant went over to the shelves and reached for a tiny jar amidst the chaos of glass and stoppers and wooden boxes.

He handed it to Cora and muttered, 'Someone has to keep track of things in this place.'

She nodded her thanks and held the jar to a lamp to examine the red-white dirt it held. No more than half a teaspoon's worth.

'What do you think this is then, Pruett?'

'Plague.'

Cora fumbled the jar onto a nearby table and stepped smartly away from it. 'What?'

'That's my theory, anyway. What else do you expect from the muck of this city?'

'You're telling me you don't know what this is, and, more importantly, you don't care.'

'Exactly right, Detective.'

'You won't mind if I take it then?'

'I think we can live without it, though I doubt you've got room in that cupboard of yours for too many—'

The door at the top of the stairs was flung open and a red-faced constable appeared above them. 'Five dead at the Derby Pump, Mr Pruett!'

Pruett groaned. 'Move this one to the back door, Bowen. I'll send someone for the burning as we go.'

'And Sergeant Hearst says to tell you,' the constable called down, 'it's a mess. Some of them was wheelwrights. They went at each other with piping and such.'

'I need you to keep the Wayward,' Cora told the stitcher.

Pruett shrugged on his coat. 'When there's five more on their way? What's so special about this one?'

'Everything,' Cora said.

'Two days,' Pruett said. 'The rate this city murders people, I won't have room for him for any longer.' He and Bowen readied themselves to leave.

Cora looked at the laces in the bowl again. One black, one white.

The door closed behind the men. She took out her bindleleaf tin and rolled a new smoke.

One black lace, one white.

She lit up, then put the small jar of dirt into her coat, her fingers brushing against the many slips of paper that lined her pocket. She didn't need to take them out to see what they were, or that the name of the Oak was written on each of them. She didn't have a choice now, did she? She'd have to go. The laces had decided her. Whoever sewed the Wayward's mouth had done so to send a message, and the colours of the laces were deliberately chosen. Of that she was certain, and she was beginning to see why.

One black, one white. The twin colours of the coats worn by the chequers: those takers of bets big and small, rich and poor. If you gave them your Senseless, Penniless, Heckling, your Curious, they'd make stories worthy of the Audience, win or lose. Had the Wayward over-played his hand and been unable to pay?

She left the cold room. Tonight she would see what the betting world knew of the dead Wayward, and learn the night's numbers while she was at it.

Three

It was raining, Painter be damned. Cora became aware of it as she left her desk, despite the lack of a window in her office. The water knuckled hard on the station roof two floors up, and was quietly finding its way inside too, no doubt. Anyone spending the night in the cells would be witness to the wet creep across the floor. In the cold room, Bowen would be putting down the sandbags again.

She was late leaving the station, but the briefing room was still noisy – the election meant long days for the constables. As she stepped into the street, there was the reason: despite the rain, there were people everywhere. And somewhere among them, the Wayward's killer. The kind of person who sewed a man's mouth shut. She quickened her step.

It wasn't just Fenest's own in the crowds. People came from far and wide for the election, though most wouldn't hear the stories. It was the occasion that drew all six realms to Fenest, to the heart of the Union. They came just for the atmosphere, and here it was, pissing all over them. She pulled up her collar and stepped into the throng.

Once every five years an election took place on her doorstep, and somehow every five years she managed to forget how awful it all was. The whole business of it: each realm sent a storyteller to Fenest and, over the course of a few weeks, those storytellers told their tales to win votes for their realms – votes cast by stones. And the prize was power. It was just as Ruth had said, all those years ago: there was power in stories and a story of power. Cora spat. Ruth hadn't hung around long enough to see what that really meant. Things were different once the easy lessons of the Seminary were left behind.

But in the election, stories *were* the means to power, because every 'yes' vote, every black stone cast for a story, got that realm a seat in the Assembly. And the realm with the most Assembly seats at the close of the election gained the power to shape what happened across the Union for the next five years, including in Fenest. Just being an administrative capital, Fenest didn't get its own storyteller or election story. Though the capital was in charge of proceedings, Cora, like every other Fenestiran, was stuck with whoever won for five long years. Until the wheel turned again and brought the next election. Until this moment.

In some ways, these weeks leading up to the first story were the worst. Newcomers to the city had to find their way among the locals. There was always a spike in cut-purses and the Brawler heard more stories in his Seat than usual. Perhaps the Wayward found behind Mrs Hawksley's was just one of the expected victims of the election. Caught in the fever pitch and consumed by the chequers' halls – betting being one of Fenest's most popular attractions. Not that things would settle down even when the election started and the stories began. Then the constables would be needed for crowd control at the story sites. Demand for seats in the public gallery always outstripped supply and it was often ugly.

The constables could get to work out here, Cora thought, dodging a group of young Perlish men oiled and tucked into their fancy clothes. Thin smoke drifted from bindleleaf held at arm's length in lacquered holders. Enjoying the last days of Perlish control of the Assembly, she guessed; the Perlish realm, both damn Duchies of them, had won the previous election. Try as she might, she couldn't remember anything about the story that had won the Perlish power last time. Their tenure as ruling realm would likely stay much more memorable: tax exemptions for luxuries while basic provisions in Fenest went unfunded. This was the state of things for the other realms too, so the pennysheets said. And here was one such dereliction now: a pothole yawned before her, full of greasy-looking water.

Cora wasn't going anywhere fast, but the rain was getting heavier. She ducked into an alley she knew she shouldn't, but she needed to make a stop before the Oak and do it before she drowned. Picking her way through piles of muck and streams of slops and who-knew-what-else took some doing. Which was why she didn't see tonight's trouble until the knife flashed towards her chest.

Two of them, a man and a woman, both as dirty as the alley they were thieving in.

'Pockets, now!' the man said.

'All right, easy does it. But you're not going to like what I've got.' Cora reached into her coat and pulled out her badge. The woman saw silver and, Poet hear her, she looked pleased – as if it might be something valuable. But the man understood. He hesitated, his knife dropping just a touch. 'That's right,' Cora said. 'Picked the wrong one tonight.'

A look passed between them. It screamed desperation as loudly as their tattered tunics.

The man lunged. Cora caught his wrist and pulled, hard, overbalancing him. One shove and he was sprawling among the alley's detritus.

They weren't tough, but they could run. The woman was gone so quick Cora started to doubt she'd been there at all. The man was up and off before Cora had even taken a step. She sifted the sodden pennysheets and rotten crates with her foot, just in case he'd dropped the knife. It was no great surprise to find he hadn't – that blade was his livelihood. Shined special for the Partner and the out-of-towners.

Cora let her breath settle back to its usual bindleleaf-induced pace and counted herself as fortunate as the Latecomer that the pair hadn't been real trouble. The Wayward hadn't been so lucky. When she got moving again she kept her wits about her, ignoring what she stepped in, until she emerged from the alleys and into an even more perilous part of the city: the administrative quarter. Least in the alleyways people were honest about stealing from you.

She made her way along wide, well-lit streets where important people walked from one important building to another. It was almost possible to pretend she was one of them. But then, when she looked up at the enormous pale stone walls and thin windows of the Wheelhouse, she felt about as small as a cutpurse impressed by a flash of silver. There was nothing about collecting her pittance of pay that made her feel important.

The Wheelhouse was squat and square, despite its name. It was home to the Commission – the civil service of Fenest. Even at this hour of the evening, lamps still burned in all the windows. The main doors were open and the front desk was manned. Clerks in washed-out purple rushed to and fro, arms overflowing with scrolls and ledgers. The Commission recorded every aspect of life in Fenest – the city, the people, the stories, all the hours of all the days. Cora was just another employee, paid, logged, weighed and measured by the Commission.

Her badge was checked at the front desk, as it always was, despite the regularity of her visits to the Wheelhouse.

When she'd first joined the police, Cora had wondered if badge-checking was a policy designed to make employees feel as if they could at any moment be rejected – a way to ensure complicity with Commission systems. Now she didn't bother wasting thought on such questions. The Commission was the Commission. It was above her pay grade to fathom it.

After all these years she knew her way through the ugly marble-floored corridors to the small office deep in the bowels of the building. She nodded to the men and women she passed, most of them blind as the Devotee behind their thick spectacles. If any of them had seen the sun this year, it was only because they were under orders to log that it still hung in the sky. No one looked healthy, least of all Henry.

He grunted a greeting as Cora entered the office. He'd put on weight again. He barely fit behind his desk, his gut resting on the top so he had to lift it to turn a page – something he did without thought. The smell of his sweat filled the room, and Cora felt guilty for letting some of it escape into the corridor.

'Gorderheim.' He strained to reach a stack of ledgers. 'Gorderheim. Gorder— yes. Every month I wonder if it'll be our last together.' He smiled, his lips thin in his face. He used to be all hands and smiles back when Cora was younger, and he was quicker.

'Don't say that, Henry. You've got another year in you, I'm sure.'

He hacked a laugh that quickly turned into a cough. 'Not 'nother election though, eh?'

'They making you do overtime?'

'And then again,' he said.

'All part of the Commission's greatest work.'

He looked hard at her for a moment, unsure if she was serious. For her part, she wasn't sure herself. What she'd said sounded like something from a pennysheet, and one that was particularly well-disposed to the Commission. There wouldn't be much relief from talking about the election now: there was a week to go until the first story was told.

And until then, the Commission's army of civil servants and bureaucrats would be drawing up lists, making lists of lists, copying everything in triplicate and filing it all somewhere in the Wheelhouse, never to be seen again.

'Between you, me, and the Stowaway, they've put me on voters,' Henry said, pride dripping down his chin alongside the sweat.

'Oh?'

'Three hundred of Fenest's finest scum and lowlifes, every district of the city represented an' accounted for.'

A pool of three hundred men and women from Fenest. For each story, fifty new names were drawn from the pool; fifty people who not only got to hear a storyteller's tale, but also had to pass judgement on it. And on that realm. Had to choose: a white stone or a black, with the prize a term in power, ruling over all the other realms and Fenest too. Were the voters the lucky ones? To listen to an election story was a privilege Cora had enjoyed before Ruth left, but to say whether that story deserved a vote, deserved seats in the Assembly? It was a burden Cora didn't want. Which was just as well: Commission staff, including the police, weren't eligible to vote. One of the few perks of the job.

'Voter lists. You're a big wheel, Henry, right enough.'

'Flatter all you like, Gorderheim.'

Cora waited, expecting a 'but' to follow. It didn't. She cleared her throat. 'As good as it is to catch up, I'm afraid I have to get to business.'

'Oak tonight, is it?'

'Where else?'

He chuckled unpleasantly. 'Lot of out-of-towners with wool between their ears and heavy purses.'

'Heavier than mine.'

'Now, now, *Detective*. The Commission compensates us *all* as per our station.' He turned his chair like a barge turned in a river. From a locked chest he produced a small stack of coins, which he placed carefully on the desktop; Commission regulations said he couldn't pass her the money directly. How they loved their pointless rules.

Cora stashed her pay inside her coat, in three separate pockets. It wasn't much, but she couldn't afford to lose it all at once – not even ringside. Most months she managed to double it or better on the same day she saw Henry.

Tonight, that would be a struggle. She had actual work to do.

'Audience save us from an election, right, Henry?'

She didn't wait for an answer, instead closing the door on the purple-clad clerk. As she strode away from the reek of stale sweat, she decided she had a second thing from that night to tell the Grateful Latecomer: this wasn't her world. The Commission, with all its petty concerns and wheels-within-Wheelhouses, was something she only had to worry about one day a month – pay day. Silence take it the rest of the time.

The rain-drenched streets of Fenest never felt so sweet as when she left the Wheelhouse behind.

Cora ducked inside the Dancing Oak. Steep stairs led down into the gloom, but she knew the way well enough. She also knew to grip the handrail when it was raining out. Making her way down, she dripped her own deluge on the steps which, worn smooth by decades of eager soles, were one of the finest waterfalls in all Fenest. If she listened long enough at the Oak's bar on such a night she'd hear a story of irrigation, pipes, and that same rain water ending up in the Oak's beer.

And tonight was a night for listening. If anyone knew about a Wayward with debts enough to make a message of his dead body, it'd be Beulah. Dancing Beulah ran half the chequers' halls in Fenest, one way or another, including the back room at the Oak. Cora hoped neither had anything *directly* to do with the Wayward in the alley. Or, at least, nothing that couldn't be worked out.

At the bottom of the stairs she avoided a man pissing his own waterfall and then pushed her way into the bar. For a moment she wondered if she had the right place, dazzled as she was by the sheen of oiled hair and beards in the lamplight. Men dressed in fashions that defied any kind of sense stood, posing, in pairs, acutely aware of when they were and weren't being watched. They laughed fake laughs and coughed politely. The women were no better.

'Amateur save me from the Perlish,' she said, not caring who heard. If they wanted to slum it when they visited for the election, fine, but she didn't have to like it. Though the more she looked, the more she noticed people from other realms among the Prized's fops and dandies.

At the bar, two Caskers were arm wrestling, as if they were the only people in the whole place. A Wayward passed her, the many pockets of his cloak full to bursting. Cora thought about stopping him, but what could she say? 'I've got a dead Wayward – you missing any friends?' She'd have just as much luck talking to the group of Seeders who were drinking strong ale with the kind of determination even the Drunkard would find unsettling.

Applause broke out like a fever. In the corner, on a stage lit by a single candle, a battered-looking man took to a piano. A few halting notes put an end to the applause. From his bruised mouth came the voice of a sweet summer girl.

She turned away and headed down the passage that led to the back room. At the barricaded door she banged twice, loud. Someone from the crowd shushed her.

When Butterman, the pennysheet hack, had said most of her sources were beyond this door, he'd been closer to the truth than he'd been his whole career. Lucky for her – lucky for a lot of people – the truth wasn't worth printing. Not that she'd tell that to the Whisperer.

She knocked again.

'What's the weather?' someone grunted from behind the door.

Cora cursed the Critic under her breath; how many times had she told Beulah such things were better left to Seminary children?

'Just let me in. I need to talk to her.'

'What's the weather?'

'Raining cocks, all right? It's raining cocks out there. Not enough to help him on the piano, mind.'

A deep belly-rumble came from the woman behind the door. 'Sure thing, Detective.' The door opened to reveal a heavily-lined face and gaps of missing teeth. 'I heard the Perlish did that to them singers,' she said, making a snipping gesture. 'Beulah's in her box.'

'Where else *would* she be?' Cora said.

As the door closed behind her, the Perlish eunuch was singing of betrayal, the kind that came from those who were loved.

The tiered booths that spread from the ring were full, every one of them, so full there was barely enough room for the chequers and the whores to ply their trades. The former squeezed through openings, looking hot in their black-and-white chequered coats. The latter were themselves squeezed as they wandered by in nothing but hats and old feathers.

A whore clumsily, deliberately, brushed against her. He wasn't the worst-looking boy Cora had ever seen. Cora cupped his chin, feeling the softness of rarely-shaven skin.

'When I'm done,' she said. 'You're upstairs?'

He nodded.

'Clean sheets, and make sure there's no one in the room when I arrive. No one. That includes you.'

She watched him move off among the crowd. He barely came up to her shoulder but he had some muscle to him. She might even sleep with him.

Passing beneath the booths, she eased her way through the press of bodies that surrounded the ring. It was as busy as she'd ever seen the back room, but at least the whole Union was out in force. Some realms made it to Fenest for the election in greater numbers than others, but a ring was as good a place as any to see the whole lot. Rustans with their lockports – metal sunk right into their skin and bones – and Caskers inked up to their eyeballs. Doe-eyed Seeders, and a few Perlish with enough sense to know where the real action was. Torn, too, though rare. Wayward rarer still. The wheel and all six spokes, the Union of Realms, as unified in the stench of bindleleaf smoke and sweat as it was in its love of stories.

Cora allowed herself a glance at the ring itself – just a look, just because she was there. Ash beetles, brought in from the Tear. An election special.

The chequers at the huge numbers-board, which hung in silent judgement above the ring, were working furiously to keep up. The lure of the ash beetle was too much for many, but three-to-one favourite was madness.

'Who'll take the beetle, who'll take it? You there— Oh, Detective.' The chequer took a step back from Cora.

'These short odds,' Cora said. 'Has the whole city gone mad?'

'I don't want any trouble,' the chequer said. 'Beulah, she—'

'She knows her business,' a man said, turning from the ring. A Rustan, by the looks of him; he wore a thick, lined coat despite the heat and his head was closely shaved. He was smoking a pipe, of all things. With one glance from the man, the chequer melted away into the crowd.

'These your beetles, then?' Cora asked the Rustan.

'Ash beetles need ash to breed – we live above those clouds, in cleaner air.'

'Lucky you.'

'We help get the beetles here, so your city can go mad.'

He took the pipe from his mouth as he spoke. At the end of the stem were two shiny metal teeth. Cora stopped herself from wincing at the sight, but she couldn't look away. He took his time replacing the ashes with fresh bindleleaf, as if the Bore was listening, and the bets continued all around them.

'There'll be some big losses tonight,' she said, allowing herself a brief glance at the ring.

The Rustan's metal teeth clicked loudly back into his mouth. 'Beetle or no, Latecomer's luck to you,' he said.

'Southerners,' she muttered, as she took the steps up to Beulah's box two at a time.

'What's your bet, Detective?' Beulah said.

Cora closed the door behind her. Beulah was sitting at a narrow window, hunched on a stool. She had a plain pair of story glasses through which she surveyed the ring below.

'Not tonight,' Cora said.

Beulah smiled without lifting the story glasses from her face. 'Tell it to the Drunkard.'

Every wall was plastered with betting slips, form tables, schedules and results from more manners of races and contests than Cora could name. The small room bulged with similarly papered shapes that must once have been usable furniture; nothing like a bed, though. Cora hoped the old chequer didn't sleep down here, making a nest for herself in the broken hopes of losers. Better she found someone warm upstairs, in the whorehouse she owned.

'So if you've not come to place a bet, what do you want, Detective?' Beulah said.

'I've got a body.'

'Lucky you.'

'I think he had debts,' Cora said.

'Dead people don't pay their debts.'

'Some debts are too big. Heard of any like that lately?'

Beulah gestured to the mess about her, the stubs that littered the floor, and those that spilled out of hanging baskets like dried flowers. 'You'll have to be more specific.'

'A Wayward. Visiting the city, I'd say. Someone wanted to send a message and used chequer colours to do so.'

Beulah chewed this over, half-reaching for something and then stopping, only to shuffle on a few feet and reach again. 'Wayward are rare at the ring. Even when they're the favourites.'

'The election?'

'Best pre-Opening Ceremony odds on an election story I've ever seen.' Shifting her stool, Beulah stood on it and plucked a sheet from the ceiling. 'See?'

Cora waved her away. 'I don't play rigged games.'

'So young, so cynical.'

'Wayward debts, Beulah, not election odds.'

'Fine.' With the precision of a wading bird at the water's edge, Beulah plucked slips from the murky detritus and came back with a grip full. 'I hope none of these are dead.'

Cora flicked through. The Wayward listed on the slips liked the horses – no surprise there. And they were stingy at it. Again, no surprise. Nothing worth killing over.

'You heard anything from the other ringmasters?' she asked.

'Those wet gossips? Nothing about a body, no. Nothing about a message.'

'Shame.'

'Is it?' Beulah said. 'I suppose it might be. Hard to give numbers either way.'

'The wisdom of the chequers.' Cora turned to leave the ringmaster. 'I hope your beetle loses.'

'One day you'll stop chasing long odds, Detective, and learn to take a sure thing when you see one.'

Cora left the cramped box and carried on up beyond Beulah, beyond the galleries and out of the back room. If she wasn't going to place a bet there was no reason to stay. She considered finding the boy she'd put on order, but there was too much to think on, and none of it felt good.

If the Wayward hadn't been killed because of his debts, hadn't been a warning to others coming to the city, then she had no idea why he *had* been killed. And that was a problem. Where to start to get the killer off the streets? Someone who took the time to sew a man's mouth might not be too shy about striking again. The last thing the city needed during an election was that kind of murder. The cutpurses and drunkards didn't go to the trouble of sewing up their victims. She doubted any of them knew how. Maybe that should be her first move; haul in the usual crowd and see if any of them could stitch.

She stepped into the street and lit a bindleleaf. By the door was a little niche dedicated to the Latecomer. At the feet of his crude wooden form were incense and pennies and all manner of scraps that spoke of stories told him here. Cora murmured a few words to the Latecomer before she left, mentioning the dead Wayward in the alley and the strange stitching of his mouth. In return, she asked the Latecomer for better luck, and as she walked away she saw that things were improving already: it had stopped raining.

Four

The next morning, Cora was stopped on the steps of Bernswick Station by a harassed-looking constable. But before she could add her own special form of harassment, might it please the Brawler, Sergeant Hearst emerged from the station.

'That's all right, Constable,' Hearst said.

The young man was either too confused or too exhausted to offer any complaint as the sergeant waved Cora forward.

'You'd best come in, Gorderheim,' Hearst said. 'Quickly now.'

'What's going on, sir?' Cora said, glancing back at the steps where more members of the Bernswick constabulary were gathering like a mob. 'Tell me no more stitched bodies have turned up.'

'Not yet. We've got a visitor.'

Hearst walked briskly past the unmanned front desk. In all Cora's years she'd never seen it empty like that. She felt a hollowness take hold of her, which grew with every echo of their footsteps.

'Had to close the station,' Hearst said. 'Not my idea, but nothing for it.'

'Close the station? For how long?'

'Keep up now, Gorderheim. We'll be closed for as long as they're here.'

'*Who?* Those two?'

Two men were standing rigid but alert at the end of the corridor. Tall as sentry towers, there was little more than a few inches between them and the ceiling. They were so wide that Cora and Sergeant Hearst had to shift sideways to pass between them to reach the door beyond.

'Gentlemen,' Hearst said with a heavy deference. He waited until Cora and he were well away before saying, 'Surely you recognise hired muscle when you see it?'

'What I *don't* recognise is why you're doffing your cap and giving them the "how you please, sir". So why don't you tell me just *whose* muscle that is?'

'The men are here with the Chambers,' a woman said behind her. Chief Inspector Sillian came down the stairs from her office on the top floor of the station. 'Outside the Audience, no one else causes this kind of havoc wherever they go.'

'Ma'am,' Hearst mumbled.

Cora found her mouth was too dry to do likewise, but managed to nod at the station's highest-ranking officer. The chief inspector had ten years on Cora, and every one of those years had been spent indoors behind a desk. Her skin was smooth. Her dark hair oiled in place, slick across her scalp, clamped around her ears. Her parting revealed a scalp as pale as the Widow.

'A Chambers?' Cora said. 'In the Audience's name—'

'Not a guest to keep waiting,' Sillian said.

That was an understatement. The Chambers were the most powerful people in the Union. Each realm had one, and whichever realm won an election, it was their Chambers who assumed control of the Assembly and had the final say over taxes, law-making, potholes... And now one of the Chambers had come to the Bernswick station. That couldn't be good news.

Hearst muttered something about refreshments and slipped away towards the briefing room. Cora made to follow him, but Sillian caught her arm.

'Detective, you'll come with me.'

The chief inspector was heading down to the cold room.

Cora had a glimmer of hope, fleeting, tantalising, that this might have something to do with the wheelwright scuffle that had got out of hand, and not her dead Wayward. Perhaps this Chambers owned a wheelwright, or the Derby Pump, or maybe they just wanted to stare at some mangled corpses.

That hope died as she descended the stone steps to where a man in the brown robe of the Chambers waited.

A man with the weathered face and slate-grey eyes of a Wayward.

Chief Inspector Sillian bowed, slow and full, a perfect example of studied deference. 'Your honour, this is Detective Gorderheim. She's the investigating officer on this case.'

The Wayward Chambers' gaze fixed on Cora. It was flat, intensely so, as if years on the Northern Steppes had left this man with nothing new, nothing impressive, to see. She could only look away as she was studied.

The body she'd found in the alleyway, only the morning before, was still laid out on the stone slab. Pruett and his assistant had done their best, but they couldn't hold off the Widow's attentions. The flesh had the usual pallor of the day-old dead, but the holes that punctured the skin around his lips were black now. With the dried blood cleaned, the effect was somehow worse than when the laces had still been there.

'Do you know who this is?' the Chambers said, his voice deep and accented, but clear.

'No,' Cora said.

'No one should, not yet.'

He put a hand on the forehead of his dead kinsman. The gold bracelet of the Chambers was unmistakable, even in the pale light of the cold room. One bracelet on each wrist, each bearing the horseshoe of the Wayward realm. Bracelets that turned to manacles when the occasion called for it. What those occasions were, Cora couldn't say. Ruth would have known. She'd have known it all – but then knowing it all was why Ruth had left. Abandoned her. Abandoned her to—

'Look at what they did to him,' the Chambers said. 'They knew his name. Who he was.'

Cora cleared her throat. 'And who was he, your honour?'

'Ento. Nicholas Ento. A name that, in a few weeks, would have shaped the Union.' The Chambers went to touch Ento's punctured lips but stopped. 'Find your place with the Audience, friend.'

'Your honour, we regret your loss,' Sillian said, her voice flat and measured, as if being near a Chambers was something she was used to. And maybe she was. Who knew the circles she moved in?

'Our loss… This is only the beginning.' He straightened and turned to them, his resolve as clear as anything could be on such a weathered face. 'Nicholas Ento was the Wayward realm's election storyteller.'

A storyteller. A storyteller had been murdered. She had never heard of such a crime before, and a quick glance at Sillian suggested that neither had the chief. As far as Cora knew, this was a first in the history of the Union. But had Sillian known the identity of the dead man all along? Was that why she wanted to keep a grip on this one?

'You're right to be shocked, Detective Gorderheim,' the Wayward Chambers said. 'Even in the aftermath of the War of the Feathers, when there was still so much distrust, even then a storyteller was held in high esteem. No one dared harm the first 'tellers as we sought peace after the war – votes instead of swords. But now, someone has committed the worst of all crimes.'

'I see,' Cora said, but in truth she was reeling.

'I doubt that. I doubt that very much.'

'Your honour—' Sillian said, trying to regain some control of the moment, but the Chambers waved her words away.

'You *see*, Detective, you're not just looking for a killer of men. Whoever did this, their wish is to kill the Wayward story, to silence us.'

'And you're not going to let that happen, are you?' Cora said, meeting the grey stare.

'The story Ento carried, it will be told,' the Chambers said.

'Is that wise, your honour?' Sillian said. 'Might it not be better to change the story, to find a new tale for the election?'

The Wayward blinked, and in that small gesture was a world of scorn. 'It is not a question of wisdom, Chief Inspector. It is a question of what is needed. The Wayward will tell the story Ento would have told, and you will find who killed Ento to ensure that no more lives are lost. We will not sacrifice our story, or another storyteller, to this election.'

The Chambers told them the body would be collected later that day by a Wayward delegation. It wasn't a request. Cora raised no objections: she was done with it and Pruett would be only too pleased to have it out of his way. She had a name now, and she knew who he really was: Nicholas Ento, the Wayward's election storyteller.

Cora waited respectfully for the chief inspector to accompany the Chambers from the cold room. Then she covered Ento and climbed back up the narrow, uneven stairs to the main floor. With each step, the picture became clearer, even as her bindle-ridden chest gave her less breath to consider what it meant. And maybe that was a good thing. She wasn't liking where those thoughts were taking her.

She'd been wrong to read the laces as a sign of the chequers. Black and white meant something else in Fenest right now, with the election coming. Black and white meant stones for voting, one of each colour weighing the pockets of those picked to hear a tale. Black for a good tale, white for bad. Black for winning seats in the Assembly, for a new Chambers to lead their realm in power over everyone else. Ento hadn't been killed for debts. According to his own Chambers he'd been killed because of his story, the Wayward realm's story, before a single vote had been cast.

And whoever had strangled him had wanted that known. Leaving the body in the alley, sewing the mouth and tipping off Butterman – if the murder *was* a message then it spoke a warning, but she needed more before she could understand it, let alone heed it.

The corridors of the station were still deserted, as was the briefing room and the front desk. She might have been the only living soul there. She waited.

It didn't take long for the boots to sound on the station's old and creaking floorboards. Sillian rounded the corner of the corridor. Without a glance at Cora, and without saying a word, she started up to her offices, which occupied the whole second floor. Cora followed her to the largest of the rooms and stood silently as the chief inspector positioned herself at the window to watch the street below.

'Once, Detective Gorderheim.'

'Excuse me, Chief Inspector?' Cora said, closing the door behind her.

'Once. That's how many times, before today, a Chambers has visited Bernswick Station.'

'Small mercies are rare under the Audience.'

'The Wayward Chambers,' Sillian said, 'comes to see the dead Wayward storyteller, who was found in your alleyway. Do tell me when we're granted the mercies, small or otherwise, Detective.'

Sillian allowed a silence to grow between them, still not turning from the window.

'You have a question,' Sillian said eventually. 'The obvious question. But it still needs to be asked.'

'Who would have known that Nicholas Ento was a storyteller?'

Sillian nodded to the street. 'Only the Chambers.'

'All six of them?'

'All *seven*,' Sillian said. 'You forget your politics, Detective. The Perlish have double of everything.'

'Of course, how could I forget the Perlish...'

'Every election the Chambers choose their storyteller from among their people, and tell their opposite numbers from the other realms. And only them.'

'Other people must know too, though, surely?' Cora said. 'The identity of a realm's storyteller is too big a thing to keep secret.'

'You're likely right. But only the Chambers are *supposed* to know until the Opening Ceremony.'

'Well, that helps narrow things down. Ignoring the Wayward Chambers, that still leaves only six people – one for each realm, plus two for the Perlish.'

'You will leave all the Chambers out of this, Gorderheim.'

'What?'

'You found a body in an alley behind a whorehouse. *Strangled*. Do I make myself clear?' Sillian said, meeting Cora's stare and holding it.

'But... you said yourself, the Chambers are the only ones who would have known Ento was a storyteller.'

'That's not what I care about. It's not what the pennysheets care about, either.'

'If you want someone else on this, that's fine,' Cora said. 'Politics, the election, I'm a poor fit for any of it.' And then quietly: 'You know my family's history.'

'I do, but you are not your parents, Gorderheim. Or your sister, for that matter. However, that history might mean you're more... more *alive* to the sensitivities of this case.'

Sensitivities? That was a new name for corruption. Her mother would have approved.

'I want *you* on this case,' Sillian said. 'You're the one who started with it, you're going to keep it. But I want you to do it the right way. The only way. Find the person who *did* strangle the storyteller. Find the killer. That's all.'

'Is that an order?'

Sillian glanced back at the street. 'We're all watching, Detective. And here's another order for you: I remain informed of all developments.'

Cora started to object, and then remembered where she was. Who she was talking to. She gave a half-hearted salute, which Sillian didn't even notice, and then left the office.

How a man or woman came to tell a story at an election wasn't something Cora had given much thought to over the years. An election happened, there were storytellers,

one realm won, and life went on. People would grumble
– the Seeder Chambers did this, the Rustan Chambers
said that, but that was people complaining for the sake
of it, encouraged by the pennysheets. Most had no idea
what was going on in the Assembly. Probably couldn't
tell a Chambers from a coach driver; until that morning,
neither could Cora.

But now she knew it was the Chambers who decided
which individual would tell that realm's story in the
election. Maybe each Chambers had a different way of
deciding? Maybe for each realm there were well-known
storytellers waiting five years just for a chance to tell a
story? Maybe... Maybe Cora had too many questions.

She needed to speak to Constable Jenkins. She needed
to speak to Sergeant Hearst. She had plenty to tell the
Martyr, the Poet, and the Amateur too. And none of them
were around to hear it.

Even so, she had to start somewhere.

Five

Cora headed for the Seat of the Commoner. It didn't matter where you were in the Union – up one of those Rusting Mountains, dockside on the River Cask, even wandering the Steppes – you'd find Seats to the Audience: places to say your piece to one of the members in the hopes you got their attention. She could have chosen other places in the city to begin, and plenty more besides in which to think through her next course of action. But if this case was as much about the election as it was murder then the Commoner would be just as willing to listen to her stories as the Widow.

Cora wasn't as devout as some she knew – the newer constables tended to have a real religious streak she didn't share, visiting a different Seat every day. She wondered if Jenkins shared their zeal. When Cora's time came, she wanted to take her place with the Swaying Audience along with the rest of them. Her life was full of stories to sway them, especially the Widow. If that pale spinster didn't welcome her into the afterlife with open arms and a spot ready with a good view, what with all the tales of death Cora brought her, then there wasn't hope for anyone. Cora knew she didn't always have the time to tell every grisly detail. She knew she wasn't the best storyteller in the Union. But still – what she told was worth something, surely?

Hopefully the Commoner wouldn't be too upset that she wasn't there just to talk to him today. She had an idea there was someone else inside his Seat who would be worth the walk from the station alone.

She admired the heavy wooden doors of the Seat as she entered: intricately carved with hundreds of people who appeared to lean out of the wood, their shoulders and heads thrust forward. She had been to her share of Seats of the Commoner and they all had crowds rendered in one form or another, whether the people were carved, painted or woven. It was hard to be sure of the nature or temperament of the Commoner's crowds. They were as indecipherable as anything to do with the Audience. To Cora, they looked as uncertain as she felt.

Huge, unlit hearths lined the walls of the Seat and most of the benches were empty. At the head of the aisle was a stone statue that was little more than a silhouette of a person: the Commoner, ready to hear everyone's tales of home, hearth, and maybe something election-related. Perhaps ready to hear Cora's tale of a murdered storyteller, and the most powerful men and women in

Fenest who might be responsible: the Chambers. There was a tall man in a plain robe dusting the statue. He wasn't wearing any shoes as he stood on tiptoe.

'Commoner's welcome,' he said. 'I won't be a minute here.'

But as she started to reply, to tell him not to rush on her account, she heard a ripple of laughter. So her tip had been right.

'Think I'll listen first,' Cora said.

The caretaker smiled. 'Commoner likes a good listener as much as a good 'teller.'

At the far end of the Seat was a group of maybe ten or fifteen children sitting on the floor: a school outing. Cora had been on many such trips in her time at school, but *her* school had been the Commission Seminary. These children looked to be from a city school, the poor kind, judging by their clothing. They were listening to the woman standing before them. She nodded a greeting as Cora sat down, but the children didn't bother to turn around. Each of them had string crossing the back of their head: they were wearing their paper masks of the Audience. This was the election, played out before her. She and Ruth had done likewise at the Seminary.

Her sister had enjoyed their lessons about the election, but she'd been good with numbers too: profit and loss, debts and loans. More of the Commission's good works. Ruth's talents explained a great deal, in hindsight. How else had her sister been able to find out the truth of their parents' dealings? Their mother and father had paid for Ruth to attend the Seminary, hoping she would carry on the good work of the Gorderheims, and instead it was the knowledge Ruth gained there that helped undo the family. They ended up telling many stories to the Weary Governess. Had Ruth known the terrible way things would unfold after she'd given the story to the pennysheets? Sometimes, when her anger was a cool and brittle thing, Cora told herself that Ruth couldn't have known. That Ruth hadn't been much more than a child herself when she left – just seventeen. But most days, Cora believed Ruth knew exactly what she was doing. And that she chose to leave Cora to deal with it.

Cora became aware the caretaker had joined her on the bench. He'd left a well-judged distance between them: not so close to cause discomfort, but close enough for Cora to share a story if she chose to. The caretaker had the shrewdness of someone who'd spent a lifetime in a Seat.

'I always hated the way the mask felt against my face,' Cora said. 'Itchy and ticklish at the same time. And the *smell*.'

'I'm sure some here feel the same,' the caretaker said, nodding towards the group. 'They're doing well to keep the masks on.'

'That's the power of a good story.' Cora studied the backs of the children's heads. It didn't take long to find the girl she was looking for, with her lank hair and throaty cough. But Cora would wait – it wouldn't do to interrupt a story in a Seat.

'I realise my age, seeing them learning like this,' the caretaker said. 'As I wore a paper mask to learn about the election, so did you, my friend, and so do they. A never-ending circle, a wheel that must always turn to save us from the chaos of the past.'

'That's been drummed into every Seminary child ever since peace was declared after the War of the Feathers.'

'And the election devised as a means to keep it.' The Caretaker stretched his legs. 'The War, now. We didn't learn much of that at my school. But I'm guessing you were Seminary-trained?'

Cora nodded.

'You're Commission then?'

It was easy logic. Seminary children were always Commission-bound. That was why parents used their good name and their good money to get them places in the Seminary as soon as the new babes of Fenest could stand. Once they'd finished their studies, they were given jobs, all of which in some way made sure the election kept happening. And that other children would come to Seats to learn the election's power.

'You've a busy time of it at the moment,' the caretaker said, with some kindness.

Another nod couldn't do justice to the truth of *that* statement, but why burden an old man with the case? It was burden enough for her.

'The War of the Feathers was my favourite lesson,' she said.

The caretaker smiled and closed his eyes, and Cora began.

'The Archduke of Perlanse died and left twin sons squabbling over power. They were young and feckless and cared only for the finer things in life. Things that fascinate the realm even now: hairpieces, jewellery, rare fruits and rarer pets. It was the last of these that sent everyone as senseless as the Brawler.

'Each brother had been given a kenna bird by their father: one red bird, one blue. I saw pictures of kennas at the Seminary, but never a real one. Flightless birds, only interested in preening their ridiculously coloured feathers and stretching their ridiculously long necks.'

'No wonder the Perlish love them,' the caretaker murmured.

'As the brothers squabbled over who would be the next Archduke, one of the kenna birds was killed – a hat pin right through the heart. I liked to tell that part of the story to myself in the dull lessons.'

She decided not to tell the caretaker how much she'd enjoyed using a quill to stab the drawing of the bird.

'The brother whose bird was killed blamed the other, swore revenge. The great Perlish houses took sides, West or East; territories were marked out, and it wasn't long before the battles started. The fighting spilled over into the neighbouring Lowlands, and many were killed, including a visiting delegation of the Torn who had the misfortune to be caught in the middle of the warring duchies.'

'All because of a kenna bird,' the caretaker said. 'It was the death of the Torn that brought it all to an end. That much I *do* know.'

'And brought the first election.'

'And so the wheel turns,' he said, opening his eyes. He gave Cora a nod of thanks and said something about the hearths, but his voice was all but lost in the noise coming from the children. Their story was going down well.

The caretaker took his leave, and Cora listened.

'And that's when Laurel leapt.' The teacher raised her hands. The children gasped. 'Right onto the back of old Madam Swanson.'

The little audience laughed.

'Laurel scampered up the lady's back and started to lick the honey from her hair!'

'No!' a boy cried, and was quickly hushed.

There was more laughter. Laurel, apparently a naughty, nimble lapdog, was causing all kinds of mayhem at an important party. The guest of honour was a stuffy duke from Perlanse whom Madam Swanson was trying to impress. The story's final flourish had the duke fall backwards into a three-tiered cake and Laurel, a lover of laps, join him. As the party – and the Audience – held their breath, the duke proclaimed that Laurel should be at every one of his parties.

A roar of applause.

Then, abruptly, the children turned serious. Each one took a pair of stones from their pockets, their coats or from the benches. The teacher-come-storyteller placed a small box in front of the children.

The shuffling of feet stopped. Now in a line, the children had a handful of moments to consider their choices and cast their votes. Each child, still masked, came forward and dropped a pebble inside, careful that no one else could see the colour of their voting stone. A silence fell, deep enough to please the Commoner, as the votes were cast and then counted.

'I'd give Laurel the lapdog two-to-one favourite,' Cora muttered to herself. 'Even if this isn't the Messenger's Seat.'

The teacher announced the result: eleven for, two against.

The children whooped and cheered. Some tried to throw their masks into the air to celebrate but the paper made it difficult. When their excitement had died down, the teacher packed up their voting box and led the class along the aisle. The girl was last in the line and tried to slip past. Cora caught her by the arm and made her sit beside her.

'Hello, Marcus.' A wave of her badge let the teacher know all was right with the world. Mostly. 'I didn't think you actually went to school,' Cora said.

'One day a week. It's nice to have a rest,' Marcus said. She was named on Drunkard's Day, poor soul. A pennysheet girl by trade, she'd helped Cora in the past and had a good set of eyes and ears on her.

'I almost didn't recognise you without your stack of 'sheets.'

The girl shrugged. 'Why, what're you after?' Her baritone, usually booming headlines across busy streets, was oddly delicate in the Seat.

'Nothing much,' Cora said. 'Just keep your ear out.'

'For what?'

Cora hesitated. The identity of the dead Wayward wasn't in the 'sheets yet. But it soon would be. Cora might as well be the one to break the story. It was *her* story, in some ways.

'The man found strangled behind Mrs Hawksley's, he—'

'Him with the mouth sewn up?'

'He was the Wayward storyteller.'

Marcus' eyes widened and she sat back on the bench. Then she grinned. 'I'll do well out of that twist. What am I meant to be listening for?'

'You hear anything about the new Wayward storyteller, or their story, from the sheet hacks or the sellers, you come to me.'

Marcus looked at the door. 'I dunno, Detective… The hacks won't like it and I got to get paid, don't I?'

'Maybe this will help: I'll take the morning and afternoon editions at the Bernswick station.'

'What editions?'

'All of them. And don't look like that, they'll be paid for.'

'A pleasure working with you, Detective.'

The girl hopped off the bench. Cora let the pennysheet girl go, but then something occurred to her.

'Marcus?'

'What?'

'You were one of the white votes, weren't you?'

'Stupid dog story. It wasn't funny.'

Cora watched the girl go. She knew it was ridiculous, but for some reason she found herself thinking of Ruth again. She couldn't seem to stop. It must be the election, and Cora getting dragged into it with Ento's death.

Her sister was a lot older than Marcus when she left, and she couldn't have been more different from the pennysheet girl. Always in school and choosing to stay longer each day than she had to, unlike Cora who was out the door before the final bell had even finished ringing. Ruth would study in the library or ask her teachers endless questions. But, like Marcus, Ruth would have hated a comic tale about a lapdog. She would have seen it as a wasted opportunity. 'There's power in stories and a story of power.' That was one of the last things Ruth had said on the night she left.

Cora kept looking at the little pennysheet girl, hoping she'd turn around one last time. But she didn't, and then she was out the door and lost to the city.

Returning to the statue of the Commoner, Cora touched his outstretched hand and then sat on a bench opposite.

'A story for you, Commoner,' she said, 'the kind you'll want to hear. The kind you'll remember. The body was left there to be found. At least, that was how it looked. But then I started making mistakes. I haven't stopped since. I haven't...'

The Poet's bells rang the hour across the city before Cora left the Seat of the Commoner and headed back to the station. By that time the disturbance caused by the Wayward Chambers had eased, and Cora held a small hope of getting something done. And there was much *to* do, even with the chief inspector's warning that she had to keep clear of the Chambers.

'Find the killer,' Sillian had said. 'That's all.'

Easier said than done.

Cora found Sergeant Hearst right where she expected: the station roof. As she climbed onto the small, flat square that sat between the great peaks of the roof, the warm wind tugged at her. Even up here there was no escaping the smell of the streets: horse muck and drains. But there was something else, something sharper underneath all that. The stink of birds.

She joined Hearst in the shelter of the chimney breast, where the pigeons roosted. He was dropping seed along a low wall, and the birds were pecking it up as quick as he could get it down.

'Keep on like that and they'll be too fat to fly,' she said. 'Drop like stones.'

'Speaking of stones,' Hearst said, 'I hear you're on election business now.' He dusted his hands of seed.

'Audience help me.'

Cora looked out across the city. The station wasn't the tallest building in Bernswick, but it gave a good enough view of the spires on the Grand Seat of the Poet, and, beyond them, the grubby glass dome where the Assembly sat, soon to be led by whichever Chambers won the election. A few streets over was the Wheelhouse: home of the Commission and its thousands of scribblers and stone-counters who made the election happen. Between them, the tangle of streets and alleys that was Fenest. Where Ento's killer was still hiding.

'Did the Wayward Chambers tell you anything useful?' Hearst said.

'You mean aside from the fact the dead man was a storyteller?'

'I had heard that.'

They were both silent for a moment.

'We've got a name,' Cora said, and ducked as a pigeon flew too close to her face. 'And an address. Lodging house where the 'teller was staying. That's where I'll start.' She made for the hatch that led back inside.

'You'll have to get something better to wear for tomorrow,' Hearst called after her. 'You can't go looking like that.'

Cora stopped. 'All right, I'll play along – go where?'

'The Opening Ceremony. This is an election case now.'

She put a hand on the warm chimney breast and a pigeon took to the air. She watched it fly silently up towards the Audience. 'Why did he have to be a storyteller?'

'Garnuck House, six o'clock.'

'Can't you go, sir? I... Well, it's not my kind of crowd, is it?'

Hearst stuffed the empty seed bag into his pocket. 'It is now. This is your case. Had that from Sillian directly.'

'But all those Commission types, their noses in the air. I won't know...'

'Won't know what, Gorderheim?'

'You *know*.' She waved at the pigeons, as if they were a demonstration of the rotten grandeur she'd likely see parading at Garnuck House.

'Take Jenkins,' Hearst said. 'She'll be useful.'

'The constable with the teeth?'

'Her mother worked for the Office of Electoral Affairs. Ran it, I should say. Jenkins knows more about that world than your average constable.'

'If her mother was that high in the Commission, how did she end up at the bottom as a constable? She could have done anything with a start like that.'

'Jenkins could ask you the same question,' Hearst said. 'You can discuss it while you're sipping your fine Perlish wine at the Opening Ceremony.'

'You know I don't drink.'

'You might after tomorrow night.'

Six

In disbelief, Cora read the pennysheet headline again: *Chambers Chases Justice to Tell the Keeper! Wayward Storyteller's Death Not a Priority*. She tried to clear her throat but ended up with a hacking cough that made her spit a yellow-black mess into the nearby bin.

Her room in the lodging house was barely furnished: a bed, a cupboard for her clothes – the few that she owned – and a washstand. She didn't even have a table or a desk. Her mother had been so disappointed by her decision to join the police force that Cora had left home not quite empty-handed, but not far off. Her landlord had offered her a chair when she'd first moved in, soon after joining up, but she'd never taken him up on the offer. There hadn't seemed much point, given that she spent so little time here. Some weeks she wondered about returning the bed.

She went back to *The Spoke*. The 'sheet claimed the reason the Wayward Chambers had been forced to sink to such a level as to visit a police station was because he had no faith the police would find Ento's killer, and that there was a lack of commitment to the truth – would the Whisperer believe it. *The Spoke's* inside knowledge of the case, being the first to break the story, meant they were perfectly positioned to cover every twist and turn, every suspect and arrest, every blunder, of which they expected many.

What utter nonsense. As if the force wouldn't try to find the killer. As if they'd have a choice! They did their best to solve cutpurse crime – why would they decide to fall short for a dead storyteller? But what else could be expected, with Butterman's name at the bottom of the column?

The rest of the evening edition of *The Spoke* was given over to the Wayward's election hopes, so cruelly dashed by the death of their storyteller. A whole column was dedicated to the chequers. Who knew how many marks had already been put down on the Wayward story to win? What would happen to the numbers now? The story was apparently going to strike at the heart of the Union – so *The Spoke* predicted – and would shock everyone who heard it. As long as the Wayward had courage enough to find another storyteller to tell such a shocking tale, they might still win. But that wasn't without its risks.

Cora tossed the 'sheet onto her bed with the rest. Marcus had done as Cora asked, after she'd seen the girl in the Seat of the Commoner, and delivered all the pennysheet editions. But Cora hadn't realised there would be *quite* so many of them: morning, afternoon and evening editions of *The Fenestiran Times*, *The Daily Tales* and *The Spoke*, plus *The Stave*, which was only printed first thing but guaranteed to contain all the day's news before it had even happened.

Grimly, she picked up another 'sheet. She'd paid for them, or rather, the station's petty cash had, so she might as well read them. Couldn't afford not to, really. The death of Nicholas Ento was an election story, and the 'sheets were alive to the election's scandals and secrets. Not all that was printed was true, but if there were grains of truth there, hints that might become leads, she needed them.

The Fenestiran Times led with a different story to *The Spoke*: the Commission's decision to use Burlington Palace as the venue for the Perlish election story. A controversial choice, according to the 'sheet, given that the palace was a strategic landmark during the War of the Feathers. The unnamed writer of the column suggested the use of Burlington was intended as a critique of the Perlish for their penny-pinching approach to power – the Commission up to its usual trick of making its views known without ever actually saying anything. Why else make the Perlish tell their story at the site where they massacred the Torn, if not to make them face their past actions? And remind the voters of them too.

But the view of *The Daily Tales* was an altogether different story. According to that 'sheet, the choice of

Burlington Palace for the Perlish venue was simply long-overdue recognition of the glorious power of Perlanse, and its place in the history of the Union.

Cora pushed the pennysheets to the floor and sat down on her now print-stained bed. Every story had a different way of being told and it was hard not to see possible connections in all of it to Ento's murder. She needed a lead, and soon.

The clock chimed in the hall downstairs; she was going to be late.

Cora kicked the 'sheets out of the way and felt the pain in her tendon. The old ache. The stitcher who came to the house the day after Ruth left had claimed he'd got all the glass from Cora's foot. Cora had never been convinced, but the pain had been part of her life for so long now, she couldn't imagine her body without it. Just as she couldn't imagine her life with her sister as part of it. The stitcher had been called back to the house just a week after he'd removed the glass, when her father had been found dead.

She grabbed her coat from the bed and briefly saw Nicholas Ento in the alley, laid out on a cape of stiffened skin. Would going to the Opening Ceremony help her find his killer? She very much doubted it, but she had to hope it wouldn't be a complete waste of time.

Cora took stock of herself. Her coat didn't look any more crumpled than usual, but she brushed mud from a sleeve – Hearst had said she needed to look presentable for the Opening Ceremony. This wasn't likely to be what the sergeant meant, but she didn't care. Cora wasn't going tonight to look 'fetching', as her mother might have said. Might have hoped. She stepped out of her room, locking the door behind her, and put the key in her pocket next to her badge.

Detective Cora Gorderheim was going to Garnuck House to do her job.

She caught a Clotham's gig, rather than one belonging to the larger coach company started by the Rustan Simeon Garnuck. That little defiance lifted her mood. As did the fact that she definitely *was* going to be late. She lit a bindleleaf and promised herself a trip to the Dancing Oak as soon as she could get away.

The driver dropped her at the main doors, or as close as he could get to them. Carriages and coaches and gigs fought for room, with people wandering between them, all heading for the wide steps up to Garnuck House. Light spilled from the open doors and tall windows, seeming to draw everyone towards the place. Cora included.

'Detective?'

Cora found herself face to face with Constable Jenkins, who was almost unrecognisable out of her bulky uniform. Tonight, Jenkins was in a sleek black dress, which showed her to be lean – the kind of leanness that helped when chasing down a cutpurse, Cora thought. The constable's dark hair was caught up in some kind of scarf, and another scarf was draped around her shoulders. Even her teeth looked different, smarter somehow, as she told Cora how excited she was to be at the Opening Ceremony.

'Shall we go in?' Jenkins said. 'We don't want to miss the dance.'

'Dance?'

'I can't wait either!' Jenkins appeared to rein in her enthusiasm. 'But if you think we should miss it, if there's something else we should be looking for... Sergeant Hearst, he said I had to help—'

Someone bumped into Cora. A woman whose back looked to have sprouted feathers made her apologies, but not before she'd looked Cora up and down and frowned. Cora shrugged herself more firmly into her old coat and steered Jenkins up the steps.

'Looks like we're getting in the way of all these eager folk. And you're one of them.'

Jenkins beamed.

'Hearst tells me your mother was high up in the Commission,' Cora said. 'Ran electoral affairs.'

Jenkins nodded. 'I grew up hearing about voting chests and tents.'

'And yet it didn't put you off.'

They came to the top of the steps and joined a slow-moving queue of bodies pressing to get inside.

'To hear the stories,' Jenkins said, 'there's nothing better, is there?'

Cora was about to mention the betting ring, the smell of blood and sweat and discarded chequers' slips, but thought better of it. 'If your mother was a big wheel, why join the constabulary? Why not go into the Commission? Top level?'

The dreamy look on Jenkins' face vanished and she looked at Cora with a kind of confidence. The kind that was hard-won.

'I wanted to make my own way,' Jenkins said. 'That's how it should be.'

Did this young woman know Cora's story? Was it just coincidence that Cora had ended up with a constable with whom she had a lot in common?

'You're right,' Cora said. 'That *is* how it should be. But it's not how it often plays out.'

'Your coat, madam?'

Cora flinched. She hadn't noticed the greying man in Commission livery standing in front of her. He was small in the crowd, which was itself small under the painted ceiling and the polished brass and the gilded walls of the entrance hall. He was holding out a hand, his face the plainest thing in sight.

'I'd rather…'

Without giving it a second thought, Jenkins took the scarf from her shoulders and tossed it over the man's arm. Then she was away into the crowd, as casual as if she was just walking by the River Stave.

'Madam?' the servant said to Cora, as one might do when encouraging a child to take their first steps.

She jammed her hands into her coat pockets and pushed past him, making sure to keep close to Jenkins.

The hall soon opened onto a large room that was filling up with guests, dignitaries and all manner of important people Cora didn't recognise – but she *did* recognise that they were important. It wasn't just the well-tailored clothes or the tastefully worn jewellery. It was the way they carried themselves: straight-backed, as if they'd never walked a street in which they'd step in something, or on somebody. The set of their shoulders, their light smiles and clean conversations suggested they didn't even know such streets existed. Not in their Fenest. Had Cora's parents still been alive, they would likely have known these people. And if Cora's mother had had her way, Cora would be part of this crowd, rather than watching it from the outside.

She and Jenkins were caught nonetheless, and were moved, slowly, into the room. Four huge chandeliers hung from the ceiling, each made up of six rings of glass-encased oil lamps: the six realms of the Union. There was no escaping the form of things.

The light from the chandeliers caught everything: people's drinks, their jewellery, even the buttons on their jackets and the stitching of their dresses. The waiters' trays flashed in the crowd like mirrors. Everything was gold-tinted. The lavish fountain at the centre of the great space only heightened the effect. Its tall spouts of water were shot through with rainbows, and they poured down on a set of unnervingly detailed dogs: a rabble caught in bronze, mid-frolic, as if enjoying a perfectly-timed rain storm.

'His great loves,' Jenkins said, following Cora's gaze.

'Sorry?' She wiped the fountain's spray from her face, then wondered if it was actually sweat. Perhaps she should have left her coat at the door.

'Simeon Garnuck. When he moved to Fenest he came to love dogs. Those there, they're modelled on his pets.'

'More money than sense,' Cora grumbled.

'Only until the Commission took it away from him. Garnuck had debts all over Fenest...' Jenkins coughed, and looked away. 'Debts that just so happened to be called in when the Rustans lost the Assembly to the Caskers.'

'Rivers, not roads, eh?'

'Something like that. Might have pleased the Washerwoman, but it wasn't the Commission's finest hour.'

'There's plenty in the running for that title.' Cora made for the nearest wall, wishing, and not for the first time, that she wasn't so tall. The job wasn't always about intimidation. Often it paid to go unnoticed.

Jenkins took two glasses from a passing server, and Cora accepted one, just to have something to occupy her hands. She asked Jenkins what kind of stories she favoured.

'*Well*,' the constable said, baring her teeth in a huge grin. She'd obviously been waiting for that question. 'My mother always said the funny ones were the best bet for black stones, but I think funnies have a cruelty in them.'

'And you wouldn't vote for that?'

Jenkins shook her head. 'I like it when things end well, for everyone. Or as near as can be.'

'Our line of work doesn't encourage happy endings,' Cora said.

'But we still look for them,' Jenkins said quietly, then sipped her drink.

For a moment neither spoke, just watched the gilded and the garish pass by.

'Wasn't a happy end for Nicholas Ento,' Cora said eventually, 'but we'll find an ending, happy or otherwise, when we find out why he was killed. Let's start with tonight. What are we doing here? All of us, I mean.'

'Right,' the constable said. She downed her drink and put the glass on a passing tray. 'Tonight is as much about the Perlish term ending as it is the start of the election. That's why the wine tonight is from Perlanse, for instance. Both duchies.'

'And why it smells like horse piss. You seem to be enjoying it. Here.' Cora handed Jenkins her untouched glass.

'The cultural item,' Jenkins said, 'that'll be Perlish too.'

'And what's that?'

'If I had to guess I'd say it would be the Hildantante. That's usually the Perlish choice for these kinds of functions. Don't worry, Detective. You won't have to join in.'

'Join in with what?'

'Oh, sorry – the Hildantante's a folk dance.'

Cora groaned. A folk dance.

'But we've got the formal opening first,' Jenkins said, 'with the parade and the unveiling.'

Cora looked around to see if anyone was smoking. A heavy-set woman stepped on her foot and the old ache flared.

'… that's why it's more difficult,' Jenkins was saying.

'Sorry?' Cora said.

'For the Perlish. As the incumbents, they have the hardest job in this election. Their story is judged more harshly than those of the other realms. They should have done a better job when they were in power, I suppose.'

'You mean not all the voters enjoyed reduced trade taxes while the Perlish were in charge of the Assembly, Constable? No cheap cheese and wine for all their balls and banquets?'

'Hard to enjoy a banquet when the sewers are overflowing,' Jenkins said, warming to her subject. 'It's as if the Perlish Chambers have their own personal roads to travel the Union – they've done nothing about the state of them in Fenest. Holes big enough to swallow a gig. And the gangs of bandits – some no older than children – in every alley. And the markets and shops—'

'And yet here we are, at a ball. Or is this a banquet?'

'Neither,' Jenkins muttered. 'They've done nothing but line their own pockets.'

'"A Perlish pocket is always lined by another's silk."'

'Perlanse is too cold for silkworms, that's why.'

'As a lover of stories, I thought you'd be less literal,' Cora said. 'Some would argue it's the Commission that should have done something about the sewers and the roads.'

'The Commission tallies how much money there is to spend. Whoever holds the Assembly decides where that money goes.'

'Wine and cheese. So, nobody is envying the Perlish storyteller then?'

'*Storytellers.* They send two.'

'Because they do everything in pairs.'

Jenkins shrugged. 'The duchies are still formally separate.'

'If the Perlish have the hardest job of winning this election,' Cora said, 'that could be a reason for one of their number to kill another realm's 'teller, if the Perlish thought that story presented a particular challenge to them.'

'I suppose the motive is there,' Jenkins said, 'though no one would go so far, surely? There are laws, and traditions, that protect 'tellers.'

'They didn't protect Nicholas Ento, did they?' Cora said.

Jenkins looked like she might have an answer to that, but then something seemed to catch her eye on the other side of the room. 'He has *some* nerve.'

Cora turned to see a familiar problem walking towards them: Butterman.

'Audience-sake, why did they let *you* in?' Cora said to the pennysheet hack.

'They let everyone in,' Butterman said, waving towards the bar where several other pennysheet writers were steadily drinking the place dry.

'No need for you lot to do any actual work, is there? You'll just make it up anyway.'

'Right you are, Detective.' He scratched under the rim of his tub hat. 'Don't s'pose you've got a word about that Chambers visit for my readers?'

'Funnily enough, no.'

'And you wonder why we get creative.'

'Accusing us of not wanting to find the truth!' Jenkins said. 'Do you have *any* idea how an investigation works?'

'I know it's mostly boring. I'm sorry, we haven't met. I'm—'

'She knows who you are, Butterman.' Cora pushed away his offered hand. 'Constable, it looks like we both need another drink.'

'But—'

'*Now*, Constable.'

'They still don't have a replacement storyteller,' Butterman said, almost wistful.

'Critic take you, don't pretend you care. Whatever helps sell a few more 'sheets, right?'

'Dead or alive, storytellers sell 'sheets.'

'This year, no,' a muffled voice said. There was suddenly the trace of smoke on the air. 'The Wayward story. That will sell every pennysheet.' A woman joined them, glancing from Cora to Butterman.

A Torn woman.

Seven

In all her years, Cora had rarely been this close to a citizen of the Tear, and those few times were usually in Beulah's dark, smoke-filled betting rings or games houses. At this moment, in Garnuck House, Cora was closer than she'd like. She could see everything.

Three small glass boxes were strapped to the woman's face. The glass was misted and smoky, like that of the older Fenestiran street lamps, and there was a flickering hint of a flame beneath. This woman had a small furnace covering her mouth. And inside it?

Tornstone.

Cora's Seminary lessons came back to her. For as long as there had been stories told, the Torn had lived in the Tear: a great rift in the earth where lava flowed freely and ash rained from the sky. Every day the Torn lived and breathed fire and smoke. That changed a people, over time. The Torn had to adapt, or they wouldn't have survived in their chosen land. A land that left them scarred – this member of the Torn was laced with a pale tracery that spoke of a long, hard life. Cora's own scars, those that made her foot a lumpen mess, were nothing in comparison to this woman's marks.

When the people of the Tear did choose to leave – which was rare outside of an election – they took a bit of it with them, so they could breathe as they did at home. If the Tear was a smoky, ash-filled sauna, then Cora supposed Fenest's air would feel like swallowing ice. Ice that tasted too much of a city, of people.

But knowing that didn't change how unsettling it was to see, in the flesh, this woman with burning volcanic rocks an inch from her face. Too close to Cora's face too.

Cora took a step back, bumping into the wall. Butterman felt no such fear.

'You know what the Wayward's story will be?' he asked the Torn woman. 'I've heard some of the Wayward come near the Tear. Not so close as to risk themselves, but—'

'Close enough,' said the woman. 'Closer than any from Fenest.' She looked at Cora. 'We come to you, yes? We come for election, though your air is weak, like Drunkard's piss.'

'That's Fenest all right,' Cora said. 'The centre of the wheel draws us all.'

The Torn laughed. At least, Cora took the louder, harsh grating sound for laughter. The woman wore a dark dress of heavy cotton that bagged about her. Who knew what fashions made sense in the Tear? Or what their bodies were like beneath?

'Wheels. You love them.' The mouthpiece flared. 'But wheels turn, and only Audience knows when they stop.' The woman made a circling gesture with hands covered in old, shallow scars.

'Time you were going, Butterman,' Cora said.

The hack looked back and forth between Cora and the Torn. 'Not even off the record?'

'As if I could trust you to honour that.'

He produced a card from somewhere in his cheap suit. 'If you want to talk to someone with *real* influence,' he said, forcing the card on the Torn woman. He headed towards the bar.

Cora took a deep breath and held out her hand. 'Detective Gorderheim. Bernswick Division.'

The Torn took Cora's hand in both of her own and pressed Cora's knuckles, quickly and firmly. Was that a Torn handshake? A curse?

'I know you, Detective,' the Torn said. 'I am Sorrensdattir.'

'You're here for the election?'

'What else brings my people to your streets? I am... you would say *advisor* for the Torn realm.'

'And what do the Torn know of the Wayward story?' Cora said, keeping her voice low.

Sorrensdattir held Cora's gaze for a moment, then looked away, into the shaking pool of the fountain.

'We know enough. Ento died for his story. A story some do not want told.'

'Why? What's it about?'

The woman walked towards the fountain. Everyone hurried out of her path, and Cora caught sight of one man making the Sign of the Tear. It was prejudice, plain and simple, and Cora knew she was as guilty as the rest of them. She'd broken up Casker bar-brawls, arrested Seeder bandits fool enough to venture into the city, caught Perlish traders who were making off with other people's fortunes. But she wasn't shying away from people of those realms in this fancy ball room. The Torn were no more dangerous than anyone else, they were just more *different*. And that was what scared people. Sorrensdattir didn't appear to notice the reaction from those around her, or perhaps she didn't care. She trailed her fingers in the water and looked up at the drops falling on the metal dogs.

'Such arrogance, Garnuck, to make rain inside. To think such things are game. Rustan should know better. Maybe he stayed here too long, in Fenest, forget the truth. Water, fire, stone – nothing stays the same forever. The Wayward, they know change comes. Others here, they don't want such a story.' Sorrensdattir glanced about her.

'I'm trying to find out who killed the Wayward storyteller,' Cora said. 'If you know something—'

A noise. A bell ringing. A ripple of excitement went through the crowd and there was a surge towards a doorway at the other end of the room. Cora turned back to the Torn.

Sorrensdattir was gone.

Instead, Jenkins was there, at Cora's elbow. 'It's time,' the constable said.

'Time for what?'

But Jenkins was heading into the press of bodies, and all Cora could do was follow.

The room broadened, the air all at once cooler, and near silence descended. At the far end was a deep balcony, half covered in shadows. Standing at the front, looking down on everyone beneath, was a figure dressed in a purple robe.

Jenkins whispered, 'Director of the Office of Electoral Affairs.'

The Director waited for the last few murmurs to subside, then he opened his arms wide and, in a deep voice, began. 'On behalf of the Commission of Fenest, let me welcome you to this, the two hundred and ninth election of the Union of Realms.'

An enthusiastic applause greeted these words, with Jenkins clapping loudest of all.

'It has been my pleasure to open the previous two elections, but, on this occasion, I stand before you with sorrow in my heart. You will have heard, I'm sure, through our great presses—' Cora caught a glimpse of Butterman picking his teeth with a fingernail '—that the Wayward people have suffered a terrible loss, and so, too, have we all. Nicholas Ento has taken his place among the Swaying Audience. His tale is for them.'

Was that a thinly veiled warning, Cora wondered. The Wayward would find a new 'teller, but would they have to find a different, less dangerous tale?

'Make room for the realms!' the Director boomed.

Another bell sounded and the people at the front, closest to the balcony, were forced to move backwards. Cora nearly fell in the sudden press of bodies. When she could see again, a pair of young men dressed in purple tunics crossed the floor. Each carried a Perlish flag: two kenna birds, one red, one blue, their long necks intertwined so that they were looking at each other.

A girl in purple followed the lads, this time carrying the Caskers' barrel. The next flag was the crossed spades of the Seeders.

Cora whispered to Jenkins, 'I always forget the Seeders' symbol.'

'You know, most *Lowlanders* consider that name a form of abuse.'

'That so?' Cora said. 'That's probably why people use it so much.' Her back was beginning to ache and it had been a long time since she'd had a smoke.

The Torn's flame came next, then the two triangles of the Rustans and their Rusting Mountains. And, lastly, the Wayward's horseshoe, which sent murmurs through those watching.

The seven young men and women who held the flags aloft remained facing the crowd, as the Director called for order.

'I hereby give notice: the wheel turns and the Caskers are the first story. Patron's Mount, three days' hence. As is custom and right under the Audience, the Caskers will display their story Hook before their tale.'

The Hook, a little teaser of the election story for the pennysheets and the chequers and the curious – and didn't the Stowaway know it! Despite herself, Cora felt her own curiosity piqued by the thought of the Caskers' story Hook, the first of the election.

'And now, ladies and gentlemen, Fenestirans and visiting friends.' The Director lifted his arms above his head.

Cora hoped, with every bindle-starved ounce of her body, that this wasn't the start of the folk dance.

'I ask you to welcome those who seek to please the Audience. Our 'tellers and your Chambers.'

The Director dropped his arms to his sides and the shadows behind him rose to the ceiling: a curtain, and behind it – all the lights in the world.

Cora closed her eyes to the glare but could still hear the gasps and cheers, and Jenkins gibbering excitedly to herself. Carefully, Cora opened her eyes, and saw all around her one thing: hunger. Suits and dresses be damned, these people would take their piece of the storytellers any way they could. Cora had seen the same look at the side of the ring, winners and losers shaking their chequers' slips as a prize fighter was led to the floor.

In the brightness of the balcony, a row of people waved to the adoring crowd.

They were standing in pairs, one person in each dressed in brown robes. She was too far away to see the gleaming bracelets, the manacles-in-waiting, but they'd be there, on each wrist. The Chambers. And each with their storyteller: the men and women *the Chambers* had chosen to tell their realm's story. And once the Chambers had chosen their 'tellers, they told only the Chambers from the other realms, until this moment when the identities of the 'tellers were revealed to all. These Chambers on the balcony had each known who, and what, Nicholas Ento was. Cora bit back a curse for Sillian and all the things that prevented powerful people getting what they deserved.

She looked across them, left to right along the balcony, and realised that each pair was standing in line with their flag on the floor below. That made it easy to work out who was who, though there were other ways too.

There was the group of four – two Chambers and two 'tellers – which was clearly the Perlish. Beside them was a small woman, with Inker's designs winding up her arms. A Casker and her Chambers. First to tell her tale this year. Next in the line were the unremarkable Seeders.

'Lowlanders,' she mouthed to Jenkins, who was too absorbed in the spectacle to share the joke.

The Torn were recognisable enough, with their smouldering mouthpieces. Beside them was a woman with a thick strip of metal covering her shoulder. Cora checked the banner below. Rustans. Next to the woman, her Chambers, whose robe hid the similar metal additions she was likely carrying.

And then just one person, standing alone. The Wayward Chambers, with a space where Ento should have stood. Cora remembered the flat gaze of the grey-eyed Chambers from the cold room.

They were all still waving, the crowd still cheering.

'Is that it then?' Cora said to Jenkins over the noise.

'There's the Hildantante. That's next I think.'

And as if summoned by the constable's words, from somewhere in the corner, music started. Behind the flagbearers, a group of men and women were forming lines. They wore brightly coloured tunics beset with bells, and conical hats, and carried strangely shaped sticks they kept banging together.

'I think I've seen enough,' Cora said.

'But the dance...'

'You can tell me all about it tomorrow, at the station. Goodnight, Jenkins.'

Cora pushed her way through the crowd, heading for the door, but that way seemed blocked. All at once she wanted to get out of Garnuck House, away from the laughing and the fine clothes. Away from the sight of the Wayward Chambers, standing alone.

A steady stream of waiters was heading in the opposite direction, away from the doorway, carrying trays of empty glasses. With no better option, Cora followed them.

They led her into a service area – tables piled with glasses and bottles, casks stowed beneath them. Waiters milled around. Men and women in aprons were hauling crates of fruit and bread. Everyone was too busy to notice Cora. She caught the coolness of fresh air and saw an open door: the back entrance to Garnuck House. She picked a way through the throng, in striking distance of getting back to the Fenest she knew. The real city. The grime and the gutters and the noise. She raised a hand to push open the door, and almost collided with a woman in a purple tunic.

'Hey!' the tunic said. 'You're not s'posed to be back 'ere.'

'Right you are, I was just leaving,' Cora said.

'Not tha' way you're not.' Despite being shorter than Cora by some way, the woman put her hands on her hips as if making up for it in width. 'Guests go out the front, see?' The woman looked Cora up and down. 'Is you even a guest?'

Cora reached for her badge. 'Actually, I'm a—'

'Oh, lay off her, Sylvie, she's with me.' A striking face appeared in the doorway.

Sylvie turned to the man. 'With you *how*?'

'Isn't it obvious? That's my sister, visiting from down south. She only wants a quick smoke before I get back to it.'

The tunic took in both of them. 'Don't look alike, do you?'

'Dawsons make beautiful men and serious women, that's the right of it.' The man grinned, which seemed to go some way to thawing Sylvie.

'All right then, just don't take too long about it. Have your reunions on your own time, see?'

Cora edged past her, following the man into the yard behind Garnuck House.

It was quiet after the noise inside, and Cora felt her shoulders soften, her back ease. She'd been tense all night, but now she was free of it – free of the election. But for how long?

'Rough in there,' the man said. He was a waiter, judging by his uniform. He was big, a few inches taller than her and well-built. A year or two younger, maybe. Smoke curled from his hand and she caught the smell of bindleleaf.

She reached for her tin, but he passed her a rolled smoke.

'Your job to be on hand with these?' she said, taking it.

'Something like that.' He lit it for her. 'You don't look like you work for the Commission. Don't look from out of town, neither.'

'And you're a Casker in a uniform,' she said, repaying the favour; his wrists were inked.

'Guess that's why we'd both rather be back here, and not in there, then. Name's Finnuc Dawson.'

'Is that a Casker name?'

'Could be,' he said.

'So tell me, Finnuc, you like your chances this election?' She gestured back towards the Opening Ceremony that was still going on without her.

'Not really, no.'

'I saw the numbers,' Cora said. 'Not so good as the Wayward, but that was a few days ago, now.'

'That's the beauty of numbers, ain't it? They never stay the same for long.'

'What does?' she said.

'If you plan on backing the Caskers, you could always wait for their story Hook.'

'You mean *your* Hook.'

Finnuc shrugged.

The Hook: Cora hadn't been to see one since she was a little girl. Not since Ruth had left.

'It'll be packed,' she said. 'Don't know if I could face it.'

'I could take you.'

'You don't need to—'

'I was going anyway,' he said. 'Like to make a day of it. Where should I pick you up?'

She waited, certain he wasn't serious. But he waited likewise. What was the harm?

'You know Bernswick station?'

'I know of it, sure.'

'Ask for Detective Gorderheim.'

He almost dropped his bindleleaf.

She smiled as she walked out into the street.

Eight

The next morning, Cora was barely through the station's door before Constable Jenkins was upon her. Cora felt tired just looking at the young woman. All that brazen enthusiasm – it wasn't right in their line of work.

'Morning, Detective.'

'So it is.' Cora hefted the stack of pennysheets Marcus had left on the station's front steps. She was beginning to regret asking for *all* the editions.

'Let me help you,' Jenkins said, and grabbed a wedge of 'sheets threatening to escape Cora's arms.

They passed the front desk, the sergeant there giving Cora a cursory nod. Cora knew the man but couldn't recall his name. Leeman, Leeson, Lewis, something like that.

'... Ento's lodgings.'

Cora stopped dead. 'What was that, Constable?'

'Nicholas Ento's lodgings, in Derringate?'

Cora gestured for her to continue.

'Sergeant Hearst gave me the address. It's on Teilo Street. Not much to report of the room itself. Very plain, very sparse, very little of the man at all, really.'

'No more than he'd carry on horseback. And his last movements?'

'The woman who runs the lodging house, a Mrs Kettleby, she says she saw Ento get into a coach on the night of the murder.'

'A late coach, from outside the lodging house?' Cora said.

'That's right. Last time she saw him, she said.'

'And what time *was* that exactly?'

'A little after midnight,' Jenkins said.

Cora felt her spirits lift, cutting through the tiredness she'd felt since being at the Opening Ceremony the night before. This was a chance, a lead.

She strode past the door to the briefing room and headed for her office.

'But,' Jenkins said, running to keep up with her, 'the landlady says it was too dark to see anything of the coach or driver.'

'And this landlady – what's her name again?'

'Mrs Kettleby.'

'Does this Mrs Kettleby have any idea where Ento was headed?'

'None whatsoever.'

'Wonderful.'

They'd reached her office.

'Where shall I put these?' Jenkins said, proffering the 'sheets.
'On the desk.'

Jenkins eyed the mess of pastry wrappers, overflowing ashtrays and yet more pennysheets that were scattered across the desk. 'Are you sure—'

'The landlady,' Cora said. 'Put it in a report.'

Jenkins set the 'sheets down and slipped into the corridor. There was a lump beneath the morning's editions, and when Cora shifted them aside she found a jar beneath.

A glass jar that held a teaspoon of red-white dirt. The dirt she'd collected from the alley where Ento was found.

She was still none the wiser as to what it was, or if it even had a part in the story of Ento's death. It was probably no more useful than the pastry wrappers on the floor. She looked around the small room with all its mess. It was a far cry from the gilded lavishness of Garnuck House and the Opening Ceremony. Thank the Audience for that.

There were only a few constables in the briefing room. They looked up briefly at her arrival, then carried on talking. Latecomer's luck, they'd left some coffee in the pot. She poured herself a cup.

The coach was a start. Nicholas Ento, the Wayward storyteller, the man with a whole realm's hopes firmly on his shoulders, had been going somewhere the night he was murdered. Going somewhere and, chances were, meeting someone. In Cora's experience a late coach either meant unsavoury habits or a romance best kept private. Each was interesting in its own way, but she didn't yet know enough about Ento to guess which was more likely. His being dumped in an alleyway behind Hawksley's whorehouse might've meant something, if Hawksley and the whores weren't certain no Wayward had paid a visit that night.

'I heard it's about a dog,' one of the constables said.

Cora looked up from the black, secretive surface of her coffee. The two constables were deep in discussion.

'Where'd you *hear*?'

'It's a dog, goes mad, see? Because they take it to the middle of that lake of theirs.'

'But their dogs like the water, don't they?'

'It's not one of *their* dogs.'

'Doesn't sound like a funny one. I was hoping it would have laughs.'

'That'll be the Seeder one.'

She was about to give them some incredibly long odds on a Seeder story making anyone laugh, when the desk sergeant appeared in the doorway.

'Detective Gorderheim?'

Lester. That was his name.

'Gig out front for you,' Sergeant Lester said.

'Gig?'

'That's right. Casker fella, it is.'

That got the two constables' attention. One opened his mouth but Cora held up a hand to stop him.

'It won't be about a dog,' she said.

Finnuc was waiting beside the gig. He wasn't in his uniform. Instead, he was wearing the ridiculous sleeveless shirts and loose trousers that Caskers seemed to favour, even when they weren't working a barge. It wasn't *that* warm yet.

'I wasn't sure you'd show,' Cora said.

'I wasn't sure you were really a detective, but you've got the coat and everything.'

'The same coat I was wearing last night?' she said. 'Last night when you *didn't* realise I was a detective.'

He grinned. 'Once you know what you're looking at...'

'Wouldn't want people mistaking me for anything else. Just like you and that... vest?'

'This vest will get us meat worth eating,' he said, 'and sight of the Hook before sundown.'

'Where are the Hooks this year?' she said.

'Don't you like surprises?'

'No.'

'Then you should read your pennysheets.'

Cora got into the gig, ignoring his offer of help. The gig rocked as the Casker sat beside her. He called to the Clotham's driver and they lurched into the road. Sitting next to Finnuc, she had to admit he did have arms worth showing off – and not just because of the swirling ink all over them. And he smelled of sandalwood, which she liked, but he'd used too much.

She took out her bindle tin and, despite the bouncing and jostling, rolled and offered him one. When he made to refuse, she insisted.

'I don't like being in anyone's debt,' she said. 'Anyone not in the black-and-white, anyway.'

The city rolled by. Everything looked so normal, so innocent, by day. Shops, street sweepers, lines of Seminary children led by a teacher. It wasn't the Fenest she knew.

'Tell me about yourself, Finnuc,' she said, moving closer to hear him over the sounds of the road.

'Ain't much to tell.'

'Then tell me a story.'

'I'm no storyteller, and for good reason.'

'Seems we're short a 'teller,' she said.

'My life's not nearly as exciting as yours, *Detective*.'

'So lie.'

'All right.' He made a show of fidgeting until he was ready. 'I wasn't born in Fenest. I can tell that comes as a shock. But I wasn't raised in Bordair, on the Cask, or on a barge neither. My mother died birthing me. My father did his best, though things were complicated. See, my mother was not his wife. He wouldn't be tied to any one berth, so to speak, and still won't; only married to get a stake in a barge. His wife didn't like him straying, she was more of a traditionalist, so as soon as he told her that I was his son – and tell her he did – she set us down on the river bank and waved goodbye. As Exiled as the Washerwoman.

'So I started life as a Casker baby on a Seeder farm. But Pa, he was no good at farming. It wasn't the hard work, he was plenty used to that, but he had no patience with the growing of things and seeing the same patches of earth day in, day out. As far as I can remember, I liked it. Those early years I saw the seasons in a way I haven't since: the beginning and end of things, life and death, everything.

'I had a hard time with the other children, but that was to be expected. Never went too far, though I had more accidents and broken bones than was normal for a farm, and farms are dangerous enough at the best of times.

'Just as I was getting big enough to hold my own, my pa decided he was done. I was ten, maybe eleven, and we'd both worked long enough to save pennies into marks. I thought we'd be going back to river life, the way he talked about it. He was always saying "on a barge" this and "we Caskers" that. I've asked him plenty of times since, but he still can't tell me why we went north instead of south, why Fenest instead of Bordair.

'The capital was hard in a different way. On both of us. I was getting bigger by the day – apparently my mother had been a real bruiser too. In certain parts of the city that gets you noticed. I started working for the wrong kinds of people and it wasn't long before the constables caught up with me. It wasn't the Steppes for me, but there are plenty of roads and bridges and walls that folks want built with free labour here in Fenest. Lucky for me it was an election year, and who had become the Casker Chambers but my pa's old wife, Captain Tennworth. The Faithful Companion had a real chuckle at that, I'm sure. Captain Tennworth felt, I don't know, a kind of guilt maybe? Enough to cross the right palms and get me free and, just as importantly, a job with the Commission.'

Cora re-lit her bindleleaf. 'How much of that is true?'

'You're right, I'm really Torn, with metal lungs so I can manage your weak, clean air.'

'Maybe you're not a good storyteller, but you're a pretty good liar.'

Nine

'Can't get any closer to the Hook,' the driver said.

Cora looked out her side of the gig and saw the truth of it – coaches and carriages, gigs and carts, all sizes and all shapes blocking the road.

'Might as well walk from here,' Finnuc said. He paid the driver, and added a fair tip given the trouble that traffic was going to be. When she mentioned it, Finnuc just said, 'I know what it's like to work like that.'

They picked their way through the stationary traffic and joined the busy pavement. They were alongside the Stave; beyond a low wall the river made its slow course through the city. People and river alike moved placidly in the same direction, both paying little attention to the other.

Shuffling along with the high and low of Fenest – of all the realms, really – Cora remembered why she hated elections: Casker mothers with babes on their hips alongside Perlish two-penny boys, Fenestirans in polished shoes queueing alongside those of the city who did the shining. The great equaliser, it was, and no one seemed too comfortable with that – not least Cora.

She felt more on edge this election than she had in the previous ones. With Ento's killer still at large, she couldn't let her guard down, whether she was in a lonely alley or jostling in a crowd. Fenest was a sprawling city, and the killer could be anywhere, could be close too, watching the case falter. It irked her that the constant stories in the pennysheets made *that* likely, wherever the killer was hiding. A woman stumbled into Cora's hip, mumbled a curse. Elections. The only good crowd was a ring-side crowd, with eyes only for the numbers and hands too busy clutching slips to cause trouble.

At last she and Finnuc reached the end of the road proper, marked by a line of barrels and a handful of bored-looking constables from another division, and they came out onto a cobbled waterfront.

'Wait, I know this place,' Cora said.

'After today, everyone will know it.'

'No, I mean from before.'

She had walked it as part of her beat, back when she was in uniform. But now it was almost unrecognisable. The tall buildings opposite the water had been transformed: gone were the boarded-up doors and shutters, the broken windows and weeds sprouting from cracks. Everything looked... if not clean, then fixed, or whole. Not new, but no longer old – not in the way she knew it. She shuddered at the strangeness of it, at the feeling that part of her past had been scrubbed away and replaced by gold-lettered shopfronts and eateries.

'Hungry?' he said.

She hadn't been. But as they approached the numerous stalls that were packed between the buildings she caught some of the smells and flavours and her stomach groaned. She'd not bothered with breakfast.

Finnuc stopped beside a roaring fire pit. A blackened piglet was turned on a spit by a young Wayward woman who rained spices on the flesh. At the next stall, huge sinta cakes were carved and handed out to a never-ending reaching of hands. Stew pots bubbled with bright colours – orange, red, yellow – flanked by towers of Seeder-bread. Holens and medlars and all manner of things from the south jostled alongside cheese and meats from the north; about as comfortable in each other's company as their producers were. But they all came together here and now, in Fenest for the election.

Beyond, through the tall windows of once abandoned warehouses, Cora caught glimpses of tables and chairs packed with people. A Rustan stood berating her companion, gesticulating with a fork gripped by a half-metal hand. At another window two Caskers stared at the river, their expressions unreadable. Around them everyone was eating, arguing and speculating. A fair amount of which would concern what the Casker Hook meant for the Casker story.

She and Finnuc took their meat and bread, wrapped in old pennysheets, and moved back into the crowd. She was idly trying to make out the headline now smeared in grease when, as if it were the theme of the day, the old collided with the new.

'Caskers bag a body! Get the story here, folks.'

Cora recognised the deep voice that carried above the crowd. Recognised why there was something unnerving about it, which was even then making Finnuc frown.

Marcus, the pennysheet girl, darted here and there as she rushed to meet the hands going up. Between transactions she belted out more baritone calls of story, of headline, of excitement. As she reached a would-be buyer another pennysheet girl appeared. She punched Marcus full in the gut, and then neatly stepped in front of her groaning, prone competitor.

'Casker tale catching! All signs point to plague! Who wants it? Who wants it?'

Marcus recovered enough to kick the other girl's feet out from under her and the two wrestled on the cobbles. The shrill peevishness of a whistle started and within moments a squarely-built constable was pulling the girls apart by their collars.

Grumbling, Cora made her way over, leaving a bemused Finnuc behind.

'I'll take that one,' she said, pointing at Marcus.

'Oh yeah?' the constable said, raising an eyebrow.

Cora fumbled around in her pocket, eventually producing her badge.

'Bernswick?' the constable said with a sneer. 'What's this to you? Besides, they all got orders not to cause any disturbance today.'

'I ain't disturbing no one!' Marcus shouted, and spat at the other girl. 'Just selling, that's all, and she come over here and starts on me. I ain't eaten, I ain't slept.'

'Selling it to the Poet, she is!' the girl said. She took a swipe at Marcus and missed, swinging into the bulky torso of the constable instead.

'This one owes me,' Cora said.

'Maybe she owes me too?'

Cora stepped close to the man, close enough to smell his rancid breath over the cooking pots, and whispered in his ear. His eyes bulged and then he promptly dropped Marcus.

'It's clear who the problem is. C'mon you,' the constable said to the other girl. 'Stop wriggling or I'll drop you in the Stave. And all that paper won't help with floating.' He dragged the pennysheet girl away through the press of people.

Marcus dusted herself down, much good it did her.

'Now you *do* owe me,' Cora said.

'Take it in 'sheets?'

Before Cora could answer, a boy barged past her and threw an armload of pennysheets at Marcus, who was bowled back to the ground by their weight. The boy raced off without a word and Marcus wearily got to her feet again. She hefted the new 'sheets more securely in her arms.

Cora saw the headline. 'Marcus, don't—'

But the roar was out before she could clamp Marcus' mouth shut.

'Constabulary no closer to killer! Storytellers at risk. Read it here.' And the girl was off again, hurrying to meet the raised hands.

'What did you say to that flatfoot?' Finnuc said, joining her. 'Never seen one look so scared.'

'I told him I knew every debt-collector this side of the Tear.'

'And he believed that?'

'Of course he did. It's true.'

They joined what Cora assumed was the queue for the Hook. Finnuc seemed to know what he was about, and made easy conversation between mouthfuls of Wayward pork as they shuffled forward every few minutes or so. He was quite taken with Marcus, who could still be heard touting her wares, and suggested the girl was one of Cora's 'informants'. She decided the lie wasn't worth the effort to convince him otherwise.

'I'm not waiting around here,' she muttered. 'Come on.' She strode towards the head of the queue, ignoring the tuts and murmurs of those she passed.

People in the purple uniform of the Commission were stationed at intervals along the line. One of them, a young man, stopped her before she reached the front. Cora showed him her badge. It seemed to be a morning for it.

'Bernswick division,' she said, and made to pass.

He put a hand on her arm – not a grab so much as unarguable firmness.

'Commission policy is to manage numbers with a queue system,' he said.

Cora shook him off. 'This is an official matter.'

'No exceptions, I'm afraid.' He gave her a tight smile. 'If you wouldn't mind returning to your friend there.'

She turned: Finnuc hadn't followed her. He knew better, she guessed, but her blood was up now.

'Are you telling me,' she said loudly, 'that the Commission's authority is superior to that of the police?'

'We all work for the Commission, Detective. But the election is a matter for the Office of Electoral Affairs. We have our orders. I'm sure you understand.'

'I'm not sure I do.'

'You wouldn't want to undermine the election in any way, would you, Detective? I'm sure your commanding officer wouldn't be too pleased to hear of that. Who is it at Bernswick I should report you to?'

Cora looked at the head of the queue, then back at him. He smiled.

She marched back down to Finnuc.

'Problems?' he said.

'Only the way the world's run.'

By the time they reached the front of the queue, her anger had cooled. Finnuc's constant talking helped. He was still talking when they stepped onto a gangway. It was wide and solid and about as permanent as anything under the Audience, but it was still a gangway.

'The Hook is on a *barge*?' Cora said.

'You could say it's our year.'

Crossing onto the deck, Cora did her best to ignore the slight motion of the river beneath her. The barge itself was dominated by a single sizable structure, like a one-room house made of wood. They stepped into near-darkness. At the centre of the room was a brown leather bag, like a stitcher's, sitting atop a stone plinth that was roped off on all sides. A lone lamp illuminated it. Cora wasn't sure what she'd been expecting, but it wasn't this.

'This is it, your Hook?' she whispered.

'So I'm told,' Finnuc said.

Once she was over her initial surprise, she had to admit the Hook did have a certain quiet power. She felt it in those around her, the small group who'd been ushered inside at the same time, and in the air of the barge. A tension, a tightness, a question hanging there, until Finnuc gave it a form.

'Wonder whose blood it is.'

The bag's handles had a smattering of red stains. She leant closer and caught the tang of metal in the air.

On the opposite side of the plinth, other visitors peered at the Hook, and more were pushing their way in from the gangway. Everyone strained for a glimpse. Apart from one person. Small, hooded, clinging to the far wall rather than trying to get closer. Whoever this person was, the Hook was already known to them. It wasn't a draw.

Cora stepped back to let others take her place near the plinth. Finnuc was talking to one of the Commission ushers, and she took the chance to circle the plinth, slowly, pretending she was heading for the door.

When she got close enough to grab the figure's wrist, she saw the inkings there, and then she understood.

The Casker storyteller. Nullan was her name, if Cora remembered that morning's pennysheet rightly.

'Brave, stupid, or both?' Cora said quietly to the woman, fumbling for her badge with her free hand.

'I wanted to see what people were making of our Hook,' the Casker said in hushed tones. Her face was only half visible from the edge of her hood. 'You can put that badge away. I saw you with the Commission boy just before. I know who you work for.'

'And I've seen a dead storyteller lying on a stitcher's slab,' Cora hissed. 'Are you looking to join him? Ento's killer is still out there. What if they decide they fancy seeing the Hook too? If someone here should recognise you, no hood is going to keep you safe.'

'Would you, Detective? Would *you* keep me safe?'

'I'd try,' Cora said. The Commission ushers called for them to move on – their time was up. Cora took hold of the storyteller's arm and escorted her to the exit. 'I'd try, just like I'm trying now.'

'Then try *harder*. Find who did this, find who hurt Nicholas.'

Hurt him? There'd been worse done to him than hurt.

'You knew Ento?' Cora said.

'I... yes, I knew him.'

They stepped off the barge and into the sunlight.

'You knew him,' Cora repeated uselessly, and then she understood. The way the woman's voice had caught just before she said 'Nicholas'. That she couldn't bring herself to say what had really happened to him. 'He went to see you that night, didn't he?'

It was a guess, but as Nullan's silence dragged on, Cora knew she was right.

'I told him not to,' Nullan said eventually. 'That we had to stop once the election started.'

'What happened?'

'I waited all night for him, worrying. I knew something was wrong.'

'You're saying he never arrived?'

She fought free of Cora's grip. 'I'm not *saying* it – that's what *happened*.'

'Can anyone else speak to that?'

'Just what are you implying? You can't... I *loved* him.'

People were starting to notice their little discussion, starting to stare. This was the last thing Cora wanted. She'd meant what she said about the killer visiting the Hook.

'Calm down,' Cora told Nullan through gritted teeth. 'You don't want a scene and neither do I. Where were you and Ento due to meet?'

Before Nullan could answer, there was a wall of purple between Cora and the storyteller. Two Commission staff. Both women. Neither looked accommodating. Cora pulled out her badge but, just as in the queue, it did little good.

'Storyteller Nullan has a tale to prepare,' said one of the purple-clad women.

'I'd say she does,' Cora muttered.

The woman grasped Nullan's elbow, making the storyteller wince. 'We'll escort you back to your lodgings, where you won't be *disturbed.*'

Nullan was led away without any further fuss, soon lost in the crowd. Cora had to trust that the storyteller wouldn't be hard to find in an official capacity, if it came to that. Though she'd have to get past the Commission security to reach the storyteller, even though she was a Commission employee herself! But there was the Commission and then there was the *Commission.* Her mother had never tired of making the distinction between the parts of it that mattered and the parts that didn't.

Cora turned back to the barge. The Casker and Wayward storytellers together, doing much more than telling stories. It was hard to imagine. There were probably rules against it, knowing the Commission. And if Nullan was lying, she might have been the last person to see Ento alive. Or the first to see him dead.

'Who was that?' Finnuc said, easing beside her.

'You wouldn't believe me, even if I told you.'

Few would. Hearst? Sillian? The Wayward Chambers? Would any of them believe that Cora's one lead, maybe even her one suspect, was the Casker storyteller?

Ten

Patron's Mount was teeming.

Cora and Jenkins had set off from the station early in hopes of beating the crowds, but they might as well have stayed at Bernswick and done some work. The stack of papers on Cora's desk was getting tall enough to challenge the Poet's Spire, and she was dodging Sillian whenever she could. She had nothing for the chief inspector – at least, nothing she felt certain enough about to say out loud.

'Caskers have drawn the crowds this year,' Jenkins said.

To Cora, the square mile of the Mount looked like a carcass covered in flies: the black flecks buzzing to and fro.

'Fenest can smell blood,' Cora said.

'What do you mean?'

What *did* she mean? Was it the red stains on the bag the Caskers had used for their Hook? Or the death of the

Wayward storyteller? Or, worse still, the chance another 'teller might be killed – right there, on the Mount? Cora didn't want to know what odds the chequers were giving on *that*. Jenkins was looking at her now, concerned.

'The Hook, the bag,' Cora said. 'From the 'sheets I've read, that mystery has everyone excited. And today we find out why.'

As their gig made its slow way down the busy road, Cora could see people gathering all along the perimeter fence. Men and women of the Union who couldn't get a place in the public gallery. They wouldn't be able to hear the story from the fence, but they'd see the storyteller in the distance, and that would be something to tell their neighbours.

'It'll be hot for them today,' Jenkins said, looking up at the cloudless sky, shielding her eyes. 'For the voters, I mean.'

'Hotter than for the rest of us? Does the sun shine on them specially, Constable?'

'Anyone in a robe is going to feel the heat. This sun.'

'Chambers too, then,' Cora said.

'But the fifty voters will have it worse. They've got to wear the masks as well.'

'Something to tell the Amateur then, isn't it? Unlucky enough to be drawn from the voting pool on a hot day.' Cora wiped her face. 'Hope it's worth the sweat.'

The gig lurched to a stop and Commission staff dressed in purple tunics climbed onto the gig's steps, demanding to see their papers. Cora pulled out her badge. Jenkins did the same on her side, and that seemed enough to get them waved through. That happened three more times until they reached the point gigs weren't allowed to go any further, just a little way beyond the main gates to the Mount.

The big tent, which Jenkins informed Cora was the garbing pavilion for the voters, loomed above them. The canvas sides were almost painfully white in the morning sunlight, secured with ropes as thick as Finnuc's arms.

'My mother practically lived in that pavilion during elections,' Jenkins said. 'She couldn't let the chests out of her sight.'

'Chests?'

'The voting chests. When the story's finished, the voters go back inside and cast their votes.'

'They don't get much time to think about it, do they?' Cora said.

Jenkins shrugged. 'It's mostly practicalities. Voters aren't permitted to talk to one another, or anyone else, about their choice. And no one else can leave a story venue until all the votes are cast.'

'They'd best be quick about it today, then,' Cora said, squinting in the sun. She and Jenkins passed two rows of empty chairs facing the Mount, front-and-centre. 'This where the voters sit?'

'Yes. There isn't usually this much security, though.'

In between the chairs and the Mount was a line of constables and a waist-high fence.

'There isn't usually a dead storyteller just before the election,' Cora said.

'I should think it's too late now for anyone to harm Nullan. At least until after she's told her story.'

'She's got plenty of stories to tell, that one.'

They reached the public gallery and a harassed purple tunic ushered them towards the few remaining seats. Uncomfortable wooden ones that Cora doubted she'd last the whole story on. She rolled a bindleleaf and looked around at this, the first story venue. Further back people had cleared space for blankets – much to the consternation of the purple tunics. And there were plenty of them, rushing about on one errand or another. Cora watched them as she smoked, doing her best to exhale in the opposite direction from Jenkins.

From where she was sitting, Cora could just make out the Commission boxes that flanked one side of the Mount. Along their tops were banners bearing the Spoked Wheel, and the six symbols of the realms, though they barely stirred in the slight breeze. The Chambers and the dignitaries and high-ups and the like would have plenty of shade in those boxes. Everyone else had to make do in the glare of the sun.

A bell rang and everyone in the public galleries stood.

'This one going to have a happy ending, do you think?' Cora said.

Jenkins gave half a smile. 'After the blood on the bag? I'm not hopeful.'

'Don't imagine the voters are, either. But then not everyone finds happiness entertaining,' Cora said, remembering a story about a naughty lapdog that turned out well, and the gruff pennysheet girl who voted against it.

'It's not just that,' Jenkins said. 'We have a serious reason for being here, and so do the voters. The Casker story will be just as much about the state of the current Assembly, the state of the Union and what they'll do about it, as it will be about that bloodied bag.'

'Sounds dull.'

'If it is then they won't win, will they?' Jenkins said, her patience clearly running thin. 'Every realm, in every election, in every story, is just trying to find that balance. Each does it differently. All to get enough black stones.'

'All to keep the realms from one another's throats.'

'That too. A thousand years of peace, all because some people tell good stories,' Jenkins said. She pointed to the garbing pavilion. 'They're ready.'

The canvas side opened and for a moment all that could be seen of the inside was a wall of darkness. Then the darkness began to move and became separate shapes of black: the hoods pulled low, the robes hanging to the floor. And the faces, oversized and fixed.

The Audience had come.

Fifty voters from across Fenest, each in a different mask so that every member of the Audience was represented and accounted for. There was the Heckler, mask painted red, his face a sloppy smile of too much ale. And the Devotee, with blue bulbous lumps for eyes forever closed to disappointment. The Critic always green, always pursed-mouthed, the Poet singing with a yellow tongue. The Stowaway and the Amateur, the Commoner and the Brawler, and all the rest; each one leaving the shadows of the pavilion to join the line of black robed figures in colourful masks moving in silence.

The Audience took up positions by their chairs but stayed standing, as did everyone else. This was why they were called the *Swaying* Audience. It wasn't just because people tried to sway them with stories, but because when they all got together like this it was impossible to keep track of them all, there were so many. Not to mention that standing there in masks and robes they did appear to *sway* – Cora had to look away when her stomach started to churn.

'Audience, welcome,' the Master of Ceremonies called from atop the Mount. 'In this, the two hundred and ninth election of our realms, we give you a 'teller who gives you a tale.'

'The Audience is listening.' The voice came as one from the robed bodies.

The Master bowed to the Audience, and then again as Nullan, the Casker storyteller, appeared.

She walked slowly around the crest of the Mount, and there was something compelling in the way she held herself, the way she stood above everyone else. She wasn't hooded now. Her arms were bare but covered in ink – what shapes or pictures Cora couldn't see.

Nullan stood silently for several moments, as if she was deciding when the quality of listening was at its peak. Her waiting made the air around her hum, a noiseless vibration. This was the dead Wayward storyteller's lover. Perhaps the last person to see Nicholas Ento alive.

The storyteller began.

'The man was dying. That was what the boy said.'

THE CASKER STORY

The man was dying. That was what the boy said.

He couldn't have been more than ten, maybe eleven years old and he'd clearly been running for some way. He held onto the doorframe as he gulped at the hot night air. His skin – not just his face, but his arms and neck and shins – was as slick as the walls of my little hut.

'He's in a bad way, Sanga,' the boy said.

I glanced back down at my desk, where a fly was settling on my stew. Half a meal was probably more than I deserved. I picked up my small bag and made to leave, but the boy didn't move.

'He's not a rich man, Sanga.'

'That's fine,' I said.

'And he's been drinking. Days, maybe.'

'Days?'

The boy checked both ways of the alley, then he lowered his voice. 'It's not that. Something... else. You'll see.' He made the sign of the Tear, defiant in the face of my surprise.

'Lead on,' I said, trying to hide my resignation at the prospect of seeing to another man near death at the bottom of a bottle.

Late summer is a despicable time in Bordair. The very walkways and lakeside shacks swell in the muggy air, everything drips despite the clear skies and tempers are less frayed, more eviscerated.

'Which bar?' I said to the back of the boy's head.

'Barge of Good Hope,' he said.

I didn't know of it, but he was sure of his way as he ducked and weaved between empty alleys and boardwalks full of evening revellers. It may have been a holiday of some sort; I always found it difficult to keep track of those.

The larger 'walks were lit by oil lamps swinging on short chains from balconies and eaves. Though soft, it was not a flattering light, and faces leered out of the crowd. Painted youngsters – some not much older than the boy I was following – made crude gestures from the balconies. It wasn't difficult to see their madams behind, more often than not waving their fans or scratching at their wigs. We passed one such establishment, the Merry Jig, where I was on the payroll. Madam Wishful saw me and pushed her way to the rail, much to the consternation of her charges.

'Sanga Jeffereys!' she called, loud enough to turn some heads. 'Is it Tuesday already?'

It was Friday.

'A hard working sanga, and worth every penny! No cheek in the Merry Jig goes un-turned by his professional fingers.'

Some of the boys and girls pantomimed just what cheeks she was referring to, and laughter rose above the general din of the crowded 'walk. I hurried to keep up with the boy and we made our way along the east shore of Bordair, passing through the busier districts. Then he turned towards the hills. The 'walks became streets, narrower than those by the shore.

'Aren't we going the wrong way for a barge?' I said.

The boy grunted, though I couldn't tell if it was in the affirmative or the negative. I was too far from my hut and, I'll admit, too curious to turn back. The only light in the streets was cast by candles inside bed or sitting rooms, and I had to squint to follow the outline of the boy even though he was only a few paces ahead.

'Were there not sangas closer by?' I said in a kind of hush, not wanting to disturb good people in their homes.

'Had to be you,' the boy said, without turning. 'They said.'

'The dying man?'

'No, his 'swain.'

That the dying man worked a barge was so much a given that the boy hadn't mentioned it until now. To have a boatswain, and one that cared enough to send for someone like me, it must be a sizeable barge – one big enough to need a proper crew and the hierarchies that went with it.

'You work the same barge?' I asked the boy.

'You might say that.'

'What would the boatswain say?'

'You can ask her yourself,' the boy said.

As I rounded a corner I almost bumped into him. He was staring up at a single-storey building that was set high into the hillside. Tall posts, bearing all the hallmarks of ex-masts, appeared to prop up the place. The frontage had a spindly railing, broken in multiple places, and there was blood on the cobblestones below.

'Sangas must be a common sight at a bar like this,' I said to the boy.

He nodded at a set of poorly constructed steps, besides which was a modest shrine to the Amateur, but wouldn't be moved himself. When I asked why, he simply said, 'Captain's orders.'

There was sense in that; I wouldn't have wanted the boy to enter such a place. I didn't want to myself. He settled against a wall of one of the dark homes, like a bird settling to a familiar perch. I took a firmer hold on my bag, as if that would be an aid against a person foolish, or desperate, enough to rob a sanga, and started my ascent. It wasn't until halfway up the steps that I noticed the silence.

The doors and windows of the Barge of Good Hope were all open, its lamps still lit, and yet not a sound came from within. My step faltered when I reached the top. The large doorway in front of me gave onto polished floors and high stools at high tables. I was surprised to see they were all of a quality, and in a state of good repair.

'Hello?' I called, pleased by the steadiness of my voice.

I stepped inside and saw a long bar, behind which a balding man was taking regular slugs from a wooden tankard while keeping it filled from one of the taps. He had blood on his knuckles.

A woman appeared in an archway in the far wall, took one look at me and then turned back the way she'd come. With little other choice I followed her. She led me past a series of small, empty nooks, before stopping at one with a bench running the length of three sides. A man lay on it; heavy-set, like every bargeman I'd ever met, with black ink running up both exposed arms.

'Are you the boatswain?' I asked the woman. She clearly was – I just needed to fill the silence as I put my bag down.

'Was me that sent the boy,' she said. 'They say you're mongrel.'

I paused, hand half in my bag. 'What would that matter?' I said.

She gestured to the bargeman. 'This ain't from around here.'

'What's your name?'

'Eliza.' She was edging back into the hallway, rubbing at something beneath her shirt.

As I began to examine the bargeman, I could see why Eliza thought whatever ailed him was not from Bordair.

He was bone dry.

I gently ran a finger along his arm, just to make sure it wasn't a trick of the ink or the smoky lamps that at once felt very close in the room. I pressed beneath his jaw, under his arms, the bottom of his feet: all dry. And not only dry, but they seemed to suck at my own slick sweat; my fingertips came away as if they'd just been powdered.

'What happened here?' I said, half expecting to be reminded that I was the sanga. But the 'swain understood my meaning.

'Dahey just dropped. Didn't see it myself, but that's the way others told it.'

'What others?' I said.

Dahey's pulse was weak, but regular.

'Some of the crew. When he wouldn't wake, I sent them out. Redmond back there, he cleared the rest of the bar.'

That might have explained the blood, both on his knuckles and in the street.

'Why clear the bar? Why not just put Dahey here out?'

Eliza pulled a necklace from beneath her shirt, a small representation of the Tear in silver and some kind of black stone, and clutched at it. I rolled my eyes at such simple superstitions.

'Was obvious he weren't right,' she said.

'Obvious how?'

Eliza's eyes were wide and almost all white.

I took her by the shoulders and said once more, calm and slow, 'Obvious how?'

'He was bleeding. From his eyes.'

'Are you sure?'

'I cleaned him up,' she said. 'Didn't do the crew no good to see him like that.'

I turned back to the prone bargeman. 'Bleeding from his eyes,' I muttered.

'And his mouth,' she added.

I wasted a moment trying to imagine what that might have been like for her to witness; as a sanga, I had seen plenty of men and women bleed from orifices, but it was enough to shake most people. A man is stabbed, and onlookers are prepared for the blood. They know it's coming and that, in some ways, lessens the shock. To watch Dahey smiling, drinking, talking, then bleeding from that very same apparatus...

'I'm sorry,' I told Eliza, which was both insufficient and all I could give her. To Dahey I might be of more use.

Taking some care, I opened Dahey's mouth and was met by three black teeth and a fat, swollen tongue. I winced at the rancid bouquet of decay, strong liquor, and partially dried blood. The 'swain had done her best with the exterior blood, though some staining was on the cheeks and she had, quite rightly, avoided inside Dahey's mouth. Some blood clung to his only molar, but came away easily. In fact, rubbing it between finger and thumb, the blood was curiously thin. I did my best to ensure Dahey wouldn't choke on his own tongue, and then inspected his eyes. There was some inflammation, but little else I could make out.

'His ankles,' Eliza said.

They were both black. My mouth was half-open, a question half-formed, when I realised the blackness wasn't ink. I lightly pressed the skin, thinking it might be swollen, but found it surprisingly hard and rigid. Both of Dahey's ankles were ringed black in such a manner.

I knew what I was looking at. I had experience treating the wounded – most often bargemen like Dahey – and so could conclude this was dead flesh.

But Dahey had no wound.

To be sure, I closely examined each ankle but could find no puncture made by man nor beast. From my kneeling position, I looked up along the body, the landscape, of this man and felt a tightening in me.

'How well do you know Dahey?' I said, trying and failing to make the question sound casual.

'Why? What's that got to do with anything?'

'Is he the kind of man who would want to live, regardless of the cost?'

'Silence have you, what does that mean?' she said.

I went to my bag and found the bone saw. I withdrew it as calmly and steadily as I could – it was not a time for Audience-worthy flourishes. Still, the clean shine of the saw's teeth was enough to make her start back.

'The decay will spread from his ankles,' I said. 'He's beyond walking but we might save him.'

'We?'

'I'll need help.'

Her steps were tentative, but she approached her crew mate. I lay a sheet from his knees up to his chin and told her not to touch anything but its whiteness.

'Hold him here,' I said, gesturing to one of Dahey's thighs. 'Firm.'

She gripped the man like it was her own life that depended on it. Her breaths were long and deep – she was doing what she could to keep herself calm, and I gave her a nod of encouragement. I took a deep breath myself and aligned the saw an inch above the blackness. I tensed in readiness. Then the convulsions began.

A fan of blood spewed from Dahey's mouth. His arms and legs flailed, though Eliza did what she could to hold him. I dropped the saw and rushed to pin his shoulders against the bench. The spasms were fierce and it was all we could do to keep him from falling. His eyes had rolled back and were as white as my sheet. The choking sounds he made were enough to thin my own blood there and then, and wake me for nights to come. I wrestled with his tongue, while his gummy gnashing matched the convulsions.

It may have lasted mere seconds, a minute perhaps, but when it was over all three of us slumped where we were: Dahey on the bench, Eliza and I on the floor. The bargeman's death rattle was as clear and mournful as any of the Poet's bells.

Once outside the Barge of Good Hope, I was relieved to find the boy gone. It was later than I realised and the sky had a lightness to it. I remembered the last sunrise I had seen, which had not been so long ago; I was aiding the labour of a young woman. How different that joyous early light had been. Now, I stumbled my way through the higher streets of Bordair, not knowing exactly where I was going but with the understanding that, just as all roads in life lead to death, all streets in Bordair lead to water.

Eliza had said their captain would take care of Dahey's affairs, little as they were: a sister, Eliza thought. No children, no wife, of that she'd been sure.

I kept to the smaller streets and 'walks. Once I reached the water I was able to orientate myself and hurry back to my hut. My stew was cold and had a thick layer of skin. I didn't care. I ate without tasting a single mouthful. I fell, fully clothed, onto my mattress and slept.

I woke in the dark to someone shaking me by the shoulder.

'Sanga,' they said, soft but insistent.

I rubbed my eyes, still heavy with sleep, and squinted at the figure standing over me. Slowly a small face fringed by greasy blond hair resolved itself out of the shadows.

'Captain wants to see you,' the boy said.

'What?' I struggled to sit, relieved that I was dressed.

'She said not to wake you until it was dark. And then not to leave until you followed.'

I managed to light my last candle and, though it was little more than a stub, I could see the boy was alone. Something in the way he sat at my desk suggested that my checking the hut for missing items was unnecessary.

'Your leethes and tars need more water,' he said, bringing me up short. This youngster, whose skin had yet to turn to pock or pimple, knew the old names of plants. And perhaps their old uses too.

'Would you?' I said, motioning to a small can.

The plants took up a good portion of my hut's back wall. The boy was careful not to overwater them, watching intently as their soil sucked the water down and then wanted no more. As he was so occupied, I set to righting myself. I changed my shirt, cleared my mouth with crushed fennel, and drank more water than all my plants combined. In the outhouse, my urine was heavy and dark and I chided myself for affording far less care to my own body than to those of others. When I returned, the boy was back at the desk.

'Did your captain say why she wanted to see me?'

'No,' the boy said.

I cast around for my boots, before realising they were still on my feet. I covered my error by looking for my bag, which was inexplicably underneath one of my pillows.

'You won't need that.'

'Oh?'

'It's not like Dahey. She wants to talk to you, is all. And the payment.'

'I see. Was she angry? About Dahey?'

He shook his head.

'Plenty more bargemen in Bordair, I suppose?'

The boy's expression hardened, and I felt a stab of shame at my foolish words. I was making assumptions about a woman I had never met, and a captain who I had never seen among her crew. He waited patiently as I fussed over the state of my hut and of my person, neither of which really required attention, but I was unwilling to answer this summons on anyone's terms but my own. I brought my bag, against the boy's advice, in case the captain wanted to see what measures I had taken – or tried to take – for Dahey. I hoped the boatswain, Eliza, would also be present. For the second time I followed the boy out among the boardwalks, but was surprised when he entered a Commission building. So surprised, I checked the crest on the front in case I'd mistaken the Spoked Wheel above the shuttered windows for a barge pilot's wheel.

The double doors were large enough for a carriage, but we entered through a small door cut out of its bigger brethren. Once inside, the air took on an officious quiet. High ceilings gave the entrance hall the illusion of a more northern chill, but I was still sweating plenty from our brisk walk.

I stalled in the face of the long tapestries that lined the walls and the unfamiliar feeling of carpet beneath my boots. But the boy walked confidently on, as if he belonged there as much as the old Fenestiran dozing at the door. When the Fenestiran stirred, I hurried after the boy.

We climbed a wide, strangely shallow set of stairs that sloped upwards for at least fifty yards, possibly more. I noticed the steps themselves didn't extend as far as the walls and, looking back, it dawned on me that these stairs, like the doors, were designed for a carriage. I stopped, dumbfounded by this obviously Fenestiran design. I could count on one hand the number of boardwalks by the shore that were big enough for a carriage. And besides issues of practicality, what did it say of a person who demanded their carriage take them not only inside a building, but up to its second floor? Was it vanity, or simple laziness? I looked up to see the boy waiting at the top.

We walked down a carpeted corridor lined by portraits of men and women with uniformly dark backgrounds. I found myself greatly affected by their sombre atmosphere. I had never considered Bordair and its inhabitants frivolous – extravagant, certainly – but that is how I felt in that corridor: as if I'd been transported to a distant place, with foreign customs and peoples that made me look at my own in a new way. I felt all this, even knowing that to simply look out of a window would reveal Bordair's fractured, quilt-like clash of hut rooftops and the water beyond.

'I don't know what your captain knows, or think she knows about me,' I said, remembering Eliza's crude assessment of my parentage, 'but I'm not Fenestiran.'

The boy shrugged. 'She's the captain.'

For him, that seemed to encompass a great many unknowns.

We proceeded down another corridor until at last the boy stopped at a small door and motioned for me to open it. If this was some kind of rite of passage, its significance was lost on me; I merely walked into the well-appointed study. A woman looked up from where she was leaning over a large, polished writing desk.

'Sanga Jeffereys. I'm glad we can finally meet in person.'

Her smile suggested she was genuinely pleased, rather than being polite, and its warmth went some way to dispelling the coolness that had settled over me in the corridor of portraits. We shook hands.

'I can see you were expecting something else,' she said. 'A busy bar perhaps?'

'No, not at all.'

'It's all right,' she said, smiling once more. 'I appreciate the fact I rarely bump into other Casker captains here. Though if you did want a drink, Perse here would do his best.'

'Thank you, I'm fine, Captain...'

'Cope,' she said, pausing, perhaps allowing a moment for my recognition or acknowledgement of her reputation. I gave none, because I had no idea who Captain Cope was beyond the short-haired, middle-aged woman in front of me. She recovered smoothly with no sign of disappointment. 'I thank you for what you did for Dahey.'

'I did very little.'

'You tried when others had refused. Relied on experience and knowledge when others were led by superstition and fear.'

I glanced at the boy Perse, wondering how many other sangas the boy had really visited before my hut, before he peddled his white lie. But I was not above a little flattery, not the day before and not there in the presence of Captain Cope.

'In the end, the Audience was all for Dahey,' I said.

'He has plenty of stories to share. Tell me your own story, Sanga Jeffereys, of that night and of Dahey's passing.'

The captain gestured to two comfortably padded seats in front of the desk. I sat stiffly. I'll admit I was a little intimidated by the shelves of scrolls and papers – even though I had little idea of what they contained. There was money and power there, in that building with its ramps for carriages and a myriad of closed doors and hushed corridors. I considered myself an educated man, who had seen a little of the world and its pains and wonders, and educated enough to know when I was out of my depth.

The captain was waiting, indulging my hesitation but clearly watching it. With a distinct lack of eloquence I recounted that evening, choosing my entering the Barge of Good Hope as a suitable beginning. The captain was not surprised to hear of the empty bar, or her boatswain's predilection for the sign of the Tear. She was, however, intensely interested in my assessment of Dahey as I found him, and how he progressed from that state to his death. At various details she nodded affirmatively and, though I couldn't see the significance those details held for her, I had the impression she missed little. She didn't ask questions or interrupt. Perhaps because of this, I made the utmost effort not to omit a single piece of information, regardless of how small or pedantic.

By the end of my tale, I was quite unsure of my audience and her opinion. Her face, lined by age, experience, hard work, or all of these, was impassive. The slight upturn of her lips could mean anything. She allowed the silence to grow, and I was glad that I had left nothing out of my retelling as I felt a strong compulsion to fill that silence. Eventually, she motioned Perse forward and whispered into the boy's ear. He gave no reaction but quickly left the room. The captain continued to smile ever so slightly, but now was looking just above me and to one side. I fidgeted.

On what errand had she sent the boy? Was he, at this very moment, escorting a crew of barge thugs down those plush corridors? Did they each carry a bone saw, ready to implement my suggested but failed remedy on my own ankles? Or was Perse leading a Fenestiran constable to the room, cuffs at the ready? I looked between the captain and the door, finding both unmoved, and then to each wall in turn hoping for another site of egress. There were two windows that might prove large enough for me. I tried to calculate just how high that carriage ramp had brought me. I tensed, ready to run headlong at a window and take my chances.

When the door opened, I jumped half out of my chair. Perse entered alone, holding a tray with a pot of coffee and a plate of small biscuits. My cheeks burned as he settled the tray on the desk, and I noticed a not-too-small stack of coins beside the pot.

'Compensation for your time and inconvenience,' the captain said. 'And for your discretion.'

It was more than I made in a season. I nodded, resisting the urge to pick up one of the Fenestiran marks and bite it. I rarely frequented places that would accept such a weighty currency, but I knew of one or two finer merchants on the west shore who might accommodate these marks. The captain sipped her coffee despite the curls of steam still rising from it.

'The payment,' she said over the rim of her cup, 'also ends all obligations you may feel towards Dahey Carver. His family have been equally compensated.'

'His sister?'

'To hear her tell it, this was the first good turn he'd done her,' the captain said without a hint of mirth. 'I understand you have no brothers or sisters.'

'That's right,' I said, though her tone wasn't one of a question.

'And your parents are both dead.'

I shifted in the seat, almost spilling my drink. 'Yes. My mother was a Casker. She died, as many did, in the winter flus.'

The captain gave me the opportunity to say more, but I didn't. We finished our coffee in a more comfortable silence than that of before. When she replaced her cup on the tray, I had the sense there was something more she wanted me to hear. So it was that when she said, 'I have a proposal for you, Sanga,' I was not particularly surprised by the sentiment, only the wording.

'A proposal?' I said. I routinely accepted requests, answered calls, and even responded to demands. Proposals were something new.

'I would very much like for you to join my crew,' she said, meeting my eye with an intensity that gave no room for humour or whimsy in my answer. That she had need of a sanga was obvious given the previous night, though for some reason it hadn't occurred to me before that moment. That she would want me was impossible.

'Captain, I thought you understood my position.'

'I do.'

I checked the door again with the feeling that something, or someone, was waiting to burst through and cast me out of the well-appointed study, out of the Commission's building, and out of Captain Cope's regard.

'Your crew,' I said, without looking at Perse, 'they wouldn't work a barge with me, let alone accept my help.'

'They will work with you, Sanga, and they've already accepted your help once.'

'Dahey was—'

'Dying,' the captain said. 'I don't care where your father came from, and neither will my crew. Of that, I promise you.'

'And what of the Captain's Concordance?' I said.

'You strike me as an observant man.' The captain leant back in her chair. 'Where we are can't have been lost on you.'

'Do the Concordance know?'

'Know what?' she said.

I gestured uselessly, frustrated by how little I understood what was happening, what was being suggested. 'They would never let me work a barge.'

'Sanga, who said anything about a barge?'

I laughed at her. I am ashamed to say that was my first reaction and it was an all-consuming one. It was also a difficult reaction to recover, and then move on, from. What else could I do?

To her credit she waited patiently until I was finished.

'My crew and I will cross Break Deep,' she said again, no different in tone or solemnity than before. But I had already laughed. Now, all I could do was stare at her in confusion and ask what I considered the most obvious of questions.

'Why?'

She smiled, for some reason pleased. 'Most people start with "how". "Why" is on one hand simple, another vastly complicated. Why not?'

'Everyone who has tried to cross Break Deep has died.'

'As far as we know.'

'As far as we know,' I conceded. 'But no one has ever returned.'

'No one has returned from the Audience, and yet we still tell them our stories. Still hold elections. Still build Seats.'

The captain poured us both another cup, as if she was only now confident I wasn't about to walk out of the study. After all, if you weren't of a similar disposition, what was the point in staying to argue with someone who had just revealed they were unhinged? But my curiosity had its limits and I wondered again how many sangas the captain had sought to employ prior to finding me.

'"Why not" is not enough,' I said, referring to myself as well as expressing my disbelief that that was enough for the captain and her crew. 'And don't talk to me of the stories they might tell.'

'Why not?' she said, smirking at her own joke. 'Wouldn't they be glorious? Swashbuckling tales of adventure and discovery.'

'Those stories rarely remember the sanga.'

'Shall we play this game, then, where I run through the obvious and you deny their appeal?' she said.

I shrugged. 'What else is there?'

'Riches,' she said flatly.

'You cannot possibly know what lies beyond Break Deep: why assume there is anything of value there?'

'Because it is more interesting than assuming there isn't.'

'And I would have my share of these assumed riches?' I said.

'My crew has always had an equal share.'

Perse was nodding before I even fully turned to look at him.

'I'm not a greedy man,' I said.

'If not the fame of the adventure, then the adventure itself.' The captain stood and picked a scroll up from the desk, a map. She pointed to the hatched section that was Break Deep. 'To see for yourself what lies beyond.'

'I look forward to hearing the stories. I wish you good fortune, Captain,' I said, collecting the stack of coins and rising from my chair.

'Because the world is dying.'

I stopped, arms still braced against the chair, and searched the captain's face for any sign she was mocking me. She was quite sincere. I walked out of the study, down the carriage ramp and out of the building.

Three days passed relatively quietly. I had no patients beyond my normal rounds, which included the Merry Jig. I administered to the young men and women there without any particular incident: one draught of the typical kind given to a woman well versed in its effects; and a younger man showing signs of something more serious that made passing urine uncomfortable. But he had the sense to approach me straight away and I gave him a suitable tonic, under advice to seek me if the pain persisted. His relief gave me some cheer. Many men avoided my help until it was almost too late.

Madam Wishful was out on an errand so a boy working the front-of-house paid me. He was too young to be put to work elsewhere in the establishment, but his rosy cheeks and long lashes indicated his future. I gave him back a penny from the little purse and he smiled with such radiance that my chest ached for what would become of him. I hurried out of the Merry Jig.

The purse from Madam Wishful was embarrassingly light, even before my act of generosity. Despite my best efforts I couldn't help but compare it to the heavy marks of the captain's money; and not just the amount already paid, but the implication of more forthcoming. A share – albeit a share of a fool's errand – had a draw that I was loath to admit, and therefore it weighed on me as all things do when we try to ignore them.

Once back at my hut, I was restless. I ate a modest meal without enjoyment, fussed over my plants and looked up at every person who passed by my threshold. I ensured the curtain was well-pulled back and my sign on full display. I paced. Frustrated with myself, I set to making a stronger mixture and ointment, should the difficulties worsen for the young man of the Merry Jig. It was a silly thing to do – the herbs would lose some potency with time, as the Tout would have it – but I had to occupy my hands somehow. I resolved to take a walk after sunset, when the air might have lost some of its stifling heat and heaviness.

When the soft knock came against my doorframe, I was deep in thought: imagining what kind of vessel, if not a barge, would attempt Break Deep. I stumbled off my stool, embarrassed by my whimsy, but the woman at the door mistook my bumbling for anger at being disturbed. She made a squeaking sound and ducked back into the alley. In my haste I somehow tangled a foot in my threadbare rug, which I carried with me beyond the hut. I called after the woman, pleading with her to come back. She was equally startled by my vehemence for her return and so we both entered my hut with flushed cheeks and duelling apologies.

'It's my brother's girl,' the woman said, without preamble. 'She won't stop coughin'.'

I began to gather my things, asking the girl's age and how long she had been in difficulty. The woman answered in a distracted manner – seemingly more concerned with my filling my bag. I guessed at the reason why.

'Don't worry yourself over my fee,' I said.

'He'll pay, my brother that is, he just don't have much. He ain't worked a barge since his wife passed, that's all.'

'Show me the way,' I said.

For the second time in less than a week I was walking the steady incline of the east hills of Bordair. We passed roughly where I judged the Barge of Good Hope to be and continued to climb. I hadn't thought it possible but the streets grew narrower and more warren-like. The air also thinned, or so it felt, and there was a faint smell of ash, and underneath sulphur, which tickled the back of my nose and throat. It was darker here. When given the opportunity I looked back to the shores of Bordair below to see sunlight on the water. The sun still had some hours before it sank below the peaks that circled the city.

'Is the air usually this poor?' I said, unable to contain my wheezing.

'Worse of late,' she said.

We stopped for a moment, not that she needed to. The ash may have gone some way to explain her niece's cough, but when I suggested this the woman made noncommittal noises and wouldn't meet my eye.

Her brother's hut was a single room, like my own, but one that had to cater to a whole family's demands. There was a curtained area where I assumed the parents slept, a pallet where the girl now lay and a small cooking pot, which hung over a blackened patch of earth. The man was kneeling with the girl's hand in his. I could see the glistening tracks of tears on his cheeks, though he answered my greeting soberly enough. I set my bag down and took the other side of the pallet.

The girl was, to my surprise, carrying more weight than either of the adults – and not just in the way that young children do. Regardless, her complexion was wan and she was shivering with fever. A damp cloth beside the father indicated they had attended her during the heat of it.

'Has anyone else seen to her?' I said.

The father shook his head.

'But my hut is so far from here.'

The girl coughed violently; her whole body shook and her eyelids fluttered.

When the fit subsided I felt beneath her jaw, finding the lumps

I'd expected for a fever of this kind. I opened her mouth and saw no sign she had been coughing blood.

'This is good,' I said, ignoring the look the bargeman gave me. 'No blood.'

'No bleeding, Sanga!' the father said, mistaking my meaning. If it were up to me, my profession would have changed its name a long time ago; the memory of bargemen could be as long as it was selective. He clutched his daughter's hand.

'Hot water,' I said to the woman. She did nothing until the father gave her a brief nod.

'But—'

'Just do it!' the father said.

She crossed the room and slipped behind the curtain. After a few confusingly tense moments, she returned with two short logs. I wondered if these were the last they had. There was a pail of water, half full, by the fire. I told her to heat it all and get more.

'The girl needs to drink as much as she can,' I said.

The woman left with the pail.

'That – that will help?' the father said, looking at the herbs I was working in a mortar.

'With the fever. What she's really battling, I can't say. But she's like a river in mid-summer: the danger comes if the water gets too low.'

He grunted at that, as if to question whether I'd ever seen a river run dry.

'I'm sorry about your wife,' I said, changing the subject. But I had judged poorly. The man flinched bodily, as if I had struck him.

'That was different,' he shouted. 'You have to help my daughter!' He stood and, across the prone body of that beloved girl, grabbed me by my collar. He hauled me to my feet as easily as if I were a child and brought me close enough to see the veined whites of his eyes. I looked down at the girl, just to be free of that gaze.

'I'm here to help,' I said.

There was a moment in which I feared he would strike me; his arms and neck muscles tensed, and I shied away as much as his grip would allow. My cowardice may have moved him, I couldn't say, but he released me and fell back beside his girl, drained. He began to sob quietly. I turned to the water, which was almost boiling now, and gave the man what privacy I could.

The woman returned just as the water boiled. Experience has taught me to always have someone, usually of the family, watching what I do for a patient. She may not have recognised the herbs but she at least could be drawn on to dispute any wild claims of black sorcery, which weren't unheard of in Bordair, especially this far from the shore. She found a bowl and took to the task of helping the girl drink. The father watched mutely.

'The infusion is best kept hot,' I said, but neither were listening. Thinking to be helpful, I crossed the room and drew back the curtain a little – expecting to find a wood pile. Instead, I found a body laid on a funeral raft.

'Sanga, no!' the woman said. She was beside me in an instant, guiding me away from the curtain and over to the door. The father was wailing now: a guttural and animalistic sound that I normally associated with dire physical pain.

I stood in the street, the nearby huts pressing in on me despite their odd silence, as the woman retrieved my bag. She pressed a penny into my palm, and I nodded.

'Keep her drinking,' I said.

The noise of the father followed me down the street. I made sure I was always walking downhill, towards the shore, but I was soon lost among the twisting maze of bigger buildings. The sun was setting ahead of me, on the far side of the lake, and I stood in its last rays and simply enjoyed the feel of them on my face. Two children, a brother and sister, ran past me playing a game only they could know. They ran along the street, neither of them wearing shoes.

My breath caught in my throat.

The funeral raft, a common practice in Bordair, had been covered by a white sheet – not too unlike the kind I used. The mother lay beneath that sheet. I had been too surprised to realise, to properly see it, at the time.

Her feet were blackened.

I cast around, trying to retrace my steps to the family's hut, but all I managed was to lose myself more completely. Few candles or lamps were lit and in the growing darkness I couldn't distinguish one street from another. I gave up. I turned downhill once more, but I was unable to avoid thoughts of the father and his likely dying daughter. I tried to lie to myself, to believe that it was just a regular fever and not the beginning stages of... of whatever this was. Whatever had killed Dahey and the girl's mother. I had never been a good liar.

I kept walking until I found a bar. Being in Bordair I didn't have far to go. Ducking under the low mantle, I entered a steamy room half full of inked bargemen and women. A couple of bored whores nursed drinks. The barman didn't look like the talkative type, so I took a small table near the back and drank until I couldn't smell the boneset that lingered on my fingertips. Which meant I was three tankards the worse when the woman sat down opposite me.

Initially I thought she was old. I was still young enough to consider grey hair the realm of the elderly despite finding them in my own mirror if I looked closely. Hers was long and wavy, held back with an ornate band. She wore a lot of rings and more than one scarf. I swore – a coarse word I won't repeat here – and went to leave. But she took my hand with a strength that caught me off guard, and almost off balance.

'Sit,' she said.

'I don't need my waters read.' I grabbed my genitals for emphasis. I was never good with ale.

'I think you do, but I'm not here for a reading.'

My outburst had not gone unnoticed: the whores sniggered sloppily into their glasses. 'Charging you extra, is she? Experience costs,' one of them said, cackling.

I sat down quickly, but the whore wasn't finished. She rose, unsteady on her feet, and came towards our table. The water-reader turned to face the girl, who stopped dead as she realised, through her drunken haze, just what the woman really was: a lecanomancer.

'You're not wrong,' the water-reader said.

'Sorry, sorry, I didn' know,' the girl said. She made the sign of the Tear, bowed her head, and then gathered her companion to leave. The bar settled back to its anonymous hush.

'Always gratifying to see respect from the younger generations,' the water-reader said.

'Respect and ignorance make for good bedfellows.'

'Shall we fence a little more, or do you want to have a real conversation?' she said.

'By all means,' I said.

'You saw it again tonight, didn't you?' In a very deliberate manner she placed her hands flat on the table, as if she were attempting to divine something from the scuffed wood. Or, perhaps, from the wet ring my tankard had left there.

'I'm sorry, just who are you?'

'Mona,' she said, with an air of finality that suggested I would need no more to place her.

'And?'

She made a tutting noise. 'I crew with Captain Cope.'

'Good day,' I said, trying to leave for the second time.

'Black feet,' she said. 'You saw it again, didn't you?'

'What of it?' I rounded on her. 'What do *you* know?' I was yelling at the older woman. Nearby, bargemen put down their drinks and stopped their conversations.

'The captain told you what was happening. She sent me to find you.'

'She spoke madness,' I said, lowering my voice.

'It will only get worse.'

'And whose piss did you stir to see that?' I hissed, the effect slightly ruined by my nervous glancing at the big-handed men to my left.

'No need to divine it. You know it too. Seen it before, haven't you?'

'Not like this,' I said.

She waved one of her rainbow hands. 'Different people up north, different problems, same kind of dying.'

'So, you want me to run from it? Join Cope's crew and leave without looking back?'

'No one knows what's out there, out beyond Break Deep. But we know what's *here*. That's my point.'

'Leave me alone.'

She took my hand in hers. 'You don't have to face this on your own,' she said. She let go, and I fled.

I woke the following day with a pounding head and an empty stomach. I remembered little of how I got back to my hut, and if I had vented the contents of my stomach I was relieved to find no evidence on my pallet or anywhere else inside. The bitter, furry taste in my mouth suggested some other location had been less fortunate. I hurried, as much as my head would allow, to heat some water. The striking of flint and steel was torturously loud and I had to grit my teeth to remove the sensation that they were shaking themselves loose.

Luckily, I already had some herbs ready to cast into the pot: a pestle and mortar was beyond me at that moment. As they boiled, I retreated to the far side of my hut; even though I knew the infusion would settle me, I found the smell unbearable. I belched tornstone. When it was ready I held my nose and swallowed, which almost choked me. I cursed myself as all kinds of fool. My mother had said my intolerance for alcohol came from my father's people, and that it was her great shame. She would openly weep when it was mentioned.

I was approaching recovery when there was a knock at my door. I considered acting the coward and keeping my silence, but my mouth had experienced enough bad tastes for one morning.

'If the peril is beyond mild, come in, otherwise Sanga Cafferney is two 'walks over,' I called, my head cradled in my hands.

'That butcher? I think not.' Madam Wishful entered in a flurry of layered skirts and wig-powder, which formed a constant fog around her. She had a handkerchief pressed to her mouth and was sweating profusely.

'A hot morning to be paying house calls,' I said. I didn't get up from my stool; I couldn't be sure I wouldn't fall off.

'Hot?' she said, taking a moment to grasp my meaning. 'Oh, yes, of course.' She dabbed her forehead, losing yet more powder, and then returned the handkerchief to her mouth. 'You look dreadful, Sanga.'

'One day I will learn to leave ale to the bargemen.'

'Yes,' she said, stretching out the word until I thought it might snap. 'Dreadful stuff.'

'Is it Daniel?'

'Daniel?'

'He was struggling to pass urine, an early infection. I have a stronger tonic here.'

'Oh, no, Sanga,' she said. 'He's fine. Pissing like a Fenestiran fountain.'

'I hope not,' I said, recalling their preference for six-spout fountains. She tittered. A noise I had never heard her make before.

'Well, to business I'm afraid, my dear sanga.'

'Business?'

'Yes, I'm ending our arrangement. Terribly sorry but nothing for it, what with recent events. I'm sure you understand.'

'I'm sure I *don't*,' I said. 'What events?'

'That poor family. I'm certain you did everything you could.' She was backing away from me, towards the door, ever so slowly. She had, I realised, been doing so since the moment she entered. 'That's what I keep telling everyone: Sanga Jeffereys would have helped that family all he could, even if he isn't a full—'

'Madam Wishful, *what* family?'

'They're calling it Black Foot, or Black Ankle, or Black Toe, something like that.'

I stood very slowly. Madam Wishful almost jumped out of the doorway.

'They all died?' I said.

'But I thought you knew? Were you not there, after all?'

'The father? The aunt?'

She couldn't say it, only nod.

'Audience welcome them,' I said.

'It's not your services, Sanga, I *want* you to know that. And I wanted to say it myself. It's just a matter of reputation. Please say you understand?'

I waved her away.

By sunset I had, one way or another, lost all my regular custom. The three other brothels that I serviced had cited the same reason as Madam Wishful, but had done so through nervous errand runners. Carla Beswick sent her sister to tell me her baby was just fine, thank you, no need to visit. Mr Driscal was feeling much better, not coughing at all, according to his grandson. All kinds of cousins, nephews, nieces, and grandchildren graced my alleyway that afternoon. Not a single one entered my hut: I could see their mothers' decrees written on their terrified faces. Many pressed themselves against the opposite wall of the alley and had to shout their messages. After the first few I drew my curtain, but left the door open, hoping to make it easier on them. But really it added to the fear – as if I had become some malignant beast, grown monstrous overnight.

The only person to come inside was Sanga Cafferney. The older man was very apologetic, only stopping briefly because of all the extra work. As he said that, he had the good grace to wince. He wanted me to know that it was just the folly of superstitious and scared people. The kind of people who didn't just burn down a house touched by plague, but a whole street.

I was too stunned to weep or break anything in anger. All day I sat at my desk as one voice after another made their excuses. Nightfall was a relief: by then I had no one left.

At least, so I thought. When a note slid under my door, I had no idea who might have been cancelling my services. I ran through a mental list, starting with patients I knew to be either alone or without family, though in Bordair that was extremely rare. Mrs Granger had already sent round her neighbour and Mrs Paulson had limped her own way to my door.

Widow's Welcome

I could have looked at the note, of course, but instead I made an extravagant dinner – at least, extravagant by my standards. I emptied my meagre larder of anything still fresh and sat down to a thick soup with dumplings, bread with butter and some dried sausage. I ate beyond the feeling of being full. As I loosened my belt I experienced a moment of vertigo, as if my three-legged stool were the spire of the Grand Seat of the Poet in Fenest. Clutching my desk with one hand, I rifled through my papers and instruments with the other. I collected every coin and small purse I could find. I counted my money once, twice, three times. It might have been enough for passage up the Cask, far enough away that people would hire me, and a small hut of my own.

I opened my small bag out onto the pallet and found a larger bag that rarely left the hut. I crossed my little floor many times, taking items from shelves to the pallet, then back again as I sorted through what was essential or too expensive to buy anew. On one such crossing, I kicked the forgotten note. In a hurry, my attention more focussed on approximating the weight of my larger mortar, I bent down and opened it.

Marley's Wharf, Berth Six. Signed CC.

I took only my usual bag. I reasoned I was likely dead, one way or another, so what good would worldly possessions do me? And, in the unlikely event I returned to Bordair, there was a chance my association with Black Toe, or whatever it was called, would keep people away from my hut in the meantime. A chance. Fear, like stone, has a tendency to be worn away by time to reveal something different yet related beneath: fascination. I patted my large mortar, knowing that it would fetch a fine price if someone was brave enough – and strong enough – to steal it.

A little before dawn I crept from my own hut. When a couple rounded the alley corner I jumped at their merriment. My palms were sweating on the handles of my bag. As the couple passed, I managed to mumble a Drunkard's greeting but they ignored me for each other.

Watching their retreating backs I wondered if I'd ever been quite so lonely.

There was a slip of water between my hut and the one adjacent. I went right to the edge of the 'walk so the toes of my boots had nothing between them and the slickly empty surface. That perception of emptiness was folly, of course; the waters of Bordair teemed with life, death, and all that existed between. I could clutch my bag, I thought, and if my will were strong enough I might drown.

'If that's what you want to do, I think the captain's given you a better offer,' someone said behind me. Mona, the water-reader. She couldn't stop me, and I doubted she would even come in after me. But having her there, watching, made it impossible. So instead I fiddled with my fly as no man had before, or would ever again.

'Then aren't I the fortunate one?' I tried to smile, but it was obvious she saw through that as well as my little pretence.

'Latecomer, Widow, Drunkard: they'll all be interested in your story, Sanga. Now, shall we?'

Mona casually offered me her arm and we walked together along mostly empty boardwalks. Even at such an early hour, I was glad that she avoided the busier parts of the city.

'They're calling it Black Jefferey,' she said, with a calm that left no room for doubt. 'They talk about it as if they're talking about *you*. As if a man has crossed their threshold and strangled the life from their loved ones. "Black Jefferey took old Mr Mason down the street, took him quick, mind." Or, "Black Jefferey better leave my two alone or I'll show him what's what."'

'My name is Jeffereys,' I said, stressing the 's' so much I made a ridiculous hissing noise.

'I don't think that matters to those taken by plague.'

She said the word in the same way as any other she'd used to outline my plight. But it seemed to shake my head, forcefully, until I had to close my eyes to stop the dizziness. I pressed a hand to my temple in a fruitless attempt to ease the pressure.

'How many have died?' I said. 'A lot?'

'What's "a lot"?'

'I should have jumped,' I said.

'Maybe. Still can.'

'Shouldn't you be trying to convince me not to?'

'How could I?' she said. 'Perhaps someone here might be able to.' She had paused at the entrance to a brothel, the last building before we were on the wharf proper and among the barges.

'I don't think so,' I said.

'It could be some time.'

'I'm no innocent, Mona. But those places – I've treated the people who work there.'

She didn't ask for specifics, didn't want details or stories – and Audience knew I had enough to get us to Break Deep and back.

There was plenty of other activity on the wharf, despite the early hour: bargemen loading and unloading, though telling the difference between the two was difficult at times. They also engaged in many tasks I could awkwardly describe but with no idea as to their purpose or effect. Even so, I felt a kind of peace at their business. I was intrigued by my own contentment but when I examined it more closely, I realised it came from a dark place: I was happy seeing people busy being alive. I jerked at this thought, and at the same time a barking started up. Mona misunderstood, and said, 'Don't worry, she knows it's us.'

We stopped at the bottom of a short gangway, at the top of which was a solid-looking Caskanese water-dog. I knew many barges employed such animals; I'd been told they had webbed paws, though I'd never inspected them closely myself. The dog turned its head towards the aft and barked again.

'All right there, Brin, I see them and so does the Messenger.' The captain came to the railing and patted the water-dog.

'Is this it?' I said, raising my voice above the din of the busy wharf.

The captain spread her arms. 'What did you expect?'

'You said...' I couldn't remember exactly what the captain had said, but I remembered the implication: the crossing of Break Deep would not be done in a barge. And yet, here was a barge.

'Said what?'

'A barge, Captain?'

'And what's wrong with her?'

'Well, nothing, of course. But.' I gestured emptily.

She laughed at my floundering. Mona didn't join in, instead standing impassively by, which was somehow worse.

'Don't fret, Sanga,' the captain said. 'We will not be making the crossing on this good barge.'

I hefted my bag and climbed the gangway. The captain had already turned back to her duties, but Mona helped me aboard.

'She says "crossing" as if she's sure there's something on the other side,' I said.

'She is sure.'

'And you?'

'Look forward to seeing if she's right.'

'That's your position, as the crew's diviner?' I said.

'It is – if they ever ask. Sanga, I'm pleased you're with us,' she said.

She kissed my cheek. I was too surprised to say or do anything. I must have worn that surprise clearly: she smiled, as much to herself as to me, and then went to join the captain at the aft. I stood there like a fool for some minutes.

I had been on plenty of barges in my life, of course, even if I had never worked as part of a crew. I was quite at home with the pitch and roll of it; my own hut had the same kind of movement, if to a lesser degree. I was also used to keeping out of the way. Bargemen, like all people, are creatures of habit and economy: they take well-worn paths that allow for the quickest accomplishment of any task. Identifying one of those routes, I found a dead spot in which to stand and observe.

The captain was talking with the pilot: a tall, long-limbed man who appeared in a constant state of nodding. I initially thought this had something to do with their conversation, but it continued once the captain had moved away. There were four or five bargemen bustling to and fro at their various duties. The 'swain, Eliza, was just below the helm overseeing their work. She met my gaze but gave no acknowledgement of having met me before, or having been by my side when Dahey died.

Beyond the barge I saw Bordair drag itself awake. Carts were set up along the wharf, mostly food and drink. Mostly drink. A woman carried a tray of pins and trinkets, likely of her own making, but she was politely ignored: bargemen had little need for possessions as far as I could see. A couple of young men – I didn't recognise them from my rounds – lazed by some nets, calling without conviction to the women working a nearby barge.

I felt a pang of regret at leaving my home, the place I had lived – in one part or another – for the majority of my life. Where I learned my trade. Where I nursed my mother until she died. I stepped towards the railing, then heard my name.

I looked about me but the bargemen were all intent on their preparations, the captain talking to the pilot once more. From the railing I saw an elderly man set against a barrel. His legs ended in stumps, just above where the knee would have been, and in front of him was a cup.

'Black Jefferey took my legs,' the man said to a passer-by. A penny clinked into his cup and he said his thanks. 'Black Jefferey took—' Another coin. I watched the man until we cast off. It was rare that my namesake did not result in a penny – he emptied his cup into a pocket twice just while I was watching. I felt oddly conflicted.

'Sanga?'

I looked round to find the boy, Perse, holding out his hand. I do believe if I'd had a coin readily available I would have given it to him.

'I'm to show you to your hammock,' Perse said, taking my bag.

I looked once more at the wharf, but the elderly man was obscured by another barge. I did not look at Bordair again.

Below deck was everything I'd imagined of a working barge: cramped, hot and noisy. A fine mist hung in the air near the ceiling. At first it was some relief, like the summer rain that fleetingly graced Bordair, but then I realised the mist was actually from the bodies that sweltered there. I ducked and swallowed back the bile that threatened to embarrass me among my new crewmates. Those ten or so paces were neither pleasant nor easy, but I would have to get used to it. Break Deep was a long way from Bordair – how long, in terms of days on the barge, I had no real idea. But I knew there were a lot of the Washerwoman's rivers between the two.

Perse stopped at an empty hammock. He made no gesture, no comment, just stood there long enough to be sure I understood and then left me. The two hammocks either side of me were occupied, one man and one woman: both large, both snoring – though more of a purr than a shuddering roar. I put down my bag as quietly as I could, which was met with a yelp. I looked to the two sleeping bargemen but saw no movement from them. Instead, out of the darkness beneath my own hammock there resolved two eyes, and a tongue.

'Hello?' I said softly.

With a grunt that spoke of significant effort, the water-dog stood and came to me. Its claws played on the wooden floor like a rhythmless spoons-man. I offered my hand, which it took to with a wet nose. Satisfied, it grunted again and returned to its position beneath my bed.

I wondered if I was being made fun of – the butt of some joke only a bargeman would find funny. But looking about me I found mostly sleeping crew, and those awake were engaged in games of dice or speaking in pairs in hushed tones. A rough estimate suggested a crew of somewhere between twenty and thirty, though it was impossible in the dim light and confines of below deck to get a proper sense of numbers. It felt like a lot to me.

In the end, I was too tired to raise an objection to the animal as a kind of bedfellow. I hung my jacket at the far end of the hammock and loosened my shirt. It was clear sleeping in your clothes was normal behaviour on a barge and, besides, that had become *my* behaviour of late. I loosened my shirt at the collar a little and then eased myself slowly onto my swinging bed. I watched my backside sink closer and closer to the dog, who, it appeared, was completely unconcerned by any event that did not directly and physically impact on her. When my weight was fully committed I was still a good few inches above the dog's back, which I'm sure the animal knew would be the case from the outset.

I lay down and was kept awake by thoughts of what Mona's rather chaste kiss meant, or didn't mean. I also spent a good while wondering just how old Mona was. As a few more bargemen stumbled down the steps to their hammocks, I decided I didn't care. My thoughts wandered to my place in a crew – something I had never thought possible, something I had never prepared for. Finally, I fell asleep with the understanding that I would now be reliant on the knowledge and experience of those around me and, until my services were needed, I was completely unnecessary. I hoped to remain that way.

That hope would have made the Audience laugh, as the majority of my hopes did. I slept through the day and was woken in the evening by a rough shaking that almost toppled me to the floor. A bargeman had apparently been careless and suffered some kind of injury. The circumstances were explained to me as I was led up on deck, but I had little understanding of the finer details of ropes and booms and the like. I managed to ascertain the woman, Shann, was very much alive, not bleeding profusely, and clutching an arm that she would let no one else touch.

I knelt by the woman, who cursed me for a heavy-footed imbecile. I hesitated, thinking that perhaps the captain had been wrong in believing her crew would accept my aid. But the woman hadn't realised who I was, being so intent on the bruise that was flowering at the end of her inking, which ironically put her flowers to shame.

'Can I?' I said.

'Can you what, piss-breath?'

I cast about hoping that the captain, or even the 'swain, was nearby to make my introduction easier. But we were in a rare moment of isolation.

'My name is... well, I'm your new sanga and I'd like to have a look at your arm,' I said, steeling myself for more curses followed by questions of my character, parentage, et cetera.

Instead, the woman turned mild as milk. 'Yes, please, Sanga.' She offered the arm tentatively to me, wincing at the effort.

I probed around the bruise, noting when she showed signs of pain, and decided the break was not too serious. I formed a splint and advised she get some rest.

'Captain has already ordered me below,' she said.

'If the pain keeps you from sleep, I can help.'

'Won't be any danger of that,' she said. She refused my help to stand.

I stayed on deck to watch the sunset, and well beyond. We were passing through the low hills that surrounded Bordair. The current appeared strong to my ignorant eyes, but the main sail was full and so was the smaller one in front – it probably had a special name. I enjoyed seeing the landscape slide by: a sense that it was always moving, always changing, despite being quite similar from one hour to the next. I was perhaps starting to understand, at a very basic and naïve level, the appeal of working on a barge; a feeling that should have pumped through my very veins had I been a true Casker. I tried to not let the bitterness of that thought ruin my simple joy.

The following days passed in much the same manner. I managed to adjust my sleeping hours to see more daylight, but that didn't stop the bargemen waking me in the middle of the night when I was needed. To think I was worried I would be of no use, little more than a passenger! There was no end to the small bumps and ailments these bargemen endured. I checked regularly on Shann, the woman with the broken arm, but she was working the day after the incident and somehow managing despite the splint. I had yet to have the opportunity to speak to the captain – who was manically busy and never in one spot for longer than a few minutes – regarding my pay. A share was promised, but I assumed there would be a stipend of some sorts. Should that opportunity present itself, I felt on solid ground to argue my worth.

We left the hills after two days and the River Cask widened with every mile. At first, the fields of the Lowlands were some distance from the river bank. But they crept closer until their rich soil was clear to be seen. Those working in the fields paid us no mind, and the bargemen appeared to return the disinterest. I, however, was fascinated by their work: the horses and the devices they pulled, their carts and wagons, their tools. I watched them every moment I could.

Other barges were a constant, of course, and I soon became accustomed to the loud greetings and rapidly shouted news that accompanied a nearby barge passing in the other direction. The first time it happened I thought someone was injured and rushed to the other side of the barge. It was news of a wedding.

We travelled mostly by sail, but there were times when the winds dropped. Poles were the solution: the entire crew except for the pilot, Darcie, were called to action. That included the captain, and me. I had no trouble sleeping any night – but after an afternoon at the pole I all but collapsed into my hammock.

No trouble sleeping, but my sleep was troubled.

I dreamt often and vividly. Images I recognised and understood tumbled into one another, became twisted and took on meanings I either didn't comprehend or couldn't bring myself to. The elderly man with no legs featured often, but he gained the face and voice of others: Dahey, the aunt who called at my hut, her niece. They said incomprehensible things to me, all the while shaking their cups, which ranged from overflowing to bottomless. I never woke in a start from these dreams, thank the Child, but was left to contemplate them in the harsh light of morning. In those moments Brin, the Caskanese water-dog that continued to sleep beneath me, would nuzzle my feet as if she felt my low mood. I had had little contact with animals in my life; my mother would not tolerate insects in our hut, let alone a pet. But I found Brin's presence strangely comforting.

The days passed, and the Cask was enormous now. It moved ponderously through the flat landscape and this easy pace not only infected the crew but also the barges we passed. No one was in a hurry, or so it appeared to me until I saw the captain. She constantly checked the river's depth in the hope that we might use the poles to speed our passage when the wind dropped. Though I couldn't hear their conversation, she was quite animated in the face of an impassive Mona. Even a water-reader could say little about the vagaries of the wind.

With no one in immediate need of me, I decided to check on my existing patients. I wandered the length of the barge, careful not to get in anyone's way, asking after burns – rope and otherwise – and various cuts. I changed a particularly bloody bandage from the knuckles of a woman who wouldn't quite meet my eye. When I suggested the blood might not have been only hers, she favoured me with a toothless grin. But I couldn't find Shann.

I managed to catch the captain in her quarters, during one of the rare moments she sat down. These she spent pouring over maps and charts that, if I looked at too closely, danced before my eyes and made my head ache. The small room was taken up by a table to accommodate these maps and, unless I was mistaken, she slept in a hammock that she stowed away during the day. That was, if she slept at all.

'Captain?' I said. When no response came I waited patiently, knowing she had heard me. Eventually she looked up and blinked rapidly. No doubt she would have found me easier to see if I'd been a small inked number.

'Yes, Sanga?'

'I can't find Shann.'

'No.'

'I was tending her arm and wanted to check the break was setting properly,' I said, still standing at the table side. I noted there were no chairs to offer me, even if the captain had been so inclined.

'Maybe that's why she banked out.'

'Banked out?' I said.

'It happens more than I'd like, but it's nothing to worry about. Another time we might pick her up on the return leg but this, of course, is different.'

'Is she all right?'

'How could I know?' she said, without malice. 'What my crew do beyond the boundaries of this barge is out of my control, as much as it might concern me. Affect me, even.'

'Don't you need her?'

'We're still afloat, aren't we?' She laughed at her own joke, though I didn't. 'Don't worry, Sanga, this is all planned for. You'll have to trust that I know my business.'

'Of course, Captain.'

'You worry for the crew, and that's good. Essential, in fact. Gerant looks to have banked out too, so you know. But we will manage just fine.'

'I see, thank you, Captain.' I turned to leave.

'I have been meaning to call the senior crew together to eat. Now that we're a little more organised.'

I glanced about the captain's quarters, trying to imagine what less organisation might look like.

'Only evening meals, of course,' she said.

'That sounds...' Arduous? Dull? Horrendous? Trying to make polite small talk with half a dry biscuit under one's tongue. 'Useful,' I said.

'I thought you would understand.' She returned to her maps, as good as any dismissal I might receive.

I spent the rest of the day in a kind of dread-anticipation of the evening. I watched the sun's descent, beautiful as it was, and wished the Audience might arrest this great tale; if not indefinitely, then at least for a while. I knew to have it over and done with would be better. How many times had I told my patients the very same regarding their treatment? But if the captain wished these evening meals to continue through to the end then there was no hope for quick relief.

The sunset was also particularly stunning thanks to the city that was starting to dominate the horizon. I didn't embarrass myself by asking one of the bargemen; I was fairly certain it was Fenest. I had heard all the stories of its vast size, its sprawl, its decadence. I had listened with the other children who cast sidelong glances at me as if I should already know of Fenest despite being born in Bordair. The bullies had later cornered me, demanded more stories and, as my imagination failed me, did what they had come to do.

'I had expected more spires,' I said, not sure why I felt the need to air the thought. Luckily, no one was near enough to overhear. I had thought the Grand Seats would be visible from afar. I had assumed they towered over the city with majestic benevolence. Instead, Fenest looked like a bloodstain: something that had spread in a way no one had anticipated or could now remedy. As someone who was considered a foreigner in Bordair, I felt strangely let down by the capital. When Perse came to collect me I was in a morose mood. I was apparently not the only one.

The table was set for six. Where the chairs had come from, I couldn't say, and even with one end of the table hard against the wall there was little space. I was ushered to a chair beside Fian, the master-of-arms whose knuckles boasted my fresh bandages. Opposite me sat Mona and Arthur: the barge's carpenter. The captain had the head, of course. Evidently we were saving the mindless chatter for when the table was full and the following few minutes were spent in excruciating silence, only broken by Arthur awkwardly clearing his throat. On the third time, the captain remarked, 'Perhaps the sanga would be good enough to look at that cough, Arthur.'

Titters went around the table, and somewhat eased the atmosphere.

The last to join us was Eliza, the boatswain.

'I've said this to you all individually,' the captain began, 'but I'd like to say it again to *all* of you: this coming together is important. Those who have crewed for me before know it is my way, and know why I consider it so valuable. Those who are new to this table I hope will come to understand.'

The bored nods of everyone other than myself marked me out as clearly as if the captain had asked for a show of hands.

'We have only one rule,' the captain said. 'Once the port is served there is no talk of the boat or the crew or any aspect of our business.'

I wondered if this was a rule I would come to appreciate or loathe.

'But until the port I'd like to hear from every one of you. Perhaps you would care to start, Arthur?'

The carpenter cleared his throat – to more stifled chuckles – and began to list a number of issues he was facing with the barge. My attention lasted all of a few seconds, but I did my best not to appear rude. Others at the table asked questions and otherwise were quite engaged by the whole process. Then the first course was served.

I was pleased to find I had been wrong in my expectation of dried biscuits and bread. A small bowl of fiery broth was passed down to me – Perse only having room to serve from near the captain. It was actually hot, in both senses, and I wondered where on the barge this was achieved, and whom the chef was.

'Darcie,' the captain said in answer to my question.

'Darcie?' I tried to imagine the gangly man below deck, long arms frantic and spider-like in the preparation of what I had to admit was a very tasty broth.

'I think, and this includes the men and women at this table, you'll find my crew full of surprises, Sanga.' The captain smiled, evidently pleased by this minor revelation.

During the soup course, Eliza grumbled her way through a report to the effect that there were no problems of discipline or duty among the crew. I did notice her hand stray towards the necklace of the Tear I knew to be under her shirt, but no one else appeared to see or, if they did, it was just an accepted habit of hers. It made *me* think of Dahey, that night, and a barge-full of memories I would rather have avoided. I didn't look directly at her again for the entirety of the meal.

Fian had similarly little to say, except that all 'inventory' was present and accounted for. When the smoked fish arrived – I didn't quite catch its name – it was Mona's turn. She placed her hands on the table. Like Eliza and her necklace, I wondered if this was a deliberate affectation or if she did so unthinkingly. I didn't know

Mona well enough yet to tell the difference; even if she knew *me* enough to kiss my cheek.

'There's little the waters tell me that you don't already know,' Mona said. Beside me, Fian *hmphed* – clearly I wasn't the only one who had their doubts about lecanomancy. We shared a look, but Mona continued. 'This is a journey fraught with difficulty and uncertainty. My readings suggest this is unchanged, even though we have begun. I cast several readings, at different points of the barge, and always the outer fourth quarter has been densely lined.' She paused, perhaps waiting for a reaction or even a sign that anyone understood the significance of this. None was forthcoming though I noticed the captain was frowning. 'The fourth quarter represents the last days of any given tale: mine, yours, that of the barge, that of the world.'

I could have been mistaken but she seemed to place a slight emphasis on 'world' in a way that made me recall the captain's words as I left the Commission's study in Bordair. She'd claimed the world was dying.

'That so many lines are drawn to the outer fourth suggests a lot of tales are about to end.'

'How many is a lot?' I said, throwing her own words back at her. However, the gesture felt hollow as she gave no indication she remembered asking the same question.

'I couldn't say.'

Fian threw up her hands. 'What's the *point* then? We don't need a water-reader to know people die each day.'

'A lot,' Mona repeated.

'Thank you, Mona,' the captain said. This had the feel of an old argument, and one she would rather move on from. 'Sanga Jeffereys?'

I sat up in my seat, suddenly aware just how badly I had been slouching. 'Yes, well, barges are dangerous places,' I said, attempting to break the atmosphere with a jest. I was met with blank stares and one or two open glares. I cleared my throat and proceeded to give an extensive list of ailments I had seen to since being on-board, stopping only briefly to explain my treatments if they might have affected a bargeman's ability to carry out their duties. Judging I had suitably bored my dinner companions, who had all turned to their fish as if, by comparison, it were worthy of the Reveller, I concluded by saying, 'And, of course, the most serious injury was to Shann, but she is no longer with us.'

No one so much as looked up from their food. Either they all knew or didn't care, and I had to assume it was the former. It did go some way to affirm the captain's claim that Shann's banking out was not unusual.

Captain Cope left long enough to be sure I had finished, and then said, 'Thank you, Sanga. With only two crewmen banked out, none of the crew should expect extra rations.' She cracked a smile at this, though it only lasted a moment. 'Water and food levels are acceptable and there are, of course, further supplies awaiting us at the ship.'

Ship.

I choked, quite literally, on the word. I made some terrible noises, but with the aid of Fian's meaty fist on my back and a number of glasses of water, I managed to recover myself. To most of the table there was little more to it, but I had the impression both the captain and Mona noted the timing of my misfortune.

I had heard stories of ships as a child. I usually liked them because, not having anything to do with Fenest, they rarely resulted in a beating from the bigger boys and girls. There were rhymes too. One I could recall a verse from but little more:

Ship a ship o' houses,
A berth full of louses.
We miss you, we miss you,
We all Break Deep.

When I looked up from my lap I found everyone staring at me, and all of them quite grave. Mona was positively ashen-faced.

'Sanga Jeffereys,' the captain said, 'do not, *ever*, repeat that rhyme on this or any other vessel of which I am in command.'

Apparently I had, without realising, murmured the childhood tune.

'Yes, Captain. My apologies.'

Eliza had her necklace fully out from beneath her shirt and was making a good effort to rub a hole in it.

The evening was beyond recovery. The fish was followed by slices of fruit. I've never witnessed port drunk so quickly or in such silence; certainly not a night to mention to the Drunkard. Arthur was the first to leave and when he stood from the table he looked me squarely in the eye and shook his head.

He was dead within the week.

★★★

The day that followed was not easy. I stepped lightly around the barge, wondering if news of my – apparently colossal – blunder had spread. There were no new injuries and I delayed checking on existing patients until the very last moment; any longer a delay and I could not, in good conscience, call myself a sanga.

I looked for signs of a damaged reputation as I saw to the small splint with which I'd set a bargeman's two fingers. He was as brusque as ever, not one for idle talk, and offered the usual hint of deference towards someone from whom he needed help. In short: no change. The same was true of the woman whose bandages I refreshed, the bargeman whose boil I had lanced, and the man who had, before we set sail, chosen poor bedfellows. Bed*fellows*: the plural was very much emphasised, and he insisted on detailing the whys and hows of the situation from beginning to end. He was utterly unrepentant. If anything, he wore his current condition as a badge of honour. In spite of myself, I couldn't help but smile along with Harry – that was his name.

I spent as much time on deck as I could during the approach to Fenest. The river was very busy and there were periods in which we moved in increments of feet in what felt like slow hours. It was much cooler here than in Bordair and the early evenings demanded a jacket, and then an overcoat.

'You're quite taken with the city, aren't you?' Mona said, joining me at the railing.

I explained my childish imaginings of spires and a kind of

glittering that would be the envy of the stars. She didn't mock me but nodded as if such fancies were perfectly reasonable.

'It's a shame we won't be docking,' she said. 'There's things worth seeing here.'

'Not docking?' I said.

'The captain says we can't delay,' she said. 'Though that's only the half of it.'

'Oh?'

'News has travelled quicker than we have. You just wait and see: we'll pass empty wharfs, keep to the middle of the river, and be watched the whole way.'

'Because of Black Jefferey?' I said.

'You have the right of it.'

I turned back to the view of the city, but my thoughts were wandering to what lay beyond. 'Whenever I've asked, no one would tell me, but I've always wanted to know why it's called Break Deep.'

Mona hissed. Then she cursed. 'Do you spend every day a fool, crafting tales for the Drunkard?'

'I don't know what you mean,' I said, taken aback by her reaction.

'We could fill this barge, and the ship, with what you don't *know*.'

'I'm sorry.'

'She's called Break Deep because that's what happens to anything that sails her.'

'I don't know—'

But she interrupted me by placing her mouth on mine.

I hadn't lied when I told Mona I was no innocent: I had kissed girls before. And been with enough women to understand what it was that drove people to each other – and what drove some of them to my threshold afterwards. And yet Mona disarmed me of this knowledge. I floundered, like a boy ambushed in the playground, and only just recovered quickly enough to not embarrass us both through inaction. I returned her kiss. When we parted she patted my hand that had remained on the railing, and it was a gesture of genuine affection. To an onlooker it might have appeared condescending, but I was left grinning like a buffoon. I was still grinning as we entered the outskirts of Fenest, but it was not to last long.

Mona was, of course, correct in her prediction that the city wouldn't welcome us, though I was sure that had more to do with her understanding of people than it did the casting of any oil on water. We joined a number of Casker barges in the centre of the river, making a slow procession past eerily empty docks. Most of the crew were up on deck and at the railings, and together we gazed silently back at the few dockhands and officers on the harbour boards. The atmosphere was one of a funeral march. A number of the crew turned away from the Fenestirans' grim pity.

But I remained there, at the railing, through the harbour and beyond into the residences of Fenest. There may have been few spires, but the buildings were grand. Mixes of wood and stone that I didn't fully understand the logic behind, not being a builder after all, but in which I could appreciate a kind of functional beauty. I was impressed – though not awed – by the size and scale of the city. I resolved to visit Fenest on my return. An easy resolution to make, given the circumstances.

I enjoyed that view of the backs of homes, the side windows that showed glimpses of pantries and studies, the little window boxes – some well-tended, others abandoned. The sun set on this more intimate view of the city and I had to move to the aft of the barge to see candles and lamps lit in the receding windows. As we left Fenest, other barges took to tributaries large and small though all leading away from the capital. We stayed the course on the River Stave.

We were two, maybe three, miles clear of the city when the dweller attacked.

I felt the first bump. I didn't know what it was, but I did feel the barge rock slightly. I took a step back from the railing. There were plenty of people on deck with me and I looked up and down the barge to reassure myself. Some did look up from their work, so I knew I had not imagined it. I thought perhaps we had hit something in the water – maybe a silt bank or the like. But no one appeared concerned, and when another bump didn't come, they went back to whatever they were doing.

Then the first shout went up.

It might have been a word, but all I heard was the sound, the tone, the alarm. Everyone was on their feet. In the near-silence that followed that cry there was such a tense stillness, the likes of which I had never experienced. A die rolled across the deck, knocked or kicked in the players' haste in standing. It came to a stop showing three pips. In that insane moment I groped for some significance in that number: neither highest nor lowest, a line that put me in mind of a triangle, et cetera. That's what I was thinking when I saw a woman dragged overboard.

She was standing only a few yards from me with her back turned. Suddenly she was falling in a way that made no sense: the wrong kind of fall for someone who had tripped over or fainted or was in pain. She hit the deck hard and then she was sliding towards the rail. The woman didn't struggle. She was limp, her arms now forced above her head as she was pulled along the deck. There was... something at her feet.

Brin started barking. More shouts, and I could make out one word above all others: dweller.

I shuddered, a kind of primal reaction that took hold of my whole body.

Bargemen were rushing to and fro about me. Some carried poles, others had knives of varying lengths, but all of them wore looks of grim determination. I felt something brush against my hand and flinched, as if bitten. Brin was by my side, the whole of her rigid and alert. She gave a low growl. I followed her gaze and saw it.

An eye so big it belonged in a nightmare – and has haunted mine ever since.

I watched in horror as its misty iris became engorged, and then slowly shrank to focus on me. I stepped back but my path was blocked. I looked my own death in the eye and did not find courage or cowardice in myself, just paralysis. Brin, however, barked her challenge. The eye slid away, and I took my first breath in what felt like hours. I knelt to commend the water-dog's bravery, when one of the dweller's long tentacles shot over the barge's edge.

My ankle burst into flame, or so it felt. The pressing, needle-like heat of a fire blossomed there and I had just a moment to register the sensation before I was pulled from my feet. I slid towards that precipice, and the eye waiting for me beyond. I reached out in desperation and caught hold of a heap of netting, which did nothing to stop me. I was making some kind of noise – a scream, perhaps.

And then, in a bolt of black muscle, Brin set upon the tentacle. She sank her teeth into that nightmarish pink limb and shook her head viciously. Again, and again, her muzzle came away in sprays of midnight-blue blood. I felt the grip around my ankle loosen. I kicked and wriggled and grasped for something, anything, but to no avail.

I hit an upright of the railing and the wind was knocked from me.

Below, the dweller flared in all its unimaginable glory. Pocked more than any pox victim, its spread of tentacles struck out at different parts of the barge. I was just one mouthful. One stubborn, likely tasteless mouthful.

I felt the boards beneath me shudder under a heavy blow and wondered if I was worth the attention of another of the beast's teeth-lined limbs. But no further bite came; I dragged my head back from the edge to see Fian tugging at a machete that was now wedged in the barge. Her hands, like Brin's muzzle, were slick with the dweller's unearthly blood.

The realisation I was free came slowly as Fian turned to some other skirmish. My ankle was still alight, still wrapped in the creature's thick muscle. I could only roll away and gulp at the air, my chest tightening with every passing moment.

That I remained as such, lying on my back as the rest of the crew defended the barge was a source of shame long after the event. I heard the screams of those less fortunate than myself: those who Brin or Fian or the captain were unable to save. But the dweller did not destroy the barge. I was told we did not destroy the dweller either, and that three men and two women were lost, Arthur among them.

I became my own patient. My ankle and lower shin were ragged: a bloody mess of loose skin and muscle. With an effort that left me panting, I eased away the end of the tentacle. Even in such a short time the dweller's teeth had marked me in a way from which I would never totally recover. And not just scarring, but an uneven gait. I wiggled my toes, wishing I could see their movement inside my boot, not fully trusting the sensation. But once I determined there wasn't any real risk of losing the use of my foot, I knew infection would be the real danger.

As soon as I could stand after the attack, I shuffled my way below deck. That I could still walk – however painfully – was nothing short of miraculous. I was vaguely aware of the frenzy of activity around me but could only focus on the simple act of placing one foot gingerly in front of the next. Men and women were shadows in the lamplight – we passed each other like barges at midnight, but without hailing. I swallowed hard against the pain and rising bile.

Below deck was as calm and dark as ever, though much of that had to do with how empty it was. The hammocks hung like abandoned spider webs; the corners favoured for dice held the memory of rattling cups and soft curses, but now they felt different to me. I took up my bag, glad that the handles meant I didn't need to break my stride or kneel: I was unsure if I would find my way back to my feet.

I commandeered the galley with no opposition. Through gritted teeth I worked, liberally mixing herbs, leaves, and water. I made a good deal of the salve – far more than my own needs – certain that others too would have felt the dweller's spiny kiss. Biting down on one of Darcie's wooden spoons, I applied the salve. My vision shrank and I fell against a cupboard.

But after the initial shock, there was a cooling sensation that was most welcome. I knew it would turn to itching, if all was well, but I did not let that knowledge ruin my small relief. I carried a cooking pot's worth of salve, what bandages I had, and one or two other useful items from my bag up on deck. I placed myself in one of the dead-spots on the barge, but in plain view. Before long I had a steady stream of bargemen to attend to. So many, that while I wound bandages and applied the thick, green salve I wondered at the number of tentacles a dweller had. I knew better than to ask anyone, but it looked to me very few on-board had avoided the dweller altogether.

When it was clear no more would come I fell exhausted on my hammock and, although I was aware of being the only one below deck, fell straight to sleep.

★★★

I was woken once again by Perse. I was relieved to see the boy: he had not come to me the day before with any wounds. He appeared as calm as ever as he led me to the captain's quarters. Had I slept the entire day, right through to another senior crew's dinner? On deck the high, warm sun dispelled this fear, but in its wake was a roiling uncertainty in my stomach. Nothing good could come of a meeting with the captain, not now.

She waved me into a chair immediately – no waiting on her maps, no standing at a loose kind of attention.

'Tell me of the crew,' she said.

'The crew, Captain?'

'The injuries. You've seen them all?'

'I believe so, yes. Eliza was clear that everyone should see me.'

'Some bargemen can be stubborn,' the captain said. She herself had not come to me and I knew she had been on deck to battle the creature. She must have noticed my look of concern, as she said, 'I'm fine. That's not the first dweller to try its luck with my barge.'

'It was hideous,' I said, recalling the movement of its enormous eye – something I had been trying hard to forget. 'And so close to the city?'

'They have been, of late.'

She told me of the men and women lost to the dweller. She also spoke of the barges ahead and behind us, apparently not attacked, who had offered us aid with repairs. They had been too far away to offer any real help during the attack.

'I didn't know Arthur well,' I said, 'but he struck me as a good man.'

'"A good man?" Maybe he was.'

'Will we return to Bordair, or Fenest?' I said.

She looked at me for a moment before answering, 'Neither.' She stood and moved behind the table.

'But we've lost so many?' I said.

'Seven,' she said flatly.

I thought that to be at least a quarter of the crew. 'Yes, seven,' I said.

'That is acceptable,' she said, her attention now on her charts.

'Acceptable?'

'Yes, Sanga, our ship is designed with the expectation there will be casualties.'

I left the captain with a heavy sickness in me.

I was on deck when the ship came into view. I realised I had been staring at it for some time, this small break in the flat line of the horizon, where the sky met Break Deep. I had thought it to be a cliff or island or some other natural phenomenon. I gripped the railing. That we would be voyaging in something so colossal terrified and appalled me. That we could build such a thing brought forth similar emotions.

'There she is,' Mona said. She knew me well enough by now to know how I preferred to waste my spare hours; I was no longer surprised to hear her voice behind me.

'Does she have a name?'

'Hubris.'

I turned to look at her. She couldn't quite keep a straight face. 'That's terrible,' I said.

'You don't want to know its real name,' she said.

'It's big enough.'

'For what?'

'No more dweller attacks,' I said.

'That would depend on how big the dwellers are out there.' She was gazing at Break Deep. She had been below deck during the attack. I wasn't sure what the rest of the crew felt about that, but it wasn't hard to think a water-reader might know a thing or two about what happened beneath the river's surface. I had wondered myself.

'How's your leg?' she said.

'It itches.'

'You're not the only one. Half the crew are scratching at themselves.'

'It's good. All part of the healing,' I said.

'You aren't moving right, though.'

'My foot-race days are over.'

It was good to hear her laugh, even if briefly. 'We'll be aboard before sunset,' she said. 'Captain wants to feed us again.'

I groaned. 'I won't go, not after last time.'

'You have to. That was the quickest senior meal I've known. This time walk in singing that rhyme, won't you?'

I took an exaggerated breath, but she stopped me, her face serious. 'Don't,' she said.

I'd had little time to think about Mona, or the kiss we shared. Now, she was so close, her face tilted slightly up towards me. I touched her cheek and, when she didn't step away, I kissed her. That felt better than thinking, or talking.

***

The ship had its own wharf. As we approached, I had the sense that it was a very lonely thing. I said as much to Mona, who was still beside me, our hands entwined, and she hummed her agreement.

'It's the only one of its kind.' The way she said it, I had the impression she was talking of an animal or flower – a living thing at the point of extinction. There was a kind of sadness to it.

Our barge was secured; now that we had stopped moving I finally understood the sheer size of the ship. It towered above us – more building than boat – and even had a balcony on the aft. The masts satisfied any need I might still have had for spires, the crow's nest high enough to tickle the toes of the Audience. The complex lines of rigging were impossible to follow, and I almost felt dizzy trying.

'Have you ever seen such a thing?' I said.

Mona released my hand and drifted away. I was too awed, too much in the ship's sway, to follow her.

The ship not only had its own wharf, but its own flight of steps, which twisted and turned up to its deck. Men and women were already climbing those steps, arms laden with crates and nets and all manner of supplies.

'Still have your doubts?' the captain said, coming to stand beside me. She felt wrong in the space Mona had left: too slight, too hard.

'She *is* impressive,' I said.

'She's our future.'

I shuddered at the cold certainty in the captain's tone as she said this. If she noticed, she made no comment. Instead, she told me to gather my things and stow them below deck on the ship. I did so, my awe now tainted with apprehension. It spoke to the power of the ship that I had, however briefly, forgotten that it was likely to be the site of my final days; mine and the crew's.

As I climbed the dock's stairs that apprehension grew into a blind panic. I gripped my bag until my fingernails dug painfully into my palm. I kept climbing only because I was unsure whether I would be able to keep my feet if I turned around. At the top there was a small gap between the dock and the ship. Only a foot of air, and water below, to cross and yet in that moment I would have felt more able to vault from one side of Bordair to the other. People went about their business on deck, paying me no mind, as if there was nothing more normal in the whole world.

I felt something brush against my leg, and then Brin was rushing across the washed wooden boards. She went straight to one corner of the lower deck, barked, then with bouncing ears she hurried to do the same in the other corners. The ship thus marked, she made her way below deck. In a strange way this show of superstition – from an animal, no less – settled me. I strode onto the ship.

The pitch and roll were far more extreme than that of the barge, but the journey from Bordair had gone some way to prepare me. I went directly to the railing, and the view was quite astonishing.

Break Deep. The effect it had on me was impossible to fully comprehend, let alone share. A painter might be able to, perhaps, but their canvas would have to be enormous, for that is what Break Deep was: a vastness beyond reckoning. It made me feel small, but that was only part of the sensation. That its beauty was a kind I had never seen before meant I could make no worthy comparisons. You had to see it. Be in its presence. Only then could we have spoken of Break Deep, and likely we wouldn't speak at all.

Night, day, dawn and dusk, I stood there or thereabouts and just watched it whenever I could. I never tired of its rolling fields and rainbow colours and razor-edged horizon.

The salt was something I had not been expecting. No adventure story said anything about salt: in the air, in the water, on every surface. Over the next few days it was always in my hair. I tasted it when chewing food and when my mouth was empty. It crusted my nostrils.

The first time I went below deck I stowed my bag and prepared myself – both mentally and, as to my wounds, physically – for the captain's dinner. I was pleased to find the ship's sense of space extended to the sleeping quarters. While there were a great many hammocks, fewer were accounted for. I dithered as to which I should choose, before realising the choice had been made for me: Brin was lying beneath a well-positioned hammock with plenty of space on either side, and even a low shelf nearby for some of my things. I ruffled her head as I settled in. I was vaguely aware of people playing dice somewhere, but they did not disturb me.

My wounds were healing well, in part thanks to my discipline in not scratching at them. In a few days I would remove what salve remained and, if necessary, apply a fresh mix. There would likely be other crewmen of a weaker character who would need further assistance.

I had just finished applying a fresh bandage when I heard

shouts above me. I hastened on deck to see what was the matter, dreading another dweller attack.

Instead I saw the dock, barge, and shoreline already some distance away. A great sail was now employed and swelling with a lively breeze.

'I didn't expect us to leave so soon,' I said to Mona, who was also on deck watching the receding shore.

'Captain won't waste any time.'

'Is that wise?'

She didn't answer. That she didn't want to talk, for whatever reason, soon became apparent. I left her there without any ill feelings; I understood well the need for solitary moments, especially when surrounded by the rest of the crew. I hoped the ship would afford me some such moments.

I wandered on deck for a while, as ever making sure I wasn't a nuisance to anyone with real purpose, and awaited the summons to the captain's table. At least I was hungry. But when Perse tugged on my sleeve to awaken me from a gazing stupor, he led me forward, not aft.

'Where are we going, Perse? What's happened?'

'Eliza is dying.'

She was in a cabin below deck. Too big for the bench-like bed, one of her arms was hanging over the edge. As well as the bed there was a small table with a lamp, and a barrel full of water. I checked her pulse and found it still reasonably strong and regular. But she was sweating profusely.

'Eliza?' I said. 'Can you hear me?'

She gave no response.

'Perse, will you fetch the captain?'

'Captain knows,' Perse said.

'Yes, but will you bring her here? Please, this is important.'

With the boy gone I stripped Eliza, except for her necklace. This was no easy task as she was much bigger than I, and quite the dead weight. I inched off her boots, then her leggings, and let out a sigh of relief when her feet were unmarked. I checked her hands too, and then her whole body just in case. I could find no black marks. She had been lashed on the shoulder by the dweller, and her wound had an angry purple colour once I peeled away some of the salve. It could have accounted for her fever. I drew some water from the barrel, so as to be ready for the moments when she did surface from the fever. All I could do was wait. And hope.

There was a knock on the door.

'Come in,' I said.

When the door didn't open, I went out myself. The captain was waiting some distance away.

'What are you doing?' I said.

'You wanted to see me.'

I looked from her to the door and back again. 'You won't come in?'

'How is she?' the captain said.

'In full fever.'

'How long has she got?'

'Excuse me?'

'I think you heard me, Sanga.'

'It could be just a fever,' I said, struggling to keep my voice calm. 'She was bitten by the dweller.'

'And if not? When will we know?'

'Are you asking me when Eliza will die?'

'Yes,' she said.

'I will try everything I can to save her.'

'You are to stay here, Sanga, until I say otherwise. I will have your things brought.'

'You must have known this might happen.'

She turned and walked away.

'We have to go back,' I shouted into the silence.

A groan behind me made me jump. Eliza was struggling to sit up, weak as she must have been, struggling perhaps in a fever dream. But her eyes were intent on something. I brought her a cup of water and she drank greedily. I filled it once more, but she ignored me. She was reaching for something, a low wail coming from her that grew and grew. She was trying to reach her toes.

'No, Eliza,' I said. 'There's nothing there.' She kept straining to see. 'No Black Jefferey,' I said, though it pained me. She stopped her struggles and blinked slowly. I repeated what I'd said, and she slumped back against the bed.

She didn't wake again.

I watched her the whole night. I still believed it was just a fever until, right in front of me, there came a black spot on the bony tip of her ankle. I rushed from where I was sitting and pulled the lamp closer. I rubbed my eyes, waiting for those earthly stars to disappear, and then looked again. Had the spot grown already? It was now the size of the fingernail of my little finger.

This was an opportunity. I had the wherewithal to realise that, and also to realise how ghastly a thought it was. With Dahey, and the family that came after, I had no idea what was happening. With Eliza, once I had accepted what the captain had already, I could make some study of this Black Jefferey and, in doing so, perhaps help the poor woman.

I counted a slow thirty and then compared the mark with my fingernail. It was now easily as big as my thumb – not just the nail, but my thumb from my knuckle upwards. I checked the other ankle and found another, smaller mark. Eliza was still in the grip of the fever, still sweating, which was different to Dahey's dryness but close to the little girl's condition. I tried to wake her, but to no avail. I futilely pressed a wet cloth to her forehead. With equal futility I looked in my bag. I knew of no herb, no mixture, no tincture for this plague. I picked up vials and packets only to toss them back. I caught the edge of my bone saw and quickly withdrew my hand. Not yet. But it did give me an idea: if I had nothing to give Eliza, perhaps I could aid her by taking something away.

Scalpel in hand, I stepped softly towards her. The blade was within inches of the black mark before I remembered exactly what that mark represented: dead flesh. I had a bottle ready under her ankle to catch the blood, but there wouldn't be any blood, not from there. Given the marks were closest to the feet, I decided to let the blood from other extremities. Eliza had good, clear veins and there was no difficulty in making an incision at the wrist. The blood flowed weakly at first but grew steady.

'There we are then,' I murmured, in reply to her feverish whimpering.

When the bottle was almost full I bandaged her hand, pressing down for a few long minutes to stem the flow. I took the bottle over to the lamp, though the flame was low and I would need more oil soon enough. I turned the bottle in what light I did have. Were there black specks there, or was it my imagination? I closed my eyes and took a deep breath. No. It was just blood – a solid, unblemished red.

I took a strip of paper from my bag and dipped it into the bottle. The blood was a little thin, perhaps, but there was nothing unusual I could see. I slumped back against the wall and waited. It didn't take long.

She bled from her eyes, just as Dahey had. I crawled to her side with a hastily snatched vial but couldn't catch the trickle down her cheek to her ear, where the blood pooled briefly, before falling like a drum beat on the floor. Then it came from her mouth.

In the end she bled from everywhere – from her face, from the wrist I held, from between her legs. The air of the small cabin was like a forge: hot and sharp to taste. When she was dead, I cleaned her and the bed as best I could. Watery blood seeped between the floorboards. I pictured it finding its way through, somehow, to Break Deep and mixing with the water. That was more comforting than the reality of it pooling somewhere below me. I closed her eyes, breaking the crust of dried blood.

With a clean cloth over my mouth I picked her up under her arms. It was not as dignified as I would have liked, but she was bigger than me. I apologised and, shouldering my way through the door, dragged her out of the cabin. Unable to carry her further I laid her down.

And then I noticed him: my second patient – second victim – aboard the ship.

Harry was shivering, his hands tucked under his arms, his teeth chattering. I had not seen this in a patient yet. He was curled on the floor, eyeing me with a mix of emotions about his face that I could not fathom.

'Can you walk, Harry?' I said, my voice muffled slightly by the cloth. I doubted my ability to lift him. I was beyond tired.

'Sure,' he stuttered. 'No dancing, though.'

I helped him to his feet and, with him leaning heavily on me, we entered the cabin. He didn't want me to see, kept trying to hide them, but his fingertips were black. This time I didn't shut the door: I wanted to see who was delivering my patients, and what they might do with Eliza. Once Harry was on the bench, I took out a sheet to drape over her body – she deserved much more, but there was little I could do. I left her necklace in place.

Harry had his hands in his armpits again. 'No, Sanga,' he said when I tried to look at them.

'I want to help you, Harry. That's all.'

'Won't cut 'em off, will you? I'll need them with the Audience.'

I stared down at this young man, with his closely shaved head and line of ear piercings, and was surprised by his inciting old-fashioned dogma. The belief that we joined the Audience in the same shape in which we died had, even in terms of Bordair's slow moving superstitions, fallen out of favour.

'I won't cut them off. I just need to look at them.'

He waited a moment before deciding I was sincere. The blackness had spread to all of his fingers, some as high as the second knuckle.

'Have you bled from anywhere?' I said.

He sniffed in way of an answer.

'I want to try something, Harry, but it won't be pleasant.'

'"Pleasant",' he echoed hollowly. 'You talk strange, Sanga. Captain said not to say anything about that, but what's it matter if I get in trouble?'

'Talk strange?'

'Do what you got to, Sanga. Just keep me whole for the Audience.'

I nodded and went to my bag. I mixed together a syrup of ipecac root and poppy milk, diluting it a little further, and gave it to Harry.

'Guessin' I don't want to taste this?' he said.

I couldn't help but smile at his spirit. 'I wouldn't.'

He threw the mixture back. It didn't take long to work, and I was ready with a bucket. He purged until there was nothing left. He slumped on the bed and his breathing was so loud I could hear nothing else. I didn't have to look very hard at the contents of the bucket to see streaks of red. Beyond the blood there was little in there that was noteworthy. I put the bucket out the door, as far from the cabin as I dared to go.

He took water gladly, though I stopped him at three cups. I asked him to take off his clothes, assisting him with his trousers and boots. To see his feet and ankles clear of black marking was of little consolation, given how the corrosion was creeping rapidly over his hands. His shivering grew more violent and I covered him as much as I could. His breathing was not only loud now, but also ragged and wet. I rubbed his arms hoping to aid the flow of blood and make him at least feel warmer. But where my hands had been he was covered in bruises, as if a person much stronger than I had intended him serious harm.

'I'm sorry, Harry,' I mumbled, quite in shock.

I watched him sleep, my eyes weary and itchy. I considered waking him and giving him more ipecac, but I couldn't see what that would achieve other than to make his last hours more miserable.

Eventually he stopped shivering. Then he stopped breathing.

That was when Fian came.

I was sitting beside the open door with my back against the wall. I must have dozed off, though I felt no more rested. I was woken by the noise of something heavy hitting the floorboards. My first thought was that Harry had rolled off the bed somehow. But he was still there, curled in on himself as if in his last moments there had been great pain. His eyes were clear of blood, at least. Fian was staring down at the sheet-covered shape of Eliza.

I scrambled to my feet.

'Fian, you have to...'

'Have to what?' she said, not looking up.

There was a woman already deep in fever lying on the other side from Eliza.

'Help me,' I said. I could think of nothing else, nothing specific, that she – or I – could do and she knew it.

Fian turned away, ignoring my pleas. But she returned soon enough, carrying a second woman; this one shivering like Harry had.

'This can't go on,' I said.

The look she gave me made the stupidity of my statement clear.

'Captain says they're to come down here. Says you're to stay here too.'

'And Eliza? And Harry?' I said.

'Overboard. What else?'

I opened my mouth to protest, but, as she had said, what else could be done on a ship? In the close cabin, with its walls and door, and the desperate intensity of seeing to the patients, I had all but forgotten we were sailing Break Deep. How many miles had we travelled? How far behind us was the safety of the known? Even if Fian would tell me, what good would it do?

She picked up Eliza as if the dead woman were nothing more than a tired child.

'I'll need more water,' I said to Fian's back. 'And sheets.'

'All right.'

'And you should cover your face.'

I waited for her in the doorway, as certain she would come back for Harry as I was that I could do nothing for the two women lying there. I punched the door frame, suddenly frustrated by my own uselessness. I wiped away my tears when Fian returned. She was wearing her bandanna across her face. Without too much effort she carried two buckets full of water, topping off the barrel in the cabin, and some sheets that may or may not have been spare sail. She also had some stale bread and bruised fruit for me. I tore into both.

'I can't stay down here all the time,' I said between mouthfuls.

She grunted as she braced to lift Harry.

'I *can't.*'

'I'll talk to the captain,' she said.

Harry flopped limply over her shoulder. There was little room and, though I pressed myself against the wall, Fian brushed past me. She smelled of salt, from Break Deep, and her own sweat.

'Wait!' I said.

She stopped; as much, I think, because of my frantic tone than any impulse to follow my orders. I pushed Harry's head to one side. There, just below the crown, was a cluster of red pinpricks, like bite marks. Beguiled as the Picknicker, I ran a thumb over them but they were hard to feel through Harry's rough stubble. They didn't fade at my touch.

'He's not getting any lighter,' Fian said.

'Of course.' I patted her shoulder.

She left, carrying Harry to his watery grave.

I rushed to my bag, my paltry dinner already forgotten, and found my shears. Both women had long hair tied back in one manner or another. To save any argument I approached the feverish woman. The other watched, wide-eyed but silent, as I went to work. The hair was tough and matted in places, but I had a habit of keeping my shears sharp. I went as close to the skin as I could without cutting it; I didn't want to look for red bites in thin sheets of blood. Finished, I grasped her uneven skull in my hands. I couldn't help registering, as inconsequential as it was at that time, that she must have suffered quite a blow as a child. I soon found what I was looking for.

A smaller grouping than on Harry, but the bites were there nonetheless. I scratched at my own scalp – a gesture I could not avoid, and it did little to reassure my other patient. The bites were once again raised, quite fierce in appearance, but I saw no blisters or pustules. The skin of the surrounding area might have showed evidence of scratching, but it was hard to say for certain. I met the other woman's eye and felt we shared a moment of understanding. Lice.

I moved the lamp closer to the pile of discarded hair. With great care I felt my way through the dark strands, alert for any white specs or anything dust-like. When I pulled apart the more matted sections there was indeed something there, but under close inspection it resembled dead skin more than lice eggs; at least, that was my opinion. The other woman was in no state to give hers. I let the hair drop to the floor. Straightening, I took up my shears.

I first took her protests to be the kind of violent shivering Harry had experienced near the end. But then she managed to croak, 'No need, Sanga.'

She pulled up a shirt sleeve, her movements awkward and jerky to the point where it was easier for me to help her. She wanted me to take off the bandage, which I had presumably applied after the dweller, though I had no recollection of her or her wound. There had been so many that night.

'What is your name?' I said.

'Merith,' she said with some difficulty.

I fetched her water, by which time she had unwound the bandage and held her arm up for me to see. Bites. I almost dropped the cup. That they were the same as those on the other woman's scalp, and on Harry's, was clear.

'When did you notice these?' I said.

'I told the Picknicker a day or so ago.'

'But you have been scratching for longer?'

She nodded, looking as if I had just said something to chastise her. I made sure my tone was soft and kind.

'How long, Merith?'

She took a moment to think. 'Three days.' She sounded sure of herself.

'And how long have you been shivering?'

'Started just this morning, Sanga, honest.'

'I need to check your scalp,' I said, reaching for my shears.

'No! Sanga, don't send me to the Audience without my hair!'

Another bargeman with outdated beliefs. I wondered if Captain Cope attracted such types, or sought them out specifically.

'I have to, Merith.'

'No, look.' She rolled onto her side awkwardly and pulled up the hair at the base of her neck. The bites were clear to see.

'And these? How long have you been scratching them?' I said.

'Don't know, Sanga, my head's always itchin'.'

I sat back, trying to think. I had to assume Merith wasn't unique:

that the bites weren't always localised to the scalp. Her arm was not particularly hairy. Many of the crew had complained about itching; my own leg itched from the dweller. I resisted the urge to check beneath my bandages, reassuring myself that I would later when I wasn't being watched by a patient.

'Sanga,' Merith said quietly. She was looking at the other woman. From her expression I knew what I would find.

I wiped the blood from the woman's eyes and covered her body in a sheet. As delicately as I could I dragged her to the other side of the space outside the cabin.

'We'll go inside,' I said. Merith was one of the smaller bargemen but she was far from frail. I reached beneath her knees and shoulders and, with her hanging onto my neck, I staggered into the cabin. Placing her down as gently as I could, I had to steady myself against the wall until my dizziness passed.

'You don't look so well, Sanga,' she said.

I waved away her concern. 'Where are you marked?' I said.

'Ain't got marks.'

I raised an eyebrow.

'Look all you want,' she said, presenting her hands. They were indeed free from the blackness. I took off her boots and rolled up her trousers. Nothing on her feet or ankles.

'Something for the cold, Sanga?' She was shivering badly again.

I fetched all the sheets I had and folded them. 'Best I can do,' I said.

I gave her water when she wanted it, and made her drink when she didn't. I ate the rest of my bread and fruit – she wouldn't take any. Though she wasn't able to talk for long, when she was awake she was keen to listen. She asked me about my life in Bordair, about being a sanga, about my parents. I could tell what she wanted to ask but, uncharacteristically for a bargeman, she was being tactful. I told her the little I knew. She wasn't surprised to hear my father was not a Casker, but couldn't believe I didn't know where he was from.

'It's okay, you not wantin' to tell me,' she said, her voice laden with coming sleep.

'I would if I could, Merith.'

I watched her sleep, as I had the others, and waited for it to happen. But there was another knock before then.

I inched open the door, dreading how many I might find lying there. Instead, the space was empty. Lara – I asked Merith the dead woman's name – was gone. Fian had clearly made an effort to scrub the blood stains from the floorboards. Now, she was waiting in the shadows, propped against the opening that led to the rest of the ship. I raised the lamp to get a better look at her, but she was too far.

'Captain says you can come up. Only for a short while, and you stay ahead of the foremast.'

'I don't know—'

'The mast at the front,' she said tersely.

As I followed the hulking master-at-arms I imagined this was not quite what she signed up for. Seeing this kind of death was not easy for me; it must have been horrendous for her. Had these corpses been barge-raiders or Seeder bandits she'd taken a machete to, or driven through with a spear-pole, our roles may have been reversed. As it was, she was shaken. Stepping on deck I could tell she wasn't alone in that.

All eyes were on me, and I felt them. Those up in the rigging, Darcie and the captain at the helm, and the rest of them on deck. No one was working beyond the foremast but I almost broke into tears when I saw Mona there, waiting for me. She was smiling, though I could tell it was strained. Fian leant against the mast and gestured me forward.

I took a great lungful of salty air and found the breeze on my face to be fantastic. I felt lighter there and I stretched my back, wondering if I had been hunched the whole time below deck.

'Hello, Orin,' Mona said.

I blinked at my own name. How long had it been?

'Mona,' I said, moving towards her. But she took a step back. As much as that hurt I could not blame her. Looking down at myself, I saw I was covered in other people's blood, Harry's sick, and the Audience knew what else. I must have appeared the very agent of the Pale Widow. To Mona's credit, she hid the horror from her face though it was still difficult to look at her knowing I could not touch her, not kiss her. So instead I gazed out at the endless rolling of Break Deep.

'Your readings said it would be this bad.' I made sure there was no note of accusation in my voice.

'I've said the whole time. Cope listened in her own way.'

'And yet you came anyway,' I said.

'So did you. It's no better at home.'

That was a terrible thought. I was a man with few friends, and no family, but there were people I was fond of in Bordair.

'I can't do anything for the crew,' I said.

'I know.'

'And the captain?'

'They call it a skeleton crew. We will go on, however few are left.'

'There's nothing out there, is there?' I said.

She didn't answer. We both stared at the waves. Even in those moments they were growing, swelling, finding an energy from somewhere. Mona looked on with a calmness that came from this being all as she'd divined. If I were a superstitious man, I might have said she was stirring the water as she stood there.

I was back in the cabin with the sleeping Merith when the storm hit. She slept longer than I thought possible in the heaving and rolling of the ship. I wedged myself beside the bed. As far as I could see she had stopped shivering, but it was difficult to be sure when the whole cabin shuddered with every wave.

And the noise. How could she sleep through the noise? The creaking, groaning and sometimes cracking of the ship was such an enormous sound it allowed no room for anything else. As bizarre as it may seem, there was one other situation where I felt the same kind of concentration of sound – as if the world had only one focus for all its cacophony – and that was assisting in childbirth. The difference, beyond the obvious, was how active I was in the face of that focussed sound. With the pitching ship all I could do was ensure the lamp remained intact, that my bag was secured, and that I myself was not a danger to any other. A far cry from aiding the birth of a new life.

The storm, however, outlasted my patience and better judgement. I made sure Merith was comfortably asleep, then crawled to the door and opened it. The space beyond was dark, but I could see there were no new patients waiting for me. I made it to the opening of the crew's quarters before Fian said, 'That's far enough, Sanga.' She lit a lamp, revealing her hulking figure still swaying on a hammock.

I had the clear impression she was guarding me and not my patients who were, after all, unlikely to stroll up on deck. At least she wasn't armed. She looked tired, her eyes sunken and hollow, her wide features thinner, more pinched than I remembered. I was suddenly embarrassed by my crawling to her, animal-like, and tried to sit with as much dignity as I could muster.

'There aren't any more patients,' I said loudly over the storm.

She shrugged. I wasn't sure what to make of that.

'Is everyone all right?' I said.

'All below deck,' she said.

I waited out the storm with her in silence. I tried to sleep but couldn't; there were too many dead faces behind my eyes. No matter how hard I tried to reason it through, I couldn't remove the guilt I felt about them all. It was just a name. I knew I had nothing to do with this plague. But there was a power in names. If the captain and Mona were right, if this Black Jefferey was running as rampant in Bordair as it was through the ship, then it would be remembered for a long time, long after I was dead. Long after any who knew me were dead. That was a heavy thing to bear.

Fian's hand on my shoulder woke me from a kind of waking-sleep.

I had been staring at my hands but not really seeing anything at all.

'Storm's over,' she said, and stood there expectantly.

I rose, my knees shaking and feet alight with pins and needles. Fian had her mouth covered. I shuffled back to the cabin: sick bay and brig.

Merith greeted me.

She was sitting upright on the bench and smiled through the effort.

'I'm hungry, Sanga.'

I felt her forehead, which was warm but not overly so. She wasn't shivering or sweating and her pulse was strong – or felt so to someone who for days had only taken the weak pulse of the dying. Before I could ask, she displayed her hands and feet to me, even wriggled her toes. We both laughed at that. It was gloriously strange to laugh, and I had to stop myself before it became sobbing.

I hurried to the crew's quarters, calling for Fian the whole way. My throat was raw and my voice weak but without the storm the ship was coldly silent. I paused only a moment at the threshold before pushing onward, confident the news of Merith would eclipse my flouting of the captain's orders. The quarters were empty. I was almost on deck when I saw them. Lines of them.

The ship had run out of sheets; some of the bodies were covered by their own clothing. There were gaps, of course, but the feet were all covered as were the faces.

I counted nine.

If the sweat running off Fian and her panting were any indication, nine was not the beginning or the end of it.

'What?' I said lamely.

'Passed during the storm.'

I caught hold of her arm but I may as well have tried to slow the wind. 'Why weren't they brought to me?'

'They're dead. What good are *you* going to do?'

'Merith has recovered,' I said.

Fian grunted and lifted another body.

'Did you hear what I said?' I shouted at her back as she climbed the steps to the deck. The head of a man jiggled against her shoulder, as if he were laughing at me. 'Merith *survived.*'

'I'll tell the captain.'

'She needs food,' I said.

'There's plenty.'

That was as close to permission as I needed, or would get. I passed the steps round to the mess. While there were clear signs of use, the polished surfaces and unsullied pots gave me a sad kind of impression. As did the quiet of the place. I did not tarry there long and took Merith some of the better bread and fruit. She was resting – I made sure it was only sleep – so I left the food by the bed.

When I returned there were six bodies still at the bottom of the steps. I made myself watch Fian carry every single one, beyond caring that I was unable to help her. With the last I followed her. I had arguments ready for her objection – arguments I'd had nearly an hour to rehearse. I was almost disappointed when she said nothing.

The clear skies were a mockery of all that had come before; the Audience had a wicked sense of humour, as if our tales weren't pitiful enough already. The warm sun on my face produced a brief happiness I had no business feeling. The scene in front of me soon chased it away.

Captain Cope was administering the Widow's last rites to the partially wrapped body. Her voice had no intonation as she spoke. Mona was there too. She sprinkled something from a bottle over the corpse before it was lowered over the edge of the ship and down to Break Deep. Fian was working the winch.

Eventually I was noticed.

'Merith is alive,' I blurted out, before I could be banished back below deck.

'That's good,' the captain said, without much enthusiasm. 'Come with me, Sanga.'

The captain's quarters on the ship were uncomfortably large. The table would have amply accommodated the senior crew as it was back on the barge, but now we would only huddle at one end. Simply put, the room was empty. Empty of character, empty of warmth, empty of purpose. The same could be said for the whole ship.

'How did this happen?' the captain said. She looked blankly at me, giving no hint, no indication of her meaning. The silence between us stretched on until I could take no more.

'How did *what* happen, Captain?'

'How did you save Merith's life?'

I considered lying but found scant benefit in doing so. 'I did nothing.'

With a nod she acknowledged my honesty. 'Then why Merith?' she said.

'I don't know.'

'Sanga, what *do* you know?'

I was about to say, 'Nothing', but that wasn't entirely the case. I told her of the bleeding of Eliza, and the voiding of Harry, and that I could see nothing in either. That neither act helped the patient. I told her of the two states that every patient experienced one of, but not the other: the shivering, dry chill and the sweating fever. Both led to the same end. And I described that end, which so frequently resulted in bleeding from the eyes. Finally, I told her of the bites.

'Lice?' she said.

'I found no eggs in their hair. Mites or fleas from rats would be more likely.'

'We have no rats aboard, Sanga.'

'You can't be sure of that.'

'I can,' she said. 'I *can* be sure. It best be you that does it.'

'I don't understand,' I said.

'Make sure the rest of them don't see.'

'See what, Captain?'

'We don't have rats, because we have Brin,' she said.

I had time to compose myself but that was little help. I wandered through what felt like an abandoned ship with a heaviness in my stomach and in my step. If I saw the captain again I may have tried to argue against what I knew to be a necessary course of action. As it was, I saw only Darcie at the helm and Fian sound asleep below deck. Brin was lying under a hammock: the one that had nominally been mine. Somehow that felt like loyalty, but I did not dwell on it. The salted meat in my hand ensured she padded along behind me.

Merith was awake, though weak, in the cabin. She smiled at the sight of Brin but then remembered where she was.

'Brin's not sick, is she?' Merith said.

'No, not sick. She's going to help me with something.'

'That's good,' she said, in the voice that people reserved for animals. She rubbed the water-dog's head until Brin decided she'd had enough and pawed the floor. The sound of her claws cut right through me and I had to look away.

'Captain wants to see you,' I said with some difficulty. 'Now you're better.'

Merith left looking steadier than I felt and every part of me wanted to call her back.

Brin sniffed the room, no doubt disliking what she found but that was a water-dog's lot, wasn't it? She was sitting calmly in the centre of the room waiting for whatever duty came next.

Duty was the word. I rolled it around my mouth as I opened my bag. I found it bitter tasting and were I to swallow it there would be no lasting satisfaction. I took out a wide, thick-handled knife, knowing this was no job for a scalpel and feeling sick at that knowledge.

She didn't look at me and in a moment of cowardice I was relieved she didn't. I knelt in front of her muzzle and stroked her tight, curled fur, wondering if even then fleas were migrating from Brin to me, if this little act of kindness would in the end condemn me. I whispered words to sooth us both.

I thrust the knife into her heart.

I did it quickly, before she could see the knife and know. Just behind the front leg; I felt the knife glance from a rib.

And then I held her to me. I held her for a long time.

I was there when Fian came for the corpse. The captain must have told her as she made no comment on finding Brin carefully wrapped. I had wept my eyes dry. We exchanged no words as I followed her up on deck.

Brin wasn't the only one to be consigned to Break Deep that day; there was another by the winch. They had found hemp sacks from somewhere to wrap the body. I hadn't thought of that, and it was better than the partial covering of clothes.

Mona and the captain were at their ceremonial positions with their faces ceremonially set. The captain was saying something. I looked up to the helm: Darcie was still there, his emaciated limbs and nodding head making him appear all the more like the effigies the Lowlanders put in their fields. Scarecrows, Mona called them. I shied away, despite there being a good distance between us. And then I realised. Fian, Darcie, Mona, and the captain.

Merith was missing. A high moan escaped me.

I fell beside the sack-wrapped body.

'No,' I said. I kept saying it, over and over again.

'It's not your fault, Sanga,' the captain said.

I tore away the sack around Merith's head. She was as pale as the Widow and her eyes were open, but no blood stains. I undid all their careful wrapping, not one of them moving to stop me. Merith's hands were unmarked. Her ankles. Her ankles.

Her ankles were covered in bruises.

I stared at those storm clouds until they crackled with pent-up lightning and swirled in malevolent colours. Someone had done their best to make Merith's ankles look like she'd been touched by Black Jefferey. To my eyes their efforts were poor, but perhaps the others saw it differently – wanted to see it differently. Perhaps one indiscriminate dealer in death was enough for them. It was the story they were ready to believe, given everything that had happened on the ship. The lump on the back of Merith's head, the blood half-hidden in her hair, told me another tale than plague.

I stayed there, trying to understand the indifferent cruelty of an Audience who would hear such a tale, until someone touched my shoulder. I flinched at the touch of Mona's hot hand. None of the remaining crew appeared any different. There was no change in their countenance and no sudden outpouring of guilty tears. I swallowed everything: the burning accusation in me; the urge to strike each and every one of them; the roar of despair that boiled in my likely tainted and weakened lungs. I swallowed it all.

I coldly rose and walked, one deliberate step after the other, until I reached the cabin. There was a pool of Brin's blood in the centre of the room. I didn't walk around it. I lay still and quiet on the bed, where crewmen had shivered and sweated and bled and died.

I might have slept in the time between lying there and hearing her voice through the door, but I couldn't be sure. What was the passing of days to me after all that happened?

'You might not understand, Orin. You might never understand,' Mona said, as clear as if she were beside the bed. Maybe she was. 'But I want you to, for better or worse. I will tell you a story. A story we both can take to the Widow.

'When I was a child, my father put a stone above the front door of our home. Carved on it were the words: "Know your place, and then find it among the Audience". When we moved, the stone moved with us. Damn how much it cost, or how much my mother tutted, the stone was taken out of one house and put in the next.

'When he died, she buried it with him. I'm not sure if that was an act of kindness or defiance. But the stone's place was with my father.

'What *place* does this ship have, Orin? Where does it fit? Not in Bordair, not here on Break Deep, nor in the nothingness beyond. It shouldn't be here. We shouldn't be here. There is no *here.*'

I staggered to the door but my hand faltered on the latch. I had to be sure of every word she said, but couldn't bring myself to see her. Instead I pressed my forehead against the door.

'Most Caskers are happy enough with their place,' she said, 'happy enough on a river, on a barge, plenty to tell the Washerwoman. A life they understand, beneath an Audience they understand. Some people: my father, my brother Dahey and plenty of others besides, we want to keep it that way.'

And in the silence that followed those words I knew why she'd killed Merith, Merith who had survived the plague. Merith who might have helped me tend the others who yet lived. Merith who was hope.

Mona wouldn't let any of us live. No matter the unpredictability of plagues or dwellers, we were all as good as dead the moment we stepped on board.

I wished that my other self would do what needed to be done. His approach was direct and unfailing, and he was everything I was not. But in this Black Jefferey failed me.

I waited as long as I could, almost starving myself in a kind of paralysis of inaction, of indecision. I could only take so much of the ensuing self-loathing, and it was that which drove me from the cabin. I stood painstakingly slowly. My legs shook from the balls of my feet all the way to my hips, as if my exposed ribs and prominent shoulders weighed a ship's worth of crew. Hunger was through feasting on my insides and instead sulked where my stomach once was. I eased the door open a fraction; it was heavier than I remembered. In my other hand I held the knife I'd used to kill Brin.

I staggered, lively as a corpse, through a dead ship.

Fian had passed, still in her hammock. Judging by the damp patch beneath her she had been one to sweat in the fever, and not that long ago. There was nothing I could do for her, except maybe cut the hammock's ties, but that felt pointless, childish even.

I saw no one else below deck, from one end of the ship to the other. Beyond the hammocks the galley was predictably empty. Though I knew I was hungry, the thought of food, of anything passing my lips ever again, made me shudder. I fled from fruit that was near ruin.

At the door to the captain's cabin I paused only briefly, feeling sure there was someone inside.

Mona was by the table, which was covered in open map scrolls, just as I had seen the captain so many times before. She seemed to understand what she was looking at, and she kept her gaze on those thin, faint lines when she said, 'Hello, Orin.'

I stepped inside and closed the door behind me. 'I realise now, I never told you my name,' I said, my back to her.

'You didn't have to. *I* chose you, not Cope.'

'Because I saw Dahey die?' I said.

'I may not believe your legend myself, but the Audience are fickle. What better way to bring plague and death to this ship, than to have Black Jefferey himself aboard?'

I turned, the knife clear in my hand. Perhaps she saw it catch the light, or perhaps she could just sense the keenness of its edge, the readiness of it.

'Is that for me?' she said.

'For us.'

'I was wrong, then, when I said you wouldn't understand.'

'I understand we both deserve the Widow's judgement. And I'll take my chances with the rest of the Audience.'

'We could wait for the plague,' she said calmly, as if discussing options for an afternoon stroll.

'You don't need to pretend anymore, Mona. I know you survived it. Why else would you be alive?'

'Oh, you know, do you? Why are you still alive then, Sanga?'

'Because I *am* the plague.'

She gave a mocking bow. 'Then I thank you, for making my role in this tale all the easier.'

'But if you were so certain there's nothing out there, why not just let Cope and her crew sail back as failures?'

'To be *sure*.'

'To be sure,' I echoed.

We locked eyes and I slowly drew the knife across my wrist. The pain was less than I had anticipated, distant somehow, and edged with relief. Blood ran like the Cask down my wrist and spread into its many tributaries around my fingers. I put the knife on the table and took a pace back.

'Would you—'

'No,' I said.

Concentrating, as if she were threading a needle, she cut both of her wrists. I left her there to die alone; another thing we both deserved.

And yet one more thing I was to be denied.

On my way back to my cabin I heard someone calling 'Sanga' from the deck. Sanga, again, weaker this time; a rattle from a voice I recognised as being more Black Jefferey's than her own.

The captain was propped against the main mast, shivering, her hands completely blackened.

I tried to laugh at her for the folly of everything she had done, everything she had said since I first met her. I wanted to laugh. But nothing came.

'Sanga. Tell me what you see,' she croaked.

I opened my mouth, but she shook her head. She pulled herself up with the help of the mast – I offered no assistance and she asked for none. I was so weak I was in danger of being blown over by the gentle breeze. I saw Darcie curled at the base of his wheel like a sleeping cat.

The captain pointed. 'Tell me what you see. I don't trust myself,' she said.

I squinted against the setting sun.

'Land, Captain Cope. I see land.'

Eleven

The Casker storyteller, Nullan, bowed and waited. There seemed to be a collective intake of breath from the crowd and then, finally, people began to clap. It seemed like thoughtful applause rather than one of any real enthusiasm. At least, that was how Cora felt as she joined in. Those she could see in the rows of the public galleries wore puzzled expressions, their brows furrowed. The masked voters would be impossible to judge but she guessed they, too, would be wondering what to make of the Casker story. But that wondering didn't necessarily mean all fifty stones would be white for no.

Cora wasn't sure what to make of it, what it might mean as the story that opened the election. She was even less sure if it had any relevance to her case. It felt like there was something to be found, some hint of the two storytellers' relationship, in the tale of the sanga, Mona, and the ship. Wouldn't Nullan find it impossible *not* to make some reference to her recent loss? But if she had, it took a greater mind than Cora's to find it amid all that talk of plague and Break Deep.

Nullan was still alone on the slope, somehow staying on her feet despite such a long story. Across the Mount, purple tunics were busy doing... something. Closing procedures, Cora supposed. The voters were all filing into their big pavilion.

'They'll be at their heaviest now,' Jenkins said.

'The masks?'

'The stones. That's what my mother says people told her, when they came back into the pavilion. The stones in their pockets felt heavier just before they were cast.'

At the end of their row, a purple tunic was calling for people to stay in their seats until the votes had been cast and the voters had removed their masks of the Audience.

'"The hammocks hung like abandoned spider webs",' Jenkins said. 'Who'd have thought the Caskers had such poetry in their blood?'

'There was more blood than poetry,' Cora said. 'Like I told you on the way here, Fenest could smell it.'

'It was a little grim, wasn't it?' Jenkins looked hot and tired. Cora imagined she looked the same.

'I've seen worse. I'm sure you have too.'

'Maybe,' Jenkins said. 'And maybe the Caskers just wanted to match the city's mood – the death of Ento.'

'Or they knew something about it.'

'You think the Casker story might be about Ento's death?' Jenkins said.

'Perhaps. Not the murder necessarily, but it's hard not to see Ento's sewn mouth as a sign someone wants the Wayward tale silenced. Plague does a good job of that, making people silent.'

'I suppose so.' Jenkins looked at Nullan again. 'A connection between Ento's death and the Casker plague...'

Cora wiped the sweat from her face. 'I don't know. You can see meaning in anything when you're short on leads. I'm sure the story has given the pennysheets plenty to talk about at any rate.'

'Oh great,' Jenkins said, as if she could already hear more shouted headlines full of plague.

Beside the pavilion a mess of purple tunics and uniformed constables were gathering. With something close to a flourish, a whole side wall of the tent was rolled up and a huge chest appeared. The chest was escorted to a constabulary coach, though where it was bound, Cora wasn't sure. Some secret safehouse known only to a handful of top names in the Commission, she guessed, given that the chests weren't opened, the votes not counted, until all the stories had been told. The Casker tale was the first, and now the votes had been cast for it: fifty black and white stones. Fifty opinions on the Casker story. Perhaps fifty seats in the Assembly for the Caskers, but Cora doubted it.

One story told, five remaining, and she was no closer to catching the killer.

Jenkins was staring at the voting chest.

'You all right, Constable?'

'Just thinking how *I* would have voted,' Jenkins said.

The voting chest was secured, and the coach departed.

'Commission people like us only have to make sure the election happens,' Cora said. 'I try not to worry about who actually wins.'

'But it'll have an impact on our lives just the same,' Jenkins said.

Cora opened her bindleleaf tin. 'Not much we can do about it though, is there?'

Twelve

Cora glanced up from the pennysheet she was reading as another group of constables rushed past her door. Something had the station all stirred up but she was too tired to seek trouble out. Let it come to her.

She'd slept at her desk last night and had been rudely awoken by Marcus delivering the early morning editions.

Brushing a scattering of pastry crumbs from the pennysheet – she'd found something stale but edible in the third draw of her desk – Cora tried to focus. The 'sheets packed as much tight print as they could into their columns, but it would have taken more than the whole pastry to obscure the headline: *Casker Opening Disaster!*

She didn't think it was *that* bad. It had certainly kept her attention on a hot day, sitting in a hard seat; what more could the Commoner ask of a story? And the snippets of conversation she'd overheard since – in the streets, in the shops, in her lodging house – were mostly positive.

The pennysheets disagreed.

She flicked through the other 'sheets. Though they said it in different ways, the opinion was the same: the Caskers had gambled and lost. They'd chosen a grim tragedy, but Cora could see why: those kinds of stories had won elections in the past. It wasn't always about entertainment – though plenty of people enjoyed sad tales. Stories like the one the Caskers had chosen this year could be damning enough of the incumbent realm – or even the Commission – to please the voters *and* the Critic. But it seemed the Caskers had misjudged things. Commission exit polls showed that only a third of those asked would have voted for the plague story. Fenestirans hadn't responded well this year to what was being labelled a 'disaster story'. Was a plague ship sailing off into oblivion too far removed from the voters? Or somehow too close? And did it mean anything for her case? Part of her wished someone would offer her a ship bound for Break Deep.

She flicked through the rest of the 'sheets. They were talking as if they knew what was inside the voting chest, as if the Caskers had lost already. But not everyone had ruled out the first story's success.

'I've got a mark on the Caskers,' Jenkins said, handing Cora a welcome cup of coffee. 'Mad not to with those numbers.'

Cora looked at the bottom of the 'sheet. 'Thirty-two to one!' She held it up to be sure. 'That can't be right. We're one story in.'

'I s'pose the chequers know their business.'

'This is why I don't bet on elections,' Cora said. 'What's all the fuss out there?' She gestured to the corridor where more uniformed men and women hurried to and fro.

'No one's saying much, not to me, anyway. But from what I can tell, something's happening in Murbick.'

'There's a lot of somethings happening in Murbick, Constable, and none of them are good.'

'This one's big,' Jenkins said.

'Not another dead Wayward?'

'Not that I've heard.'

'Thank the Audience.' Cora let out a breath she hadn't realised she'd been holding.

'It's something to do with controlling a crowd,' Jenkins said. 'They're calling in help from across the city.'

'Not you, though?'

'Sergeant said no, not me, nothing to take me away from this case.'

And thank the Audience for that too, Cora thought. Constable Jenkins had proved herself an asset so far and Cora couldn't spare her. Not if she was going to have any chance of finding Ento's killer before the election ended.

'Well then,' she said, 'any luck finding Nullan?'

'She hasn't been back to her lodgings since the story. I left someone I trust there in case she shows up.'

'I need to talk to her. Where would a Casker storyteller go after telling their tale? A bar? Docks? Back up the river?'

'I don't know, but he might,' Jenkins said quietly, nodding to the doorway.

Cora almost fell out of her chair.

Finnuc Dawson was standing there, a bloody handkerchief pressed to his forehead.

'You look pale as a Perlish milkmaid,' Finnuc said, with a lopsided grin.

'What happened?' Cora said, making her way over to him.

Finnuc peeled away the handkerchief, wincing as it pulled at a nasty gash at his temple. 'Someone threw a bottle, threw more than one actually. I was getting into a gig. Just glad they didn't hurt the horse.'

'Jenkins, get Pruett.'

'But he's—'

'Just do it!' Cora said. She eased Finnuc into her chair, which creaked alarmingly under his weight, and took a closer look at the cut. It wouldn't be easy to stitch, so close to the bone. 'Why would anyone throw a bottle at you?'

'It's why I was coming here in the first place. I wanted to know... I wanted to be sure you were safe.'

'Me?' Cora said.

'With what's happening in Murbick,' he said, 'I was worried.'

'Just what's going on? The station's like a tumbled wasp nest, and now *this*.'

'Started last night. Folks in Murbick think—' Finnuc sighed. 'They think they've got Black Jefferey.'

Cora opened and closed her mouth twice before saying, 'From the story?'

'From the story.'

'But that's…' Cora wasn't sure *what* it was. Impossible? Some kind of joke? 'There's always been strange types down there.'

'First count put the queue at two hundred,' Finnuc said.

'Queue?' Cora said. 'Queue for what?'

'There was a sanga, but they torched his house with him inside.'

'But it isn't real!' Cora said. 'It was a story, for Audience-sake.'

'The other local stitcher was overrun within hours, so the Commission closed off part of the city to manage the problem.'

'And all this has happened since yesterday?' she said.

'Would you sleep if you thought you had the plague?'

'Wait.' Cora closed her eyes, as if that might help her make sense of what she was hearing. It was too early for this. 'What about you? You're saying someone threw a bottle at you because of the story's plague? Because you're a Casker?'

'The Commission is telling all Caskers to stay off the streets. The talk is that Bordair's gone and Caskers brought Black Jefferey to the city. Likely be in the 'sheets by this evening.'

'That's crazy!' Cora said. 'Black Jefferey isn't *real.*'

'Must feel real to those sick people.'

'So where's the Commission putting them?'

'Burlington Palace, I heard. Close enough to Murbick, but not too close.'

Burlington Palace. She had seen that name recently. She picked up a pennysheet from her desk. 'But that's the Perlish venue,' she said, finding a list of venues in a chequer's odds.

'It *was*.'

Cora put the 'sheet back on the desk. At the Opening Ceremony, Jenkins had said it was the Perlish who had the hardest task to win the election, and now the Commission had turned their story venue into a plague hospital. If the Perlish *were* responsible for Nicholas Ento's death, life wasn't getting any easier for them after the act. Was the commandeering of Burlington somehow connected to the death of Ento? She couldn't make it out, not yet.

'What's that?' Finnuc said, pointing at Cora's desk.

'What's wh—' She noticed the small glass jar, the one with the dirt scraped from the alleyway where they'd found Ento. 'That? Good question. I don't know, really.'

'You don't know. No wonder your office is so neat and tidy.'

'Funny,' Cora said. She picked the jar up, turning it this way and that to get a better look at the reddish dirt inside. 'When I took it from Pruett's cold room, he said... he said... I need to see this plague for myself,' she said.

'He said *what*?'

'Never mind. *I* need to see Burlington Palace.'

'I'll take you.' Finnuc went to stand but Cora stopped him, a hand on his arm.

'Don't be ridiculous. You're hurt.'

He tried to laugh away her concern but stopped when he saw her face.

Giving a low cough, Pruett's assistant Bowen edged into the cramped office. The youngster looked harried and lacking in sleep. Cora knew how that felt.

'Pruett making you do the grunt work is he?' she asked the assistant.

'Something like that,' Bowen said, and set down a cloth wrap from which the tips of sharp things gleamed.

'Just wait, can't you?' Finnuc said to Cora. 'Let the stitcher do his work and then I'll come with you.'

Cora stepped aside for Bowen. 'You said yourself the streets aren't safe.'

'That's why I want to help—'

'They aren't safe for *you*, Finnuc. You're a Casker in a city dealing with a Casker plague from a *Casker* story. The Commission is right: you shouldn't have even come here.'

Bowen wetted a cloth and wiped the blood from Finnuc's head.

'That'll be a nasty scar,' Cora said. 'Won't make you any prettier.'

'I haven't told you one of my stories this time, have I?' he said.

'Thrown bottles and imagined plagues, I think that's story enough for one day.'

'There's one where I kissed a pretty woman when she was at work.'

The stitcher's hand stilled for a moment, but he clearly thought better of making any comment and carried on his work.

She looked down at Finnuc, searching for any sign he was mocking her. He stared back, as earnest as she'd ever seen the Casker. Any Casker.

'I'll save that story for another day,' she said.

Thirteen

It took her the better part of the morning to make her way through the busy streets. Cora watched those streets warily, as if an angry mob might be around the next corner; she doubted the outbreak of Black Jefferey, a story's plague, not Finnuc's bleeding head. That had looked all too real.

By the time she reached Burlington Palace, the sun was high and relentless. It was turning out to be a hot spring day – just the thing for frayed tempers and sick folk. She shook her head. How did she get mixed up in all of this?

At the arched entrance to the ruined palace she was stopped by a constable. He was from Uppercroft, judging by his badge.

'Keep five paces back,' he said. 'Now, what signs do you have?' His voice was partly muffled; he had a cloth tied across his mouth and nose, above which his eyes were ringed with darkness that spoke of exhaustion.

'Signs?' she said.

'Coughing, expelling, fever.'

Cora stepped forwards, and the constable stepped back. His hand reached for his baton.

'I told you to stay back!'

She took out her badge. 'I'm Detective Inspector Gorderheim, from Bernswick.'

'I don't care who you—'

'It's all right. I'll deal with this, Constable.' A woman came through the archway. She wore a stitcher's apron that might once have been white, but now was a mottled, faded mix of browns and reds.

'Are you in charge?' Cora said.

'Here? As much as anyone can be. Miriam Damer.' She went to offer her hand out of habit, then seemed to realise the absurdity of the gesture.

'This was supposed to be a venue,' Cora said.

A wail sounded from somewhere beyond. Cora noticed a thin plume of distant smoke: maybe the sanga's house that Finnuc said had been burned by the mob.

'Only tale being told here is one of death,' Damer said. 'Can't see that getting many votes.'

'I came to see it for myself,' Cora said.

'You want a *tour*?'

'Please, it could be... it could be important.'

The stitcher stared at her for a moment, then grabbed a bucket from next to a brazier and shoved it at Cora. 'Take a cloth,' she said coldly. The bucket held squares of flannel floating in a milky liquid. 'Helps keep the smell at bay.'

'Will it stop anything else?' Cora said.

Damer shrugged. 'You're better off keeping your distance. Don't touch anything or anyone.'

Cora covered her mouth as she followed Damer through the arch and past Burlington's old gatehouse – though barely any gate or house remained. Jagged walls stopped abruptly, leaving dark gaps and the sense that Cora was only seeing a fragment of what once was. The remnants were stained by moss and streaked by bird droppings; perhaps that was all that kept the walls upright.

'I haven't been here since my Seminary days,' Cora said.

'We teach our children history,' Damer said, 'so we can forgive ourselves for forgetting it.'

Cora glanced at the blood-spattered woman. Perhaps her line of work lent itself to that kind of talk. She strained to remember her lessons, surprised to find she wanted to prove the woman wrong.

'It's harder to recall our history when it's changed, or re-named,' Cora said. 'Burlington wasn't a palace. It was military – a castle.'

'Not much of a castle now.'

'No. It's old, though, older than all of Fenest, my Seminary master said.' Cora touched the stone wall. A wonder it felt no different to any other wall. 'Before the city, this was the border between those ridiculous Perlish duchies. They ruined it, as they ruin everything, with their fighting. Big battle, this one, ended the War of—'

'The War of Feathers,' a little boy said, peering round the wall at them. His eyes were wide beacons blazing out of a grubby face.

'That's right,' Cora said. She made to ruffle his blond hair but stopped when she saw how thickly matted it was. In her remembering, she'd forgotten why she was there – what now resided in Burlington alongside all that history. 'You don't look so Perlish. What do they teach *you* in school about the war?'

He looked from Cora to Damer, and back again. 'We fought them too. My uncle Jorian, he says no one thanks us for "starting this whole mess of a wheel".'

'Whole mess of a wheel?' Damer said.

'That's what he says.'

'Go on, then, go play.' Damer shooed the boy out from under the archway.

'Jorian, that's a See— a Lowlander name, isn't it?' Cora said.

'Likely.'

They came out onto a grass track lined by shin-high walls that suggested the shape of rooms. Men and women were sitting against those walls while children chased each other, playing their unknowable games, but in an unsettling silence.

'Lowlanders, Caskers, fair few Rustans too,' Damer said. 'No Torn yet, far as I know, but the rest of the south is here.'

Cora saw the truth of that easily enough. Among the muted crowd were plenty of inked Caskers. The sun caught the dull metal of Rustan lockports and Widow-knew what else. The children looked to be mostly bare-footed Lowlanders.

'They don't look like they have the plague,' Cora said.

'*They* don't. Not yet anyway. Those are the relatives,' Damer said, gesturing up and down the area beyond the archway, where the old Palace had become a makeshift camp.

People huddled in groups around their belongings – Cora could see that now. Canvas and leather bags full to brimming, hand carts similarly laden, and anything that could be carried. Those who met her eye had a hollow look. Constables from all divisions moved among them, there to keep the peace. Was it really the election that had brought these people to Fenest? They didn't strike Cora as the type hoping for a seat in the public galleries, ready to queue and jostle for the chance to hear an election story. But what else would have brought them?

'It can't be easy sleeping in the open like this,' Cora said. 'Don't they have anywhere to go while they wait for the sick to recover?'

'Do you think they'd be here if they did? They've come to the city and the city offers them no shelter. Besides, most want to be near their sick families. Wouldn't you?'

Cora pictured Ruth among the sick, no one beside her, no one who knew her name. She deserved her fate.

'Detective?' Damer was frowning at her.

'And what about the sick themselves?' Cora said. 'Are you really seeing black hands and feet?'

'That, and everything else you'd expect,' the stitcher said. 'Vomiting, fever.'

'All this because of a story,' Cora said.

'No. Not because of a story. Because of a plague. Could have started in Bordair, or in the Lowlands, or right here in Fenest – on any road or river between. But it's plague.'

'So why are people blaming the Caskers and their story?'

'Same reason we blame a messenger that brings bad news. But I'll tell you just what I told *her*: one person, one story, can't be responsible for a plague.'

'Her? You mean Storyteller Nullan?'

'She wouldn't leave so I put her to work washing bedsheets.' Damer gestured to a far wall of the ruins.

'I'd like to talk to her,' Cora said.

The stitcher looked like she might object, and then evidently decided it wasn't worth the effort. They came to the first of many rows of tents that stretched across the grounds of the ruined Palace. 'Tent' was perhaps too grand a term: the shelters weren't much more than canvas lean-tos that looked to have been put up in a hurry. Several other stitchers rushed back and forth with buckets and blankets.

Damer parted the canvas of one of the tents. 'You can tell me afterwards if you still think this plague is just from a story,' she said.

'I...'

'Remember: don't touch anything.'

Inside the tent, the smell hit Cora first, even through the herbal-scented cloth at her mouth. A cloying, fetid smell. She felt bile rising at the back of her throat. She gagged, wanting to rip the cloth from her face and breathe fresh air. Then she took in the horror before her: in the gloom, bodies writhed on pallets, emitting low moans. Their contorted faces suggested they would be screaming, had they the strength.

Something touched her. She turned to see a hand clutching her coat, a young boy hunched on the nearest pallet. His mouth opened and closed on silent words. A white paste coated his tongue and had crusted at the corners of his mouth. His shirt was soaked; with sweat, or something else, she didn't know.

The boy's hand slipped from her. His eyes rolled in his head and his body convulsed.

'Move!' a stitcher said, knocking her out of the way as he rushed to put a bucket under the boy.

He was just in time. A stream of hot, brown liquid poured from the boy's mouth. The stench worsened. A low gasp escaped his lips, and then... nothing. His eyes were wide and his mouth open. After a moment of quiet, the stitcher covered the body.

Outside, the wind had picked up. A cart was sent for and the boy's body was loaded on – just one more roll of canvas among many. His feet were marked black, as were the others that stuck out from the bottom of the rolls. Cora couldn't help thinking of Sanga Jeffereys. She damned to Silence Nullan, her story, and the plague it had foretold.

She pulled off her coat and threw it on top of the cart.

The dead boy had touched her coat, but it was more than that. *She* had to be more than that if she was going to finish this case. She'd used that coat in so many ways, sometimes to hide behind, at other times to announce who or what she was. But that didn't fit anymore. Not with the kinds of stories she was dealing with.

Damer followed the cart between the rows of tents and more black-marked bodies were added. And then the wind changed direction. There was something strange in the air; thick, it darkened the day. Cora looked for clouds but instead found ash. A heaviness high above, blowing from the fire at the far end of the Palace. That was where the cart was taking the boy and the others. Flames she had thought were a sanga's house, still burning after the mob, were much closer. These flames were for the bodies.

Cora hurried along the makeshift path to the other side of Burlington Palace, breathing as lightly as she could, the cloth in place across her mouth. Damer had pointed her in the direction of where the linens were washed and seemed to understand that Cora wanted a private conversation with the storyteller. Obviously, the stitcher had enough demands on her time. Cora envied her none of it.

Soon enough she heard water slushing about in buckets, the whine of old mangles at work. There were a few men and women going about their chores, but Cora recognised the hood of the Casker. Cora could hardly blame the woman for wanting to remain anonymous, even as she helped – not everyone would be as understanding as Damer.

'You're a hard woman to find,' Cora said, 'except when I'm not looking for you.'

The storyteller visibly stiffened but didn't stop stirring a huge vat full of bedsheets. The water was the colour of cheap red wine.

'Detective, you know so little of storytellers,' Nullan said quietly. 'I am wherever my story can be found.'

'Perhaps you should both sail off into Break Deep, then?'

'You might be right.'

'Why even bring such a bleak story to the election? Did you really think it would get enough votes?'

'Tragedies win as often as funnies. You ask me why. Given your job, Detective, I'd have thought you knew all about our morbid fascinations. We each have such darkness inside us.'

Cora stopped the woman's hands on the wooden paddle. 'I need you to tell me what happened the night Ento was killed.'

'I already have.'

'He was coming to your lodgings that night, wasn't he?' Cora said, still holding the small Casker. She smiled at a man as he passed, his arms full of filthy linens.

'No,' Nullan said.

'Then where?'

Nullan mumbled something.

Cora jerked back the woman's hood. 'Where?'

'Corner House. It's a—'

'I know what Corner House *is*.' She also knew *where* Corner House was, and it was a long way from Hatch Street, where Ento's body was dumped. 'What did you do when he didn't arrive?'

'I already told you! I waited all night for him.'

'In the room?' Cora said.

'Where else? I wasn't there to drink, or to... We were supposed to be keeping it secret.'

'But someone saw you, someone gave you the room.'

'The madam. She was discreet,' Nullan said.

'I don't doubt it. And she'll tell me you didn't leave at all that night?'

'Why don't you ask her?'

'Oh, I will,' Cora said. 'Did Ento ever tell you about the Wayward story?'

'What? No, of course not.'

'Nothing at all? He never mentioned it, not once?'

'Maybe, in passing.' Nullan stared into the distance. 'But it was more like a feeling.'

'A feeling.' Cora grasped the Casker's hood once more.

'Change. That's what took hold of him; a great change is coming, he said. He was just the harbinger. Do you know that word, Detective?'

'I know it's rarely good,' Cora said.

'You might be right. Ento's story would have shown what is to come, what can't be stopped, out there, in the world beyond this small city. That scares some people.'

The Torn woman, the one Cora had met at the Opening Ceremony, said something similar about the Wayward story. Both Nullan and the Torn were clear on two things: change, and fear.

'But what was the story *about*?' Cora said.

'It wasn't like that, we couldn't talk... we weren't 'tellers when we were together.'

Cora put back the woman's hood, her thin hope of staying hidden. 'Neither of you are 'tellers now.'

Fourteen

She deserved this. That was what she kept telling herself every time the gig stopped and she briefly considered getting out before she reached the Oak. She deserved this and, after everything that had happened, she deserved a lot more besides.

It was nearing midnight by the time she got there but the streets were still busy, what with it being a warm night. The driver had to crack his whip more than once when a drunkard, Heckling or otherwise, stumbled too close to the horse. She couldn't shake the feeling she was being watched – Ento's killer was out there still. Was it the drunkard in the road, the whore fanning herself in a doorway?

She told herself it was what she'd seen at Burlington that was making her think this way. That and the crowds. It wasn't only the stuffy air that had driven all and sundry out of their homes and into the streets of Fenest: it was the election. The city was full to bursting. More than usual for the election? It was hard to be sure. But she saw it everywhere she went, this over-fullness – coaches making slower progress because of the bodies in the road, queues in the shops. Even at Burlington, with the horrors there, people from afar had crowded the place. There was no escaping it, and the Oak was no different.

She headed straight for the ring.

Three fights came and went, and Cora kept her pennies in her pockets. She hadn't been paying attention to form and didn't know who was presenting what these days. It didn't take long to lose that understanding. It took much longer to get it back. But when a breeder's name she recognised came up, and the numbers looked right to take some out-of-towners' money, she placed a few bets. Nothing big. Just to get the feeling again. The hooded cockerels were brought in.

The first two she had money on were quick, one-sided affairs. The victorious birds were lauded by winners and losers alike – ringside was always a place that enjoyed dominance. Cora was wrong about one of the fights but had hedged her numbers so she still came out on top.

The last of her bets was with spurs. Nasty one, too, with well-matched birds. The crowd cheered all the louder in their ignorance. The breeders weren't cheering so much. They'd make their money but even the winner of this kind of fight was not long for this world. Finally, a blood-splattered bird, swaying on its clawed feet, crowed over the fallen. Cora won two marks. She didn't stay for more.

Three flights of stairs up, she knocked on another door – softly this time. A girl in her undergarments, eyes downcast, welcomed her to Beulah's pleasure house, where delights untold await, no desire too—

'Hush now, girlie, I've been here before,' Cora said.

'Can I help you with anyone in particular?'

'I'd heard his name was Lucaszia.'

'Luca is popular tonight. Could I suggest—'

'Tell him I want no one in the room when I enter, and the bedsheets clean. Actually clean.'

Cora slumped onto one of the sofas, which was mostly cushions. She tossed a few aside to get comfortable. The lounge was opulent, in a tasteless way – everything muted and dark, reds and purples, no surface untouched by lace or silk. Even the walls bulged with hangings.

She wanted to roll a smoke but couldn't find her bindle tin. She patted down her trouser pockets and then went to look in her coat.

Her coat wasn't there.

Her hand froze, mid-air, and she remembered the cart, the rolls of bodies, the ash of Burlington Palace. The thickness on the breeze. She'd thrown her coat on that cart because of the plague; the young man in the tent had touched her, Black Jefferey had touched her.

Despite the warmth of the evening and the heat of the bodies packed into the betting ring beneath the whorehouse, Cora felt cold. Without her coat she was exposed, and that wasn't a good feeling. Not in her line of work. She folded her arms across her chest. That coat had been with her since she'd made detective. It carried the scars and the stains of all the cases before this one. But this case, Ento's death, was different to those others. It was the election, it was the Chambers, it was plague. The boy at Burlington had made the choice for her, but it was the right one, because without the coat she felt lighter, somehow. It wasn't just losing the weight of the cloth. It was about not hiding beneath it.

But she was still without smokes; when she'd thrown away her coat she'd also thrown away her bindle tin, leaf and all. She coughed to clear her throat but couldn't get rid of the memory of that smell. Of that place.

She was going to give up the leaf. After Burlington, it didn't feel like she had much choice in *that* matter either. She fussed with the sofa cushions some more to distract herself, and she waited. At last, the girl came to summon her.

Luca's room was on the top floor. The girl opened the door for Cora and then left. Cora vaguely recognised the room from years ago – well before Luca's time. There was no one else inside, as she'd demanded. The bed was in the corner, away from the eaves, with a lamp set to low beside it. She pulled off the covers and ran a hand over the sheet. Dry, and none of the scurf or roughness that spoke of use. None of that, just the feeling of her hard, worn hands on starched cotton.

She checked over the room, like she did every time she slept in a bed that wasn't her own, but this time she was more thorough: under the bed, behind the privy screen and in the wardrobe. She opened every drawer and lifted out the clothes, jewellery and the like. There was nothing to worry her. Nothing sharp – not even a razor or a letter opener. No secret pots of powder or droppers full of who-knew-what. None of the kinds of things people liked to hit each other over the head with – no vases, mantel clocks or plant pots. If the boy wanted to hit her with a table, or the short bath tub, so be it.

There was a soft knock at the door, and he came in.

'Lock it,' she said.

'It doesn't—'

'Yes, it does. And don't worry, it's for me, not you.' The feeling she'd had earlier, of being watched, was still with her.

He twisted the handle twice over and a *click* echoed in the room.

He waited there, letting her look at him. He was wearing a simple white shirt and breeches. None of the flounce and flair she saw at the ringside. Beulah's hand was evident in that – as it was in the preparation of the room. She knew what Cora wanted.

Cora went over to him. He smelled of rose water. She ran her fingers through his sandy hair, then felt behind his ear. He, too, was clean.

She pulled his shirt over his head. His chest was well-defined and muscular, but not overly so. He wasn't a heavy-set boy; not a boy who'd worked a plough or loaded a barge. He had a body for use between the bedsheets. His skin was perfect. Not a mark or blemish, and no ink.

She stepped back and sighed.

'Those too,' she said, gesturing to his breeches.

He undid the button and let them fall to the floor. Naked, standing there, prick to the wind, without a hint of self-consciousness.

'Turn around,' she said.

Hairless back, taut buttocks. No ink.

'You'll sleep facing the wall.'

He nodded.

'You don't snore, do you, Luca?'

'No, Detective.'

'Good. Now, get into bed.'

She undressed down to her undergarments, her trousers and shirt a pile on the floor, and joined him.

As she pulled up the cover she found herself thinking of Finnuc. A Casker, no longer safe on the streets of Fenest – and he had the cut to prove it. She hoped he was doing the sensible thing and staying at home, wherever that was. She couldn't even send him a note.

With her back to Luca, Cora shifted until she touched him: his shoulders, the base of his back, the balls of his feet against her calves. She felt his warmth – he roared like a fire. For the first time in days, weeks maybe, she relaxed. It all drained out of her, from her muscles and her nerves and her very bones, soothed away by the heat of a young man.

She slept soundly enough to interest the Widow.

Fifteen

Cora left before anyone else was up. Nothing so depressing as a whorehouse in the first light of day – the harshest light for a place that did its business in the borrowed kindness of night time. The boy, Lucaszia, mumbled something as she pulled on her clothes, then shrugged the bedclothes over his head. She left him some pennies by the door. For his purse, not Beulah's.

It wasn't just the staleness of early morning in a whorehouse that made Cora get going. She wanted to be across town before the streets became too crowded. She didn't remember having to do that in other elections, busy as they were.

The air had a chill she felt sharply without her coat, but she hurried along to warm herself up. The coat was gone. She was facing the day without it.

Cora caught a gig and settled in for the journey across to Derringate, the part of the city where Nicholas Ento had lodged. She went to roll a bindleleaf before remembering she had given it up. She could still taste the ash of Burlington Palace, as if it were caught between her teeth. This case was bad enough and now it was taking away the few pleasures she had left. To distract herself from the lack of smokes, she picked up the pennysheets left on the floor of the gig. They were yesterday's, but better than nothing, even if one of them was *The Daily Tales*.

If she'd wanted to forget about what she'd seen at Burlington, the 'sheets weren't the place to go. *The Daily Tales* had little else to report. The cause of the plague was clear, said the unnamed writer: those coming to the city from outside its gates were to blame. A certain *kind* of person, for which Cora read 'poor' and 'southern'. The 'sheet suggested a more selective entry policy was needed for future elections, 'to protect the safety of Fenest'.

Cora scrunched the sheet into a ball and threw it over the gig's side. With any luck another gig would soon trample the 'sheet and its message into the muck; little good it would do in stopping the spread of such ideas. Even now, over breakfasts and first smokes, there would be people in Fenest saying to one another that southerners brought disease, because they were poor, because they were dirty, and so it only made sense to keep those people out... Her parents would have been loud in saying such things. Ruth wouldn't have though. Cora picked up the other 'sheet from the floor.

The Fenestiran Times took a different view of the plague. What could be more certain than sickness if people were left with nowhere to stay? The plague at Burlington was the result of the city's neglect, not a fact of southerners being where they shouldn't. That led neatly to the Perlish and their failure to invest in necessary things like new houses, more water pumps, drains. Which led back to the election. Like always.

And back to Ento's death too. The plague had been foretold by the Caskers in their election story, which meant it had to be connected to the murder somehow. If she could find the killer, she could find answers about the sickness – what it meant beyond people dying just in Fenest. Audience knew if that would put an end to pennysheet guesswork.

The gig came to a stop and the driver called down: they'd reached Derringate.

Cora walked the last part of her journey, to Teilo Street where Ento had lodged. The 'sheets talk of plague had reminded her too much of Burlington and she wanted to clear her head.

Derringate was a nice part of the city. A quiet, respectable part. Fresh paint everywhere, even on the fences and iron railings. Cora reached the lodging house in Teilo Street and knocked. The paint on the door appeared new; no scuffs along the bottom, no dust or grime in the panel corners. A family was taking advantage of the warm spring morning on the green. Cora wondered why the parents weren't at work or the children in school. Then she realised she had no idea what day it was.

She turned back to the door, ready to knock again, but there was an elderly woman standing there tapping a fan in her hand.

'Yes?'

'Mrs Kettleby?' Cora said, taking out her badge.

The woman peered closely at it. She was smartly dressed in a dark dress and silver graced her ears and wrists. There were lines at the edges of her eyes, and her lips seemed at their ease when pursed.

'I told the girl everything I know about Nicholas Ento, *Detective* Gorderheim.'

'I thought you might have remembered something else since then.'

'No.'

'Then maybe you'd indulge me,' Cora said, 'and talk me through what you saw the night before Ento was found dead.' She rummaged in her pockets for her notebook. 'You know these youngsters, rushing all the time, forgetting all the important things.'

Kettleby raised a plucked eyebrow at that. 'All right, Detective, you can come in. But wipe your feet.'

Cora did, noting the new carpet in the hallway and on the stairs beyond. 'Business is good then, Mrs Kettleby?'

'The election,' she said with a lazy wave of her fan, as if those two words could account for everything and anything. These days, Cora was inclined to agree.

The thin woman led them into a small sitting room at the front of the house. Nicely done, with soft leather seats each with their own side table and a ready stack of pennysheets – that morning's editions.

'So,' Cora said, 'why don't you tell me about your house guest? About Nicholas Ento.'

Mrs Kettleby looked hard at Cora, but instead of objecting she gestured for her to take a seat, and then sat down opposite.

'I didn't see much of the man. He was up early for his... wanderings. I suppose they're *all* like that.'

'You mean the Wayward? So I'm told. Did he ever say where he went on those trips?'

'Hardly. I dare say I would rather *not* know. Though he did seem to favour the Seats.'

'Really? Whose?' Cora said.

'The Commoner and the Widow.'

The first was to be expected, Cora thought, given why Ento had come to Fenest: the Commoner would have been sympathetic to his task as the Wayward storyteller. But the Widow? Had Ento feared for his life?

Mrs Kettleby flicked open her fan which, to Cora's surprise, was rather lurid. 'My husband likes to travel,' she said by way of explanation. The lithe figures did have an exotic look about them.

'Did Ento ever discuss his reasons for coming to Fenest?' Cora said.

'Detective Gorderheim, this is a respectable lodging house. I do not *pry* into the affairs of my guests.'

If that was to be believed, it made her unique among landladies across the Union. Cora cleared her throat.

'Of course,' Mrs Kettleby said, 'I was as shocked as everyone else when I heard he was a storyteller. And the awful things in the pennysheets. His mouth—'

'I gather from Constable Jenkins that you saw Ento leave the house that night. The night before we found him.'

'I was reading the evening editions in here, as I do most nights before bed. Sometimes the guests join me but that night I was alone. I heard a coach draw up outside.'

'Do you know what time that was?'

'A quarter past midnight. I'd heard the clock chime.'

'And then what happened?' Cora said.

'Well, nothing. Not right away, which I thought quite strange. I didn't hear the door of the coach – no one stepping out or getting inside. And then Mr Ento came hurrying down the stairs.'

'Hurrying?'

'Still putting on his jacket. Ridiculous man – his handkerchief was flailing about like a pennant in a squall. He didn't even stop to bid me goodnight.'

'He didn't see you?'

'I don't believe so,' Mrs Kettleby said. 'He usually told me when he would return. I deadbolt the door at night, you see.'

'So he regularly went out late?'

'I wouldn't say regularly, but yes, he was out from time to time. I assumed he found another, warmer bed on those occasions.'

Mrs Kettleby might not be one for prying, but she was certainly one for assumptions. It rankled some part of Cora that landladies' gossip was right more often than not, but this wasn't the first time she'd used such a source.

So, Ento had left the boarding house knowing full well that Mrs Kettleby deadbolted the door. That went some way to corroborate Nullan's story of a night planned with Ento at Corner House.

'You looked out to see the coach, though?' Cora asked.

'Well of course I did! Coming that late, stopping right outside the house.' Mrs Kettleby fanned herself. 'I knew my neighbours would be asking about it in the morning.'

'Did you notice anything particular about it?' Cora said.

'I could barely see the blasted thing. Couldn't even tell you how many horses it had.'

'But you said it drew up right outside.'

'It was between the lamps,' Mrs Kettleby said.

Cora went to the window and shoved aside the thick lace curtains. There was a street lamp maybe twenty paces off. She looked in the other direction and spied a second lamp, but that was even further away.

'Your own light,' she said, 'above the front door. That was out by the time Ento left?'

Without needing to turn around she knew Mrs Kettleby was bristling; Cora could hear it in the creak of the leather chair.

'Business isn't so good I burn oil all night.'

'And the coach – none of its lamps were lit?'

'Not inside or out.'

That was unusual for hired coaches. Cora turned to face the landlady, to be certain of her understanding.

'No lamps, even when Ento got in?'

'That is correct, Detective.'

'But you *did* see Nicholas Ento get inside the coach?'

'Yes, and before you ask, I know it was a coach and not something smaller. That girl you sent round kept asking *that* question – so often I wondered if she was hard of hearing.'

'Yes,' Cora said, 'I've wondered about that myself.'

Cora left the lodging house and stepped back into quiet, leafy Teilo Street in Derringate where Nicholas Ento had begun a journey he would never return from. Now she needed to find a coach herself.

The coach that carried the Wayward storyteller to his death.

Sixteen

Easterton Coach Station was a strange place. Cora had felt that before, the few times she'd had to visit the place while working a case. It was the clash of it. The small office – little more than a room where the fare clerk worked – and behind it a huge space filled with coaches. So much land that had escaped being built on as the city sprawled. It was rare, and it wasn't right, somehow. Reminded her of being in a Seat, and yet none of the Audience were at Easterton to hear her stories. Just coaches and gigs coming and going, horses being led into and out of their traces, drivers hailing one another or cursing when their way was blocked. The air was full of the creak of wood and the smell of leather.

She stepped inside the office. The square room was small, and three of its sides were lined with a deep counter top. With a couple of drivers before her, leaning on the counter to tell the clerk their fares, the office felt even more cramped. Cora hung back in the doorway and listened.

'Uppercroft to Bank Street,' said the slim woman in the uniform of Garnucks: the rusted red colour matched the Rustan who had set up the company. 'Seven trips between Bank and the Hook barge,' she said, 'then to the Wheelhouse before coming back here.'

The fare clerk was writing on a large square of paper. He wore the pale purple of Commission underlings: those whose work wasn't deemed important enough to get the full, deep purple of senior staff or the tunics of election staff. But everything was important, in some way, to the Commission. Every mile of Fenest crossed, every mark earned. It all had to be recorded.

'You didn't go through Murbick on the way back?' the clerk said to the Garnuck's driver, without looking up.

'I'm not wanting to join the Audience just yet,' the woman said. 'Even if the constables hadn't blocked off the streets and there was a way through, I wouldn't risk catching anything.'

'I heard people are offering double if you can find a way through the blockades,' the other driver said. 'Might pay triple to get close to Burlington.' He was older than the woman and wore the pale grey uniform of Clotham's.

Cora wasn't surprised to hear a driver from the smaller coach company talk of higher fares for grubbier, riskier journeys. That was the only way they could compete.

The woman took a step back from the Clotham's driver and eyed him with disgust. 'Damn you to Silence if you bring any of that sickness here.' Then she jabbed a finger at the clerk behind the counter. 'It shouldn't be allowed, Pete. These penny-grubbing bastards ought to be barred from Easterton. I've said it before.'

'And don't think I haven't heard you.' The clerk looked at the woman over the tops of his half-moon glasses. Pete, she'd said his name was. 'You know how those Perlish Chambers like to drive up the competition.'

'Don't get me started on the Perlish, Pete. The roads! Whoever comes next has got to do something about—'

'These fares all from this morning?'

'They are. Coach fifty-eight twenty-three.' She untied the coin purse that sat on her hip and handed it to the clerk, who briskly counted the coins and made a note on the paper. 'You want to put gloves on for touching Clotham's dirty money,' she said, tying her coin purse back on. She passed Cora on her way out, glowering, as if Cora might also try to bring plague to Easterton.

Cora moved further inside while the Clotham's driver gave his fares to the clerk. She recognised those little stories all too well: short trips to whorehouses and chequers' halls, from stitcher rooms to the docks. So many stories within those journeys. She didn't want to know them today. She had enough to do with the dead Wayward and his single, final ride.

'And how can I help you, Detective?' Pete said, once the Clotham's driver had left.

'I'm here about a fare that's already been paid.' She gave him the date the Wayward storyteller had left his lodging house. 'Coach arrived just after midnight.'

'Which company?'

'Could be any of them.'

He reached down and opened a hatch in the floor, then, with much grumbling that Cora knew was for her benefit, descended into the fare archives that stretched beneath the small office. He returned with several ledgers: thick blocks of square pages sewn together. She thought of Ento's sewn lips. Perhaps she was about to learn his secrets. The reason he'd been strangled and dumped and silenced. A thin sheen of sweat appeared on her palms and made the pages stick to her as she leafed through them.

'Those cover eleven o'clock until one,' Pete said. 'What address?'

'I'll find it.' No need to go advertising the specifics.

He shrugged. 'Suit yourself. I got enough to do here. Audience send me a Casker Assembly – they know how many people it takes to run things.'

'Let's hope enough people vote for them, then,' Cora said.

'If it was me casting a stone, if I didn't work for this lot—' He tugged at his Commission uniform '—I would've given the Caskers a yes, even if the story was dull enough to sober the Drunkard.'

'It certainly wasn't dull,' Cora said.

'Heard it, did you?' He gave a low whistle. 'They barely let me leave the office these days.'

A group of Clotham's drivers came in then and Cora was pushed into the corner with her records while they relayed their fares to the clerk. An achingly dull job that would be. Day after day, hearing parts of the city listed over and over until they became a meaningless babble. No longer places.

She was beginning to experience that herself as she searched through the fare records for the night Ento left Mrs Kettleby's for the last time.

But there was no fare recorded for just after midnight on Teilo Street, where the lodging house was. Cora checked further back, to eleven o'clock, in case Mrs Kettleby had made a mistake in judging the time. Nothing. And nothing later in the night either. The landlady had no obvious reason to lie about a coach collecting her lodger, or the time it had arrived. Perhaps Cora needed to try a different angle. Start from the story's end.

She called over the noise of the Clotham's drivers to ask for the records for Hatch Street and Green Row, where Ento had been found. Pete scowled at being interrupted but did as she asked, grumbling back down the stairs. Cora felt the curiosity of the drivers and, when the clerk handed her the new records, she turned her back to hunch over the papers.

She checked the fares from midnight onwards, which was easy, given that there were fewer that time of night. Time of *morning*, she corrected herself. She saw her own trip from the station to the alley when she'd gone to see the body, but nothing else that had gone that way. She shoved the ledger away from her. Maybe she'd been foolish to expect whoever had dumped Ento in the alley to use a recorded coach, but people were often stupid, and when they weren't they were just as often arrogant.

The coach had to have existed. Even though there was no record of it at the start or end of the journey, Ento was last seen climbing into one outside Mrs Kettleby's lodging house and was found several miles across the city. He had to get there somehow. But this coach was a shadow, always slipping around the next corner, always just out of her sight.

The last driver left the office. Two more were inbound but Cora closed the door on them.

'Hey, you can't do that!' Pete said.

'Looks like I can. I want the records for private coaches.'

'Clue's in the name,' he said with a greasy smirk. 'Off the record.'

Cora grabbed him by his shirt and hauled him half over the counter.

'All right, all right!' he said. 'No need for—'

'What about the Commission's coaches?' she said.

'Kept separate, they are, honest. I'll get them for you.'

But there was nothing in the Commission fare records either. She went through them again, not caring when she tore pages in her growing exasperation. Then she asked the question she knew she shouldn't.

'What about the Chambers? Are their journeys recorded here, along with the Commission nobodies?'

The clerk nodded, eager to keep her placated. 'They all go in the same records. All the coaches. Well, I guess not *all* of them.'

'What do you mean?'

'We're not supposed to use them, the coaches withdrawn from service. They're too old, and too big.'

'Too big?'

'It's the width. They don't fit the newer parts of the city, which is most of it. One of them got stuck, few years back now. Wedged in an alley. The woman inside had to cut a hole in the roof and climb out.'

'But they do get used,' Cora said.

'Sometimes, when we're really pushed.' He touched his shoulder, wincing. She hadn't been *that* rough with him. 'Not many of them are fit for the job, though they're all still taking up room at Tithe Hall.'

'No one records those trips,' Cora said, 'because you're not supposed to be using those coaches?'

'Exactly, so you won't tell— Hey, now, where are you going?'

'Tithe Hall.'

'You can't get anywhere near there today,' Pete said.

Her hand on the door stilled. She turned back.

'Don't you read the pennysheets?' he said.

If she had a mark for every time someone said that to her, she'd be able to buy the press that printed *The Spoke* and get the constables to smash it to pieces.

He grinned. 'Place is sealed until tomorrow.'

She fought the urge to haul him back over the counter and make him talk straight. 'Why?' she managed to say through gritted teeth.

'It's the venue for the Lowlander story.'

Seventeen

Cora was at Tithe Hall at dawn the next day. The day of the Seeder story.

The Easterton clerk, Pete, was right: the place was sealed off. From her spot in an alley opposite, Cora counted twenty-five purple Commission tunics at the Hall's main entrance, and a fair few constables to manage the queue for the public gallery that was already snaking down the street. There would be more purple tunics at the rear too, in the yard. On a normal day that was where traders parked their wagons: Wayward bringing livestock; fish from the Caskers; Seeder fruit and vegetables; and sometimes Perlish 'white gold' – that was what they called their cheese. Rancid stuff, far as Cora was concerned.

But no one would be selling anything today. The yard was shut, its gates locked. Her badge had been no use when she'd tried to jump the queue to see the Casker Hook. She couldn't see why it would be any use here either. There was no chance of climbing over the yard's walls, which were half as tall as the Hall itself. And according to Pete at Easterton, that yard was where the old Commission coaches were kept. Her only lead and here was the election blocking her way. Everything seemed to come back to it.

She wished she had some bindleleaf. She missed the feel of it on her fingers, in her chest, even on her tongue. To distract herself she went over the pieces of the case, trying to make them fit into a story. She had the beginning and the end, but not how to get from one to the other. Ento was seen getting into a coach on Teilo Street at around midnight. Nullan, the Casker storyteller, expected him at Corner House but he never appeared. Had he planned to disappoint her, or was he waylaid on the journey?

Most of her thinking put suspicion on the driver of Ento's coach, but she couldn't rule out the coach being attacked by someone else, planned or otherwise. Coaches were known to be boarded as they passed alleyways, the thieves waiting in the shadows, and it happened often enough for Garnuck's and the like to avoid certain parts of the city. Usually it was just purses taken, rarely kidnapping or murder. If that was how Ento had died, caught in a hold-up that went wrong, then it was nothing more than bad luck a storyteller was killed.

But then there was the mouth.

The message of Ento's sewn mouth; that wasn't chance, that was something else. Which brought her back to the driver again, back in the centre of things. She had to find the coach that took Ento from Teilo Street, and the person who drove it.

She turned up the alley, away from Tithe Hall. There might just be another way into the yard.

It took her a few minutes to get her bearings among the jumble of backstreets, but eventually she found the boarded door she was looking for. On the wall above was a rusted lamp, the glass broken and the oil-wick long gone. No lamp-man called here. Cora checked up and down the alley, then pulled at the fitting. It moved smoothly out of the wall, at odds with the broken look of it, and slipped just as smoothly back.

Nothing happened. No movement, no sound in the alley. But somewhere behind the boarded door, a bell would be ringing.

She waited, hoping that codes and phrases were no longer the fashion, or at least reserved only for the Dancing Oak. Minutes passed and she was starting to think she wasn't wanted. Then the boarded door swung open and she stepped inside, into darkness.

'You're too late for last night's games,' someone said in a gruff voice. A voice more used to hawking pennysheets than acting doorman.

'But not too early for today's,' Cora said.

Marcus said something in reply but her words were lost inside a yawn.

'I don't know why you choose to sleep in a games house,' Cora said.

'Beulah keeps the fires going and the stew pot full. Worth a lot, that is.'

The pennysheet girl led Cora down a narrow corridor towards the glow of candle light in the distance. Dark wood and a plush red carpet tried to make the corridor more cosy than claustrophobic, but Cora wasn't buying it. She heard a shout and then muffled laughter from somewhere deeper inside the building.

'I'm not stopping,' she said to Marcus' back.

'Of course, Detective.'

'I mean it, I just need to see Beulah. I want one of the back doors. One of the more... sensitive ones.'

'Oh yeah? Who you hiding from?'

'Never you mind.'

They came out of the corridor into a large, square room with carpeted staircases leading from all four corners.

'Wait here,' Marcus said, heading up the stairs towards where the better games were played.

Cora paced the room. There were expensive paintings and tapestries on every wall, but it was the stuffed animals that gave her pause. One in particular: a huge creature that loomed over her. No matter how many times she had seen it she hadn't become used to it. All spines, claws and scales, it was terrible to look at even knowing it was stuffed – a favourite of the Dissenter. She had known its name, a long time ago. The creature came from the Tear, she was sure of that much. But she'd come to know too many living, breathing monsters since then to remember.

More muffled laughter from beyond the staircases, then the unmistakeable noise of furniture being kicked over. She heard a door open somewhere, but the metal clank that followed told her it wasn't Beulah on her way.

A Rustan woman came down the stairs. She was already telling her story to the Brawler, who was always ready to listen to a good betting tale. Between muttered curses about bad hands and loaded dice, the woman's metal lockports clanked. Cora watched her closely; you never quite knew where you were with Rustans. Someone who was happy to replace a leg bone with a metal splint might be just as happy to add knives to their wrists. Cora couldn't see any of this Rustan's additions, covered as they were by a long coat made of some kind of animal hide, but the noise told her this one was more metal than bone.

'Do yourself a favour, friend,' the Rustan said as she headed for the passage that led to the street. 'Take your money and run. This house is rigged.'

'The Brawler loves a bad loser,' a voice called down the stairs. It was Beulah, with Marcus just behind her.

The Rustan left, but not before she made a gesture that Cora could well believe meant something pretty strong in the Rusting Mountains.

'This had better be good, Detective,' Beulah said, coming down the stairs. 'I have some players to placate.'

'I need a back door,' Cora said.

'Our mutual friend here could have helped you with that.'

'I need a back door for Tithe Hall,' Cora said.

'I see,' Beulah said. 'There are easier ways to hear the Seeder story, not that it has a chance.'

'What are the num— No, don't tell me, I don't want to know. I need to get into the *yard* behind the Hall.'

Beulah sighed, and the slips in her many pockets rustled. 'A favour.'

'What?' Cora said.

'It'll cost you a favour. Of my choosing, when the time comes.'

'Beulah, don't be ridiculous. Ask for something normal: name a figure and I'll pay it. A debt that needs collecting. Maybe a—'

'I hope you can climb walls, Detective.' The diminutive ringmaster turned to leave.

'Fine! A favour. Just... within reason.'

'When have you known me to be anything *but* reasonable?'

Cora and Marcus waited respectfully as the ringmaster wrote out a slip, as if this were simply another of Cora's side bets.

'East side or west?' Marcus said.

'I... I don't know.'

'West's safer. You come out behind the old water troughs. East is closer to the Hall; won't be carts loading today but might be purple tunics.'

'West it is then,' Cora said.

And with that the girl grabbed a candle and set off deeper into the games house, towards the passageways.

Cora emerged, blinking, into the light of day. A heavy *thunk* made her spin round, but there was nothing to see except a battered wash tub that now hid the entrance to the tunnel. It was just one among many dented tubs and cracked barrels repurposed as water troughs for the cart horses bringing wares to market. If anyone decided to move that one *particular* wash tub, and if they found the tunnel, and if they were foolish enough to go down it, into the unlit twisting turns that were more dead ends than ways back, then they were no threat to Beulah or her games house. They'd only be found by the stench of their rotting corpse.

The old troughs hid Cora as she took in the sizeable yard. The hulking stone square of Tithe Hall dominated the far side. Purple tunics stood at the rear entrance. And on the other side of the yard, dark shapes brooded in the morning light.

Commission coaches. Black, the Spoked Wheel picked out in white on the doors.

Shouting came from the rear entrance to the Hall.

'What?' someone called.

'Voting chest's arrived!'

She risked a glance over the water troughs. The double doors at the back of the Hall were still open but there were no longer any tunics to be seen. Now was her chance.

She slipped clear of her hiding place and hurried to the corner of the yard.

The old Commission coaches might have borne the same black-and-white livery as the ones that toiled through Fenest now, but that was where the similarity ended. Where the current coaches gleamed, with polished lacquer and brass, these were dull. Five of them, all with their paint chipped and peeling. Boards broken, some with drooping roofs, others with doors hanging from their hinges.

Cobwebs, dust and damage – all things that shouldn't have been on working coaches. But there was something missing that *should* have been on a coach, right at the front. She checked all the coaches. Each was missing something that was on every *other* coach in Fenest, regardless of whether it was company-owned or Commission. It was against the law to drive without them.

Lamps.

So here was the proof, as far as Cora could tell, that it *had* been one of the old Commission coaches that had come to Mrs Kettleby's house. The reason the landlady couldn't see any details of the coach wasn't because the driver didn't light his or her lamps – there weren't any *to* light. These older coaches didn't have the fittings.

And that had to be why whoever collected Ento used an old coach rather than a new one, that and the fact the old coaches weren't recorded by Easterton. Two kinds of cloaking. Whoever came for Ento wanted to be traceless.

In front of Cora now were five old coaches in varying states of disrepair; Ento could have been killed in any of them. She pulled the handle of the closest one, but it was stuck.

There was a noise – inside the coach.

She stiffened, waited. It came again: a scrabbling sound, and then a whine. Someone was inside. Cora gripped the handle, took a deep breath, and pulled.

The door opened with a shriek of metal and then something big and heavy and white was on her.

Kicking, scrambling, it was so close to her face she couldn't see it. Only the colour, and teeth that gnashed and snapped. She could smell its meaty breath – feel that breath against her cheek. She flailed, punching uselessly at solid muscle with her free hand.

She reached for something else, anything, in the gravel of the yard. There, hard and metal and with an edge, she slammed it against the dog's head.

Again. And again.

The yelp cut right through her. She'd hit something important, maybe an eye or an ear, and the dog was off, its weight gone. The way it moved, its head listing to one side, and the noise it made – she almost felt sorry for the thing. It headed straight for the open doors of the Hall. Shouts from inside reached her; catching that stray would keep the purple tunics busy for a while.

Cora got to her knees and stayed there, catching her breath, letting her heartbeat slow. Her hands were deep in the long grass and the weeds that had grown round the coaches. Looking more closely at one of them, she saw that a thick bramble coming through the wall had ensnared its back wheels. These old, forgotten coaches hadn't moved for a long time, since they'd been taken off the streets. Or rather, these *five* hadn't moved. At the end of the row, deep, empty wheel-ruts and flattened weeds told a different story.

There was a sixth coach, and it wasn't here.

She grabbed hold of a wheel and hauled herself up, then looked inside the coach the dog had been living in. It would have been fancy, once: a tiny brazier in the corner; well-padded seats covered in velvet; thick curtains to keep out the cold, as well as any unwanted attention. The dog had got in through a hole in the roof and had made itself at home. The seat's velvet was ripped, the stuffing frothing out. But time had done its work too. Mould bloomed across the wooden panelling and the curtains were holed with rot. Rags, only held on their rail by the cobwebs, though still drawn open by—

Cora climbed into the coach. She tucked her nose into her elbow against the stench. She reached out a hand, and as she touched it, she knew. No thicker than her finger. Not coarse, not rough, but well made. A length of cord, gathering what remained of the coach's curtain.

Pruett's description of the murder weapon came back to her. *A thin length of cord. Not too roughly made.*

This was how the Wayward storyteller had died: the curtain cord pulled tight around his neck. Ento had been killed inside the coach that came for him.

Eighteen

Eventually, despite her discovery, the smell drove Cora from the coach. She took a moment as a welcome breeze stirred the yard. She now knew how Ento had been killed. She still didn't know who had garrotted him with that cord, or why. But now she was closer to finding out; if she could find the right coach, she could find the driver.

First she had to find a way out of the yard.

Going back through the tunnel without Marcus to guide her wasn't an option. Odds were good on her getting lost and becoming another body connected with this case. No way out from the yard: the walls were too high, and the gate was locked as well as barred. Nothing for it but to go through Tithe Hall itself. Thankfully the double doors at the rear were still open and unattended. As she drew closer, she heard the murmur of the crowd inside; so the story hadn't started yet.

The Seeder story. About to be told, right there, right in front of Cora.

She slipped inside. Ento had been killed, his mouth sewn shut, to silence his story. The other realms, *their* stories, they were all part of it. Whatever Sillian said about simply finding the killer, Cora had to work out *why* Ento had been killed. She had no choice but to listen.

It was hot and rank in Tithe Hall, so many bodies pressed into close quarters. The high ceiling and thick stone walls did little to help. The Hall was big, but smaller than the Mount. Maybe it made sense to tell a Seeder story in such a place, where people made good on the living they scratched from the earth.

Directly opposite her, the front entrance was crowded with people trying to get into the public gallery. Constables had formed a barrier by the entrance and purple tunics shouted for order. Few people seemed to be getting through into the Hall itself. Cora moved a little closer, skirting the Commission box, which already held the Chambers and their aides, and then she saw the reason for the delay, for the crowd pushing.

The purple tunics were checking people's hands and feet as they came in: Black Jefferey, still being told. She'd had some time to think on what the Caskers had done in telling that story. Like most sensible folk in Fenest she now understood that the Casker story hadn't cursed them all by conjuring a plague. Nullan was just the messenger, telling a city what to expect of the coming days. The harbinger – that was the word Nullan had used, though she'd been talking of the Wayward storyteller when she said it. They were both harbingers. Perhaps all storytellers of any worth were. And was that the end of the story – a plague to come? Or was there something else Cora wasn't seeing? It might not be plague that had brought people to Fenest in the first place. What if there was another cause, the plague only the symptom? And Ento's death part of it.

Cora looked around the Hall at the tiered rows of benches, at the 'tellers platform and at the heaving bodies, jostling for room. She recognised a large, lumbering figure: Henry from the pay department at the Wheelhouse. He'd found a way to get inside – the result of some favour, no doubt. The Commission ran on *that* currency.

But Henry might regret coming to Tithe Hall, as might Cora herself; if one of those purple tunics should find a blackened ankle or finger, there'd be a stampede. She slunk back towards the rear doors and wedged herself into a corner. She stepped on something soft and caught a sickly-sweet smell. An over-ripe sinta, softened to a pulp, edged out from under her boot. She might be in the dirt but at least she was close to a way out. She'd stay to listen, but she wouldn't let a story kill her.

It was loud in the Hall. Those already in the gallery had to shout over one another to be heard. But there wasn't much chatter from the Commission box, by the looks of it. The Chambers were there, wearing their robes and all stony-faced – though she counted only six of them. The Chambers for the Seeders was missing, most likely with the storyteller they'd chosen personally, from all the Seeders who could tell a story that year. Milling among the rest were aides and lesser Commission staff, one of which was Sorrensdattir: the Torn woman Cora had met at the Opening Ceremony, and who had seemed to know something of the Wayward story. Perhaps she had a few ideas about the other stories too. Cora made a mental note to ask Jenkins to find out where the Torn woman was lodging.

A bell sounded and the noise of Tithe Hall dropped away.

The Audience entered, their colourful masks looking, leering, and weeping in every direction. They took the seats left empty for them, for the voting stones now in the pockets of their robes.

And then the Seeder storyteller stepped into the quiet that waited for him. He was broad in the back, tall and young – much younger than Nullan, the Casker storyteller. His hair was cut close to his head, and what was left of it looked reddish. He wore Seeder colours: brown, dull green, a mustardy-yellow. Colours of the land. A sharp collar and worked cuffs. Work clothes, perhaps, but cut from better cloth for this special day.

He was nervous. Even from where she was standing, Cora could see the storyteller's hands had a tremble. When he cleared his throat the sound was thin, weak.

That didn't bode well. A murmur went through the crowd and Cora felt their restlessness. Could this young Seeder manage what his realm asked of him?

The storyteller cleared his throat again, this time with more purpose, and then he began. With each word, his voice became stronger, as if the story led him to certainty.

'The talents of the boy Ghen were first noted by his mother.'

THE LOWLANDER STORY

The talents of the boy Ghen were first noted by his mother. It was she who watched him pinch off the early buds of myrtleberry branches without crushing the comings of the second, better berries beneath. She who saw the swiftness with which he cut back the sinta branches after harvest. Unlike his heavy-handed father, Ghen lost none of the young fruit, even though the blades were large in his nimble fingers. This was in his twelfth year of age, and his seventh year working all seasons in the fields the family leased from Hend, who owned much of the land in the valley at that time.

It was his mother who had the idea, but she waited another season, to be sure. Then she wrote to Sot, her sister, suggesting Sot should visit. It had been years since Sot had come to the house, despite the fact she lived nearby – only over the hill and two lanes more. But Aunt Sot was a busy person, too busy to come to the fields Ghen's parents farmed, and too busy to be visited. Ghen wasn't sure *what* it was that kept Aunt Sot so busy, but it wasn't farming and therefore it wasn't something his parents spoke of.

But his mother did speak often of Aunt Sot's wealth: her good linens, and how she could drink Greynal every night if she wanted to, rather than only on harvest days to toast the Neighbour like they did. Aunt Sot could *bathe* in Greynal if she liked, so his mother said. At these words Ghen's father sighed and stared sadly at the walls of the kitchen that needed tempering, the cupboard doors hanging not quite square, and, somehow, stared past those doors to the damp creeping at the back of those cupboards. And then he went out to walk the edges of the fields. The rest of the family knew he must be left to do so alone. His walks eased his worries, of which he had many.

None of his worries were the fault of Sot, of course. Ghen knew that it was Hend who kept his family poor, kept them from bathing in Greynal. It was because Hend's rents were high.

Ghen's parents farmed well: they were good tenants who brought forth row after row of myrtles, glossy sintas, medlars that lasted two seasons once boxed and put to rest in dark barns, red holens when everyone else in the valley only managed green, and even figs, which, as everyone in the valley knew, were vulnerable to blight. Yes, Ghen's parents were excellent farmers, and this was a source of pride for Ghen when he met his friends Rit and Melle by the river, his work for the day done. He loved to tell them of the first medlar flower opening, to list the number of sinta barrels he'd filled in a single day. Rit and Melle had their own news too, of course: news of yields and prices, but their families' lands didn't thrive the way Ghen's did, even though they owned their fields. Ghen's parents' success made his chest swell with pride, and made Rit and Melle envious, because they were each of them children of the Lowlands and they lived to see the land flourish.

And flourish it did, with the help of Ghen and his sisters, but still they were poor. However high the prices for medlars, however many rare red holens Ghen's mother managed to sell on market day, there was never much money left at the end of the month to set aside for buying the land from Hend, which Ghen's parents yearned to do. After the rent was paid and a few pennies spent on the things the family couldn't do without – new shoes for Ghen's sisters one month, sinta nets another, and every month the poultice from the Wayward woman who lived by the bridge, for his younger sister Elin's cough, which never went away – there was little in the jar kept under the floorboard by the stove. And pennies didn't buy land, and so his father went walking round the fields, and his mother's anger fell on Sot, because she was better off, because she wasn't around to hear and, most of all, because Hend was not to be cursed. Everyone in the valley knew that.

Ghen had only hazy memories of his aunt. He thought of her as being rather like a tool that wasn't often used. A turnpoke, for instance, needed one year in three when the holens showed their leaves at last. He thought she might have dark hair.

One day, towards the end of summer, rather than cursing Sot for her wealth, his mother said she'd written to her, asking her to come for the sinta harvest. When she said this Ghen's father left the house and banged the door shut behind him, needing once again to walk the fields.

Aunt Sot won't come, Ghen thought. She'd not come when his sisters were born, or when Elin's cough was so bad even the poultice from the Wayward woman didn't help and his mother thought Elin would die, so why would Sot come for the sinta harvest? One thing Ghen did know for certain about Sot was that she didn't farm.

'Maybe she works in the long house,' Rit said.

The children were in the river, which was low after the summer months; small islands of exposed sand sat between the channels. They were looking for mostins to trap and sell to the Wayward woman by the bridge. She paid a penny for three or exchanged them for a poultice: seller's choice.

Rit idly poked a stick into the sand at his feet but nothing moved. The evening felt as hot as the day had been and the three of them were tired from their work in the fields. It took less effort to imagine what Sot did for a living than to trap mostins.

'You think Sot works for Hend?' Ghen said.

'He has forty men and forty women in the long house kitchen,' Rit said.

'*Kitchens*,' Melle said. 'Hend has ten of them, and ten dinner tables. He eats a plate at each one for every meal. That's why he's so fat. Quick, Ghen – the jar!'

A mostin was emerging from the sand, its wings shifting the grains, its legs pulling free. This was the best time to catch them, when they were slow and unused to the light. Ghen gave the jar to Melle, who planted it over the still wriggling mostin with practised swiftness.

While she held the jar in place, Ghen pushed the lid under the confused mostin, scooping both it and a handful of sand into the jar. The creature would have to be cleaned before it went to the Wayward woman; she was very particular about that. That would be Ghen's job. He had the nimblest fingers, both Rit and Melle had told him so.

'I'm not sure about Sot working in Hend's kitchens,' Ghen said, pulling another jar from his bag. 'You can't afford to bathe in Greynal if you work in a kitchen.'

'She could blend,' Rit said, resting on his stick.

'My father says that pays well,' Melle said. 'The prices they pay in Fenest. And it'd mean Sot would have the Greynal for bathing.' She used her hands to scrape back the sand.

'Maybe,' Ghen said. 'But why would anyone want to have a bath in Greynal?'

Melle gave a cry of delight as her fingers caught the wings of another mostin. Ghen readied a jar but Melle's hands faltered.

'Dead,' she said. She took Rit's stick and turned the creature over, tearing a wing as she did so.

She stepped across one of the water channels to a fresh patch of sand. Ghen knew he should follow, be ready with a jar, but the dead mostin was still lying there. It wasn't right to leave it like that so he quickly reburied it. As he stood he realised Rit was watching him, his blue eyes narrowed.

'Ghen!' Melle shouted, and both boys hurried over.

The mostins came thick and fast after that, and soon all but one of the jars he'd brought contained a live creature. Their wings batted the glass walls, leaving smoky marks of fint. That was why the Wayward woman wanted them, because fint healed all sorts of ailments. Ghen put the jars carefully in his bag and Melle helped him sling it across his back. Rit carried the sticks. Dusk had settled so it was time to start for home. Sunrise would come soon enough, and each of them would be out in the fields to greet it.

'Maybe Sot's idle,' Rit said as they walked. 'She doesn't farm herself, and she doesn't help farm your land.'

'My aunt is not idle!' Ghen snapped. He felt Melle slip her hand into his.

'Idleness doesn't make you rich, Rit,' she said.

Rit snorted. 'If she *is* rich. How can you be sure that's true, Ghen, when you haven't seen her for years? She could be letting a field lie fallow and your parents know nothing about it.'

Melle squeezed his hand.

'My mother says your figs have blight, Rit,' she said. 'Whose idleness let that come?'

The next day, coming in from an early walk round the fields, Ghen's father held a sinta. He had found it beneath a tree, the first to fall, which meant that it was time to harvest the crop.

'First I'll thank the Neighbour for his generosity, then I'll send for Sot,' his mother said, smiling like she'd never smiled before when speaking of her sister. 'Tomorrow. She can decide then.'

At these words Ghen's father went straight out to the fields again. Before joining him, Ghen cleaned the sand off his trapped mostins, ready to take to the Wayward woman by the bridge. Sinta harvesting would mean he wouldn't be able to go to the river for a little while, even if Aunt Sot did come to help. Perhaps his mother wanted Sot to watch Elin and the baby Lyra, who were still too young to work. He still didn't believe Sot would actually come but part of him hoped she would. Then he could find out what she really did, and then he could tell Rit and Melle. Especially Rit.

When his work in the fields had finished for the day, he packed his jars of mostins into his bag. As he left the house he saw his father walking the sinta field again. He'd walked it every spare moment he had since Ghen's mother had written the first note to Sot – far more than he usually did. Was he worried about blight but didn't want to worry the family in turn? Perhaps the blight from Rit's fields had spread. Maybe Sot was some kind of blight healer and that was why she was coming to his parents' fields. That would be a job that paid well, Ghen thought, for blight meant a field had to lie idle for two seasons to ensure the disease had gone, and no Lowlander would want that.

He realised his father was looking at him. Ghen turned so his father could see the bag on his back and know where he was going, why he couldn't stop. He waved. After a moment his father raised his hand to him, then leant against a sinta tree. He must be so tired, Ghen thought, working so hard, doing so well with the land. And yet Hend's high rents left the family only able to lease rather than own. Rit had once said that a man or woman without their own land couldn't call themselves a Lowlander; Rit had heard this from his father, and the words made Ghen burn with shame. Now, he turned away and headed for the bridge and his poultice pay, leaving his father to the care of the trees.

The Wayward woman was in her tent, as she usually was at that time of day. Though she was still young her eyes were weak, so when she travelled the valley she made sure she returned to her tent by the bridge before the light began to fade. Not much of a Wayward then, Melle said. But many were glad the woman stayed in the valley; she was the closest thing to a stitcher in those parts, and she charged far less.

As he neared the tent she called out to him, as she did when she heard the glass jars clinking in his bag.

'How many jars today, Ghen?'

'Nine,' he called back.

He stopped by the tent's flap – the nearest thing to a door, he supposed. He never went in until she invited him. She liked to get the coins ready first and, as the tent smelled so strange, he didn't like to be inside any longer than could be helped. He had nothing against the Wayward, as some did in the valley. It was the creatures she kept in there, dead and drying, and the ointment bottles of fint scraped from the mostins. Fint might help Elin's cough but it made his eyes burn.

'Come in where I can see you, Ghen,' she called.

The tent was full of light; lamps hung from each corner, from the middle of the ceiling and were set round the floor. He blinked furiously, knowing that would help his eyes grow used to the brightness. When he could see again he sat on the upturned crate near the Wayward woman, trying not to look at the gresta birds hanging near his face. Their puckered skin showed in red lumpy patches between the remaining feathers.

'Only nine jars today,' she said.

He could see the pennies glinting in her hands, ready if he chose to take them, rather than have the poultice. Her hands were stained with brown marks. He wondered if they ran over her wrists and up her arms, which were hidden by the sleeves of her shirt: made of a green material that made him think of the river in winter.

'I had to turn the medlars,' he said, 'and the sinta barrels needed cleaning out.'

'You work hard, Ghen. Do you like it, being in the fields?'

Her question stunned him. He was a Lowlander, no matter what Rit said about his family. Lowlanders farmed. There was no 'like' about it, it was life. Unless you were Aunt Sot. The Wayward was waiting for him to answer, her round, unlined face tilted towards him.

'Yes,' he said, not knowing what else to say. How to explain that the fields and their crops were in his thoughts from the moment he woke to the moment he fell asleep? That in his dreams he tied back sinta branches, turned medlars, cleared the holen beds of weeds. That even now, as he sat in her tent and felt the prickling behind his eyes that the fint brought, his fingers itched to dig deep into the ground, to cup the living things growing there and to make them turn a profit. But the Wayward wouldn't understand. She dealt in death. She'd kill the mostins once she'd scraped the fint from their wings. What she did with the bodies afterwards, he didn't want to know.

'Would you like to do something else, away from the fields?' she said.

He pulled the bag onto his knees and began to lift the jars out, gently, trying to keep the mostins' wings from banging the glass.

'You clean them so well, losing the sand but not the fint,' she said. 'You take great care, unlike so many Lowlanders I have seen at work.'

Ghen didn't know why she was speaking to him about such things. Usually he got out the jars, she inspected the mostins and then she paid him. Nothing more was said, or needed to be. He'd already been inside too long on this visit. The fint was making his eyes stream. The dead grestas seemed to have shifted closer to his face.

'I'm sorry there's not more,' he said.

'And there will be fewer from now on.' She held up one of the jars and the mostin inside it suddenly woke and banged against the glass. It left such thick smears of fint that it almost disappeared behind them.

'Why? Are the mostins dying?' As he said the words Ghen's stomach dropped, thinking of the poultice for Elin's cough.

The Wayward woman shook her head. 'How shall we do this – pennies or the poultice?'

Each time he came she gave him this choice, but he had only ever chosen the poultice. It was on the tip of his tongue to say he'd take that, but he found himself thinking of his exhausted father resting against the sinta tree, of his mother asking Aunt Sot to help with the harvest. Of Hend. A week without the poultice wouldn't make too much difference to Elin, would it?

'The pennies,' he said to the Wayward.

She didn't seem surprised by this, only looked at him for a long time, so long that Ghen wondered if the coins had ever really been a choice; that there was only one answer to her question. But then she pressed the coins into his hands.

'Goodbye, Ghen,' she said, which was also different to their usual, wordless parting.

'I'll be back after the harvest,' he said.

'Yes,' she said, but she said it quietly, and he didn't think she was saying it to him.

She stayed by the tent flap as he walked away. When he came to the bend in the lane he looked back and she was still there, outlined in clear, bright light, as if the sun were rising behind her.

His parents were on the porch when he drew near the house. They were sitting without any lamps and, after the brightness of the Wayward's tent, the darkness was a relief.

'There must be another way,' his father said, but his voice was strange. It was wavering, catching on something – tears. His father was close to tears, and that stopped Ghen in his stride. He'd never heard his father cry before, and he certainly didn't want to see it.

'We'll take a fourth field from Hend,' his father said. 'Red holen prices are going up. We can plant more.'

'Another field will only give us more rent to pay, and more

labour needed to pay it,' his mother said. Her voice was her voice, no change.

Ghen's father sniffed in the darkness.

'Don't upset yourself,' his mother said. 'We don't even know that Sot will take—'

Elin's cough sounded and his mother was opening the door, a soft light giving her back her features. Before she could go inside, his father spoke again.

'It's not too late. Surely we can wait, talk to Hend.'

Elin's cough grew louder, and Lyra's cry joined it, bringing his father to his feet as well. He put his hand on Ghen's mother's shoulder and tried to turn her to him, saying her name softly.

'Let's see what Sot offers,' his mother said.

And they were gone into the house.

Ghen came to the porch. The cane chair was still warm. He worried to hear his parents worry. He took out the coins the Wayward had given him. Every penny in the jar under the floorboard got them closer to buying the land from Hend, his father said. In the morning Ghen would give the coins to his parents. He counted the coins out, enjoying the weight of them, but there were too many.

She had paid him for twelve jars instead of nine.

When his mother pushed open the door to his room the next morning, she was surprised to find him already washed and dressed, sitting on the edge of his bed.

'It's early yet,' she said. Steam curled from the cup she carried, sent the tea's sweetness round the small, bare room. 'Your father's not long awake.'

He held out the pennies. She put the cup down on the little bench where he kept his few things: a slingshot he used against the birds that beaked for seeds in the soil; his pruning gloves; a spiralled shell that Melle had given him. She said it came all the way from Bordair.

'Money from the Wayward,' Ghen said, as his mother took the coins. 'I chose the money this week. For the jar to buy the fields.'

His mother sat down on the bed beside him.

'Thank you,' she murmured. She said nothing more, but she didn't get up to leave, not even when the sound of Elin's cough drifted into the room. His mother simply stared at the coins now in her hands.

'It's right that I work the land, isn't it?' he said.

She looked up quickly. 'Why do you ask that?'

'The Wayward said something. I didn't understand. It doesn't matter.'

His mother put the coins in her pocket and stood.

'It's just that, they have the sight,' he said, 'don't they?'

'Who?'

'The Wayward.'

'They say some do.' His mother handed him the tea. 'But the one by the bridge, she can't see much at all, can she? Don't let your tea go cold now.'

★★★

Ghen was so distracted by the Wayward's words that it was only when a cloud of dust appeared at the bottom of the lane that he remembered about Sot coming. He peered through the branches of the sinta he was stripping of fruit, watching the dust cloud get closer. His father was working in the tree next to him. He, too, stopped at the sight of the cart, his hand stilling on an unpicked sinta.

Ghen's mother went to open the gate, calling to his father to watch the girls on their blanket at the edge of the trees. He and Ghen climbed down their ladders but his father didn't watch the girls; instead he watched, as Ghen did, the cart driving through the gateway. The cart had an awning. Their cart had long ago lost its well-patched top; they went to market with the rain dripping square on their heads. The horse now being pulled to a halt by the house was a fine animal with high withers and a high-stepping gait. Such horses were bred for their looks, not for pulling any kind of weight, and their good looks were costly. As costly as taking Greynal baths, Ghen guessed.

Sot climbed down from the cart and tied the horse to the porch rail. She opened her arms to embrace Ghen's mother, but his mother stepped neatly away. They stood feet apart as they spoke, his mother avoiding Sot's eye.

Ghen saw he'd been right remembering that Sot had dark hair. She wore trousers of thick, blue twill and a cream shirt with sleeves that stopped below the elbow: not quite farming clothes, but not dress ones either. Perhaps she really had come to help with the harvest.

His mother and Sot both turned and looked at him, their conversation at an end.

'Back to it then,' his father said, suddenly stirring himself and moving quickly. 'Up the ladder, lad. Off you go now.'

But before Ghen could do as he was told, Sot was walking towards them.

'How long has it been, Eam?' she said to his father.

'Good of you to come,' he said, although the way he spoke made the visit sound anything but good.

Sot smiled and touched his shoulder. His father started backwards.

'And this must be Ghen,' she said, not noticing Ghen's father recoiling. Or not minding.

She was younger than his mother. He realised he hadn't known until that moment which of the two was the elder. But now it was clear. Sot's skin was smooth, her dark hair unmarked by grey. She stood straight when his mother's shoulders curled from years of weeding.

Sot held out her hand. It took him a moment to realise he was supposed to shake it. Her palms and fingertips were rough and coarse like his own: working hands. She kept hold of his hand, turned it over and looked at his palm, straightened each of his fingers in turn. He didn't know what to do. His father had turned away and was shaking a barrel half full of sintas to knock out the dead space. The fruit rattled loudly against the staves.

When the sintas had all been thrown down into the soft landing of the nets, the tree branches bare, his mother and father began to toss the fruit into the barrels. Ghen had expected that Sot would sit with the girls on the blanket, but his mother had taken them inside once Sot had arrived, and Sot stayed in the field. Ghen was still up the ladder and had lost sight of her on the ground below. She must be helping his parents collect the fruit, he thought. How long until her back began to ache and she went inside to rest? Not more than two barrels, surely. Though her hands were working hands.

He felt a tremor go through the ladder and looked down. Sot was there, one foot on the bottom rung.

'You don't need to steady it,' he called. 'The feet are in special holes.'

But she wasn't listening. She was climbing up.

The ladder shook with their shared weight and Ghen gripped a thick sinta branch.

'What are you doing?' he shouted down.

If she could hear she ignored him for she kept on climbing. There was no sign of his parents on the ground below. Was his aunt some kind of simpleton? Was that why she never came to visit, and why they never visited her?

Her dark hair came level with his shoulders and then there was her face, smiling up at him, a little red and sweaty in the heat.

He stared at her in astonishment.

'It's a wonderful view up here,' she said.

He swallowed and said, 'This is really only a one-person job.'

'It's been a long time since I cut back and tied off any sintas,' she said. 'You'll have to show me how it's done.'

He waited a moment, testing whether she was serious, but she made no move to go back down the ladder, and he couldn't very well get down himself until she did.

He firmed his grip on his blades and told Sot, 'You have to scrape the old wood back. If you try to cut it out then you might cut the new wood beneath. It takes a little while but it's much better for the tree.'

She nodded, and the eagerness of her expression encouraged him to continue.

'Like this.' He laid one of his blades gently on the branch nearest him and then pulled it towards him. A sliver of wood, thinner than a gresta feather, lifted from the branch and floated to the ground below. 'Keep your wrist light so you don't go too deep. When you've got the hang of it you can use both hands.'

'Show me.'

He did as she asked and the old wood flew from the tree. In a matter of moments he had one branch completely cut back and satisfaction flared in him. He couldn't tell if his aunt was impressed. She seemed to be in a hurry.

'And tying off?' she said.

'But I haven't finished this tree's cutting back yet. You have to cut back before you tie off, otherwise you might not get all the old wood. You might seal it in and then the next crop of sintas will be poor.'

She waved away his concern and the ladder lurched. 'Yes, yes, I see, but just show me how it's done. You can undo it afterwards, can't you? I just need to see how you do it.'

Ghen gave a short sigh. Why had his mother written to his aunt to come when she didn't respect the right way of doing things? No wonder she didn't farm herself. He did as she asked though, only to stop her from making the ladder lurch anymore.

'You need some of this tongut – Mama has it. She measures out the lengths. Pull it taut like this,' at which he pulled the gnarly string between his hands, 'and wrap it round the branch, starting close to the trunk. Tuck the little branches in so they get tied off too. That way the fruit grows closer and has a sweeter flavour. Our sintas are well known for that in the valley.'

He waited for her to say yes, so she'd heard. But she was staring at his hands, unused tongut still wound round his fingers.

'Tie another branch,' she said, without looking up.

He'd cut back a quarter of the trees when his mother called him for lunch. He tied his blades to the branch he was working and climbed down the ladder. There was no one else in the field, and a good many sintas still lay in the nets, waiting to be stowed in barrels. He wondered what his parents had been doing while he'd been in the trees. It couldn't be that they were idling. Maybe Elin's cough was bad, and his father had gone to the Wayward.

When Ghen came to the house he saw that Aunt Sot's cart was gone. He'd been so engrossed in what he was doing, he hadn't noticed her leaving. It was always like that when he was using his hands. It didn't matter if he was cutting back the old sinta wood or cleaning the sand from the mostins' wings; it was the doing that mattered. The touch and the movement of it.

The kitchen smelled of honeytons – his favourite cake, and one his mother only made for birthdays because the honey that set the cake was the expensive kind, from Hend's hives.

When he asked his mother why Sot had gone, she told him to

sit down. She explained what was going to happen, and she did it quickly. In two days Sot would be back. She'd agreed to wait for him to finish the harvest before he joined her workshop.

'Workshop?' Ghen said.

'She'll teach you,' his mother said.

'Teach me what? What does she make, farm tools?'

His mother hesitated and looked to his father standing by the stove, Lyra in the crook of his arm, Elin holding his hand. He pulled Lyra to him and buried his face in her hair.

'Yes, in a way,' Ghen's mother said. 'Sot makes Tillers.'

Ghen didn't know what that meant. The word sounded like someone who worked a field – who tilled the ground. That was a good thing, surely, for all that was to do with fields and yields and earning money from the crop was good. But how could Sot make people to work the fields? And the way his mother said the word made it sound like a bad thing. Like Tillers were dangerous. And yet he was going to work for Sot. Why were his parents sending him away?

He was full of such questions but his parents had no answers for him. He didn't want his bread and cheese, or the honeytons his mother pressed on him. He wanted to know what he'd done wrong to deserve being sent away.

'Sot will explain,' his mother said. 'And you won't be far away. Only over the hill and two lanes more.'

His father made a noise that sounded like a sob, but one he caught before it could fully sound its pain. 'I hope one day you can forgive—'

'One day,' his mother broke in, 'you'll understand why.'

★★★

He was relieved when lunch was over and he could return to work, hoping that once he was using his hands in the trees again he would be able to make sense of it. But as he untied his blades and scraped two fine slivers of old wood into the air, soft and light as mist, he wondered if it was his hands that were the problem. That was what Sot had been watching. Not the blades, not the wood, and not the tongut. She didn't care about sintas. She cared about these Tillers, whatever they might be.

As the light faded and he could no longer see the wood well enough to cut, he climbed down the ladder. He told his parents he was going to see Rit and Melle. They both nodded dumbly, and he had the feeling that if he'd told them he was going to chop down all the sinta trees in the field they would have let him. It had been the oddest day and he wondered if he had fallen asleep after his mother had taken the coins from him that morning, and was still asleep, surely, for nothing was right.

Of the three farms, Ghen's was furthest from the river. He came to Rit's first, and found him sharpening a pair of blades in the barn. That Rit's family had a barn had always impressed Ghen, but today he didn't linger in the doorway to admire the tall stacks of hay, the rows and rows of shining blades and turnpokes. He needed to get to the river as soon as he could. They could talk safely there with only the Washerwoman to hear them.

'But my dinner will be ready soon,' Rit said. 'Gresta pie.' He hung up his blades and was making for the door.

'Please, Rit. It's important.'

Ghen was surprised to hear the tremor in his voice. It had been threatening to come out since his parents had told him what was going to happen. Rit looked surprised too.

'Have you got blight?' he said in a whisper.

Ghen shook his head. 'It's worse than that. Or I think it is. I don't know. We'll call for Melle on the way.'

She was already halfway through her dinner when Ghen knocked, but one look at his face and she was out of the door before her parents could say a word.

'What's wrong?' she said once they were on their way.

Ghen shook his head. 'At the river.'

It was important to be away from the fields. He didn't know why but that feeling was a strong one, and with so much he didn't understand, he held fast to it.

There would be no mostin hunting. Melle and Rit sat on the bank; he stood in the shallows, moving the water with the toe of his boot. They waited for him to speak; Melle with patience, Rit throwing stones into the water.

'I found out what Sot does,' Ghen said at last.

Rit's hand froze in mid-air, holding a stone. 'It's blending, isn't it? I knew it.'

'No. Not blending. She makes Tillers. My mother told me. She says I have to work for Sot.'

'Oh Ghen,' Melle whispered.

'What is it? Do you know what they are?' He splashed towards where she sat on the bank and was astonished to see her flinch from him.

'Tillers are for burying people,' Rit said.

'Burying who?' Ghen felt faint with panic as he pictured his parents lying dead in their beds.

'Everyone,' Melle said. 'You've not been to a Last Planting, have you?'

Ghen shook his head. 'Mama wouldn't let me go when Grandfather Lar passed. She said it would be too sad, but I think she just wanted me to stay at home with Elin.'

Melle looked like she'd say more but instead she drew her knees to her chest and hugged them.

Rit gave a low whistle. 'So, Sot makes Tillers. No wonder she never came to visit.'

'It's bad, isn't it?' Ghen said. He was suddenly cold. Freezing cold, every inch of him.

'It's bad, all right,' Rit said. 'People like Sot make money from things that don't grow – from dead wood. And they plant them, like they're crops. But they're not. Tillers are dead things, and if your hands touch them then you're dead too. You'll never make anything grow again.'

'Well then, I won't make Tillers,' Ghen said. He sat next to Melle on the bank.

'Don't work for Sot,' she said. 'Run away, if you have to. You can live in our barn. I'll bring you food. No one has to know, it'll be a secret.'

'A Tiller maker,' Rit said. He threw his stone into the river, just where Ghen had been standing.

'I won't go,' Ghen said to Melle. 'Don't worry. My parents can't make me. Nothing has to change.'

They were each silent then. The only sound was Rit throwing stones.

When night fell, they stood to go home. Ghen wished for Melle's hand for the walk back but she kept her hands in her pockets all the way.

When he woke the next morning, Ghen wondered if perhaps it *had* all been a dream and he'd have plenty to tell the Child. Everything in his room looked the same, and if nothing had changed in the world around him, how could it be true that he was leaving? There was his slingshot, there was the shell from Bordair that Melle had given him; at the thought of Melle keeping her hands in her pockets he pushed the blankets off. He had work to do.

In the kitchen he found his father darning; Elin and Lyra played at his feet.

'What about the sintas?' Ghen said.

His mother laid a pile of clothing on the arm of his father's chair. 'We'll be out to join you as soon as we can.'

'But what's more important than collecting the fruit?' he said.

'We have to get your things ready,' his father said. He bit off the thread he was using. A jagged line of large stitches ran across the knee of a pair of trousers, barely patching the tear. Ghen realised they were his own trousers. His father handed them to his mother, who laid them in an old sack, and then reached for a shirt from the pile. Ghen's shirt.

'So it's true then,' he said.

'Of course it's true,' his mother snapped, her harshness making Lyra look up from her game. 'Why wouldn't it be?'

'Because I don't *want* it to be!' Ghen shouted, and the tears came then. They ran down his face as thick as if the Wayward woman had painted his cheeks with fint.

His father held him. When Ghen had sobbed himself to a kind of peace, he said softly, 'There's no other way. I see that now. You will too, in time.'

'What are you talking about?' Ghen said.

His mother eased him from his father's arms and walked him to the door. 'You'll only be on the other side of the hill.'

'Why? Tell me!'

She was opening the door. 'You go and start the cutting back. We'll be out in no time. Take a honeyton with you.'

'Because of Hend,' his father whispered.

He would do as Melle said and run away. Once he was up the ladder and felt hidden by the leaves, he thought about how he would do it. But as soon as he began cutting back the old wood, such thoughts became less certain. At first, he listed the things he would take with him – the slingshot, socks, a knife good enough for the Partner – but then he only saw himself with a bag. And then the bag faded and there was only him walking, and then he wasn't thinking of anything at all but the blades in his hands and the wood lifting, floating to the ground below, to lay wherever it wished. He couldn't run away. The sintas needed to be cut back and tied off. The fruit had to be collected and barrelled, before it went bad, and he might have to do that himself. His parents had forgotten who they were, what had to be done. Ghen was the only true Lowlander left in the three fields he knew to be home. And so it was that he worked every waking hour up to the moment that Sot arrived to take him, thinking only of the land.

She came early. He heard a cart in the lane but waited for his mother to fetch him from his room. He knew it would be her and not his father, like he knew there was no point him running away. They would only find him, wherever he was, and give him to Sot anyway. And that was Hend's doing. Hend's fault, all this. Ghen got up and put Melle's shell in his pocket.

His mother didn't knock. She opened the door quickly, and said just as quickly, 'Time to go, Ghen,' as if him leaving was a poultice that must be ripped off in one fast pull to avoid prolonging the pain. And she did feel pain, he could see it in her face, the way she wouldn't look at him.

The kitchen was empty. He could hear a cheery prattling coming from the porch: Sot. His father was there, holding the girls. He put them down to embrace Ghen, but Ghen felt himself to be as hard and unyielding as a holen root. His mother handed him a cloth bag.

'The honeytons,' she said. 'I thought you'd like something from home to help you settle in.'

He took the bag and managed to thank her. With one finger

she swept the hair that was hanging over his eyes. When at last he was able to look at her, he saw that she, too, was crying, and a small part of him was glad, even as he was wretched beyond any wretchedness he thought could exist in the world.

'Take care of him, Sot,' his mother said, but she kept looking at Ghen as she spoke. 'He's a good boy.'

'Mama...' he said.

She closed her eyes and stepped away from him.

'It's only for a little while, isn't it?' he said. 'I'll be back soon. Won't I, Mama?'

Elin pulled at her skirts, mewling, and his mother picked her up. She didn't look at Ghen again.

'It's not like he's dying!' Sot said.

His parents flinched and Sot threw up her hands.

'Time we were going, Ghen,' she said, setting off down the porch steps.

She helped him climb into the cart and he was glad because his legs were shaking. All of him was shaking. Rit's words were loud in his ears: *you'll never make anything grow again.*

Sot took up the reins. 'Don't look back,' she murmured. 'It won't help.' And the cart lurched forwards.

He did as she said and kept his eyes on the lane, trying to memorise every stone, every tree. They were flashing by too quickly. He couldn't catch them all. He was losing them. He craned his neck to see the broken cart wheel left long in the grass, and without meaning to his eyes sought the porch. It was empty. They hadn't even waited until the cart was out of sight.

At the bridge he asked Sot to stop.

'We can't go back,' she said, but she stopped all the same. 'Once you're going forwards, better to keep it that way.'

Ghen got to his feet but made no move to jump down. He picked up the cloth bag of honeytons and hurled it into the river. Let the Washerwoman have them.

'Your mother always was a terrible baker.'

He didn't reply, just watched the bag flounder in the shallows. There wasn't enough depth or current to take it from sight. He thought about finding a stone and throwing that at the bag, to at least cover it somehow, but Sot was waiting to cluck the horse on.

The Wayward's tent was in sight. He should go and see her, let her know he wouldn't be able to bring her any more mostins. But then he remembered that she already knew.

'I'm ready,' he said.

'Good boy.' Sot flicked the reins, and they were on their way again.

From the bridge the lane climbed and crested the hill, and then Sot had to press heavily on the foot brake when the cart raced down the other side. Over the hill and two lanes more: that was what Ghen thought of when anyone mentioned Sot, and now here he was, making the journey himself. The lanes were long and narrow, the surface thick with weeds. It clearly wasn't a way many people travelled by cart.

He caught a glimpse of red tiles among the green tree tops and presumed this was the workshop, though the trees screened the building beneath. Sot drew the cart to a halt and climbed out. Ghen followed her down a path. He wondered what kind of trees these were, standing so tall and so thick with blossom but barren of fruit. Then he saw a flash of orange on the ground a few feet ahead. He hurried over. It was as he thought: a sinta, but the fruit was small and shrivelled. Gnarled branches and fruitless blossom: two signs, he knew, of idleness. Rit had been right when he said Sot left land idle.

Sot called him from further along the path and he ran to catch up, the ruined trees a dark canopy above him. They came to a square building with a porch. Sot climbed the steps and each one let out a terrible groan, the groans of people dying, Ghen thought. The fruitless sintas above watched him and he thought they might as well be dead too, the use they gave. Death was everywhere here and so he would be death too. He'd never make anything grow again.

Sot held the door open for him. He climbed the groaning porch steps and his feet took him closer to the door, closer to the end.

'Come on, there's no need to be afraid,' Sot said.

He didn't believe her but he forced himself to step inside. The walls were lined with shelves and on the shelves were—

He closed his eyes. Sot squatted in front of him.

'Now listen, Ghen, you need to forget all the nonsense you've heard about what we do here. Your parents, your friends – they need Tillers, and that means they need people to make them. We provide a service, that's all. And an excellent one, at that. Now, open your eyes. You're no good to me blind.'

She moved to the centre of the room where there were several short wooden benches, each with a stool to accompany them. And on the benches were small sets of blades. Without realising what he was doing, Ghen reached for the pair nearest him. They sat in his hands neatly, not as heavy as his sinta blades, the metal finer.

'How do they feel?' Sot said.

He dropped the blades on the bench and stepped away.

'I'm not staying,' he said. 'I don't know why I'm here and I'm needed at home.'

'You're needed here, Ghen,' she said, with gentleness.

'I'll help with your sinta trees and when they fruit again I'll go home.'

'The order list is full and there are only so many hours in the day. If we're late with Tillers for one Last Planting then Canna will have the upper hand.'

'You don't understand, I have to *grow* things.'

'Such crude Tillers that Canna's workshop turns out,' Sot muttered to herself. 'Not that it can even be called a workshop. The *work* is clearly absent.'

Despite himself, Ghen's hands were once more straying to the blades on the bench. He wanted very much to use them, to feel he was doing something good again.

'Those are mine,' a voice said.

Ghen dropped the blades a second time. A man was standing on the other side of the bench. A young man, with dark eyes and thin lips. The beginnings of a sandy beard coloured his cheeks but that was thin too. All of him was thin.

'Ah, there you are,' Sot said. 'I was just giving the boy the tour, such as it is.'

'Sounded to me like you were telling him about someone else's workshop,' the young man said, and he raised his eyebrows at Sot. 'Someone you said you weren't going to worry about anymore. Only this morning you said that.'

Sot steered Ghen beyond the benches to the far end of the room. 'Yes, well. The best intentions sometimes need time to action. This is Wyne, by the way.'

'I'm sorry I touched your blades,' Ghen said to Wyne.

'Blades?' Wyne frowned.

'He means the rooters,' Sot said, and then to Ghen: 'Wyne's been here so long he's forgotten there are other words beside rooters and Tillers.'

But Wyne couldn't have been older than twenty-five, Ghen thought. Had he been in Sot's workshop all his life? He wondered if she let him go outside. Wyne *was* very pale.

Sot opened a door in the far wall. Ghen looked inside: a small room with two low beds. One was bigger than the other and took up most of the space. The second was wedged into a corner, small enough only to need a sack to cover it. Ghen had the feeling it was really Wyne's room.

'I should have thought to ask your mother for blankets,' Sot said. 'I'll get some, don't worry. Just as soon as we've cleared the order list. One slip and Canna will have it all.'

'What was it you said this morning?' Wyne called.

'Audience hear me,' Sot said under her breath. 'And may the Poet be deaf to Canna's stories.'

She went back to the benches and Ghen followed, wondering where it was that Sot took her baths in Greynal. There was another door nearby, left half open, and inside he could see a similar room to the one he'd just looked in, with the addition of a table heaped with papers.

Wyne was fiddling with something on the far wall.

'We rise and sleep by the order list,' Sot said. 'If the list is full then the days are long. If Canna has his way and our order list is empty then you might get more sleep, but that's not going to happen because Canna's work is so poor.'

'Sot!' Wyne said over his shoulder. 'There's no helping you!'

Sot groaned and said, 'Wyne, you're right. There is no helping me. And there's no helping foolish Lowlanders who don't know quality when they see it.'

'I give up,' Wyne said.

Ghen had the feeling they'd had this conversation many times before. He felt a smile creep over his mouth at their bickering. He swallowed it away. He didn't want to be there.

Wyne held out a pair of the small blades that Sot had called rooters. 'These are yours,' he said to Ghen.

Ghen took them and felt the same good feeling as before. His hand itched to use them, but then he remembered that he wouldn't be making anything grow.

'Well, now that you're equipped we can get on with some work,' Sot said.

'Only for a little while,' Ghen said, 'and then I'm going home.'

He caught Wyne looking at Sot, but she shook her head. She went to the shelves on the opposite wall and took one of the figures, setting it on the workbench in front of Ghen. He couldn't put off looking at it any longer. The time had come. But still he was afraid.

Sot met his eyes above the figure.

'Wood, that's all they are,' Sot said. 'Just think of them as sinta branches.'

Ghen nodded, and looked down.

The figure was a foot tall. It had a head, legs and arms, hands and feet. Everything a body needed, including working clothes. It was standing, one arm stretched out in front at shoulder height, the hand holding a tiny bushel of wheat. Ghen could make out the individual stalks.

When he made no move to touch the figure, Sot picked it up and put it in his hands. Ghen stiffened but didn't drop it. The wood was planed smooth, soft against his palms. There was no paint on it, no colour at all, not like his sisters' doll, which had garish red cheeks and lips, and hair of blue wool. This figure had detail though: buttons on the shirt, the lines of the lips, all carved in tiny grooves. Ghen turned the figure over in his hands, looking for the joins between the limbs and the torso, the hand and the wheat. But he couldn't find any.

'It's a single piece of wood,' he said.

'One of Wyne's best,' Sot said with pride, setting the figure back on the bench. A blush crept into Wyne's pale cheeks. 'Now, Ghen, tell me how much you know about Tillers.'

'They're for Last Plantings, Melle said. She's my friend.'

'Good.'

'But Rit – he's my other friend – he said that if I make them, I'll never make anything grow again.'

Sot sighed. 'This is my sister's fault. She always was one for keeping the real world at bay. When our father died, that was the time for you to learn about what I do, Ghen, about the whole business of it. I told her you were old enough to come to the Planting. It does no good to shield children.

'Wyne, put the kettle on. And Ghen, you listen to me. Tillers are for the good of the land, just as we Lowlanders are. We're Tillers, and Tillers are us. All one and the same.'

'I don't understand.'

'When a person dies, Tillers pass on their care for the land. We plant one for each month of the year so that the land is never left without the deceased's attention.'

'So they... they *help* the land?'

'Exactly. Tillers are the way we pass on our love. We put them in the ground—'

'With a *dead* person?'

'Yes, with a dead person. We put them in the ground and they become guardians of the land. That way, no one lets their land lie fallow. Even when someone is no longer here, their love and their knowledge live on. What we do is a service, Ghen. People need us, however much they might not acknowledge it.'

There was a shout and then a smash. Wyne stood in a circle of clay shards. He stared at the cup handle he was holding, as if he had no idea what it was.

'Your mother tells me you're not clumsy, Ghen,' Sot said. 'Which is another point in your favour. I'll make the tea, Wyne. We don't have enough cups left for you to break any more.'

But at that moment there was a knock at the door.

★★★

The caller was a man about Ghen's father's age, wearing a coat just as patched as his father's, a hat just as battered.

'I... I've come to place an order,' the man said.

'Welcome. Please come in.'

He took off his battered hat. 'You can arrange it out here, can't you? My friend said you would.'

'Of course.' Sot swept back inside and collected three Tillers: the one on the bench that Ghen had been looking at, and two others from the shelves. Each was made of a slightly different shade of wood. 'Wyne, fetch me a new form. Now, name?'

'Tarn. It's Arth Tarn.'

'And is this order for an imminent Last Planting, Mr Tarn, or are you looking to pay in parts?'

'That one.' He clutched and unclutched his hat, keeping his gaze on his feet.

'Which?'

'Parts. I want the best for my wife, you understand. I want her to know that she'll still be able to watch over the fields when the time comes.'

He glanced up then, and something in Sot's expression gave him courage to look at the Tillers she was holding.

'I understand,' she said. 'Well, there are two decisions you have to make. The first concerns wood. Unt is the cheapest, followed by affa and then this hundred-year-old rennwood is our most expensive option.'

She held out the Tiller made of the darkest wood and Tarn flinched.

'I can see it very well from here, thank you. I want my wife to have a spade, but it has to have a long handle. She's tall, you see. And her favourite spade, it has a chip in the right-hand side. It's important that their spades have the chips.'

'That won't be a problem, but it does push the price up. That said, if you buy a tool with custom detail then we'll add clothing for free.'

'And what would that price be, then?'

'Twelve Tillers in rennwood with custom tools is thirty marks.'

Ghen gasped. Thirty marks would take his parents months to save. Tarn was taken aback too. He ran his hat through his fingers frantically. But Sot wasn't put off.

'Rennwood without custom tool detail is five marks less.'

'The spade. She has to have that, or we'll be lost.'

'Perhaps the affa would be more suitable, for twenty marks. You won't find better value in the valley.'

Wyne reappeared with a sheet of paper. He sat down at one of the benches and Ghen perched beside him. The page was marked with as many rows as his parents' holen field but no writing.

'The affa, yes,' Tarn said. 'I think we can manage that. I want her to have the best, the rennwood, but...'

'I understand. Many of my customers choose this option.'

'They do? Oh, that's good.'

'And clothing?'

'I'll check with my wife. She wants to decide that herself. I can do that, can I, tell you when I next come?'

'Certainly. But I'll need a deposit now, to place the order.'

The man shoved his hand in his pocket. 'I have it. My friend said you had to have a little bit for it to be written down.'

'That's right.' Sot held out her hand but the man put two coins onto the porch rail. 'Next month the same,' she said, in a voice that had lost some of its earlier warmth. Tarn didn't notice in his hurry to be gone; he was already halfway down the path.

'Is his wife dying?' Ghen asked.

'We're all of us dying,' Sot said, shutting the door. Wyne made way for her to sit down and she began writing in the paper's empty rows. 'That's the first custom-tool in nearly three months. Wake up the fire, will you, Wyne? But be careful!'

'But why does he want the spade made with a chip?' Ghen said.

'Because Mr Tarn believes it will make his wife's Tillers more powerful. The wisdom is, the more detailed the Tiller, the more the land will yield.'

'You don't believe that?' Ghen said.

'It's not about what I believe. People can believe whatever they want, if they've got the money to pay for the work.'

'But what about people who haven't got the money?' He was thinking of his parents, and of himself, of course, among all the other thoughts swirling through his head: Last Plantings, the land, yields.

'In *this* workshop,' Sot said, 'there's a Tiller for every coin purse, no matter how light that purse might be.'

'Canna can't make the same claim,' Wyne called from the hearth. 'Your aunt does right by people who have little, Ghen. That's one reason why the order list is most often full.'

'A few more chipped spades wouldn't hurt,' she said. 'Go and show Ghen the wood, and bring some affa branches back with you. Better let Ghen get them down though.'

Wyne led Ghen round the back of the workshop and down a well-worn path through more of the fruitless sintas. The sinta's large dark leaves became interspersed with smaller, pointed leaves of a much lighter colour, and there were red leaves among the trees too, shaped like stars, and the trunks became more slender. When the sintas disappeared completely Wyne came to a halt. They were in a mixed orchard of trees Ghen had never seen before.

'What fruit do these give?' Ghen asked.

'Tillers.'

'But these trees must have been planted generations ago, before Sot was even born.'

'Of course they were. There's been a workshop here for years. Before Sot there was Dand, before Dand there was Jin, before Jin—' He shook his head and laughed. 'I sound like an apprentice storyteller. There have been Tiller-makers as long as there have been Lowlanders, and those old masters are buried right here, in the orchard, their Tillers helping the trees grow. This here is the rennwood.' Wyne patted a thick trunk with a reddish bark. 'And this is affa, and this is unt,' he said, pointing to two other kinds of trees. 'Not every workshop uses all three.'

'Wyne, who is Canna?'

Wyne went to lean on the rennwood tree but misjudged where it was, only just managing to catch hold of it before he fell. He turned to stare at the big tree trunk, with no sign of embarrassment, as if he thought the rennwood had moved.

'Canna?' Ghen said, to remind him.

'Hm? Oh. He owns a workshop a few hills over. His Tillers aren't as poorly made as Sot says they are, but he only offers one kind: the expensive kind. Most people can't afford them so they come to Sot.'

'That's good for Sot, isn't it?' Ghen said.

'Not really. She's done the sums. She has to make eight of the cheapest Tillers for every one of Canna's expensive ones. And eight Tillers take a lot longer to make than one Tiller.'

'Sot should only make expensive ones then.'

'And what would the people who have little do then, Ghen? The only way she can afford to keep going is to make more Tillers. And that's why you're here.'

Wyne started down the path again and they came to a low wooden structure. Inside were axes and saws, as well as hide gloves and chains. Sawdust littered the floor like snow and the smell of cut wood was heavy on the air.

'We drag the branches and the trunks here,' Wyne said, 'and cut them into useable sizes. This is the main wood store, but we keep some in the workshop for ready use.'

Wyne went to the back of the shed where there were several large, bulky shapes covered by sacking: the same as the sacking on what Ghen had supposed to be his bed. Underneath was a huge pile of wood, chopped into lengths of varying sizes and stacked neatly. Wyne reached for a piece of wood and Ghen could see that if he took it, the whole pile would come tumbling down.

Ghen leapt forward. 'Sot said I should do it, remember?'

He lifted a length of wood safely from the pile and gave it to Wyne, and kept doing so until Wyne said they had enough.

'It's Sot that stacks the wood,' Wyne said as they made their way back to the workshop. 'She cuts it as well. I'm none too steady with the saw.'

'So how do you manage to carve buttons and the like on a Tiller?' Ghen said.

'That's different.'

'Because the saw's big and the blades – the rooters – are small?'

'Maybe. All I know is I never drop anything when I'm making Tillers. I never cut myself or trip. It's like my hands become someone else's hands.' Wyne hunched himself over the wooden branches in his arms. 'I don't expect that makes any sense.'

'When I turn the medlars and cut back the sinta trees, it feels more right than anything else in the world,' Ghen said. 'But that's making things grow, not making Tillers.'

'We do that too. Well, we plant trees as well as cut them down. Two trees for every one that we cut. That'll be your job, Sot says. I always drop the seed bag and then the birds are on me.'

'Planting? So you *can* still grow things!'

'Don't let Sot hear any more of that talk,' Wyne said. 'Making Tillers is growing. Think of it that way. It might help you like the work.'

'Do you like it?'

Wyne shrugged. 'I'm good at it,' he said, but with sadness, as if being good hurt him somehow.

***

Ghen was to have his own bench, between Sot and Wyne's, so that each could keep an eye on him and he in turn could watch what they did. The first item on the order list was for a Last Planting in two days' time, for which the family of the dead had ordered the cheapest Tillers.

Sot put a few lengths of wood on each bench. 'This is unt.'

Ghen grasped his rooters and readied himself for instruction, but Wyne and Sot cradled their cups instead. Wyne told Ghen to do likewise.

'Always warm your hands first,' he said. 'It'll help you find the way the wood wants to be shaped.'

Ghen didn't understand what this could mean. The wood would be shaped however he wanted to shape it. Once he got his rooters to it, he would be in charge. But he did as Wyne said and cupped his hands round his tea. The feeling it gave him was one of home: of coming in from a day in the fields in winter, his fingers stiff from being in the cold earth. His mother or father would put a cup of tea on the table and set Ghen's hands round it, for they were too stiff for him to do so himself, his fingers like claws. And then slowly the heat would work its way into his bones.

Sot and Wyne were good enough to ignore his tears.

When his hands had swelled with warmth from the clay cup, soft as clay themselves, Sot told him to pick up a length of unt.

'Run your hands all over it and you'll know where to begin.'

'What if I don't?' he said, hoping she'd say that would mean he was a failure at Tiller-making and she'd have to send him home.

'You will,' she said. 'I saw you in the sintas, remember.'

Ghen ran his hands over the length of wood. He didn't expect anything to happen, but he wasn't sure what else he could do other than play along. He didn't belong in the workshop; he belonged on the land, helping his parents get the most from their three fields. Helping them save so they could buy the land from Hend.

Ghen's thumb snagged.

There was nothing to see on the wood itself. The surface was smooth – no splinters, no lumpen knots. He ran his thumb back and forth over the same spot and still it caught on something. *Shoulder*, said a voice in his head. He dropped the wood on the bench and sat on his hands. He screwed his eyes closed too, so he couldn't even see any shapes, let alone touch them.

He didn't know how long he sat like that, Sot and Wyne on either side of him, saying nothing. He didn't know how long it was until his hands beneath his backside twitched, slipped back to the bench and he found himself picking up the rooters. They felt right in his hand, just like when he climbed the ladder to the sinta branches and cut back the old wood. He could see the branch in front of him, feel the softness of the old wood and the firm resistance of the new beneath it. He needed to let the new wood come through. The tree needed it. His parents and the girls needed it. He ran his blades over the old wood and a sliver floated free, then drifted to the nets below. Except they weren't nets. They were floorboards. And the wood in his hand wasn't a sinta branch attached to a sinta tree. It was a length of unt.

'It's just like cutting back and tying off,' Sot said. 'Watch Wyne if you're not sure, though something tells me you'll find your own way.'

Ghen repeated Sot's words in his head as if he was telling the Audience. *Cutting back and tying off. Cutting back and tying off.* He thought of working the trees, of turning the medlars, of weeding the holens. He thought of home.

Sot had made four Tillers and Wyne five by the time Ghen had carved the shoulder for his. Sot said they would break for dinner, though it wasn't much of a break, just long enough to eat some bread and cheese and something that might have once been a holen. It had been dried so long the colour had gone as well as the flavour so he couldn't be sure.

They were sitting close to the meagre fire. The last of the daylight was fading and Ghen wondered where the candles were. Given the small amount of food for dinner and the sacking that covered his bed, Ghen had a feeling there wouldn't be money for lots of candles.

'You don't have baths in Greynal, do you?' Ghen said to Sot.

Wyne turned to face the flames, trying to hide a smile.

'Whatever are you talking about?' she said.

'Mama said you were rich, so rich you could bathe in Greynal.'

'Your mother's a fine one to talk about wealth,' Sot said. 'I know dinner's not much. Meals here will be a little rustic for the time being, given our recent outlay of expenditure.'

Wyne grumbled. Sot must have spent too much money on her fancy cart, Ghen thought. Its awning had taken meat from Wyne's belly, and from his likewise.

'But if the orders keep coming in,' Sot said, 'meat should be back on the table before too long.'

When they returned to work, he saw that at least Sot hadn't overstretched herself beyond candles. She lit five: one for each corner of Wyne's bench, and one for herself.

'Wyne, I'd like you to do some close work to show Ghen. Use the Tillers in the second order. A few are bodily ready.' She took two rennwood figures from a shelf and put them on Wyne's bench. Their torsos had been left shapeless and their heads were empty of features. 'Sit at Wyne's bench and watch, Ghen. You'll be doing this soon enough.'

'I'm only here for a little while, remember?' he said.

Sot went into the other bedroom and shut the door without answering.

'What's she doing in there?' Ghen asked.

'Accounts, I expect.' Wyne stretched his back and resettled his thin frame on his stool. 'She has to make sure all the part payments are recorded right. Canna doesn't offer paying that way so that's something she has over him, but it takes up a lot of her time. Now, see on the shelf there, the little knife. Can you bring it over?'

Ghen did as he was asked and then pulled his stool next to Wyne's.

Wyne turned the tool this way and that in the candlelight so that Ghen could see it properly.

'We call this a dresser,' Wyne said. 'See the hatched part that runs the length of it? That's for shaving the wood, to give clothes a base texture. And the finely pointed end does the detail – buttons and cuffs, and hair if it was ordered. This Tiller is to have a thick coat with a fur-lined hood. He felt the cold badly in the end, his daughter said.'

'How can you make fur from wood?' Ghen said, thinking the two things couldn't be more different.

'Watch.'

Using the hatched part of the dresser, Wyne began to scrape the Tiller's shapeless torso; thick, downward strokes like he was peeling a holen. The torso became more clearly defined, and Ghen could soon see the outline of a coat. With a few quick movements, Wyne worked the arms into sleeves, and then what at first looked like a hump on the Tiller's back became the soft folds of a hood. From Wyne's hands, the coat grew.

All the time he was shaping the Tiller, Wyne was completely absorbed in the work. The dresser moved so quickly it was often a blur to Ghen, but it never slipped. Wyne never made a mistake. A few times the dresser hovered over the Tiller briefly, as Wyne considered how to proceed, but never for long.

As Ghen watched the coat appear he wanted to try for himself, and Wyne seemed to understand.

'Your turn,' Wyne said, holding out the dresser for Ghen to take.

'But I'm not ready.' His own unfinished Tiller lay on its side on the bench behind him, still looking more like an unt branch than a human figure.

'Sot says you're good with your hands. You'll be fine.'

Ghen took the dresser knife and gripped an unclothed rennwood Tiller in his other hand. He marvelled afresh at the smoothness of the wood, the neatness of the hands and feet. His pulse was racing but with excitement, not fear; he couldn't wait to grow his own coat for the poor, cold man.

His scrapes were slow, Wyne advising him as to depth, angle, smoothness, and the coat began to appear, and so Ghen's confidence grew. He began to scrape faster, and with every stroke he felt more strongly the same sense of rightness he felt when working in the fields. The familiarity was as welcome to him as his own bed, as his mother's fingers sweeping his hair from his eyes. He was himself again.

'Careful,' Wyne said.

But it was too late. The dresser slipped and the point scored a deep scratch through the Tiller's chest.

Ghen dropped the dresser with a cry and stumbled from the bench. Wyne stared down at the wounded figure.

'Sorry, Wyne,' Ghen whispered. 'I ruined your Tiller.'

Wyne ran his thumb over the scratch. Then the door to Sot's room opened.

'Everything all right?' she said.

Wyne laid his palm flat over the Tiller's damaged chest. 'Fine.'

She eyed them both, as if waiting for more, but when nothing else was said she nodded and shut the door again.

Wyne peered at the scratch on the Tiller for a moment then began to scrape the damaged section. 'This one might have to be a bit slimmer than the others, but we'll put him at the back and no one will notice.'

Ghen sat down again and watched Wyne. He wasn't ready yet. He wasn't as good as Wyne. Would he ever be, he wondered, surprised by his own longing. It doesn't matter, he told himself. It doesn't matter because I'm going home, back to the land.

The candles had burned low by the time the damaged Tiller was wearing a new coat, all sign of his wound gone. Wyne stood the two figures side by side.

'A perfect pair,' he said.

In the low light Ghen couldn't see any difference between them. Each wore a coat with thick cuffs that sat just above the hands and buttoned just below the neck. The hoods lay neatly behind each head, the striking fur lining made by carved, wavy lines. Ghen ran a fingernail across the fur and felt the fine ridges. The fur was hard, but it looked so soft.

Wyne got to his feet and stretched; Ghen heard his joints popping. He put the two rennwood Tillers back on the shelf.

'Time we were turning in,' he said. 'Sot will have us up early enough tomorrow.'

'Should we say goodnight to her?'

Wyne shook his head. 'She won't want to be disturbed if she's still doing the accounts.'

He blew out all but one candle, which he carried towards the room with the two beds. As the flame passed the Tillers on the shelves they grew long shadows that looked to be marching across the room, following Ghen to bed. He shivered, and shivered again when he saw his bed with only the sacking to keep him warm. At home he'd had a blanket spun from the wool of Rit's sheep. He was worse off here, where his mother had believed there were such fine linens. Surely if she'd known she would never have sent him to Sot.

'Here,' Wyne said, taking a blanket from the larger bed and giving it to Ghen. 'It might be a while until Sot remembers to get you one. I had months under sacking when I first came.'

Ghen thanked him and got into bed. The blanket was thinner than the one he had at home, but it was still better than the sacking. Wyne blew out the candle. Tired as he was, Ghen didn't think he'd be able to sleep for a while.

'How long have you worked for Sot?' Ghen asked.

'Years now. I came when I was your age.'

'What did you do before that?'

There was the sound of Wyne turning over, the blanket moving. 'I don't remember.'

'You are a Lowlander though, aren't you?'

When Wyne didn't answer, Ghen guessed he must have fallen asleep, but then Wyne's voice called softly through the dark.

'Goodnight, Ghen.'

Ghen lay in the darkness, willing sleep to find him. When he heard Wyne's breathing slide into low, steady sighs, he reached for his trousers on the floor. In the pocket was the shell Melle had given him.

His tears helped him to sleep, in the end, for they tired him out enough to forget. He dreamt of the Wayward woman in her tent by the bridge. He was holding a mostin-catching jar and she was pouring marks into it, more than the jar could ever hold but still she poured. The coins bounced off the jar, off Ghen's hands holding it, and piled at his feet. It was more money than he'd ever seen in his life but in the dream he was sad, because he knew that however much money he had, it wouldn't be enough.

***

Enough for what, he thought on waking. But the dream wriggled like a mostin as he tried to catch it, and then Sot was shouting that it was time to get up: the order list was waiting.

When Sot set a bowl in front of him, Ghen was surprised to see the porridge had the bright blue of myrtleberries swirled through it, and in the middle was a slice of sinta.

'Is that right?' Sot said. 'Your mother told me how you like it, but the berries broke apart when I put them in.'

He took a spoonful. The taste wasn't quite the same – Sot's milk wasn't as rich as what they had at home, and the porridge had been allowed to thicken more than he liked – but he told her it was perfect.

After breakfast they set to work. Sot told them their first task was to finish the cheap Tillers begun the day before: their Last Planting was fast approaching. Ghen was determined to complete his Tiller. If he had to work for Sot for a while then he wanted to make the best of it, prove that he was as good with his hands as she thought he was.

Wyne and Sot made two more Tillers each, bringing the total to eleven, and then both came to stand by Ghen's bench while he finished his: the last one. He'd been working steadily all morning, not rushing, not after the injury he'd done the rennwood Tiller.

'A natural,' Wyne said.

Ghen experienced an odd sensation, which he could only describe as a pronounced pulling: pulling because he was pleased and devastated at the same time. *Torn*, he thought, and made the sign of the Tear. Sot and Wyne stared at him, and he excused himself to the porch where he sat and waited to feel better. They let him be, for which he was grateful, as he could not have explained the feeling.

From the porch he looked out on the poor fruitless sintas, which made him feel worse still. How long would he have to stay in this place where land was left to fall idle? He resolved to make Sot give him an answer, but as soon as he went back inside she called for his help.

A large wooden box was in the middle of the floor. Sot was pushing lengths of sacking into it while Wyne lined up the twelve Tillers on the nearest bench.

'Come and hold this in place,' Sot said to Ghen.

He knelt on the floor next to her and pressed the sacking into the corners of the box, but it wouldn't lie flat, flailing like it was a grass snake. Sot began putting the Tillers in the box, each one standing upright and facing the same way. They wobbled on the uneven, wilful sacking. Ghen held them steady while Wyne wove more material between the figures, swathing them until they were hidden. Lastly Sot fitted a lid on the box and noted in chalk: *Ulla*.

Together Ghen and Wyne pushed the box to the front door.

'We'll leave it here, ready for the morning,' Wyne said.

'Will the family come for it then, for the Last Planting?'

Wyne frowned at him. 'We take it. We put them in the ground. Did Sot not tell you? No one else will touch them.'

Ghen was just absorbing this when Sot put a length of wood in his hand. It wasn't unt or rennwood. Affa, he guessed.

'These are to have long, curly hair,' she said.

'By when?'

'Three days. But the Ulla Last Planting will take up most of tomorrow morning, so it's two and a half days, really.'

'Aunt Sot, when am I going home?'

'You're helping your parents more by being here than if you were still in their fields.'

'But they need me.'

'That's right.'

'But the fields, Aunt Sot.'

She walked back to her bench. A stack of affa lengths waited on his.

They worked all day and into the evening again. Ghen had fashioned the body of a Tiller from the affa wood by the time Sot said they could go to bed. The hair was still to be carved but that would be Wyne's task; Ghen wasn't at that stage yet, but he would be soon, Sot said. Yields would increase with him there.

But only for a little while, Ghen thought. Because I'm not staying.

In the morning Wyne told him to put on his best clothes, or the best he had. He emptied the sack he'd brought with him and found his dark-blue twill trousers, the ones he'd patched himself, rather than allowing his father's large, wobbly stitches, which were oftentimes worse than no stitches at all. The only unpatched shirt he had was stained at the back. Blood, he told Sot when she threw up her hands in horror.

'My father caught me with his sinta blades. It was an accident.'

'I'm sure it was, but you can't wear that to a Last Planting. Wyne, you'll have to lend him something.'

'But Wyne's much taller than me!' Ghen said. 'His clothes won't fit.'

'Do your best,' Sot said to Wyne. 'Tuck him in. Pin him, if necessary. When we've been paid for the Ulla Planting I'll take him to town and buy him a suit.'

She was talking like Ghen wasn't there to hear, but he heard all right.

'I don't need a suit for Plantings because I'm not staying. I'm *not* staying.'

Sot stared at him for a long moment and Ghen was sure she was about to shout at him, but she just shook her head and walked out to the porch. Ghen would have preferred it if she *had* shouted at him; at least then she might acknowledge what he was saying.

'This one isn't too long,' Wyne said.

Wyne held up a cream shirt with a rounded collar. The nicest shirt Ghen had ever seen. He felt the same pulling, tearing feeling again, but there was no time to be by himself until it passed, like before. It was time for the Planting.

The box was heavy and needed both Wyne and Ghen to lift it into the cart. Sot lashed it so it couldn't move, just as other people lashed their barrels and hay. Wyne and Ghen climbed up and sat next to her. Sot looked Ghen over.

'Not bad at all.'

She was smartly dressed too, changed out of her usual working clothes. The cart's hood above them was clean of mould and birds' dirt. The three of them made a tidy package, as his mother would have said. No one would suspect the sacking over his bed, the dried holen well past its best that made up their dinner. This Sot who flicked the reins and drove down the lane could well have afforded to bathe in Greynal.

Ghen was hoping the Last Planting might take place near home so he could ask Sot to call there. Even to be back just long enough to walk the fields would have made him feel better, he was sure. But when the cart reached the bridge Sot took the wrong fork in the road. All he could do was whisper hello to the Wayward woman's tent as they passed, which helped a little.

They were soon well beyond anywhere that Ghen recognised, but then he hadn't seen much of the valley beyond the river. The land looked similar, of course: field after field after field, and houses like his always nearby with washing flapping on a line and smoke curling from chimneys. He took comfort from the sameness, but he found it interesting to see gates tied with blue twine instead of red, and round windows instead of square. Sot turned down a lane that led to one such round-windowed house but stopped the cart well before they reached it.

'Wait here,' she said. 'I'll find out where the Seed Bed is.'

It was a big farm: he could see eight fields, no – nine. And a glass house for winter fruits.

'Will they let us go in the glass house?' he asked Wyne, who was fiddling with his cuff, rubbing it between thumb and forefinger. 'Wyne?'

'They won't let us touch anything apart from the Tillers,' he said without looking up.

'Maybe if Sot asks.'

'They won't,' Wyne said sharply.

Ghen looked down at his own hands. What could be so bad about them that people didn't want to be touched by him?

'I'm sorry, Ghen, for being short with you. It's just, no matter how many times we serve a Planting, it never gets any easier.'

'What doesn't?'

'You'll see.'

Sot came back then and said the Seed Bed was two fields over, behind the house. She took a stake from the back of the cart and drove it into the ground, for tying up the cart. She'd brought something like a barrow too, which Ghen and Wyne managed to get the box into.

'You'll just watch today, Ghen,' Sot said, setting off with the barrow, 'so you can see how a Last Planting is done. Given your mother's fear of even telling you about the ceremony, I'm assuming everything you see today will be new. If you have any questions, keep them to yourself until we're on our way home again.'

Their path took them past the house and along a field planted with wheat. Ghen's pace slowed as he looked at the heads, trying to work out the variety, but Sot chided him to keep up.

'We must be in place before they come out.'

'Who?'

'The Grieving.'

Wyne hadn't said a word since they got out of the cart and was still fiddling with his cuff, the action frantic now, as if he was trying to rub the material away.

'What's the matter with your shirt?' Ghen asked.

'Nothing. It's fine.'

As best Ghen could tell, Wyne was anything *but* fine, though he let Wyne be as they walked.

They came to the end of the field and Ghen saw that a deep trench had been dug next to the last of the wheat. A ladder had been left inside. Ghen guessed this was the Seed Bed but he didn't understand the ladder; it wasn't as if the dead person was going to need to climb out. Someone was waiting nearby: a woman in a red tunic with flowers wound through her long, brown hair. Sot greeted her, and the woman let Sot shake her hand, giving no sign she didn't welcome the touch.

Ghen turned to Wyne in triumph. 'See! That woman doesn't mind touching Sot. I might be allowed in the glass house.'

Wyne stood very still, rigid almost.

'That's the Sower,' he told Ghen. 'People fear her almost as much as they fear us.'

Wyne and Ghen lifted the box from the barrow and set it at the end of the Seed Bed. Sot took a few of the sacking twists out, so that the Tillers' heads were visible.

Ghen reached in to help, but Sot took him by the shoulders and marched him off a few paces.

'What did I say? Just watch. Hands behind your back. Head up. Now, don't move. They're coming. Wyne – for Audience-sake, try to ease up on the misery. There'll be more than enough from the Grieving. The boy was only sixteen.'

Wyne cleared his throat and straightened his shoulders, and all the fidgety discomfort he'd shown since arriving at the farm lifted. It was as if he'd had a stern word with himself and the anxious part had listened. Just in time too, as a line of people was making its way towards them. They passed Ghen one by one, and one by one he took in their sadness. A man and a woman, his parents' age: pale and glassy-eyed. Two boys, brothers, by the look of them, crying but trying to hide it. An old woman clutching the hand of a little girl who skipped at her side, as if this was an outing. Then men – too many to count. Heads bowed, hands behind their backs, just as Sot had told him he must stand. These were the Grieving then. They took up places next to the Seed Bed but all eyes were on the house.

Now four more were coming – two men, two women. Between them they carried the body on a sling, each holding one end of two long poles. The body itself was wrapped in a finely worked cloth and, as it neared him, Ghen could see it was covered in coloured threads that formed twisting roots and stems and buds and leaves.

The four carriers arrived at the Seed Bed and the Grieving stepped back. Then something happened and Ghen knew why his mother hadn't even told him about Last Plantings, let alone taken him to one.

The noise that broke free from the parents was the most terrible sound he'd heard in his young life. It was closer to a scream than a sob, and through it ran pain: pain, clear as a bell. A flock of birds rose as one from a tree nearby, startled by the sound. The man dropped to his knees and the woman sank next to him. They reached out to the body lying in the sling, as if they could somehow convince the boy to rise.

Then something happened that took Ghen's breath from his throat: Wyne climbed into the Seed Bed.

The carriers lowered the body down to him, feet-first. Despite his horror, Ghen edged closer so he could see. Wyne was guiding the body to a standing position against the back of the trench, so that the body looked down the field and to the house beyond it. But as the body reached the earthen wall, the wrapping around its head slipped free. Gasps and new cries of anguish came from the Grieving, and Wyne hurried as best he could to tuck the cloth back in.

But Ghen had seen the skin of the boy's face.

His cheeks were burned and blackened, the bone visible as a milky slash. Singed patches were all that remained of the boy's hair. Wyne managed to cover the boy again but Ghen couldn't forget what he'd seen.

Wyne bowed his head and waited as the Sower moved among the Grieving saying softly the name of the boy, who was Cai, and asking the Audience to welcome him, for the tales to run long, for Cai's own tale in the valley was now ended. The Grieving continued to cry as the Sower continued her walk. Even the little girl who had skipped her way to the Seed Bed was now in tears.

The Sower came back to the head of the Seed Bed. 'Widow's welcome, Cai was a good custodian of the land. No field left idle.'

'No field left idle,' the Grieving said as one, Sot joining in softly.

In the quiet that followed, Sot took a Tiller from the box and passed it down to Wyne. He positioned it carefully in front of the dead boy. He did the same for all twelve figures, arranging them in three rows of four, all looking the same way as the boy: down the wheat field. Wyne took his time, making sure the figures were the same distance from each other, that none fell on the uneven floor of the Seed Bed. He was as careful with the Tillers now as he had been when making them, and Ghen was full of admiration, because how awful it must be in the ground like that, with the burned boy, all his family sobbing above. It would be like being dead yourself, Ghen thought. And this was why Sot had taken him, the reason she had made him leave the fields. This was his task now. He would be Wyne, climbing into the earth.

He was running. He didn't care about seeing the glass house anymore. He didn't care about anything besides getting far away from Sot.

The bridge and the Wayward woman's tent were in sight when he heard the cart behind him. He was too tired to run by then, but he kept walking without turning around.

'Ready for a lift?' Sot said, drawing alongside him.

He'd thought she would be angry with him; that she wasn't left him somewhat confused, and his stride faltered.

'Running away – you're not just punishing yourself, Ghen.'

'Then who else am I punishing?' he said.

Sot let the reins fall slack in her lap. Wyne was seated beside her: pale and slick with sweat, his eyes closed.

'We've got work to do,' Sot said. 'The order list is full. I need you, and Wyne needs you. Please.'

He looked once more at the Wayward's tent. 'Just for a few days. That's all.'

'It gets easier,' she said.

He climbed up next to Wyne. He touched his friend's shoulder, and Wyne pressed against him like he was bone-cold and Ghen was a fire. It didn't look to get any easier at all.

★★★

The next two days passed in a blur of wood and blades. They rose, they ate, and made Tillers. They ate, made Tillers, ate again. They made Tillers then they slept. Ghen had no idea of the time but he knew it was passing because the number of Tillers grew, and Sot crossed things off the order list.

There were few breaks in the work besides meals and sleep, and Ghen found himself looking forward to going for wood with Wyne, and it was good when people called to make their part payments, or to place an order. Some people knew exactly what they wanted when Sot answered the door. Rennwood Tillers holding buckets. Affas with peaked hats. A scar on a cheek. Only one boot. Sot never questioned their choices or refused their demands, and she dealt with everyone the same way, regardless of how much money they had.

At the end of the second day, a knock came late, just as they were going back to work after dinner. Ghen was so tired he didn't turn around to see the caller and he didn't listen to the conversation, either. All he wanted was to go to bed and wake up at home. But then he heard a word that made him spin round so fast he knocked the Tiller he was working to the floor. The name the buyer had said, Ghen knew it. *Lart.* That was Melle's last name.

Her grandfather was on the porch with Sot. Ghen rushed out to him, gabbling about Melle.

'Melle's fine,' her grandfather said. 'She's upset about Hinny, of course.' The old man pulled a sob back inside himself. 'But she's fine. She misses you, Ghen, I know that.'

Ghen couldn't bear the sad way Melle's grandfather was looking at him. It's because his wife has died, Ghen told himself as he slunk back to his bench and took up his rooters. At his side Wyne worked a piece of rennwood with swooping, sliding strokes; himself again, after the ordeal of the Last Planting. But Ghen hadn't forgotten the way Wyne had sweated and been sickly pale. Ghen hadn't forgotten the burned boy's face.

Melle's grandmother had placed her order years earlier, the balance long paid off. Once Melle's grandfather had informed Sot of the Last Planting's particulars and taken his leave, all that was needed was for Sot to find the right payment form. She brought a pile of the sheets from her room.

'Hinny Lart,' Sot said. 'Rennwoods. Each to hold a sinta. Ghen, you'll do the fruits.'

'But I'm not good enough with the rennwood yet. The wood's too hard.'

'It gets softer the more you work it. And you know sintas like you're grown from the same root. You'll carve them, and Wyne will help if you need it. Two days until the Planting. We'll start in the morning.'

Ghen went to bed feeling torn again. He was anxious about the rennwood Tillers, wanting to do a good job for Melle's family, but pulling him another way was a lurch of excitement at the thought of seeing Melle again, and it was that that made him get out of bed again.

Sot was startled to find him already at his bench when she rose.

'How long have you been working?' she said, rubbing a hand across her eyes. She picked up a porridge pan that was lying on the floor, and a nearby spoon. 'I see you've attempted to feed yourself.'

'Couldn't sleep,' he said, without looking up.

Sot stood by his bench where six rennwood Tillers stood in a neat line, all facing the same way, as if they were already positioned in a Seed Bed. She picked one up and examined it.

'This is fine work, Ghen, but you need to sleep. I can't have you keeling over in the Seed Bed.'

Ghen dropped his rooters on the bench with a thud. 'The Seed Bed?'

Sot yawned and wrapped her shawl more tightly round her shoulders. 'I want you in this time. Wyne takes them hard – I don't like to make him do too many in a row. With you here we can fulfil more orders, and more orders mean more Last Plantings.' She picked up one of the Tillers. 'The definition on these sinta leaves could be sharper, I think, but otherwise, impressive work.'

'The rennwood is good for working fruit.'

Sot put her hand on his shoulder. 'You see now, you don't need to break your back in the fields to make something grow, Ghen.'

Ghen shook her off. 'I'm not like you,' he said with tired resignation. 'I'm going home, remember?'

A sound made them both turn. Wyne was standing in the doorway to their room.

'You must tell him, Sot,' Wyne said.

Ghen looked from one to the other. 'Tell me what?'

'That you'll be in the Seed Bed,' Sot said. 'That's my decision, and while this is my workshop, you will both respect my choices.' She turned to Wyne. 'Is that understood?'

Wyne closed the door without answering her. Sot stormed out

of the workshop and Ghen was left with the Tillers, the finished and the half-made. With a heavy heart he picked up his rooters and went back to work. So often since coming to Sot's workshop, that felt like the only action left to him.

Melle's grandmother's Last Planting was to be in the early evening. That had been the old woman's favourite time of day, the time she had chosen to walk her fields and check on her sheep. Ghen was still without a suit, despite Sot's promise to buy him one, but at least he had Wyne's clothes to borrow, which were better than his own. He wanted to look smart for old Mrs Lart's Last Planting. For Melle.

When they arrived at the house there was a lamp burning in every window. Fiddle music drifted from the open front door as they unloaded the Tiller box. In time with the sprightly jig Ghen heard many hands clapping, and whistles and bells.

He nearly dropped his end of the box as he and Wyne guided it to the barrow. Sot happened to be close by and caught the weight just in time. When the box was safe in the barrow and Wyne was wheeling it towards the Seed Bed, Sot spoke kindly to Ghen.

'This one will be different. It's a celebration of a life well lived, not mourning one cut short. Hinny Lart was eighty-six and died in her own bed, in her sleep. She didn't suffer at her end, and her family won't suffer at her Planting. It won't be like the boy.'

Ghen nodded, trying to catch hold of Sot's cheerfulness in the hope it would ease the worry that made his stomach churn, his head light.

'And there's Melle,' he said. 'I'll see Melle tonight too.'

Sot patted his shoulder. They followed Wyne along a path marked with lanterns. Garlands of flowers ran through the branches of the trees they passed, and the sheep in the adjoining field had ribbons tied to their tails. Sot was right, it *was* a celebration. And he decided to do his best in the Seed Bed. For Melle.

It was a different Sower than the previous one. This was a stout man with no hair on his head to wind flowers in, but he wore a red tunic and talked with Sot while they waited for the Grieving to come, just as before.

Wyne and Ghen set the Tiller box by the Seed Bed. Ghen caught sight of the ladder in the trench and felt his knees tremble.

'Just remember to breathe,' Wyne said, 'and don't rush. Better to do it slowly and get it right. None of the Grieving are in a rush.'

Wyne was right – they really weren't in a rush. The music continued to play in the house and the hands continued to clap along. The Sower pulled a pocket watch from his tunic and sighed. The shadows lengthened.

Ghen wondered if Melle knew he'd be there, if she was excited to see him. Her grandfather had said she missed him, and that had to be a good sign. He took comfort from this thought, and from the music and the flowers in the trees. Melle was his friend. Melle would always be his friend.

There was more light, suddenly, as the back door opened. Shadows made their way towards the Seed Bed. They brought the music with them, singing Hinny Lart to her Bed. The shadows came closer, walked past him, and became people at the side of the Seed Bed. Ghen searched for Melle's face among them, and when he found it his heart leapt. She seemed to seek him too, and when she saw him her mouth opened, and if he had been closer he thought he would have heard a little sound fall from it. A sound of pleasure, he was sure.

He stood straight as his Tillers while the Sower intoned his words and wound his way through the Grieving. There was no sobbing, no pain. When the Sower praised Hinny Lart's care of the land, the Grieving called out that she did care, yes she did. They nodded and told the Audience she'd shared a great many tales with them.

Ghen knew his moment was coming. He listened for the last of the *No field to lie idle* calls to be uttered. And then he climbed down the ladder.

The Seed Bed felt much deeper than it had looked from the ground. Wyne was far, far above him; Ghen would never be able to reach to take a Tiller. He felt dizzy and put his hand out to steady himself, but his hand met only soft, wet earth.

'Breathe, Ghen!' Wyne whispered.

Ghen took a few deeper breaths and felt steadier. He was aware of something above him. It was Hinny, wrapped in the sheet and being lowered feet-first into the Seed Bed. He caught hold of her feet and guided the body. But the bearers above let the weight go too soon, before he'd eased the body backwards against the Bed wall, and it fell against him, knocking him hard.

His feet struggled to find purchase on the soil and he started to slip. He was going to fall in the mud with Melle's dead grandmother on top of him. Frantically he shoved the body away from him and managed to get it in place, looking down the field. He gave a cry of triumph but immediately caught himself.

He felt like he'd been in the Seed Bed a long time. As Wyne passed the first Tiller down, he murmured to Ghen that he was doing well.

'But slowly, remember?'

Ghen did his best to place the Tillers with care but he wanted to get out of the Seed Bed very much. Once, he was sure he saw Hinny's hand twitch. He had only placed three Tillers, leaving nine to go. He made himself look at them rather than Hinny. At the fruit they held, that he had carved. Carved for Melle. He said that every time he took a Tiller from Wyne, every time he set it down in front of Hinny. *Carved for Melle.* The words helped him set a pace. *Carved for Melle.* She helped him, though she was far above him now.

When all the Tillers were in place he said it one more time, so that he didn't scramble out of the Seed Bed in a way that would be disrespectful, and then he climbed the ladder. Wyne helped him out of the Bed and then helped to keep him standing. He looked for Melle's face again, but darkness had come, and he could no longer make out who was who among the bodies of the Grieving. Then they began to tell stories of Hinny, and he found Melle through her voice. Her tale was one he already knew, about how her grandmother had taught her to tie her bootlaces when everyone else had given up hope that Melle would ever learn.

'She made a story of the tying,' Melle said. 'Told me there was a tree, and a gresta making a nest in it. The gresta had to swoop round the tree, under the branches, to collect her twigs, and when she had enough she pulled them into the nest. When I told myself the story my laces were tied. I still tell it to myself now.'

The Grieving laughed, and so did Sot and Wyne, and Ghen was more glad than he could say to share that laughter with people.

When all the tales were told, the Sower stood at the end of the Seed Bed where Hinny's head was and called her by name, asking her to watch over the land, to make sure its story was one of strong growth and high yields.

The Grieving then made their way back to the house. There was no music now, or singing, just low voices sharing more stories. The four people who had carried Hinny's body to the Seed Bed stayed to fill in the trench; the noise the earth made as it scattered onto Hinny's head and shoulders, onto the Tillers, made Ghen shrink back.

The Sower took his leave with mutterings about missing the last ferry home, and Sot, Wyne and Ghen walked to the cart.

'I haven't seen Melle,' Ghen said. 'Can I, just to say goodbye?'

Sot looked reluctant, but after a moment she nodded. 'You be quick, Ghen. No bothering anyone.'

He was away to the house before she'd even finished speaking. The light still poured from the windows and the music had started again. He had to knock three times before the door opened. Melle's mother took a step back when she saw who it was. The fiddle music slipped out of time, and stopped. He was aware of many sets of eyes on him, but no one spoke.

'Melle?' he said, feeling only as tall as a Tiller beneath her mother's glare.

'You get away—'

'It's all right, Mama,' Melle said, slipping past her.

Ghen felt joy surge through him. It *was* all right.

'Don't you be long with him, you hear?' her mother called after them. She stayed watching from the doorway.

Melle walked with him across the yard but would go no further.

'Is it bad, Ghen, working for Sot?'

He was surprised to hear himself say that it wasn't so bad. 'I like the work. Making Tillers, it's just like growing things.'

'But how can it be? You only work with dead wood, for dead people.'

There was a rising note of anguish in her voice that he tried not to hear.

'It's only for a little while,' he said.

'Is it?' she said, surprised, and pleased. 'When will you go home?'

'I don't know. But I will. Sot can't keep me forever.'

Melle's shoulders slumped. 'You should have hidden here, in the barn.'

And then she was walking away, back to her mother.

Sot found him in the barn, in the hay bales. His face was red from the scratching of the hay, and from the tears. He let her gather him up and guide him to the cart where Wyne was waiting. There were no lanterns now. The three of them were in darkness.

'When can I go home, Sot?'

He murmured it over and over again. He would say nothing else, and neither would he stop asking. At last Sot ran out of patience.

'You want to go home, Ghen? Fine! We'll go now. Your house isn't far, and I'm sure Wyne won't mind the detour. He's been on at me about it for long enough.'

Ghen uncurled from where he was lying in the back of the cart.

'Do you mean it?' he said.

'If it will make things any easier then yes, I mean it.'

'I'll walk back,' Wyne said. 'Set me down by the bridge.'

'In the dark?' Sot said. 'Will you be safe?'

'I'd rather risk bandits than be part of this.'

'Part of what?' Ghen said.

Ghen threw open the front door, and his parents and the girls looked up from heaped, steaming plates in surprise. His father said his name with such warmth, such longing, that Ghen had to grip the doorframe to stay on his feet. Sot stood quietly behind him.

'Did I forget someone's birthday?' Ghen said, taking in the well laid table. There was roast hennie fowl with holens and squash, all covered in rich gravy, and bowls of other vegetables, and thick bread. Waiting near the sink was a tall cake, topped with cream and tiny red berries he didn't even recognise.

'Ghen? What's going on?' his mother said.

'I've come home, Mama.'

'It's bad, isn't it?' his father said. 'Making them.'

'Is he not working hard enough?' his mother asked Sot.

'I'll be in the cart,' Sot said in a low voice. 'Do it now.'

'There's no need to wait for me,' Ghen said. 'I'm not going back.'

'Sot!' his mother said, getting to her feet. 'You can't do this. We've spent nearly all of it. We had an agreement!'

'There was nothing in that agreement about me having to do your mothering for you. Tell him now or he stays. You've already left it late enough.' Sot walked back to the cart.

'What agreement, Mama? What are you talking about?'

She snatched a spoon from Elin, who was looking to drop it on the floor. 'You just— It was supposed to—' She gave a strangled cry and turned away from him.

It was then Ghen noticed the cupboard doors were hanging straight, and the walls had been tempered. The pans by the sink were shiny with newness. The more he looked, the more he saw: the thick rug by the stove, the stove itself now bigger. New, well-stuffed chairs.

And then he realised Elin wasn't coughing.

'How did you...'

'There's money for some better things,' his mother said. 'We're not saving now, see.'

'Why not?' he whispered. But he already knew.

He climbed up next to Sot and they both sat in silence for a time. No one came after him from the house.

'They bought the land from Hend,' he said.

She nodded.

'And the money, that came from you. For me.'

She nodded again.

'So it's not just for a little while that I'm working for you. It's forever.'

'It's for as long as you want these fields to thrive,' she said, gesturing towards the dark. 'If you leave the workshop, they have to pay back the money. The longer you stay with me, Ghen, the better it is for them.'

'You've worked out the account.'

She flicked the reins and the cart rumbled forward. 'Of course I have.'

'And how long until the debt's paid off, until I can leave and they can keep the land?'

'Think of it this way, Ghen. Wyne is halfway paid.'

Ghen was glad the order list was full. The work kept his hands busy and when his hands were busy his mind emptied out and then he was saved from thinking about what Sot had told him. But as the next few days passed, he found that in the pause between finishing one Tiller and picking up the next length of wood, he couldn't help watching Wyne: Wyne, who was perhaps ten years older than he was. Wyne whose hands made such beautiful things, but whom no Lowlander would touch. Wyne who was halfway paid.

Ghen worked faster, harder, but not for Sot and her orders. He worked to tire himself out so that when he got into bed he could sleep rather than lie awake staring at Wyne's back.

One morning, Ghen drifted into a kind of waking-dream. He watched Wyne's utter concentration in his work, the Tiller and the rooters and the man as one. Then his thoughts turned to Melle, and a moment later his mother and father crowded in beside her, followed by Elin and Lyra; even Rit shoved his way in. But all at once they stiffened, lost their features, became silent, wooden figures. The world he knew before was gone.

He needed to get outside, to see the trees. To see something living.

He called to Sot that he was going for more wood. She was in her room, working on the accounts, and didn't answer. She'd said little to him since the visit to his parents, spending more time than usual with the order list, the part payment forms and her columns of figures. She forgot to call them for dinner, when it was usually only her who remembered they should eat, and when she did remember, she ate little herself. Just ran a thumb across her lip, backwards and forwards, staring into the hearth, which was more often cold than lit. Ghen could almost see the sum she was working, as if her concentration had conjured it into the air. He could tell that the figures weren't adding up.

Wandering through the orchard he found himself thinking about the Wayward woman, and the dream of the coins bouncing off the mostin-catching jar. She'd known everything: not just that he would leave the land, but about the price paid for him too. She'd sent him the dream, with the Child's permission. Maybe she knew what would happen next, what he should do. He shook the thought away. The only thing that was going to happen was him working for Sot.

He stayed outside for as long as he thought he could without being missed, then walked slowly back to the workshop, and all too soon the porch came in sight. He climbed the steps to the door, and then he heard the voices.

For a moment Ghen wondered if he'd come back to the right workshop. The fire was lit, the flames tall and bright. The kettle was on and the remaining cups were set out on a bench, together with a kind of dried biscuit Sot had unearthed from somewhere. Wyne stood by the hearth, poker in hand, watching Sot talk to the women.

There were two of them. The elder was a short, fat woman in a wool dress with a fur stole around her shoulders, pinned at her breast by a glittering red stone. She wore red leather gloves, the leather so fine Ghen could see the softness of it. She had been crying, he thought, and still tightly clutched a handkerchief. The younger woman was closer to Wyne's age. Her hair was the colour of the sun, her eyes the colour of early myrtleberries. Sot held a rennwood Tiller and was explaining about the tool it held, what they could do for personalised Tillers. The woman with the handkerchief nodded without seeming to listen. The girl's distraction was much more pronounced: she looked all around her, mouth open in wonder.

The kettle began to shriek, but Wyne gave no sign he could hear it. He kept staring at the girl. Ghen pushed past him to reach the hot rag they kept nearby, and Wyne came to with a start. His eyes widened and he lurched at the kettle, reaching out.

'The cloth!' Ghen shouted.

But it was too late. Wyne picked up the boiling kettle by the handle. He dropped it straight away and looked at his hand as if amazed by the angry red mark that swelled there. Ghen ushered

344

him to the water pail in the corner and shoved Wyne's hand in. Wyne yelped like a kicked dog, and some understanding of what had happened came into his eyes.

'My apologies,' Sot said to the woman with the handkerchief. 'Wyne there is very gifted when it comes to making Tillers, but such skill comes at a price, I've found. This is one of his pieces.'

The woman looked around the workshop with distaste. The young girl was watching Wyne and Ghen, her head tilted to one side. The light streaming through the windows made her hair gleam.

The skin on Wyne's palm was rising to a blister. The image of the burned boy in the Seed Bed flashed into Ghen's head.

'The Wayward at the bridge,' Ghen said. 'She'll have a salve.'

Sot shook her head and mouthed 'not now' at him. 'Can I offer you Greynal?' she said to the woman. 'To drink to your husband's memory.'

Ghen was amazed. Since he'd come to the workshop Sot hadn't even offered buyers tea, let alone Greynal.

The woman walked the length of the workshop, her long dress sweeping the floor. It wasn't a working dress. It was a dress bought from a lifetime's work.

The girl darted after her, bending to pull something caught in the wool.

'Grandmama, the shavings.'

The woman yanked her dress from the girl's fingers. 'Don't fuss, Pinna!'

The girl shrank back between the benches, head bowed.

'Mistress Sot, as you know, my husband was an important man

in the valley,' the woman said. 'He tended his land, and the land he rented to tenants, with great care. And many of those renters don't look after land properly, I can tell you.'

'Of course,' Sot murmured.

'I want my husband to have Tillers who reflect his stewardship, and his many talents.'

She swept down the workshop again. Ghen had the feeling she was used to people standing and listening to her. And doing as she said.

'That's why I've come to you, Mistress Sot. I've heard about the detail your workshop offers – personalised tools, real-looking hair. Well, I want more than that.'

'More?' Sot said.

'My husband wasn't just a farmer, Mistress Sot. He *was* a farm. I want his Tillers to show that.'

'You want us to make a whole farm?'

'In essence, yes. Everyone else has one model of Tiller replicated, isn't that right? Well I want fifty Tillers, each holding a different tool, each wearing different clothes. I want horses pulling ploughs. Sacks of seeds. I want everything my husband did, made in wood. Can you do that, Mistress Sot, you and your workshop?' She looked over at Ghen and Wyne still huddled by the water pail as if she doubted they could make a cup of tea between them, let alone all the figures she wanted.

'I... we've never...'

'Because if you *can't* make them then I will go to Master Canna. He would not be my first choice but to get what I want I will do whatever it takes.'

346

Sot put the rennwood Tiller back on the shelf. 'We can do it, Mistress Hend.'

'Good. The Planting will be in five days. Pinna will arrange the items with you. She knows what I want.'

Pinna nodded without lifting her head.

'Your granddaughter is welcome at the workshop any time,' Sot said.

Wyne seemed to forget his burned hand then and stood grinning.

'Tomorrow morning, Pinna,' Mistress Hend barked.

Pinna's gaze flicked to Wyne, only for a second but Ghen saw it. Mistress Hend opened the door and was away without another word, Pinna scurrying after her.

As soon as the door had shut behind them, Sot rushed to Wyne's side and took hold of his hand.

'How could you be so foolish?' she said. 'And with this order to complete, an order that could safeguard the future of this workshop. Five days! Oh Wyne.'

Wyne wasn't listening. He was staring at the door. Ghen wasn't listening either; three words rushed round his head, drowning out everything else.

Hend was dead.

Sot was reluctant to let Wyne go to the Wayward. She didn't want to waste a moment when Mistress Hend's order was so large.

'And so complicated!' Sot said, throwing up her hands. 'We don't even have the final list, not until that girl comes tomorrow.'

'Pinna,' Wyne said cheerfully, as if his blistered palm gave him no pain at all. 'Her name is Pinna.'

'Why did you say we could manage it if you don't think we can?' Ghen said.

Sot sank onto a stool. 'Because we have to try,' she said. 'If we get it right then we'll have more orders than we know what to do with. Once people see Hend's Tillers, what we can do, I won't ever have to worry about Canna again.'

'If that happens then you'll need more makers,' Ghen said. 'You'll have to find some other boy to buy.'

If Sot heard him then she gave no sign of it. 'Let's have that tea.'

As he picked up his cup, Wyne realised the problem he was facing: he couldn't make anything with his hand as it was.

'Let Wyne go to the Wayward,' Ghen said again. 'It'll save time in the long run.'

Sot tapped her thumb nail against her cup's handle for a moment, then finally agreed. 'I'll take him in the cart. You ready some rennwood, Ghen. We can at least start on the figures while we wait for the details from the girl.'

They left a few minutes later, Wyne still in a daze. It was, Ghen thought, putting the rennwood on his bench, the first time he'd seen anyone fall in love. He was surprised by how clear, how obvious it was. And that it had happened to both Wyne and Pinna, almost at the same time! Ghen felt in his pocket for the shell Melle had given him. If there was hope for Wyne then maybe there was hope for Ghen too.

★★★

Wyne returned with his hand bandaged in a blue patterned cloth. Ghen could smell the fint of the salve, his eyes watering as Wyne passed him. Ghen wanted to ask about the Wayward but a fever of work was on Sot, a fever that appeared to be mostly panic, and she hurried the rooters into Ghen and Wyne's hands, brooking no idle chatter.

Wyne winced as he fitted the handles of his rooters over the bandage. Sot hovered at his side, waiting to see if he could wield them as before. He scraped a length of rennwood, then nodded at Sot.

She was visibly relieved. 'Figures then. We'll work on getting a set made and then we can add the detail tomorrow, once we know what Mistress Hend wants.'

She set to work. Ghen did likewise, and they stayed like that until the light went. Sot said they should break then, and eat.

'I bought some meat the Wayward had trapped.'

Ghen nearly fell over himself in surprise.

'We need to keep our strength up for this order,' Sot said. 'I'm accounting for it as an investment.' She went to stir up the fire.

Ghen stretched out his back and glanced at Wyne. The bandage was dark with blood.

Sot cursed the Wayward, all the while eating a roasted gresta thigh she'd bought from the woman.

'It's not the Wayward's fault,' Ghen said. 'Wyne should be resting his hand, not making Tillers.'

'There's no time for that,' Sot said. 'Bind it with fresh cloth,

Ghen. At least you won't charge me just short of a mark to do so.'

Wyne didn't move or make a sound as Ghen unwrapped the Wayward's blue cloth. It was Ghen who did the wincing when he saw the bloodied, raw mess of flesh.

'Doesn't it hurt?' Ghen asked.

Wyne turned to look at him, slowly, as if he was only barely aware he was being spoken to. 'Hmm?'

'Your hand, Wyne!' Sot shouted. 'Wake up! Please, you need to wake up. I can't do this without you.'

He smiled at her, but it was the woozy smile of a drunkard. Or a fool.

They worked well into the night, and only when Ghen fell asleep at his bench did Sot say they should go to bed. He felt as if his head had barely touched the pillow when Sot shouted at them to get up again. They'd already been at work for more than four hours when there was a knock at the door.

Wyne jumped up to answer it, dropping his rooters and knocking over his stool as he went. Sot hurried in his wake, setting things right, muttering worry.

It was Pinna.

'I have a list,' she said. Her voice was shy, girlish.

She pulled a well-crumpled sheet from her pocket and held it out to Wyne. Her hand was shaking and a blush flamed her cheeks. She made no move to come inside the workshop, just stood looking at her boots.

Ghen couldn't understand Wyne's fascination with Pinna.

She was so wispy and wet. She wasn't like Melle, he thought, and felt a pang that made it even more difficult to watch Wyne and Pinna so drawn to one another. Wyne now reaching for the list, Pinna not wanting to let go, their fingers so close to touching.

'Come in, Miss Hend, come in,' Sot said.

She had to bodily push Wyne out of the way. Pinna giggled like Elin and Lyra did, as if she were a babe, and waited just inside the door to be told where she should place herself.

'We'll sit by the fire,' Sot said. 'Ghen – the kettle. Wyne, you just sit quietly. Now, let's see what your grandmother would like us to make, Miss Hend.' She read through the items on the list and her face grew pale. 'There's quite a lot here.' She swallowed. 'Fifty Tillers, well we knew that much, and at least we have some of them made already. Each to wear different clothes, and carry a different tool. There's a separate list for those. A turnpoke? I don't even know what that is.'

'I do,' Ghen said, pouring water into the cups.

'Thank goodness for that.' She carried on down the list. 'Eight pairs of horses, each to pull a cart. To go in each cart: four sacks of different sizes, more tools, a miniature Tiller.' She looked at Pinna. 'A Tiller for a Tiller. Is that really what she wants?'

'Oh yes,' Pinna said, nodding vehemently over her cup. 'And Grandmama always gets what she wants.'

'I see.' There was no sound for a long moment, other than the crackle of the fire, and then Sot clapped her hands together. 'We'd better get to it then, hadn't we? Thank you for bringing the list,' Sot said.

Pinna looked at Wyne. She seemed to make her mind up about something then, for instead of getting up to leave, she said, 'I think I should stay. I'll send the cart back.'

'Stay?' Sot said. 'But there's no need. We have the list, and Ghen here knows tools like a man four times his age. I wouldn't want to impose on your time, Miss Hend. There must be much to do at home with the Last Planting so close.'

'Oh no,' Pinna said airily. 'I can stay as long as I like. And Grandmama did say I was to make sure you got the Tillers how she wants them.'

For a moment, Sot was at a loss as to what to say. After all, she couldn't throw Pinna out. Then she produced a smile from somewhere. It was far from warm but it was a smile, at least.

'Of course, Miss Hend. Ghen will stoke up the fire and I'm sure you'll be quite comfortable here.'

'I shall watch you. I want to see how it's done.'

Ghen had no doubt which of them in particular Pinna would watch, and sure enough Wyne brought Pinna's chair to his bench. He pulled it out for her to sit down, like she was a great lady, which made her giggle again.

'No good will come of this,' Sot muttered.

The morning became the afternoon and the work continued apace. Ghen had thought Pinna would grow bored of watching Wyne scrape a length of wood. Even the fine, close work of buttons and hair became dull after a while, unless you were watching to learn. Unless you were a Tiller-maker. But Pinna's interest was so intense, so constant, Ghen began to wonder if perhaps she *did* want to make Tillers.

Wyne worked as he always did: with swift precision, undistracted by anything else around him. Even Pinna sitting so close gave him no cause to look up from the wood, and that gave Sot some comfort, at least. They might get the order done in time.

The daylight was fading when they heard a knock at the door. Ghen opened it. A man was on the porch, dressed in working clothes. Ghen could smell the freshly turned earth that clung damply to the man's boots. He said his name was Audley and that he'd been sent to fetch Pinna home for her dinner.

The man Audley eyed Pinna sternly from the porch as she gathered her shawl and the other things she'd managed to scatter across the workshop: a small bag of deep red cloth, a folded fan, a dried medlar flower. As she was heading to the door she stopped and turned around. She gave Wyne the medlar flower and whispered something in his ear. Wyne smiled and nodded. And then, in front of all of them watching, she touched Wyne. Not by accident. Not because she was forced to do so. By choice, and happily, she put her hand on his arm and squeezed it.

The next morning Pinna was back. It was Ghen who let her in this time. He caught sight of Audley driving the cart down the lane, leaving Pinna for the day.

Just as before, she sat close to Wyne, who worked even faster than usual with Pinna there. As the morning ran on, the wooden figures piled up on Wyne's bench: carts and horses, bags of seeds.

The new items requested by Mistress Hend posed no challenge to him, and the speed at which he produced them impressed Sot enough that she actually smiled once or twice and remembered lunch.

Ghen tried his best not to be distracted by the besotted pair. Sot had asked him to make the tools requested by Mistress Hend, most of which Sot had never heard of. He finished a turnpoke and was reaching for another Tiller, ready to shape the blunt wood the figure clutched into something definite and named. But then he noticed Pinna holding a Tiller; Ghen had never seen anyone from outside the workshop touch one.

That night Wyne slept with the medlar flower pressed to his lips, and Ghen clutched the shell Melle had given him.

The next morning it was Sot who got to the door when the knock sounded.

'Miss Hend,' Sot said, firmly. 'We appreciate your time with us, but I feel sure you're needed at home.'

'It's quite all right, Mistress Sot,' Pinna said. She caught sight of Wyne over Sot's shoulder and a huge smile blazed across her face. 'I've told Grandmama you need me here. That I'm helping.'

'You told her you're *helping*?'

Pinna eased her way past Sot, who in her worry had lost her resolve.

The day passed much as the others had passed. The three Tiller-makers worked on their pieces and the fourth watched and murmured, and sometimes tried her hand herself. The crumpled list Pinna had brought with her became a crumpled mess of lines as Ghen called out the finished figures and Sot crossed them off.

'The only things left are the Tillers' own Tillers,' she said. 'Fifty to do by the end of tomorrow, and what are they to look like? Miss Hend, did your grandmother tell you if the smaller Tillers were to have tools like their companions?'

But Pinna wasn't listening. She cradled Wyne's burned hand between her own and unwrapped the bloodied bandage. The burn wasn't healing, and it was no wonder, the work Wyne was doing.

Ghen and Sot watched in silence as Pinna gently pressed the burn, feeling for swelling. Wyne gazed at her. Pinna lifted Wyne's hand to her lips.

'Miss Hend!' came a shout from the doorway then Audley was striding across the room. He grabbed Pinna's arm and pulled her roughly to her feet. 'It's bad enough you're in this place, touching these, these *things*. But being so free with one of the makers.' Pinna struggled to free herself, but Audley's grip was too strong. 'It's wrong, Miss Hend!'

He half-dragged her to the door, while the rest of them could only watch. Wyne, stricken, rose from his bench, his burned hand reaching for her.

'Wyne, remember what we talked about,' Pinna cried. She tried once more to twist free of Audley. 'Tomorrow!' she called from the porch, and then she was gone.

The air was slow to settle in the workshop.

'Wyne, what have you done?' Sot whispered.

★★★

Ghen slept well that night, the best night's sleep he'd had since first coming to Sot's workshop. When he woke, Melle's shell was warmed from where he'd slept with it pressed to his chest. Wyne and Sot both looked to have passed an uneasy night. Deep shadows sat beneath their eyes.

Ghen made the breakfast, not that either of the others seemed hungry, and then he and Wyne went to their benches. They were up hours earlier than Pinna usually came, and Wyne said they should start on the Tillers' own Tillers: Hend's Last Planting was the next day. He and Ghen talked about the figures in great detail before they started, on occasion asking Sot what she thought. But Sot only stared into the fire.

'We'll make a few bodies of different sizes,' Wyne said, 'and then when Pinna comes she can pick which one she thinks Mistress Hend will prefer, and then we can get on with the fifty.'

They both fell to working then, and as was always the case Ghen was soon lost in the making, in the feeling of the rooters in his hands. When he had made three Tillers in different sizes he went to the water pail for a drink. It was then he noticed how light it was outside. Pinna hadn't come. Every so often Wyne glanced at the door.

It was time for lunch and still Pinna hadn't come. Wyne opened the door to the porch and looked out. He stayed there, waiting. Ghen took him some bread and cheese which Wyne ate standing up.

'She'll be here soon,' he said to Ghen.

He didn't come back inside when he'd finished eating. Ghen left the door open and went back to his bench. Sot finally examined the Tillers' own Tillers they'd made that morning.

'This one,' she said, holding up the smallest figure. 'We'll make them this size.'

'But we don't know which one Pinna will choose,' Ghen said. 'We should wait.'

'She's not coming, Ghen. And we've got work to do.'

Sot and Ghen worked through the afternoon and into the evening, and still Wyne stayed on the porch. By midnight they'd made just over half the number of small figures Mistress Hend had requested, and the Last Planting was at first light.

Sot took Wyne blankets, and even a cup of Greynal. 'To keep out the cold,' she said. 'But we need you, Wyne. To get the order done in time. Please.'

Wyne gave no sign he even knew she was there. Sot wrapped the blanket round his shoulders and set the Greynal close to him.

'I'm sorry,' she said.

She gave Ghen some Greynal too, and knocked back a great slug herself. She caught him staring in wonderment at the bottle.

'If not now, then when?' she said. 'If we keep going then we might make it.'

Ghen resettled himself on his stool and his muscles immediately resumed their previous positions, as did his aches.

He didn't know how long they'd been working when Wyne stumbled in. He sat at his bench without speaking, staring at his rooters as if he'd never seen them before. Sot guided them into his hands. She gave him a short length of rennwood and explained how she'd decided to make the Tillers' own Tillers. She and Ghen went back to work.

But no movement or sound came from Wyne. Sot ignored it for a little while, but at last turned around in exasperation. 'Please, Wyne! We only have until first light.'

'I can't,' he said. 'My hands. I can't.'

'It's the cold,' Sot said. 'You've been sitting outside half the night, what do you expect? Ghen, put the kettle on.'

All work stopped while they waited for the kettle, and then waited while Wyne carefully warmed his hands on the clay cup. He picked up his rooters again and made to scrape the rennwood, but the rooters were awkward and clumsy in his hands, as if his hands were someone else's. When he finally brought the blades against the wood all he did was scratch it.

Sot dropped her own rooters with a cry.

When she'd composed herself she put Wyne to bed, telling him it would all be better in the morning. It was just a temporary problem, that was all. The burn, the cold. The one thing she didn't blame, the one thing she *should* have blamed, was Pinna.

Sot shut the bedroom door and returned to the bench. 'How much time do we have left?' she asked Ghen.

He opened the porch door and looked out. 'Three hours until first light.'

'We need to allow an hour to pack everything and get to the Seed Bed, so that's two hours left for making. Another Greynal and we might just manage it.'

'What about Wyne?'

'We'll worry about him later. Right now it's Hend we have to think about.'

As the time for leaving drew near they were still missing some of the smaller Tillers. Sot rushed around packing boxes with sacking, packing the sacking with wooden figures, leaving Ghen to furiously scrape and carve and do the close work. His exhaustion and the Greynal had left him with a strange kind of clarity. He was able to work without even being aware of what he was doing.

'We're still two short,' Sot said. 'Bring your rooters in the cart, Ghen. You'll have to make as we go. But get changed first, and quickly!' She bundled him to the bedroom door and flew into her own room to do the same.

It was dark in the room. Ghen hoped that Wyne was asleep and that sleep would help him. Ghen edged round the bed, trying to find his Last Planting clothes but in the dark everything looked like a blanket.

'Hurry up, Ghen!' Sot called through the door.

He had to light a candle, there was no way round it. As the light flared he saw Wyne's eyes – wide and white and staring. He held the medlar flower against his lips.

'Wyne, are you coming? Pinna will be there.'

'Then I shouldn't be,' he said quietly.

'Why not? If you talk to her then it'll be all right. I know it will. It has to be.'

Wyne closed his eyes and shook his head. Sot shouted for Ghen again. He stumbled into his good clothes and stumbled back out into the main room.

'Quick – help me with the boxes,' Sot said.

They flew down the lane, the cart bouncing and jouncing, Ghen still carving and scraping. Sot bemoaned their rushing and their untidiness as they careered along, and the sky grew lighter.

'The best chance I've had in years and this is what we're reduced to – making Tillers on the road. Canna would laugh himself into an early Seed Bed if he could see this. We just have to get there in time. The work – the work is good.'

All the way to Hend's farm she fought with her hopes and her despair and Ghen made the last two of the Tillers' own Tillers, and gave each the same tool: a pair of rooters.

He finished just as the cart clattered into Hend's yard. Or rather the first yard, for there was light enough now to see that Hend's farm had plenty of yards, with huge barns and stables and tool sheds flanking each one, as if his farm was many smaller ones put together. And beyond the yards and the buildings were the fields. Rolling green stretched for miles, every inch covered in trees, glass houses, ploughed lines, leafing crops, and when there wasn't green there was yellow wheat. The yellow of Pinna's hair.

But the place was empty of people. No one crossed the yards. No one dug in the fields. A pall of silence hung over everything.

'Where's the Seed Bed?' Ghen said. His words felt thick in his mouth.

'I don't know. Pinna was meant to tell me. It could be anywhere. We're so close, but – damn that girl to Silence!'

A woman came hurrying from the barn, wiping her hands on her dirty apron. Sot hailed her and told her they had the Tillers for the Planting.

'The next field, first of the wheat. You'll have to hurry. They'll be leaving the long house any time now.' The woman altered her course so as not to pass too close to the cart.

'Quick, Ghen,' Sot said, 'we'll take the barrow from here.'

He got down and helped her load the boxes onto the barrow, but all his movements were slow, drawn out.

They found the Sower – the same bald one from Melle's grandmother's Planting. He was pacing along the Seed Bed, watch in hand and cursing. When he saw Sot and Ghen approaching he shook his head.

'Not quite your usual standards, Mistress Sot.'

Sot wiped her hair from her sweaty face. 'Shut up, Nex, and help me.'

The Sower was so stunned he did as she said and began moving the boxes to the end of the Bed. They were almost all in place when Sot gave a cry. The Grieving were on their way.

They fumbled the last of the boxes next to the Bed and took their places. Sot was puffing, red-faced, her shirt untucked and dirt streaked up one arm. But she wore a look of triumph.

Ghen scanned the faces of the Grieving as they came to the Seed Bed. There were so many people, standing four deep, so many faces. But none of them was Pinna's. Surely, if she was there, she would have been at the front?

And then he found a face he knew. A furious face. Mistress Hend. She was glaring at Sot.

When it came time for Hend to be lowered into the Bed, it was Sot who climbed down the ladder to receive the body. Ghen didn't blame her wanting to escape Mistress Hend's ire. He almost wished he could do so himself. Almost.

When Hend was standing firm at the back of the Seed Bed, looking down his field, Ghen began handing Sot the Tillers. She set out one row of five, and then Ghen took from the box a cart loaded with tools and bags of seeds, together with a pair of horses to pull it. And a miniature Tiller. There were gasps from the Grieving. People pressed forward to see. The look on Mistress Hend's face changed to one of pride.

Ghen handed the cart and horses down to Sot who positioned them with a full-grown Tiller. The horses' legs were slender, with delicate knees and neat hooves. Wyne had made them so well.

It took a long time to set out everything Mistress Hend had ordered. When it was done the Seed Bed was full of wooden figures. A whole farm's worth, sitting at Hend's dead feet. Sot climbed out and took her place beside Ghen. She had to lean on him to stay upright; he was so tired himself, he wasn't sure he could hold her through the stories. He didn't listen to them. He already knew all there was to know about Hend.

At last it was done and the Grieving were making their way back to the long house. Mistress Hend left with them, without a word to Sot. At the back of the crowd, one of the last to leave, was a familiar figure. Audley.

Ghen caught up with him, ignoring Sot's calls.

'Where's Pinna?' he asked.

Audley took a step back before he answered. 'Gone, hasn't she.'

'Where?'

Audley started walking again. 'I don't think that's any of your concern, is it?'

Ghen grabbed him by the arm and Audley shuddered to a stop, holding his arm as if he feared it would fall from his body.

'She's where that brute can't get her. Mistress Hend sent her north, out of the valley. If you had any sense you would get away too, boy.' He stepped further away from Ghen. 'Or perhaps it's too late.'

Ghen turned on his heel and went to help Sot pack up the boxes. The people who'd carried Hend to the Bed were now filling it in. As they shovelled earth onto Hend's head, Ghen's thoughts raced, turning over what might have happened to Pinna, and to Wyne. What he *hoped* had happened. Pinna was gone, and Wyne had stayed at the workshop rather than come to the Last Planting. Perhaps it was all part of their plan. Even now they could be together, on a road taking them far away.

He said nothing to Sot; she looked beyond talking after the strain of the last few days. Ghen himself felt better as the morning wore on. It was he who drove the cart home and Sot who lay in a heap in the back, rattling around with the empty boxes and the sacking.

The Wayward woman was waiting for them on the porch. She peered hard at Ghen as he climbed the steps.

'You've grown,' she said.

'I'm no taller.'

'I paid you, Wayward, didn't I?' Sot said, opening the door. 'For Wyne's hand?'

'You did, Mistress Sot.' The Wayward stared past her, down the steps. 'But who will pay for the young man's Tillers? And what do you put in a Tiller-maker's Seed Bed? Tillers with their own Tillers, perhaps. Tillers with rooters in their hands.'

Sot faltered in the doorway. 'Where is he?'

'By the bridge. Hanged himself from a rennwood tree, but I couldn't see well enough to cut him down.'

By nightfall Sot lay slumped by the cold hearth. Ghen took the half-empty Greynal bottle that lay on the floor beside her, then gathered what else he needed: the order lists, a lantern. He went to the woodshed, found a shovel and dug a hole in the orchard, near where they had buried Wyne, and dropped in the shell Melle had given him. Then he hitched the horse.

By the time he reached Hend's land, the lamps were out and everyone appeared to be in bed. Even in the darkness the fields had a glow of growth and prosperity to them, all of which Hend and his Tillers were now watching over in his Seed Bed. Ghen found the newly-turned earth easily enough. He set down the lantern and the half-full bottle of Greynal next to the spot where Hend lay, and started digging.

It was more work to dig down to a Seed Bed than to fill one in, he soon realised, and he thought there was some meaning in that, because he was undoing that which should not be undone: digging up crops that weren't ready to be harvested. Betraying the land, because Hend was down there, with all his Tillers, to look after the land, wasn't he?

And here was Ghen, below the surface now, his hands blistered and slippery with blood on the shovel's handle, cold and hot at the same time from the sweat pouring down his back and finding the chill of the early morning air.

Here was Ghen, his shovel striking something firm, something yielding when he jabbed the shovel's blade in deeper.

Here was Ghen, clearing the last of the earth from the Tillers with his hands, feeling and not feeling the sting of the dirt in his wounds. His blood in Hend's land. Wyne's blood was here too. Hend had killed him. Ghen couldn't kill Hend, because he was already dead. Here was his heavy, lumpen form, tilted against the Seed Bed wall. No, Ghen couldn't kill a dead man.

But he could kill a dead man's land, and that was the same thing, really.

He climbed back out, using Hend as his ladder, and retrieved the Greynal, then poured it over the newly exposed Tillers – all of them. All his and Wyne's hard work.

Wyne. Ghen sobbed. For himself as well.

He struck a flame from the shovel's blade and set the order lists alight. He dropped them into the open Seed Bed. The Greynal-soaked Tillers were soon burning. He watched the flames, watched them take the cloth that Hend was wrapped in. He stayed by the Seed Bed until the smoke grew too bad. It was light by then, but only just. There would still be time. He turned and looked at the farm. The wooden barns. The fields of wheat.

He struck another flame.

Nineteen

'I don't want to know,' Cora said, without looking up from her desk.

Jenkins pulled a chair closer and perched on the edge of it. 'But these numbers for the Lowlanders. You wouldn't believe—'

'I *said* I don't want to know.'

'Your loss, Detective. Quite literally, I'd say.'

The pen stilled in Cora's hand. 'Even without a happy ending?'

'It's looking to be an election of tragedies so far.'

'And it started with Nicholas Ento. But we might be getting somewhere, at last.'

Leaving out her trip through Beulah's place, Cora told Jenkins about the old Commission coaches at Tithe Hall. About the one that was missing.

'And you think that's where Ento was killed,' Jenkins said, 'inside the missing coach?'

'If we can find that, we can find who killed him.'

'Any idea where to start?'

'Do you think you'd still be sitting here, Constable, telling me about chequer odds, if I did?' Cora stood and reached for a coat that was no longer there. 'We have to find the coach, to find out who killed him.'

Jenkins, too, got to her feet. 'Where are we going?'

'*I'm* going outside.' *For a smoke*, she almost added. 'I need to clear my head.'

And before the young woman could utter another word, Cora headed for the door.

She'd reached the bottom of the station steps before she heard her name. For a moment she considered not turning around, pretending she hadn't heard, and walking quickly away from whatever trouble was behind her. But then she felt a soft touch on her arm.

'I was hoping you'd finish about now.'

It was Finnuc. He led her to a bench where he'd left a couple of pennysheets and a half-eaten pastry.

'You been waiting for me?' she said.

'No, I just...'

'Should you even be out on the street?'

'What?' he said. 'Oh, *that*. No one's throwing things at Caskers anymore. The Seeder story gave people something else to think about.'

'Your cut is looking better,' she said, touching the side of his face.

'You said it wouldn't make me any prettier.'

'That sounds like something I'd say.'

'Did you see the Seeder Hook?' he said.

'The mostins? No.'

'Would you like to?'

'Now?' she said, glancing at the darkening sky.

'Or not, if you have plans.'

Plans. She had plenty of those but they all involved finding a killer. She didn't make plans for the smaller things: what she was going to eat, where she was going to sleep, what she might do with an evening.

Finnuc appeared to take her silence for reluctance. 'It's not the same as seeing them before the story,' he said, 'but it would be just us. No crowds.'

'I'm not breaking into the Hook barge, Finnuc.'

He feigned hurt. 'Is that what you think of me? I know one of the crew that swaps over the Hooks, that's all. Says it's worth seeing again.'

'Are they in jars?' Cora said.

'What? Looking for more jars of dirt to keep on your desk?'

'The mostins. In jars, like they were in the story.'

'I don't know, I didn't hear it. You were there, at Tithe Hall?'

She nodded.

'Would you have voted black or white?'

'Black,' she said, quick enough to surprise them both.

'Really? Why?'

'It was... moving, I thought. Who hasn't had some kind of family tragedy?'

An awkward moment passed between them.

'Didn't know hearing election stories was a perk of the job,' he said, and wolfed the last of the pastry.

'It *is* the job these days.'

'Because of the storyteller? The Wayward? So *you're* the one working that case. How—'

She waved away his words. 'That's the last thing I want to talk about.'

'Mostins then? I'll get us a gig.'

'No!' Cora said, grabbing him before she could stop herself. 'No gigs, no coaches. I'd rather walk.'

He gathered his pennysheets and fell in beside her.

As they walked through the square, then down the winding streets of Fenest, he asked about her day, about the doings of Bernswick station. There wasn't much to say as she refused to talk about Ento, but he sympathised when it came to paperwork – he was a Commission employee, after all. They crossed Puscun Road, passing inns and Seats, whorehouses and bakeries, all alive with chatter and the ever-present cries of the pennysheet sellers. Turning off Puscun in favour of quieter streets with less traffic, she led the way to the River Stave. Lamps were being lit in windows, on the street, and on coach-fronts. A city trying to light up the dark. She hoped one day it would be better at it.

They stopped at a crossroads and waited for a coach to go by. She stared at it, at the driver, at its lit lamp.

'Everything all right?' Finnuc said.

She had clenched her fists without even realising. She needed to stop thinking about work. She needed a distraction, and he was right there.

'Tell me another story,' she said.

'Haven't you had enough of them lately?'

'Not yours.'

When they reached the other side of the road, he began.

'I was an orphan, abandoned in the outer-most reaches of West Perlanse,' he said. She didn't stop him, didn't mention his last story of growing up on a Seeder farm, just listened as they walked.

He was taken in by a Wayward storyteller, a middle-aged woman, who wandered the more remote parts of Perlanse. She told stories for money, which had been, and still was, illegal there – odd people that the Perlish were. She plied her trade mostly in draughty barns and poorly-lit huts, but sometimes villagers wanted to listen in their own homes. These were usually the wealthier members of the communities. When this happened, it was Finnuc's job to supplement his and the Wayward's income.

He was well-schooled in this role. He knew which items of jewellery – men's and women's – might be mistaken for lost rather than stolen. He could recognise a rare map scroll among shelves of the everyday kind. And, most importantly, he knew the timings of all the bangs and crashes and booms that peppered the storyteller's tales; these weren't election stories with their strict rules against such things. So, young Finnuc knew exactly when to risk moving furniture or to stretch for the top shelf or, as would often be the case, when to sneeze. They were dusty places his nimble little hands probed.

But all good things must end. Finnuc's young arrogance was infectious and eventually wore out the Wayward woman's natural caution. They ventured too far south, to places with too many people who lived in too big houses. One such night, when the woman began a particularly bawdy tale of big-breasted, accident-prone Seeders, Finnuc crept through the huge house. He had already opened three bedroom doors to no ill-effect, finding some choice items, so when presented with a fourth door he didn't hesitate.

Neither did the dog.

Easily as big as a small pony, it was all Finnuc could do to keep it from ripping out his throat. No amount of aped Seeder grunting and bottom-slapping on the part of the Wayward could cover the dog's barking. When they found Finnuc he was backed into a corner, atop a bed, a ravaged pillow between his hands and his pockets full of silver.

They couldn't do a thing to the storyteller without admitting their illegal audience – these weren't clever or cunning people – but Finnuc was fair game. He had since forgiven the Wayward teller, but as they dragged him off he cursed her to the Widow and the Poet and any who would listen. As he all but rotted in a Perlish dungeon he vowed to the Weaver revenge on all storytellers, and all dogs.

Years later, when a Commission employee by the name of Tennworth found him, he was little more than rags and ribs and that revenge. So twisted had he become, he could only bark. Scrabbling around his cell on all fours he had become what he most hated. Whether it was pity or curiosity or the perceived challenge, he was brought out of that empty-seated underworld. He was fed, helped to grow strong, helped to reconnect with his Casker heritage, and learned to talk all over again.

'And I've been working for the Commission ever since,' he said.

'If it were up to me, you'd be back in that Perlish dungeon,' she said, smiling.

'The story wasn't *that* bad.'

'No,' she said, 'they're getting better.'

'Still don't much like dogs,' he muttered.

'Not even Caskanese water-dogs?'

'That's not funny.'

No, after all that had happened following the Casker story, it probably wasn't. She almost told him about the dog living in the old Commission coaches in Tithe Hall, about it jumping out on her, to lighten the mood. But then she realised that wasn't funny either, almost getting her throat ripped out, and the silence between the two of them was an easy one. Something worth enjoying.

They came to the river bank and walked a little way along it, the only people there. The Hook barge was dark and silent except for the lapping of the River Stave against its side. The buildings opposite were shuttered, their chairs and parasols packed away. The only evidence that this was, and would be many times again, one of the busiest places in the city was the scattering of crumpled food papers and pennysheets.

Finnuc's friend was waiting on the gangway – another burly Casker from the looks of him. And from the bored way he was leaning on the rail, he'd been there some time.

'Didn't think you were coming,' the man said.

'We decided to walk.'

The man raised an eyebrow at that.

Finnuc pressed a few coins into his hand. 'Are they still in there?'

'You'll see for yourself. Or not,' the man said, taking two damp strips of cloth from the railing.

'What are those for?' Cora said.

'Some react to the fint – sets their eyes watering,' he said, giving them each a cloth. 'If it gets bad, going blind as the Devotee helps.'

'Not much use coming if we can't see when we're inside,' she said.

'Then I hope you can handle it better than me.' He nodded to Finnuc and left them there.

Finnuc turned the cloth over in his hands. 'What's fint?'

'Oh, come on,' she said, dragging him towards the big doorway of the barge. Since she'd been there last, for the Casker Hook, the Seeders had hung mesh curtains and nets everywhere. Cora had to step through them to properly get inside.

'What's that smell?' Finnuc said, pushing the last curtain aside.

She opened her mouth to answer, but the words wouldn't come.

In front of them was an unnaturally still scene. Across the floor were husks of dead mostins. Broken wings, sharp-looking legs, twisted antennae in their hundreds. Branches hung from the ceiling but they were drooping and tired, their blossom turned to rot and ruin. All colour was gone, and the only light in the room came from a mournful moon breaking through the mesh at the windows.

All the mostins, dead.

As Cora stepped further inside there was a crunching sound. Grimacing, she lifted a foot to see half a wing stuck to her boot sole.

'Cora... I didn't know,' Finnuc said. He sneezed and rubbed at his eyes.

'Put on the blindfold,' she said.

He did as he was told. 'This is nothing like I'd heard it would be.'

'They don't last,' Cora said. 'Nothing does.' She felt compelled to see the full extent of it but took care where she trod. Finnuc's blindfold meant he crushed corpse and wing alike with a rhythm that sounded like a kind of monstrous chewing. 'Stay there,' she said.

Some parts of the room were worse than others, as if the mostins had come together in their final hours. These strange, beautiful creatures had died for Fenest's amusement, for a spectacle, for a Hook. It would please the Widow, and perhaps the Brawler – but what of the others? And what did *she* make of their sacrifice? Ento wasn't the only one to suffer at the hands of the election. Cora could almost hear Ruth, on that last night, telling her what was wrong with the Commission, the city, the whole Union. Seeing this, Cora might, for a moment, agree with her.

'Put up your blindfold if it's getting to you,' Finnuc called. 'It does help a little.'

She felt a kind of itchiness all over, but it wasn't the fint. All the death, all the suffering – she needed to believe there was something else.

'Everyone said they were beautiful, before the story,' he said.

She ducked between the fint-covered branches.

'I thought you'd like them. My friend, he told me they'd land on your hand.'

She walked quickly towards him, not caring anymore what she stepped on.

'And it wouldn't hurt, he said. Just prickled a bit.'

She kissed him, felt his shock in his lips, along his big arms, down through his waist as she pulled him closer.

He stumbled back, reaching for his blindfold.

'No, leave it,' she said.

She led him towards a wall. He kissed her, pushing her back against the wooden boards. A puff of fint surrounded them. Tearing open his shirt, she kissed his chest again and again until she bit him.

He took hold of her, against the wall, and eased into her. She groaned and pushed back. She felt his thighs beneath her, strong and solid, and she wrapped herself around him. Her eyes started to stream and sting from the fint, so she closed them. He moved deeper into her and she raked at his huge back, his skin beneath her nails, wanting him to feel the hurt as well as the good. She bit his ear through the blindfold. But even that wasn't enough. She forced herself harder and faster on him.

And then he shivered and she felt the end of it. He held her there, both panting and covered in fint, with streaks down their faces. She started to laugh. He lifted his blindfold and blinked until he could see her.

'That was different,' he said.

She eased away from him and fastened her trousers. 'You won't get used to it.'

Twenty

The Seat of the Pale Widow wasn't the closest Seat to the Hook barge, but the walk did Cora some good, putting a bit of distance between her and Finnuc. She couldn't think about him, about what they'd just done, not yet. There were too many other things going on.

The Widow's doors were bare apart from a single design: a sickle moon, hanging low, close to the hummocky line that was the earth. A moon for winter. A moon that marked the beginning of a new phase, after an ending.

Cora made her way down to the carved figure of the Widow at the far end of the Seat, passing one or two other people murmuring their own stories, eyes closed, attention fixed on their tales. She sat on a bench and tilted her head back to take in the full figure of the Widow. She was huge here – at least three times Cora's height – and carved of an appropriately pale stone. Cora had come to tell the Widow about the coach, about the cord, about Ento – a story in need of an ending. But instead she was thinking of a tale that was over long, long ago. It was all because of the Seeder story, and the boy Ghen who left his family. He hadn't had a choice, but Ruth had, and she'd chosen to go. Did she ever regret what she'd done?

'Ruth was always making trouble,' Cora told the Widow. 'Soon as she could talk she was telling everyone that they were wrong. I got a lot of it at home, but it was worse at the Seminary. She would argue with the teachers about anything. Even you.

'For some classes the whole Seminary came to the main hall. In one of those classes, Madam Vendler told us that people who live on the Northern Steppes are known for their devotion to you. That they visit your Seat three times a day, and in telling you their stories they find a kind of peace. But Ruth, sitting two rows back from me, she couldn't let that pass without comment. She stood up and asked just who Madam Vendler was talking about – the nomadic Wayward, or the poor Union prisoners unjustly sent to the Steppes, sent there to live and die in camps.

'Everyone turned to look at Ruth when she said that. I wanted a second Tear to open in the floor and swallow me. Why did Ruth always have to do that, make things difficult? And she didn't stop there. She went on and on about the way the prisoners were kept, how few of them had any way to return once they'd served their time. What finally got Ruth sent out was the question she asked not just of Madam Vendler, but of the whole Seminary. She stood there, in the main hall, and said, "How can this be a just system of government?"

'I couldn't have been more than twelve, which meant Ruth was seventeen. A bad age. Old enough for dissatisfaction but still too young to know what to do with it.

'I had no answer to her question, of course. No one did. I just wanted to go home and pretend I didn't have an older sister. Selfish, difficult, unreasonable. Those were the words our parents used to describe Ruth and, right then, when Madam Vendler looked as if her heart might stop with rage, I agreed with them.'

How did that particular day end? Sitting in the Seat of the Pale Widow, Cora couldn't remember. It was only a little while later that Ruth stole the papers from their parents' study and then disappeared. That event loomed so large in Cora's memory that it eclipsed much else from that time.

'Nothing was ever the same again,' Cora said. 'The papers Ruth took made it clear our parents had been misusing funds in the Commission trading hall where they worked. Embezzlement, that was the word people used. "Thieving" was the better one.

'For years my parents had been at it. Where the money had gone, no one was sure. Some pennysheets claimed it was used to prop up farms in the Lowlands hit by blight. Others said it was chequer debts, or bribing Perlish tax inspectors to leave wagons unchecked. Nothing was ever proved, apart from the theft itself, but that was enough.

'My father didn't last a week after the story became public. My mother claimed his heart gave out from the stress, but it was more likely helped along by the tincture he bought in Murbick. I found the bottle under his bed, weeks after. The Coward's Cordial, the 'sheets called it. I called it Ruth's Revenge.

'My mother tried to find Ruth, but not because she wanted her daughter back, and not because she feared for Ruth's safety. She wanted to limit the damage Ruth could do, because she wasn't sure what else Ruth knew.

'I remember a man coming to the house. It was after dark, and he used the back door. He and my mother sat in the parlour and talked in low voices. I didn't know who he was but he smelled of horses, and of the night, somehow. Later, much later, I learned he was a searcher. My mother had paid him to find Ruth, but he never did. The only lead they ever had was that she'd been seen going north in a Wayward caravan to the Steppes.' Cora laughed at this memory – it was still so foolish, please the Drunkard. 'If my mother had listened to Ruth at all during that time, *really* listened to her, she would have known that Ruth would never go to the Steppes. Not by choice. Ruth argued for the rights of prisoners, for shutting down the camps, but she would never have gone to the Steppes to help them. Everything was a cause for her back then. I would have told my mother that.

'But no one was listening then. Least of all to me.'

Cora closed her eyes, the gaze of the Widow too much to bear in that moment. When she opened them again, she kept her own gaze on her boots.

'Some in Fenest wondered if my mother should have been sent to the Steppes herself. But of course it never came to that, which only proved Ruth right. This whole place *is* rotten to the core.'

Cora stood, and felt the twinge in her foot. She deliberately put her weight on it, pushed down so the pain worsened. Her vision frayed at the edges. The Widow seemed to grow taller.

'Much good knowing that did any of us, in the end.'

She limped out of the Seat, back into the spring sunlight, and back to a case that lacked its own ending.

Twenty-One

'You wanted to see me, Chief?' Cora said, walking between the stone examining tables.

Chief Inspector Sillian was standing at the far end of the cold room, in full uniform and looking immaculate. She stared down at one of the empty tables. Though they were all bare it wasn't hard to guess why she'd summoned Cora down here.

'Strangled, according to your report,' Sillian said.

The slabs of stone were clean and had been recently polished by the looks of it. Cora so rarely saw them that way; it was the bodies she came to see. Somehow this was worse.

'With something thin, like a cord, your report says.'

'Pruett thought so.' Cora looked about the room, but the examiner and his assistant were nowhere to be seen. That didn't seem like a coincidence.

'Where is it, Detective?'

'Where's wha—'

Sillian held up a hand, cutting her question short.

'Behind Tithe Hall,' Cora said.

'Excuse me?'

'I don't have the murder weapon, but I'm confident it was a curtain cord of an old Commission coach. The kind they leave to rot behind Tithe Hall.'

'I see. I suppose that is progress, of a sort. But who put that cord around the storyteller's neck?' Sillian said.

Cora didn't answer, didn't think she had to: it was obvious she hadn't found who had killed the Wayward yet. But as the silence stretched between them, she realised Sillian was going to make her say it.

'I don't know,' she said.

'You don't know. Perhaps it would be useful to tell you something that *I* know.' Sillian finally turned to face her. 'With every day that passes we come closer to the Wayward story. Every day we *haven't* arrested the murderer we come closer to the Wayward Chambers razing the entire Bernswick division to the ground. And if it comes to that, Detective, I will do everything in my power to make sure *you* are inside Bernswick when they do.'

'Chief, I—'

'You have made a start,' Sillian said. 'But time is running out, Detective. Bring me the ending.'

Cora was dismissed. She spared one last glance at empty stone slabs and then left, her boots loud on the flagstone floor.

This story was a bigger disaster than that of the Caskers, and a more personal tragedy than the Seeders'. She was getting somewhere, it was starting to make sense, but time had always been against her. She wanted to break something, but there was nothing to hand, nothing nearby, only the two most permanent things under the Audience: stone and death.

'You've been staring at that most of the morning,' Hearst said.

'That's not tr—' Cora caught sight of a pair of constables behind him, going into the briefing room with plates of lunch in hand, and realised the sergeant was right. She had been staring at the jar of dirt for more hours than she cared to admit, but her mind had been roaming. Back to the alleyway where Ento was found. Back to the Hook barge. Thinking about a different kind of dirt there. One that made her eyes sting and her body itch. Made her impulsive.

'Gorderheim?'

'Sir?'

Hearst stepped forward, into her office proper. 'I said, what's the progress? On the Wayward murder. Remember that? The case you're meant to be solving?'

''Sheets aren't likely to let me forget it.'

'And neither is Sillian. What have you got that I can give her?'

'You ever done something sooner than you'd wanted to, Sergeant? Too soon, and then it was ruined?'

'I'm not sure I understand.'

'Neither do I.' She opened a drawer of her desk and went to drop the jar in it.

'Nor do I understand why you're treasuring bird droppings,' Hearst said.

Cora's hand froze. 'I don't...'

'Why, in the name of the Audience, have you got that?' He gestured for her to pass him the jar.

'I found it in the alleyway next to Ento,' Cora said. 'Bird shit?'

Hearst held the jar up to the light. 'Far as I can tell.' He unscrewed it, sniffed it and grimaced, then quickly put the lid back on. 'Definitely. Dried, old droppings.'

It was so obvious now. So obvious that no one had said anything, not Jenkins nor Pruett or anyone – that, or they hadn't realised either. She'd been carrying around evidence of one thing only: birds defecated. And they did it on the walls of alleyways sometimes.

'Don't often see it with the red like this, though,' Hearst said, handing it back to her. 'Not in this part of the city, anyway.'

'Blood, I thought. Ento's.'

'I doubt that very much.'

'Oh?' Cora said.

'You might not see it up on the roof, with my lot, but I've seen this before. That bird,' he pointed at the jar, 'was poisoned.'

'But who poisons a bird?' she said.

Hearst gave a grim laugh. 'We all do, Gorderheim. It's across the city. But if I liked a wager, like you, I'd put my marks on tornstone.'

There were more than a few marks riding on this case – had been, right from the start. 'Tornstone,' she said.

'Could be any kind of heated stone or metal work, mind, but that's where I'd start.'

'Anywhere in particular?'

'There's a place in Tonbury,' Hearst said. 'Had a few run-ins with the owner, years back now. But she might be amenable to some gentle questioning, just to keep on the right side of things. You know the sort.'

'Only too well.' Cora stood and shoved her chair under her desk.

While Hearst scribbled down the address, Cora yelled for Jenkins.

'When you get there, you'll see it,' Hearst said, handing Cora the note. 'The birds will be painting the walls red for you, Widow help 'em.'

'Blood and shit, and Fenest blending the two.' Cora paused in the doorway and turned back to Hearst. 'That's what you can give Sillian by way of a report: blood and shit.'

Hearst had told Cora to start in Tonbury. She didn't know it – didn't know where the rings were, didn't know the whorehouses from the boarding, or in which alleys trouble waited. Jenkins, likewise, was unfamiliar with their destination. And disgusted too, by the change in the city that met them as they crossed into Tonbury. The hacking and spluttering of those on the pavements drowned out even the carts and gigs that rolled past them. Plumes of smoke rose above the crooked roofs and straining gables.

'So this is where clouds are made,' Cora muttered. Her breath felt hot in her chest.

Jenkins was coughing, but managed to say, 'That people *live* in these conditions.'

'I doubt they have much choice,' Cora said, looking at the cracked window panes and sheet-roofs.

'Detective – over there.' Jenkins pointed to a warehouse door as they passed.

White dirt, flecked with red, all over the wood. Hearst was right.

'It's everywhere,' Jenkins said, twisting in the gig. 'Front doors, street lamps, roofs.'

'And coaches?' Cora took a deep breath and felt her lungs burn. It was like she was smoking a whole tin of bindleleaf at once. 'The dirt was on the wall of the alley where Ento was found, at just the right height for a door opening and catching on the stone.'

'The door of a coach too wide for such a new, narrow street,' Jenkins said.

'An old coach, taken out of service. It could well have set off from this part of the city to collect Ento on the night he died. And it could have returned here too, once the deed was done. If we can find the coach, we can find the driver.'

Jenkins could only nod, her eyes streaming.

Their driver set them down in the street behind the one Hearst had suggested and said he wouldn't go any closer, 'What with the fumes.' Cora paid the man and didn't bother arguing. What more could you expect with Garnuck's? And they were close enough. The worsening air confirmed it.

Cora headed down the street, Jenkins just behind her. Her eyes started to sting – worse than from mostin fint – so she almost missed the shop Hearst had told her about. At the door she told Jenkins to wait outside.

'Let's see how we get on before we wave a uniform in front of anyone. I'll call you if I need you.'

Jenkins nodded once more. If she could talk in the foul air, she seemed to decide it wasn't worth the effort. Cora wondered about leaving the constable on the street, until she got inside and found it to be worse.

The heat hit her first, then a strange smell, as if the air was honey and someone was doing their best to burn the lot of it. It wasn't much of a shop at all. There was a sad set of shelves, mostly bare, and a counter with a few glass bowls and vases but really it was a workshop. A woman waved for Cora to wait. She pulled a poker from a furnace, bringing a piece of the sun with it. She turned it this way and that and then put it back, thank the Audience.

The glassblower was sweaty and dirt-streaked in her heavy leather apron, and she had a look about her that made it clear she suffered no fools.

She took Cora in, and said, 'You lost?'

'Could say that.'

'Well, you are or you aren't. Which is it to be?'

'That depends,' Cora said. 'I'm looking for somewhere that works with tornstone.'

'That so?'

'It is.'

The woman licked her lips, then glanced at the door where Jenkins' shadow was just visible: a darker cloud in a storm of them.

'I might know a place like that, I might not. Would you know the right word—'

This was getting her nowhere – Cora needed answers, not questions. She pulled out her badge.

'Hey, now,' the woman said, 'I didn't know nothing about it.'

'Constable,' Cora called.

Jenkins slipped inside and had the sense to stand against the door. Her height, and her barring the way out, were enough to set the glassblower talking.

'Thought they was using it safe, like they're meant to. I only bought a few ounces at a time, for the fancier pieces, taxes paid and all.'

Cora had no idea what she was talking about but had played enough hands to know when a bluff was called for. 'We just want to speak to some of the customers.'

'What's the Commission going to do, close us all down because White Rock couldn't keep the bad air inside? How's that fair?'

'Fairness? Now that's a more difficult one. Above our station in life, wouldn't you say, Constable?'

'I would, Ma'am,' Jenkins said.

'But what *is* more our station is your supply of tornstone.'

'It's not people like me you ought to be bothering,' the woman said.

'Oh? And who *should* we be bothering?'

The glassblower's eyes narrowed. 'Them at White Rock. They got coaches coming and going all hours.'

'Coaches?' Cora said. But the woman was in her stride.

'Who knows what they're up to? It'll be some Perlish doing – you mark my words. That's where you should be, Detective.'

'That's for me to worry about, but you—'

'Making a racket when decent people are trying to sleep. I got to get up in the morning – I got orders!'

'Speaking of which,' Cora said loudly, to stop the woman's noise. 'I'll need to see your supply.'

The woman hesitated, then turned and led Cora past the furnace into a small stockroom. Chests and straw were scattered everywhere. The glassblower used a ladder to reach the highest shelf, which held an assortment of metal pails. From behind these she produced a small box. She eyed Cora warily as she stepped down, but handed her the box.

It was heavy. Cora brushed the dust from the lid, revealing the inked words *White Rock of Fenest*. Inside were pouches of dark powder.

Tornstone. The same that burned as lumps in the glass boxes strapped to the faces of the Torn, and the fiery pebbles the Tear itself sent high into the air, only to rain down on the people of that place and burn them. It was burning Fenestirans too – its people and its birds – but from the inside.

'I got it from White Rock once a year,' the woman said. 'Sometimes not even that.'

'To do what?'

'Just a little cut-glass work. For the Perlish.'

Cora snapped the lid shut.

'Are you going to take it?' the woman said.

'That depends.'

'On what?

'Miss Harriet?' A small boy was behind her. He clutched a broom and looked exhausted, but that might have just been the dirt.

'Not now, Louis!'

'I dun out back.'

Cora glanced at the glassblower. 'I'd say he's finished for the day, wouldn't you, *Miss Harriet*.'

'Early tomorrow, Louis,' the woman said with a grimace. 'Deliveries as usual.'

The boy bobbed his head and then ran for the front door. On seeing Jenkins he faltered, but the constable smoothly moved aside for him and he was away, no doubt worried Miss Harriet might change her mind. Jenkins resumed her post.

'I don't make him do nothing dangerous,' Miss Harriet said, 'not like they did at White Rock.'

'He looked healthy enough to me,' Cora said carefully, making sure the woman caught her meaning that the boy should stay that way. She handed her the box. 'I can't see this being much use to me, if you tell me how to find White Rock.'

Back on the street, turning corners as they'd been directed, Cora saw more and more of the red-flecked bird droppings. They'd started as sporadic embers on the soot-covered walls and roofs, but the closer they came to White Rock the more that fire came to life. She saw a few of the birds themselves, many of them pigeons, like those Hearst fed at the station, but these were gaunt, skittish.

'They look uncomfortable in themselves,' Jenkins said.

'Much like the people of Tonbury,' Cora said. 'This must be White Rock.'

They had come to a huge set of gates – locked. The pigeons seemed to coo disapproval as Jenkins read the Commission closure notice fastened there.

'*Unsuitable and unsavoury practices.* No wonder tradesfolk are worried about getting caught with tornstone.'

'But since when has the Commission worried about anything unsavoury, especially when there's money to be made?' Cora said. She tried the padlock but it was sturdy and shiny-new; none of this felt right, none of it was the Commission she knew. 'They don't close businesses and they certainly don't *spend* money doing it.'

There was something here that the Commission didn't want people to see. Cora checked both ends of the street: empty.

'How are your climbing skills, Constable?' she asked, making sure her shirt was tucked into her belt. Best not to risk anything that could snag.

Jenkins' gaze drifted to the row of spikes on top of the gates. 'Is this wise, Detective?'

'Coaches, Jenkins. We're looking for one that likely set off from this part of the city. That woman who nearly turned our lungs to steaming lumps of stone says she's seen coaches here. I'd say we don't have much of a choice.' Cora wedged her foot between two bars and used the central beam to bear her weight, feeling the old twinge in her tendon, and thinking of Ruth as she always did when the pain came. But the gate seemed strong enough. They'd soon find out.

It wasn't easy, or graceful, but she managed not to impale herself on the top and landed on the other side without breaking any bones. Jenkins, looking reluctant, scaled the gates with ease.

'I think you've done this before,' Cora said. 'Misspent youth while your mother ran Electoral Affairs?' She was pleased to see the constable look shame-faced. 'Come on. Let's see what the Commission decided to lock up.'

A wide drive led away from the gates and curved around the side of a tall brick building, the front of which was hidden from the street. Cora and Jenkins followed the drive to a courtyard full of conveyances.

'Just carts,' Jenkins said. 'Not a place for coaches, it seems.'

'Silence take them,' Cora said.

White Rock was a large, U-shaped building. Surrounding the carts were hitching posts, barrels stacked and not, and many more things Cora didn't recognise. Strange vats that could have been for storage, except they appeared to have their own chimneys – as if there weren't enough chimneys on the building itself; she counted sixteen before giving up.

Jenkins checked the covered lean-tos that clung to the brick walls of the main building. 'Nothing here,' she called over.

And there was nothing in any of the carts either, or in the barrels. A sack had caught between the wheels of a cart. Cora fished it out and felt the weight of something in a bottom corner. She reached in and her hand met a hard and gritty lump. Even before she pulled it out, she knew what it was.

Tornstone was only dangerous when it was heated. Cooled like this, it looked harmless enough. She dropped the tornstone back into the sack and dumped both on the ground.

She joined Jenkins by what looked like the main doors – a tall pair, wide enough for the carts to enter, likely for loading and such.

'Thoughts, Constable?'

Jenkins turned a full circle of the courtyard. 'It's not been stripped bare, not exactly. Whoever worked here, they've been moved on to somewhere else.'

'With all this left behind? And who knows what else inside.' Cora tried the doors but they seemed to be barred on the inside and would only thud against the frame. 'No climbing over th—'

A noise. Something falling with a thud and then a clatter.

There was someone inside White Rock.

Twenty-Two

'It came from this way!' Jenkins was running around the side of the building, away from the drive and the gate they had climbed.

Cora followed, but in the poor air she was slow. All those years of smoking bindleleaf.

She rounded a corner to see Jenkins' uniformed legs disappearing into a broken window. A crate was just below it; a regular access way then, for whoever was using White Rock now. As much a trespasser as she and Jenkins.

The constable was now lost from sight but Cora could hear her shouting at someone to wait. Cora jogged to the window and peered inside. Though the light was weak she could make out still, dark shapes – furnaces and foundry-type workings, she guessed. They were silent, like beasts in slumber. And Jenkins, on her hands and knees beside one, scrabbling under it.

'Audience-sake, stop kicking me!' the constable shouted at the furnace. 'I'm only trying to help.'

But then she was struggling to stand because she was gripping the shirt of one filthy, flailing creature.

Jenkins dragged the child out from under the furnace.

'Get off me! Get off!' the boy shouted. His hair was matted, his face dark with dust and who knew what else.

'Where did the others go?' Jenkins said.

'Others?' Cora said.

'There were a few of them – I couldn't see properly. Think they got out through the back. This one didn't move so fast.'

Cora thought about heaving herself through the broken window but decided against it. She told Jenkins to unbar the main doors, and a few minutes later Cora was inside, face to face with the boy while Jenkins clung to his thrashing form. He was dressed, but only just – rags hung from his limbs. He seemed older than Marcus, the pennysheet girl, around thirteen, but thinner.

'What's your name?' Cora said.

'Silence take you!' the boy spat.

Jenkins looked appalled and gave the child a shake. 'What sort of way is that to talk to someone who wants to help you?'

'You don't want to help me. You just gonna make me move on, like everyone else in this city.'

'This city?' Cora said. 'You're not from Fenest?'

'So everyone says. "Go home," they says. Like I can go back.'

'Back where?' Cora said.

'Sweetpool.'

'That's a Seeder town.'

'*Lowlander*,' the boy said, with some pride. Jenkins flashed her a grin.

'All right, a *Lowlander* town, and in the far south at that, isn't it?'

'Near Bordair,' Jenkins said.

Another southerner who'd left his home and come north. It was hard to see through the dirt if the boy had any black marks on his hands or feet, but if he did it was probably too late to worry. Jenkins had touched him. Cora had breathed beside him.

'Family?' Cora asked the boy.

He looked at the floor.

'So what are you doing here?' Cora said.

'Eating. Looking for work. You got anything I can do?'

'That depends. First you tell me your name.'

The boy chewed his lip and thought about it. 'Tam.'

'Right, Tam, next you're going to tell me and nice Constable Jenkins here what you and your friends have seen in this place. What's been going on here?'

The boy looked confused. 'Nothing. That's why we sleep here. They left enough wood in the burners that we been warm.'

'They?'

'It was empty when we first broke the window.'

'You've not seen anyone here since then?'

'Not 'til you two came,' Tam said.

So, White Rock had turned out to be a dead end.

'Well, you can't stay here,' Cora said, and the boy's eyes widened. 'I know someone who'll give you a bed in exchange for some labour. Not the seed-sewing kind though. Beulah's more in the... entertainment line.'

Now it was Jenkins' turn to stare at Cora.

'Don't worry, Constable. There are plenty of jobs Beulah needs help with.'

Before the boy could protest, or even worse, thank her, Cora was on her way back outside. But something by the door made her stop. A crate, and on it a word, burned into the wood.

Tennworth.

She knew that word, but from where? The Seeder story, perhaps? She scratched at her nose, as if removing the itch there would do the same for that tickling memory. No, not the Seeder story. Some other tale.

There were more crates nearby, all with the same word on them. Casks too.

Tennworth.

'Do either of you know what this means?' she asked Jenkins and the boy, pointing to the nearest crate.

'I've seen it,' the boy said. 'When we go over the back wall, we're in the yard.'

'What yard?' Cora said.

'I think a better question might be *whose* yard,' Jenkins said. 'Looks to me like a name.'

Cora turned to Tam. 'This yard, can you get there from the street?'

'Guess so,' he said. 'I never went that way. Go right from the gates, maybe.'

They left the building and returned to the daylight, and it was then Cora noticed that Tam was wincing. There was a rip in his shabby trousers, the stark red of fresh blood beneath.

'Do they still make constables do basic stitching?' she asked Jenkins.

The constable sighed. She reached for the small pack that, by Commission regulations, was attached to her belt at all times. 'I'll see what I can do.'

'Good. Then wait for me here. I won't be long.'

'Where are you going, Detective?'

'To test my memory.'

She left the way they'd entered, climbing back over the gates. The glassblower had talked of coaches, and though there were none to be found at White Rock, they might not be far. Having come all the way to Tonbury and breathed this bad air, she might as well look around a bit more while Jenkins patched up the lad. And there was that name catching at her. *Tennworth.* She knew it, though she couldn't think why, and to see it here, in the part of the city where the dirt had come from – it couldn't be coincidence. Those were the stories the Audience liked least of all.

Back on the street, Cora turned right, as the boy Tam had suggested, and followed the perimeter wall to see how far White Rock went. It was certainly a big enough building, but she didn't see any more entrances. Eventually it became other businesses: a cobbler, a cooper, a winery. She glanced at the wooden signs and brass plaques as she passed. She stopped.

Tennworth's.

The winery was closed, not by Commission order, like White Rock, but because it was always closed that day of the week, so the sign said. There was a tasteful figure of the Patron beside the door, with none of the usual detritus found at street-side shrines. Despite being in Tonbury this was a respectable establishment, the merchant's word his bond, and the Patron was all ears for that. There really was a story for everyone. She peered through the window; a small shop, lined floor to ceiling with shelves of bottles. Something of the Perlish to it. She tried the door, just in case, but it was locked. Stepping back, she looked up at the dark windows of the upper floors.

It was then she noticed the carriageway.

It was open – no doors or gates – just a shadowy mouth leading, she guessed, to some kind of yard behind. She looked at the name plate again. *Tennworth. Tennworth.* Where did she know that name from? It was on the edge of her thoughts, just out of reach. Like the yard beyond the dark. A few steps more might make the difference.

She kept close to the wall, using it to steady herself as she picked her way over the broken and uneven cobbles. The remnants of yesterday's puddles pooled between them. She was about to call out when she heard a horse whicker from somewhere ahead, and stopped. She waited. No other sound came.

'Hello?' she called.

No answer. Cora looked back the way she'd come, back to the street, and asked herself what she was doing. *Tennworth*. It was pulling her on. She kept walking and when she emerged from the carriageway, out from the darkness and under the gaze of the Audience once more, she found an answer, waiting for her.

Wood, painted black, the door specked with the dirt she'd found next to Ento's body. A boxy shape – too wide for the city that had come after it. The front seat missing the lantern found on every other of the kind that had replaced it. Horses in their traces, ready to drive again.

She had found the old Commission coach.

Ento had been killed inside it. And his killer?

Someone was standing on the other side of the coach, the top half of their body hidden by the open door. She could only see their legs, clad in the purple livery of Commission uniform. Cora heard a voice murmuring inside the coach, then the door was slammed shut. The figure came into view on the other side of the horses, and then she knew why the name Tennworth was familiar. It was from the stories of the man now staring at her, a driving whip in his hands.

Finnuc.

Twenty-Three

'I never asked what it was you did for the Commission,' Cora said. Her voice sounded different somehow, distant but quicker, as if her thoughts were moving too fast for her mouth. 'You're a driver, then.'

He licked his lips. Those lips that had kissed her yesterday. That she had *let* kiss her.

'Among other things,' he said.

'Such as?'

'Nothing you'd want to hear about.'

'I think I might. Why don't you tell me why you're in possession of an outdated Commission coach? A coach I've been searching for. A coach where a man was killed. Nicholas Ento. I know you know that name. You asked me about him. Yesterday.' She swallowed. 'On the way to the Hook barge.'

'Cora...'

'The Wayward storyteller found in the alley behind Mrs Hawksley's. His mouth stitched up. Tell me what you know about *that*, Finnuc.'

He wouldn't look at her. His hands tightened on the whip. 'You won't understand.'

'Try me.'

'I had to… I owe her everything. *Everything.* Can you even understand what that's like? To be so much in one person's debt. A person who could crush you, as if you were nothing.'

He looked at her then, and she was taken aback by the despair written across his face. Finnuc was no longer the burly, bullish Casker she had come to know in the last few weeks, who had held her against the wall of the Hook barge. The man before her had wide eyes, trembling hands. But she made herself look past those things and thought of Ento. Of the black and white threads that ripped through his flesh. Of Nullan who had waited for him.

Another question came to her. A bad one. One she had to ask even as the words threatened to come out as bile.

'Is this why you… Why we… The Hook barge, all the rest of it. It was just to get close to me, to find out what I knew.'

He opened his mouth to speak but there was a noise, from inside the coach.

There was someone else there.

'Who—'

'I'm sorry, Cora. For all of it.'

He sprang forwards and made to swing himself into the driver's seat. Cora was only a second behind and caught him by the shirt. She yanked him off the step and they both fell to the cobbles. He was back on his feet first, but he'd dropped the whip.

Cora grabbed it and flung herself at Finnuc's back again. With a struggle, she got the end of the whip around his neck and pulled hard.

Finnuc spluttered a choke. He fought but soon enough she felt some of the strength go out of him. His hands fell away from the step up to the driver's seat. She kept pulling and they staggered backwards together, falling to the ground. She thought of Ento's throat, the purple ring left by the curtain cord. Finnuc would bear the same. But he would live.

They were wrestling on the cobbles, Finnuc's hands flailing as he fought for breath. Cora used her knee to push him face down. She pulled his wrists behind his back and tied them with the whip. His breath was ragged, his whole body shaking. Her hands too.

But it was over.

Then a noise, movement. The horses were pulling away, the coach lumbering behind them. Cora looked up. Someone was in the driver's seat.

She scrambled to her feet. 'Stop! Police!'

She grabbed the handle of the door and shouted again. The driver turned.

No – it couldn't be. It couldn't—

She fell from the coach, hitting the cobbles, tasting blood. She didn't move. Couldn't move. Could only watch as the coach clattered away, out of the carriageway and into the labyrinth of Fenest.

Ruth.

It was Ruth driving the coach.

Twenty-Four

'Why?' she said.

Finnuc didn't look up from the table. The lamp she'd brought into his cell flickered as a draught blew down the corridor, sending shadows across his face. For a heartbeat she couldn't see what she had done to him, could only see the shape of him. Then the flame strengthened and revealed the nasty purple mark around his neck. And there was a nasty irony in that too, given what Finnuc had done to Nicholas Ento. Widow welcome it.

'Why, Finnuc?' she asked again. She pulled her new coat tight. It was cold in the cell. And it smelled of piss – a kind of steam wafted from the pot next to his pallet. 'Was it because of the Wayward story?'

'Why else kill a storyteller?' he muttered.

'It wasn't just any old election story, though, was it?'

He shrugged.

She reached out and grabbed his hair, yanked it. He flinched, and she saw surprise in him as much as the pain. She would hurt him if she had to.

'Everyone said Ento's story was about change,' she said, and slowly pulled his hair so his head was forced back at an unhealthy angle. The purple mark around his neck stretched. 'The Wayward Chambers. Your own storyteller, Nullan. Even a Torn I met once. Great change, they said, and some don't want to hear it.'

'Guess not.'

She released him. 'I don't need guesses, Finnuc. There's no time for that. I need the Wayward story. And yours.'

He shrank back from her. 'Aren't you tired of the stories yet?' he said. 'Aren't you worn out by the endless drivel we tell each other, that we tell the Audience?'

Cora glanced into the corridor beyond the cell. Jenkins was at the far end. There if Cora needed her but sharp enough to realise her superior needed some privacy. That Cora had more than a professional interest in this man had surely been clear when Jenkins arrived in the carriageway, drawn by the shouting. Cora hadn't been able to say much that was useful then. The shock of seeing Ruth – *was* it Ruth? – left her all but jabbering. But now, the following day, Cora had found her tongue. And she had questions.

There was no sign of Hearst, not yet. He'd given her this last half an hour to get Finnuc to talk, and even that was hard-won. The sergeant was no doubt having to answer to Sillian for it. But this was the final chance. Finnuc had refused to co-operate since his arrest but Cora had to try. For the case. But for herself too. And maybe for him.

'You're lucky not to be hanged for what you did,' she said. 'Killing a storyteller. The pennysheets were calling for capital punishment to be reinstated.'

'That would have been something for the Audience – first public execution since the War of the Feathers.' He laughed, but he was relieved, she was certain of it. Relief was something she could work with.

'It's the Chambers you've got to thank for the reprieve,' she said. 'Word is, some of them wanted hanging to stay in the past. String one Casker up, who knows what that might lead to.'

'Nothing good,' he said. 'So I'll be sent to the Steppes then. Well, I've built a few walls and dug a few holes in my time.'

'Even if that doesn't kill you, when the Wayward who live there learn of your crime—'

'I'm not a fool, Cora. I know what's coming.'

'Then what have you got to lose by telling me?' She opened a bindleleaf tin and started rolling. The tin wasn't hers, may the Insolent Bore forgive her; she'd borrowed it from a constable on her way to the cells. 'Start with who Tennworth is.'

'You don't know?'

'No one does, apparently. Not even the people who work in the winery.' That particular mystery, and Finnuc's silence on it despite the punishment that awaited him on the Steppes, had *really* bothered Sergeant Hearst. It had also helped win Cora this last chance of getting an answer. The idea someone could both exist and yet be utterly unknown was... unsettling.

'I've already told you who Tennworth is,' Finnuc said. 'Many times. Or weren't you listening to my stories?'

'Tell me again.' She passed him a lit smoke.

He stared at the lamp's flame for so long she wondered if he was done, lost to her completely. But then he took a deep drag on the smoke and began.

'I was young when she changed everything, as I told you before. Just a child. My mother was a Casker, my father a Fenestiran. We lived here, in the city, and he ran a baker's shop. Nothing special, but his loaves were—'

'Where, Finnuc? Where was this bakery?'

He wasn't expecting interruptions. Everything was different now. How could it not be?

'South end of the city,' he said, 'not far from Tithe Hall actually. We weren't rich, but we managed. Until one day, when a bunch of your flatfoot constable friends turned up with an eviction notice, signed and wheel-stamped by the Commission. Said my father owed money to pretty much everyone who had it to lend. I remember his face, right at that moment, as he lifted his gaze from the notice and then looked at her. At my mother. See, he'd never borrowed a penny in his whole life. It was something he prided himself on, running a business debt-free.

'"Another man's money is like his wife – you can pretend they're yours, but they're always his," my father told me. Most days he told me. I would nod and say, "Yes, Father." As serious as any little boy could be. And all the while the Audience was laughing at him. He deserved it, really. He didn't run the business, *she* did. He was the one who could bake passable bread, but my mother could make passable sense of a column of numbers.

'Soon enough, shouting started. I heard some of it. Grain shipments had been mislaid. Order forms forged. Errors in the accounts ignored or disguised.'

Cora opened and closed the bindleleaf tin, as if checking for something. She wouldn't let him see her face. For all she knew, this detail of the story might be just for her. For her parents, and for Ruth. He carried on.

'Even imaginary employees on the payroll, Patron take her! All right under my father's nose. When they really got into the arguing, I was turfed out. But not before the worst of it.

'My mother, she'd been carrying on with another man. He—'

'Finnuc, I'm not the Audience. This doesn't have to be a good story, just a true one.'

'Do you want to know, or not?'

'Fine,' Cora said, glancing into the corridor again. 'But get to the point.'

'My father, well, you can imagine.' Finnuc whistled. 'He barred the doors and locked the shutters, both of them still inside. Me on my own in the street. I tried to get back in, but I was just a boy. I pried at the wood, banged the boards until paint chips fell about me like snow. My mother didn't realise what was happening. Neither did I, not really. Not until it was too late.

'There were words, at first, among the screams.

'Smoke started to escape around the edges of the shutters and the big double doors. Then there was just her noise. My father didn't make a sound the whole time, not that I heard.'

Finnuc stubbed out his bindleleaf on the wall.

'The smell,' he said. 'It's hard to describe. Burned bread comes closest, maybe, but there was something else under that, somewhere under all that smoke. Sickly and sweet.'

She knew that smell. Burlington. Burning the victims of a plague that was forewarned by the Caskers, and a Casker here in front of her, telling her about *another* fire, years before.

'The heat too. It pushed me back to the other side of the street. But there was no escaping it.

'I looked away. This I remember as clear as anything else: the sun was setting behind the Poet's Spire, applause in oranges and reds. They approved, all the Audience.'

'That's when she found you?' Cora said. 'Tennworth.'

'There, sitting on the street, rocking back and forth and ignoring the blaze. Despite feeling it on every part of me. She was an important person, I could tell that right away. Her hair was clean and she didn't have dirt under her nails.'

'Important how?'

'You know, Cora,' he said. 'You've always known. Blind as she is, the Devotee knows. Drunk as he is, the Heckler knows. Senseless. Restless. Curious. They all know. The Wayward Chambers, he knows too, and that's the kind of bitter twist the Audience really savours. Like a fine wine.'

'Tennworth is a Chambers.'

'And no one can do anything about it. Or the whole wheel stops turning.'

'So Tennworth's not...' Cora mumbled. *Ruth*, she shouted in her head. *Ruth Ruth Ruth*. Even though she knew nothing about her sister since she'd left, Cora knew Ruth wasn't a Chambers, because Cora herself had stood beneath the balcony during the Opening Ceremony and seen them, one by one. But nothing seemed certain anymore. Had she truly seen her sister the day before, after all these years, driving that old coach? It was a glimpse in a moment of chaos. Perhaps Cora had smacked her head on the cobbles without realising.

'Not her real name, no,' Finnuc said, misunderstanding her.

'So what *is* Tennworth's name?'

'You're a detective. You'll figure it out.'

'Tell me who made you do this, Finnuc. Tell me and maybe I can keep you here, in Fenest.'

He laughed, but it was all sorrow. 'And would you visit me?'

She didn't know the answer to that, and didn't want to think on it. 'Before, in the carriageway, you said you owed her. She helped you. All your stories end the same way: Tennworth kept a young orphan from the wrong kind of trouble. Gave you a job. More than one, in fact.'

'That's how it was.'

'Are you telling me that killing Ento was just following orders?' Cora said.

'Will you sleep easier knowing that Ento wasn't the first time? Or that the man my mother had an affair with was a Wayward?'

'Sounds as if it helps *you* sleep easier.' She lit another bindleleaf. 'You used the name Tennworth in all your stories. You wanted me to know that name. You were trying to tell me who was responsible.'

Finnuc shrugged. 'If you say so.'

'But if you won't tell me about Tennworth, let's talk about the part *you* played in this tale. You picked Ento up at his lodging house in Derringate, then what happened?'

'You know this story, Cora.'

'You strangled him in the back of that old coach.'

'Then dumped him in an alleyway, stitched lips and all.'

'Those lips,' she said. 'What was his story, Finnuc?'

He closed his eyes and sat back against the damp cell wall. He was as calm as she'd ever seen him. 'Ah, now you want something the Audience *do* like.'

'What?'

'A good Hook.'

'Is that what Ento's body was? A Hook?'

'Not how the Wayward had planned, but as good as. You're right: there are people who don't want the Wayward story told.'

'Because it's dangerous. But *why*?'

'Because it's the truth, and the Whisperer knows it. What could be more dangerous than that?'

Cora slapped the table. 'Silence take you! Tell me the story.'

'It's not mine to tell. But we'll all know it. We'll be living it, soon enough.'

'Living what?'

'The south is falling apart, Cora,' he said, looking her right in the eye. 'Black Jefferey is just the beginning, the opening story. They're trying to warn you, warn everyone, the only way they know how. The only way they can. The only way you'll listen. Before it's too late.'

'The south? How bad?'

'I hear it will make life in the Tear look like a summer picnic.'

'But why try to stop a story that would warn people, that would help them? Who would—'

The cell door behind her opened.

'Gorderheim?' Hearst said.

'Nearly done, sir,' she said without turning around.

A pause. 'The coach is here. I can't keep—'

'Thank you, sir. I won't be long.'

When they were alone again, Finnuc grinned. 'You'll need to watch him,' he said. 'He thinks he's helping you. Those are the people who'll hurt you most.'

'Like you.'

'Another story you already know.'

She stared at him, trying to take in all that he'd said. She'd come into the cell wanting to help him, give him a chance to stay in the city and stay alive. Now, she wasn't so sure. But she did know she had nothing else to say.

She opened the cell door. In the corridor she could hear the hum and clatter of the station. Jenkins was still standing guard at the end. Beyond her, the normal way of things carried on, as they always did. But that wouldn't be Finnuc's fate. He wouldn't last long on the Steppes.

'I'm sorry,' he said, so quiet she almost missed it. 'Sorry for what we had.'

She paused, about to tell him *she* was sorry too. But instead she banged the cell door behind her and walked quickly away.

She didn't remember the walk back to her office but that was where Sillian found her. The chief inspector picked her way through the mess on the floor until she was close to Cora's desk.

'He's confessed?' Sillian said.

Cora nodded.

'Good. It took longer than I would have liked but you got the right result in the end.'

'The right result?'

'Really, Detective? I believe this is quite clear.' Sillian's gaze was cold. As cold as the Steppes would be for Finnuc. 'I asked you to find the person who killed the Wayward storyteller, did I not?'

'You did, Ma'am.'

'And in the cells we have a Casker who has confessed. He will be duly punished.'

'Yes, Ma'am.'

'So what *is* it about this situation that presents difficulty?'

Cora gripped the edge of her desk, forced herself to breathe. 'Nothing, Ma'am,' she heard herself say.

'Good, then I trust—' Sillian glanced at the door as a pair of constables passed. In a low voice she said, 'I trust that I can count on your discretion in this matter?'

'Yes, Ma'am.'

'I have informed the pennysheets. The story should make the evening edition and that will be the end of the matter.'

'The end of the story?' Cora said.

'The end of the story,' Sillian said.

★★★

Alone again, Cora closed the door and leant against it. Her thoughts were churning and nothing made sense. Finnuc's words, Sillian's. It was all a mess. Finnuc said he'd been working for a Chambers when he killed Ento, which was done so the Union wouldn't find out the truth: that the south was 'falling apart'. This Chambers had rescued him from the streets around Tithe Hall. The south end of the city.

That felt like a lot of *south*, even just thinking it over.

Critic hear it, doubt was starting to take root.

Hadn't he looked right at the lamp's flame before telling his story? The fire at the bakery. The fiery sunset behind the Poet's Spire. Had he just used what was there to shape his lies while the time ran out?

What about the rest of Finnuc's story? Was the south really in trouble? Was a story worth killing over?

But then something came clear through it all.

There's power in stories and a story of power.

Ruth had told her that when they were children. The words were as true then as they were now. And Ruth herself – there was a chance she was back, and connected, somehow, to the murder of the Wayward storyteller. There was only one thing Cora was certain of, more certain than she'd ever been since she started this case: a Chambers was involved.

Cora had solved a murder, but that wasn't the end of the story – no matter what Sillian said. This election, this city, all the people caught in between...

She had more work ahead of her, and there would be much to tell the Audience.

Acknowledgements

We would like to thank the following people, all of whom supported this book and made it possible:

Our agent, Sam Copeland, for unfailing faith.

The team at Head of Zeus, in particular our editors Sophie Robinson Madeleine O'Shea and Laura Palmer, who believed in this story and helped us make it better.

Our families – without you we wouldn't have started writing, and we certainly wouldn't have made it this far.

Ollie Bevington, who told us our next book should go big or go home.

Jonathan and Ele Carr, and your wonderful cat Kiro, for friendship and hospitality in Italy where we began this story and likely moaned about it a lot over good coffee and even better ice cream.

Our early readers, Katy Birch, Tom Francis, Iain Cameron, Tricia Jones, Kate Wright – without your help we wouldn't have found where we needed to go.

Katherine would like to thank the Royal Literary Fund for awarding her a Fellowship during the writing of this book, which gave her much needed time.

David would like to thank the University of South Wales and his colleagues in the English and Creative Writing Department for all their help and support.